Holy Fire

A Novel

BRUCE STERLING

BANTAM BOOKS

New York Toronto
London Sydney Auckland

HOLY FIRE

A Bantam Spectra Book / October 1996

SPECTRA and the portrayal of a boxed "s" are trademarks of
Bantam Books, a division of Bantam Doubleday Dell Publishing Group, Inc.

Library of Congress Cataloging-in-Publication Data

Sterling, Bruce.
Holy fire : a novel / Bruce Sterling.
p.   cm.
ISBN 0-553-09958-2
I. Title.
PS3569.T3876H6   1996
813'.54—dc20   96-15139
CIP
AC

Published simultaneously in the United States and Canada

*Bantam Books are published by Bantam Books, a division of
Bantam Doubleday Dell Publishing Group, Inc. Its trademark,
consisting of the words "Bantam Books" and the portrayal of a
rooster, is Registered in U.S. Patent and Trademark Office and in
other countries. Marca Registrada. Bantam Books, 1540
Broadway, New York, New York 10036.*

PRINTED   IN   THE   UNITED   STATES   OF   AMERICA

BVG   10 9 8 7 6 5 4 3 2 1

Holy Fire

M ia Ziemann needed to know what to wear at a
deathbed.

The net counseled simplicity and sincer-
ity. Mia was a ninety-four-year-old Californian medical economist, while the prospective deceased, Martin
Warshaw, had been her college sweetheart some
seventy-four years previously. Mia could expect some
prepared statement. There would very likely be a bequest of some sort. Conversation would involve an
attempt to put Mr. Warshaw's life into retrospective
order, to supply the sense of grace and closure so desir-
able during life's final chapter. She would not be asked
to witness the actual moment of death.

A deathbed reunion of long-separated lovers was
a challenge to etiquette, but the late twenty-first century shone in social tidiness. Dilemmas of this sort
were exhaustively debated in endless rounds of calls
for commentary, working papers from boards of experts, anecdotal testimonies, ethics conventions, sworn
public hearings, policy manuals. No aspect of human

existence escaped smoothing over by thoughtful, seasoned, and mature counsel.

Mia studied as much of this material as she could stomach. She spent the afternoon reacquainting herself with Martin Warshaw's financial and medical records. She hadn't seen Martin in fifty years, though she had followed his public career to some extent. Those records of Martin's were most revealing and informative. They had made his life an open book. This was their purpose.

Mia reached a decision: black flats, support hose, a reactive girdle and cuirass, a knee-length silk dress in maroon and gray, long sleeves, high collar. A hat definitely seemed in order. No gloves. Gloves were recommended, but gloves seemed too clinical.

Mia had a blood filtration, a skin enzymation, a long bone-deep massage, a mineral bath, and a manicure. She had her hair cleaned, laminated, volumized, styled, and lacquered. She increased the saturated fat in her diet. She slept that night under a hyperbaric tent.

Next morning, November 19, Mia went into the city to look for a decent hat, some kind of hat that might truly suit her circumstances. It was a cold autumnal day in San Francisco. Fog crept in off the Bay, oozing through the leafy cliffsides of the office highrises. She walked and shopped, and shopped and walked, for a long time. She saw nothing that could match her mood.

A dog was following her up Market Street, loping through the crowd. She stopped behind the shadowed column of a portico and stretched out her bare hand, beckoning.

The dog paused timidly, then came up and sniffed at her fingers.

"Are you Mia Ziemann?" the dog said.

"Yes, I am," Mia said. People walked past her, brisk and purposeful, their solemn faces set, neat shoes scuffing the red brick sidewalks. Under the steady discipline of Mia's gaze, the dog settled on his haunches, crouching at her feet.

"I tracked you from your home," bragged the dog, panting rhythmically. "It's a long way." The dog wore a checkered knit sweater, tailored canine trousers, and a knitted black skullcap.

The dog's gloved front paws were vaguely prehensile, like a

raccoon's hands. The dog had short clean fawn-colored fur and large attractive eyes. His voice came from a speaker implanted in his throat.

A car bleeped once at a tardy pedestrian, rudely breaking the subtle urban murmurs of downtown San Francisco. "I've walked a long way," Mia said. "It was clever of you to find me. Good dog."

The dog brightened at the praise, and wagged his tail. "I think I'm lost and I feel rather hungry."

"That's all right, nice dog." The dog reeked of cologne. "What's your name?"

"Plato," the dog said shyly.

"That's a fine name for a dog. Why are you following me?"

This sophisticated conversational gambit exhausted the dog's limited verbal repertoire, but with the usual cheerful resilience of his species he simply changed the subject. "I live with Martin Warshaw! He's very good to me! He feeds me well. Also Martin smells good! Except not . . . like other days. Not like . . ." The dog seemed pained. "Not like now. . . ."

"Did Martin send you to follow me?"

The dog pondered this. "He talks about you. He wants to see you. You should come talk to him. He can't be happy." The dog sniffed at the paving, then looked up expectantly. "May I have a treat?"

"I don't carry treats with me, Plato."

"That's very sad," Plato observed.

"How is Martin? How does he feel?"

A dim anxiety puckered the hairy canine wrinkles around the dog's eyes. It was odd how much more expressive a dog's face became once it learned to talk. "No," the dog offered haltingly, "Martin smells unhappy. My home feels bad inside. Martin is making me very sad." He began to howl.

The citizens of San Francisco were a very tolerant lot, civilized and cosmopolitan. Mia could see that the passersby strongly disapproved of anyone who would publicly bully a dog to tears.

"It's all right," Mia soothed, "calm down. I'll go with you. We'll go to see Martin right away."

The dog whined, too distraught to manage speech.

"Take me home to Martin Warshaw," she commanded.

"Oh, all right," said the dog, brightening. Order had returned to his moral universe. "I can do that. That's easy."

He led her, frisking, to a trolley. The dog paid for both of them, and they got off after three stops. Martin Warshaw had chosen to live north of Market in Nob Hill, in one of the quake-proofed high-rises built in the 2060s, a polychrome pile. It had been ambitious, by the garish standards of its period, with vividly patterned exterior tiling and a rippling mess of projecting bay windows and balconies.

Inside the building it was narcotically tranquil. The lobby offered an interior grove of hotly fragrant orange and avocado trees in portable two-ton polychrome pots. The trees were hoppingly alive with small, twittering flocks of finches.

Mia followed her canine escort into a mural-crusted elevator. They emerged on the tenth floor, onto pavement set with stone cobbles. The building's internal lighting glowed in superrealist mimicry of northern California sunlight. People had hung laundry inside the building's sweet breeze and light. Mia worked her way through the big potted jacarandas and bought a shrink-wrapped pack of dog treats from an automated street shop. The dog accepted a bone-shaped lozenge with polite enthusiasm.

Fragrant wisteria vines were flowering on the stone veneer of Martin's apartment. The heavy door shunted open at a single knowing touch of the dog's paw.

"Mia Ziemann is here!" the dog announced heartily to the empty air. The living room had the sanitary neatness of some strange old-fashioned hotel: potted palms, a mahogany media cabinet, tall brass floor lamps, a glass-topped teak table with spotless untouched glassware and hermetic jars of mixed nuts. A pair of large rats with control collars were eating lab chow from a bowl on the table.

"May I take your coat?" asked the dog.

Mia shrugged out of her tan gabard and handed it over. She was wearing what she usually wore to shop: tailored trousers and a long-sleeved blouse. Informal clothes would have to do. The dog gamely engaged in complex maneuvers with a hatstand.

Mia hung her purse. "Where is Martin?"

The dog led her to the bedroom. A dying man in patterned Japanese pajamas lay propped on pillows in a narrow bed. He was asleep or unconscious, his lined face sagging, his thin, lifeless hair in disarray.

At the sight of him, Mia almost turned and ran at once. The impulse to simply flee the room, flee the building, flee the city, was as strong and raw as any emotional impulse she had felt in years.

Mia stood her ground. Confronted with the stark reality of encroaching death, all her advice and preparation meant precisely nothing. She stood and waited for some memory—any memory—to hit her. Recognition came at last, and the dying face fell into focus.

She hadn't seen Martin for more than fifty years. She hadn't loved him for more than seventy. Yet here was Martin Warshaw. In what was left of his flesh.

The dog prodded Warshaw's hand with his cold nose. Warshaw stirred. "Open the windows," he whispered.

The dog tapped a button near the floor. Curtains rolled aside and floor-length windows shunted open onto damp Pacific air.

"I'm here, Martin," Mia said.

He blinked in grainy astonishment. "You've come early."

"Yes. I met your dog."

"I see." The back of the deathbed rose, propping him in a sitting position. "Plato, please bring Mia a chair."

The dog gripped the bent wooden leg of the nearest chair and lugged it over clumsily across the carpet, puffing and whining with the effort. "Thank you," Mia said, and sat.

"Plato," said the dying man, "please be quiet now. Don't listen to us, don't talk. You may shut down."

"May I shut down? All right, Martin." The dog sank to the carpeted floor in deep confusion. His long furry head fell to the carpet, and he twitched a bit, as if dreaming.

The apartment was spotless and dustless and in suspiciously perfect order. By the look of it, Mia could tell that Martin hadn't left his bed for weeks. Cleaning machines had been at the place, and civil-support personnel on their unending round of social checkups. The deathbed was discreet, but to judge by its subtle humming and occasional muted gurgle, it was well equipped.

"Do you enjoy dogs, Mia?"

"He's a very handsome specimen," Mia said obliquely.

The dog rose to his feet, shook himself all over, and began nosing aimlessly about the room.

"I've had Plato for forty years," Martin said. "He's one of the oldest dogs in California. One of the most heavily altered dogs in private ownership—he's even been written up in the breeders' magazines." Martin smiled wanly. "Plato's rather more famous than I am, these days."

"I can see that you've done a great deal with him."

"Oh, yes. He's been through every procedure I've been through. Arterial scrubbing, kidney work, liver and lung work . . . I never tried any extension technique without running it through good old Plato first." Martin folded his bony, waxlike hands above the covers. "Of course, it's easier and cheaper to do veterinary work than posthuman extension—but I needed that sense of companionship, I suppose. One doesn't like to go alone, into . . . medical experiences of such profundity."

She knew what he meant. It was a common sentiment. Animal bodies had always preceded human bodies into the medical frontier. "He doesn't look forty years old. Forty, that's a very ripe age for a dog."

Martin reached for a bedside slate. He brushed at the reactive surface with his fingertips, then brushed his fingers back through his hair—a gesture she recognized with a shock of déjà vu, after seven long decades. "They're wonderfully resilient animals, dogs. Remarkable how well they get on with life, even after becoming postcanine. The language skills make a difference, especially."

Mia watched the dog nosing about the bedroom. Freed from the heavy cognitive burden of language, the dog seemed much

❦   B r u c e   S t e r l i n g

brisker, freer, less labored, somehow more authentically mammalian.

"At first, all his speech was very clearly machine generated," Martin said, tugging at a pillow. Color had begun to enter his face. He'd done it with his scratching at the touchscreen, and with his bed, and with the medical support gear he was using, wired into his flesh beneath the pajamas. "Just a verbal prosthetic for a canine brain. Very halting, very . . . gimmicky. It took ten years for the wiring to sink in, to fully integrate. But now speech is simply a part of him. Sometimes I catch him talking to himself."

"What does he talk about?"

"Oh, nothing very sophisticated. Nothing too abstract. Modest things. Food. Warmth. Smells. He is, after all, just my old good dog—somewhere under there." Martin gazed at his dog with undisguised affection. "Isn't that right, boy?" The dog looked up, thumped his tail mutely.

Mia had lived through a long and difficult century. She had witnessed massive global plagues, and consequent convulsive advancements in medicine. She'd been a deeply interested witness as vast new crypts and buttresses and towers were added to the ancient House of Pain. She had professionally studied the demographics of the deaths of millions of lab animals and billions of human beings, and she had examined the variant outcomes of hundreds of life-extension techniques. She'd helped to rank their many hideous failures, and their few but very real successes. She had meticulously judged advances in medical science as a ratio of capital investment. She had made policy recommendations to various specific organs of the global medical-industrial complex. She had never gotten over her primal dread of pain and death, but she no longer allowed mere dread to affect her behavior much.

Martin was dying. He had, in point of fact, amyloid neural degeneration, partial spinal paralysis, liver damage, and kidney nephritis, all of which had led through the usual complex paths of metabolic decline to a state his records neatly summarized as "insupportable." Mia, of course, had read his prognosis carefully, but medical analysis was a product of its terminology. Death, by stark contrast, was not a word. Death was a reality that sought people out and put its primal stamp on every fiber of their beings.

She could tell at a glance that Martin was dying. He was dying, and he was offering her platitudes about his dog rather than harsh truths about his death, because his strongest and most genuine regret in life was leaving his dog. Demands, obligations, forced you to survive. Survival was an act of obligation to lovers, to dependents, to anyone who expected survival from you. A dog, for instance. What year was this, 2095? Martin was ninety-six and his best friend was his dog.

Martin Warshaw had once loved her. That was why he had arranged this meeting, why he was launching sudden emotional demands at her after fifty years of silence. It was a complex act of duty and rage and sorrow and politesse, but Mia understood the reality of the situation, just as she understood most other things these days: rather too well.

"Do you ever do mnemonics, Mia?"

"Yes. I've done memory drugs. Some of the milder ones. When I need them."

"They help. They've helped me. But they're a vice, of course, if you push them." He smiled. "I'm pushing them hard now. There's a lot of pleasure in vice when there's nothing left to lose. Would you like a mnemonic?" He offered her a fresh pad of stickers. Factory-sealed, holographic backing.

Mia peeled one free, examined the name and the dosage, and smoothed the sticker to her neck. To please him.

"You'd think that after all these years they'd have found a mnemonic that would open your soul like a filing cabinet." He reached into a bedside table and pulled out a framed photograph. "Everything just in its place, everything organized, everything indexed and full of meaning. But that's too much to ask of a human brain. Memories compact themselves, they blur. They turn to mulch, lose all color. The details go. Like a compost heap." He showed her the photo: a young woman in a high-collared coat, lipstick, eyeliner, wind-tousled brunette hair, squinting in sunlight, half smiling. Something guarded in her smile.

The young woman was herself, of course.

Martin gazed at the photo, wrapped in mnemonic like a psychic blanket, and then he looked up at her. "Do you remember much about the two of us? It's been a long time."

"I can remember," she told him. That was almost true. "I wouldn't have come, otherwise."

"I've had a decent life. The thirties, the forties . . . those were terrible years for most of the world, dark years, awful years, but they were very good years for me. I was working hard, and I knew that it mattered. I had what I wanted, my career, a place in the world, something real to say, and a chance to have my say. . . . Maybe I wasn't happy, but I was busy, and that counts for a lot in life. It was hard work and I was glad it was hard work."

He studied the photo, slowly, meditatively. "But for seven months, back in '22, the year when I took this picture of you . . . Well, admittedly, our last two months were pretty bad, but for five months, those first five months we had together, when I loved you and you loved me, and we were young and life was fresh—I was in ecstasy. Those were truly the happiest days of my life. I've come to understand that now."

It seemed wisest to say nothing at this point.

"I married four times. They were no worse than a lot of people's marriages, but they never really took. My heart wasn't in it, I suppose. A marriage always seems such a good idea when you're about to commit one."

He placed the photo aside on the bed, face up. "I'm very sorry if this is an imposition," he said, "but to put it into perspective, here at my finale, it's a very great privilege. To have you here with me now, Mia, physically here, to be able to tell you this straight to your face, with no pride, no spite, no selfish pretense, nothing left to lose or gain between us—it truly eases my mind."

"I understand." She paused, reached out. "May I?"

He let her take the picture. The paper behind the glass was crisp and new—he had reprinted the photograph recently, from some old digital source he'd kept on file somewhere, for all these years. The young woman, standing outside in some campus environment, all California palms and rain-stained marble balustrades, looked innocent and excited and ambitious and shallow.

Mia stared very hard at the young woman and felt a profound vacancy where there should have been some primal sense of identity. She and the girl in the picture had eyes of identical color, more or less the same cheekbones, something like the same chin. It was like a picture of her grandmother.

The mnemonic began to affect her. She felt no lift or tingle from the drug but life was slowly enriched with mysterious symbolic portent. She felt as if she were about to tumble into the photograph and land inside it with a splash.

His voice recalled her. "Were you happy with that man you married?"

"Yes. I was happy." She peeled the emptied sticker from her neck with finicky precision. "It's long over now, but it did last for many years, and while Daniel and I were a couple, my life was very rich and authentic. We had a child."

"I'm glad for you." He smiled again, and this time it was a smile she could recognize. "You look so well, Mia. So much yourself."

"I've been very lucky. And I've always been careful."

He gazed sorrowfully out the window. "You weren't lucky when you met me," he said, "and you were right to be careful with me."

"You don't have to say that. I don't regret any of our history." With deep reluctance, as if handing over a hostage, she gave him the photo again. "I know that we parted badly, but I always followed your work. You were clever, you were very creative. You were never afraid to speak your mind. I didn't always agree with what you said, but I always felt proud of you. I was proud that I knew you before the rest of the world caught on." That was true. She was so old that she could still remember when they called that kind of work "films." Films—long strips of plastic printed with darkness and light. The memory of film, the sense and the substance of the medium of film, brought her a nostalgia sharp as broken glass.

He was insistent. "You were right to break with me. I realized later that it wasn't about Europe at all, or about a way to change our lives. I only wanted to win that argument, I wanted to

carry you off to some other continent and make you live my life."
He laughed. "I never changed. I never learned any better. Not
since I was twenty years old. Not since I was five!"

Mia wiped at her eyes. "You could have given me more time
for this, Martin."

"I'm sorry. There's simply no time left. I've faced down
everyone else already. You were always the hardest to face." He
offered her a tissue from a drawer in the bedside.

She dabbed at her eyes, and he leaned back, his patterned
shoulders denting the pillow. The neck of his pajamas fell open,
showing a blood filtration web across his chest. "I'm sorry that I'm
better rehearsed than you are, Mia. It was unfair of me to do this;
but I'm a dramatist at heart. I'm sorry that I've upset you. You can
go now, if you like. It was very good to see you."

"I'm old now, Martin." She lifted her chin. "I'm not the
young woman from that photograph, no matter how well or badly
we remember her. You can stage your scene just as it pleases you,
I won't walk out. I've never been crass."

"I plan to die this evening."

"I see. That soon?"

"Yes. Everything nicely tied up, very civilized, very politic."

Mia nodded soberly. "I respect and admire your decision.
I've often thought that I'll go the very same way."

He relaxed. "It's very good of you not to argue with me.
Not to spoil my exit."

"Oh, no. No, I'd never do that." She reached out and deliberately placed her palm against the chilly back of his hand. "Do
you need anything?"

"There are details, you understand."

"Details. Of course."

"Heirlooms. Bequests." He gestured precisely at the empty
air. "I have a bequest for you, Mia—something I think is right
for you. It's my memory palace." A castle in virtual sand. "I want
you to take possession of my palace. It can shelter you, if you
ever need it. It's ductile and it's smart. It's old, but it's stable.
Sometimes palaces can make a lot of trouble for people, but mine
won't make demands. It's a good space. I've been very discreet

with it. I've cleaned it out now—except a few things that I couldn't bear to erase, things very special to me. Maybe to you, too. Mementos."

"Why did you need such a big palace?"

"That's a long story."

Mia nodded a permission, and waited.

"It's a long story because I had a long life, I suppose. They caught me out back in the sixties, you see. The big net investigations, the financial fraud scandals." He was enjoying this chance at confession. He was swimming in mnemonic. "I was out of the directing game by that time, but I was very involved in production. I lost a lot of good investments in the legal mess, certain things I'd put aside. I didn't ever want to get stung again, so I took some serious measures after the sixties. Built myself a serious, genuine palace, the kind the taxmen couldn't reach. Kept my palace up ever since. A very useful space. But it can't help me now. The government won't cut me any exemptions for my liver and my thymus. And the amyloid thing, that's a syndrome with just one prognosis."

He frowned. "I hate when people play too fair, don't you? There's something nasty happening when there's so much justice in the world. . . . They won't outlaw alcohol, they won't even outlaw narcotics, but when you go in for a checkup they take your blood and hair and DNA, and they map every trace of every little thing you've done to yourself. It all goes right on your medical records and gets splashed all over the net. If you live like a little tin saint, then they'll bend heaven and earth for you. But if you act the way I've acted for ninety-six years . . . Ever see my medical records, Mia? I used to drink a lot." He laughed. "What's life without a drink?"

It was, thought Mia, life without cirrhosis, ulcers, and cumulative neural damage.

"The polity. The global polity, it's like a government run by your grandmother. A wise and kindly little old lady with a plateful of cookies and a headsman's ax."

Mia said nothing. She herself had a treatment rating in the ninety-eighth percentile. She was sure that Martin must know this stark and all-important fact about her life. The polity was a government run by, and for the benefit of, people just like herself.

"Martin, tell me about this palace. How can I access it?"

He took her hand, turned it palm up, and steadied it. He traced a touchscreen gesture with a trailing fingertip against her palm. Mia was awash in mnemonic now, and in his withered grip around her wrist she felt an ashen remnant of what had once been, many decades ago, a powerful eroticism. A lover's touch, rich with youth and heat.

He released her. "Can you remember that passtouch?"

"I'll remember it. The mnemonic will help me." She was determined not to nervously rub the wrist that he had gripped. "I like those old gestural systems, I used to use them all the time."

He handed her his slate. "Here. Set the palace to your thumbprint. No, Mia, the left hand. That one's better, not on so many records."

She hesitated. "Why should that bother me?"

"I've just given you the key to a fortress. You and I deserve our privacy, don't we? We both know what life is like nowadays. People like you and me, we're a lot older than the government is. We can even remember when governments weren't honest."

She pressed her left thumb to the slate. "Thank you, Martin. I'm sure your palace is a very great gift."

"Greater than you know. It can help you with another matter, too."

"What's that?"

"My dog."

She was silent.

"You don't want poor Plato," he said, downcast.

She said nothing.

He sighed. "I suppose I should have sold him," he said. "But that thought was so awful. Like selling a child. I never had a child. . . . He suffered so much on my behalf, and he's been through so many changes. . . . I thought of everyone I knew, but there was no one . . . among those very few people still alive that I call my friends. . . . No one I could really trust to take proper care of him."

"Why me, though? You scarcely know me, these days."

"Of course I know you," he muttered. "I know that you're very careful. . . . You were the biggest mistake I ever made. Or the biggest mistake that I never made. The regret's much the same, either way." He looked up, cajoling her. "Plato never asks for much. He'd be grateful for whatever you gave him. He needs someone. I don't know what he'll do, once I'm dead. I don't know how he'll take it. He's so smart, and it costs him so much pain to think."

"Martin, I'm very flattered that you should choose me, but that's too much to ask. You just can't ask that of me."

"I know that it's a great deal to ask. But the palace will help you, there are useful resources in there. Can't you try him for a while? He's no longer a mere animal. I haven't allowed him that luxury. You could try for just a while, couldn't you?" He paused. "Mia, I do know you. I've seen your records, and I know more about you than you might imagine. I never forgot you, never. Now, I think that Plato might help you."

She said nothing. Her heart was beating quickly and oddly and there was a faint whining ring of tinnitus in her left ear. At moments like this she knew with terrible certainty that she was truly old.

"He's not a monster. He's just very different, very advanced. He's worth a lot of money. If you couldn't bear having him around, you could sell him."

"I can't! I won't!"

"I see. That's your final word?" A long judgmental moment passed between them, full of intimacy and bitterness. "You can see what I'm like, then, can't you? Seventy years between the two of us—they're like one day. I haven't changed at all. Not me—and not you, either."

"Martin, I have to be honest with you. It's just . . . ." She glanced at the dog, lying peacefully in the corner with his narrow canine head on his crossed paws. Then, horrifyingly against her will, the truth began pouring out of her, in jerks. "I don't have any kind of pets. Never. My life's not like that anymore. I live alone. I had a family once, I had a husband and a daughter, but they're gone from my life now and I don't talk to them. I have a career, Martin, I have a good job in medical research administration. That's my responsibility, and that's what I do. I look at screens and I work in economic spaces and I study grant procedures and I weigh results from research programs. I'm a functionary."

She drew a ragged breath. "I walk in the parks, and I study the news every night, and I always vote. Sometimes I look at old films. But that's it, that's everything, that's how I live. I'm the kind of person you can't stand, and that you couldn't ever stand." She was weeping openly now.

He looked at her with pity. "An animal companion could help you, though. I know that he's helped me. We owe something to animals, you know. We've jumped over the walls of the human condition by climbing on the backs of animals. We're obliged to our animals."

"An animal can't help me. I don't need any attachments."

"Take the chance. Change your life a little. People have to take some chances, Mia. You're not living, if you don't take some chances."

"No, I won't. I know you think this might be good for me, but you're wrong, it's not good. I can't do it. I'm not that kind of person. Stop asking me."

He laughed. "I can't believe that you just said that. That's exactly what you said the very last time we argued—those were your very words!" He shook his head. "All right, all right. . . . I always ask too much of you, don't I? It was stupid of me to ask this. I'm full of meddlesome plans for other people who still have lives to live. You don't like to take chances. I know that. You were always careful, and you were wiser and smarter than me. Bad luck to you that the two of us ever met."

An empty silence stretched between them. A little foretaste of the silence of death.

He roused himself. "Tell me that you forgive me."

"I do forgive you, Martin. I forgive you everything. I'm

sorry I wasn't right for you. I never could do what you needed from me. I never gave you what you asked from me. Please forgive me for all that, that was my fault."

He accepted this. She could see from the flushed look on his pallid face that he'd reached some long-sought apotheosis. He'd said everything that he wanted to say to her. His life was over now. He'd wound it up, packed it away.

"Go your way, darling," he told her gently. "Someone that I used to be truly loved someone you used to be once. Try not to forget me."

The dog did not rise to see her to the door. She left Martin's apartment, numbly retrieving her purse and coat. She walked the vivid summer brightness of the halls. She took an elevator, she entered the chill of the autumnal city. She reentered the thin but very real texture of her thin but very real life. She stepped into the first taxi she found, and she went back home.

———————

Mercedes was in the apartment, cleaning the bathroom. Mercedes came into the front room, carrying her mop and her septic sampling equipment. Mercedes wore her tidy civil-support uniform, baby blue jacket with red epaulets, slacks, and discreetly foam-soled shoes. Mercedes had fifteen elderly women on her civil-support rounds and came by twice a week to tidy up, usually in Mia's absence. Mercedes called her civil-support work "housekeeping," because that was a kindlier description than "social worker," "health inspector," or "police spy."

"What's happened to you?" Mercedes said in surprise, setting down her mop and her bucket of gel. "I thought you were at work."

"I had a bad experience. A friend is dying tonight."

Mercedes slid immediately into a role of professional sympathy. She took Mia's coat. "Sit down, Mia. I'll make a tincture."

"I don't want a tincture," Mia said wearily, sitting at the corrugated, lacquered cardboard of her kitchen table. "He made me take a mnemonic. I'm still on it, it's nasty."

"What kind?" said Mercedes, tugging off her hairnet and slipping it into her jacket.

"Enkephalokrylline, two hundred fifty micrograms."

"Oh, that's just a nothing little mnemonic." Mercedes fluffed her dark hair. "Have a tincture."

"I'll have a mineral water."

Mercedes rolled Mia's tincture set to the side of the table and sat on a kitchen stool. She decanted half a liter of distilled water, and methodically set about selecting and crushing dainty little wafers of mineral supplement. Mia's tincture set was by far the most elaborate and most expensive kitchen fixture that Mia owned. Mia didn't consider herself a possessive and materialistic person, but she made exceptions for tinctures. Also—to be fair—she was fond of decent clothes. She also made certain exceptions for the cardboard covers of old twentieth-century video-game and CD-ROM products. Mia had a minor weakness for antique paper ephemera.

"I suppose I'd better talk about it," Mia said. "If I don't talk to somebody about it, I won't sleep tonight. I have a checkup in three days and if I don't sleep tonight it will show."

Mercedes looked up brightly. "You can talk to me! Of course you can tell me about it."

"Do you have to put it all in your dossier?"

Mercedes looked wounded. "Of course I have to put it in the dossier. I wouldn't be honest if I didn't keep up my dossiers." She fed a hissing gush of bubbles into the mineral water. "Mia, you've known me for fifteen years. You can trust me. Civil-support people love it when their clients talk. What else are we here for?"

Mia leaned forward, propping her elbows on the table. "I knew this man seventy years ago," she said. "He was my boyfriend then. He kept telling me today that we haven't changed, but of course we've changed. We've changed beyond recognition. He's consumed himself. And me—seventy years ago, I was a young woman. I was a girl, I was his girl. I'm not a girl anymore. Nowadays I'm someone who used to be a woman."

"That's kind of an odd way to put it."

"It's the truth. I'm not his woman, I haven't been anyone's

woman for a long time. I don't have lovers. I don't love anyone. I don't look after anyone. I don't kiss anyone, I don't hug anyone, I don't cheer anyone up. I don't have a family. I don't have hot flashes, I don't have monthlies. I'm a postsexual person, I'm a postwomanly person. I'm a crone. I'm a late-twenty-first-century techno-crone."

"You look like a woman to me."

"I dress like a woman. That's all very calculated and deliberate."

"I know what you mean," Mercedes admitted. "I'm sixty-five. Pretty much past it. Not too sorry to see it go. Being a woman—the really hard part of womanhood—it's not the sort of life you'd wish on a friend."

"It was very wearing," Mia said. "He was very polite about it, but just being near him exhausted me. The worst part was that there's no clean break between me and my earlier life. My romantic life, my sexual life. I could remember how exciting it had been. How flattering. Being pursued by some large energetic insistent good-looking boy. How it felt when I let him catch me. The mnemonic made it all a lot worse."

"Most people would say that clean breaks are bad for you. That you have to come to terms with that aspect of your former life, and integrate it so you can put it to rest and get beyond it."

Therapeutic suggestions irritated Mia in direct ratio to their tact. "I did have to come to terms with my earlier life today. I'm not a bit happier for it."

"Are you sorry he's dying? Are you grieving?"

"I'm a little sorry." Mia sipped the mineral water. "I wouldn't call this grief. It's too thin for grief." The water felt good. Very simple things conveyed most of the pleasure in her life. "I wept some today. It felt really bad to cry. I haven't wept in five years." She touched her swollen eyes. "It feels like there's membrane damage."

"Was there a bequest?"

"No," Mia lied smoothly.

"There's always some kind of bequest," Mercedes prodded.

Mia paused. "There was one, but I refused it. He had a post-canine dog."

"I knew it," Mercedes said. "It's the pet, or the house. If they die really young, then maybe they worry about their kid. People never invite you to a deathbed scene unless they want you to tidy up for them somehow."

"Maybe they just want *you* to tidy up, Mercedes."

Mercedes shrugged. "I tidy up. Tidiness is my life." Mercedes was always very patient. "I can see there's something else you want to get off your chest. What is it?"

"Nothing, not really anything."

"You just don't want to tell me yet, Mia. You might as well tell me about it now. While you're still in the mood."

Mia stared at her. "You don't have to tidy me up quite so thoroughly. I'm perfectly all right. I had a shock, but I'm not going to do anything strange."

"You shouldn't say things like that, Mia. The situation is very strange. The world is extremely strange now. You live all alone and you don't have people you can trust to advise you and prop you up. Except for your work, you're not fulfilling any social roles. You could go off-kilter real easily."

"When have you ever known me to go off-kilter?"

"Mia, you're smarter than me, and you're older than me, and you're a lot richer than I am, but you're not the only person like you in the world. I know a lot of people just like you. People like you are brittle."

Mercedes waved her blue-jacketed arm around the apartment. "This stuff you've been calling your life all these years, this isn't normality. It isn't safety, either. It's just routine. Routine is not normality. You're not allowed any so-called normality. There's no such thing as a genuine normality for a ninety-four-year-old posthuman being. Life extension is just not a natural state of affairs, and it's never going to be natural, and you can't ever make it natural. That's your reality. My reality too. And that's why the polity sends me around here twice a week. To look around and tidy up and listen to you."

Mia said nothing.

"Go on and be that way," Mercedes told her. "I'm very sorry you had a hard time today. A friend's death can hit us harder than we think. Even dull people can't keep the same routine forever, and you're not dull. You're just very guarded, and very possessive of an old-fashioned emotional privacy that no one really needs nowadays."

"I'll take that under advisement."

Mercedes looked at her solemnly. The silence stretched. Mercedes was not deceived. No woman could be a heroine to her maid.

"By the way," Mercedes said at last, "that nasty strain of fungus is back in your bathroom. Where have you been walking?"

"I walk for exercise," Mia said. "I just drift around town. I don't keep track."

"Try leaving your shoes outside the door for a while, okay? And don't take long showers. That Coccidioides is hell."

"Okay. I'll do that."

"I have to leave now," Mercedes said, getting up. "I've got another round to do. But you call me if you need anything. Call me anytime. Don't be embarrassed to call. Being called is good for me."

"Okay, Officer," Mia said. Mercedes made a face, collected her gear, and left.

———

Martin Warshaw was put to rest on the afternoon of the twenty-first, out in the old mass grave in Palo Alto. The day was bright and clear and the sprawling grounds of the former plague site had never looked greener, calmer, or more contemplative. Mia recognized no one at the ceremony. No one took the trouble to recognize her.

The nineteen elderly people who attended the ceremony were all very much of a type. Hollywood people had never been afraid of the knife. The Beautiful People had always been particularly eager to seize on any artifice of youth. Fifty years ago, people of this sort had been medical pioneers. Now they were genuinely and irretrievably old. Their primitive techniques, the biomedical cutting edge during the 2030s and 2040s, were hopelessly dated and crude. Now they truly looked the role of pioneers: very scarred and tired and hardscrabble.

Attendants opened the hinged white lid of the emulsifier, took the thin shroud from Martin's wasted, puckered body, and slid him, with reverent care, feetfirst into the seething gel. The scanners set to work, Martin's final official medical imaging. Gentle ultrasonics shook the body apart, and when the high-speed rotors began to churn, the emulsifier's ornamental flowerbeds trembled a bit. Autopsy samplers caught up bits of the soup, analyzed genetic damage, surveyed the corpse's populations of resident bacteria, hunted down and cataloged every subsymptomatic viral infection and prion infestation, and publicly nailed down the cause of death (self-administered neural depressant) with utter cybernetic certainty. All the data was neatly and publicly filed on the net.

Someone—Mia never discovered who—had asked a Catholic priest to say a few words. The young priest was very eager, and meant well. He was very exalted on entheogens, so filled with fiery inspiration that he was scarcely able to speak. When the priest finished his transcendant rant, he formally blessed the gel. The tiny crowd drifted from the site in twos and threes.

A necropolitan engraved Martin's portrait, name, and dates onto the emulsifier's cream white wall. Martin Warshaw (1999–2095) had become a colored patch the size of the palm of Mia's hand, neatly ranked beside three hundred and eighty-nine other people, the previous occupants of this device. Mia tarried, gazing across the bright rows of funereal photoengravings. The sweet presence of all these human faces made it seem almost a kindly machine, a machine that meant well.

Mia summoned a taxi at the edge of the cemetery grounds. While she waited, she spotted a fawn-colored dog skulking in the oleanders. The dog wore no clothing and displayed no particular signs of intelligence. She stared at the dog as she waited for her taxi, but when she tried to approach him, the dog vanished into the bushes. She felt vaguely foolish once the dog had gone. Large brown dogs were common enough.

Mia left the taxi at the tube station, ducked under the conduit-riddled Californian earth, and emerged at the Public Telepresence Point at Coit Tower. Telegraph Hill was her favorite site when she was away from San Francisco. Whenever she traveled she'd link back to this site periodically, for a restorative taste of Bay Area urban sensory access. Mia had done telepresence to sites in cities all over the world, but she never fell in love with cities unless she could walk them. San Francisco was one of the world's great walking cities. That was why she lived in San Francisco. That, and a great deal of habit. She set out on foot.

On the Embarcadero, Mia sipped a hot frappé in a crowded and noisy tourist café. She wondered glumly what her former husband would have thought of the day's events. What he might have thought of Warshaw's final ceremonies. Martin Warshaw had been the only genuine rival that Daniel had ever had. Would there have been some lingering trace of male jealousy there, maybe some slight satisfaction? Mia wondered if her former husband kept her in mind anymore—or if he ever thought coherently about anything or anyone at all. Daniel was in a very strange space in northern Idaho, a space beyond real possibility of contact. Mia could have called her daughter, Chloe, in Djakarta, but there was no comfort in that. Chloe would only pick at her batik and utter harangues about turns of the wheel and spiritual authenticity.

A long stroll toward Fisherman's Wharf—Mia had managed not to think about work all day, and that was a novelty for her and, in its own way, a great accomplishment—and she arrived at her destination, a metal-clad two-story town house. A weathered redwood sign in an overgrown hedge identified the place as a for-profit netsite. Mia paid to get through the door, and once inside the cavernous building she slid a cashcard into a clock.

The proprietor ambled up. He was a lanky old gentleman, well into his second century, all knees and elbows, with a sharp beak of a nose, two absurdly large and efficient hearing aids, and a shapeless fisherman's cap. The fisherman's cap was an affectation,

❦ B r u c e   S t e r l i n g

since Mr. Stuart's scaly, corrugated skin had not seen prolonged daylight in decades. He wore a short-sleeved bile green shirt and a pair of oil-stained trousers, their belt loops hung with fold-out multitools on little metal lanyards.

Mia had not visited this netsite in thirty-seven years. The town house had been extensively rebuilt: floors and walls knocked out, windows bricked over, outer walls copper clad to reduce stray emissions. Still, Mia was unsurprised to discover the very same owner, still in the very same business, at the very same locale, and wearing what seemed to be the very same clothing. Mr. Stuart had always impressed her as the sort of man who could easily outlast a mere building.

Stuart himself looked much the same, although his nose and ears had swollen visibly in the past few decades. Growth hormone treatments and steroid adjustments were one of the more sensible and low-key life-extension strategies. Men's noses and ears tended to swell quite a bit under that regime of treatment. Something to do with male steroids and progressive ossification in the cartilage.

Mia looked the place over. Gray sound-absorption baffles hung from the ceiling, beneath colored spaghetti tangles of power cables and fiber optics. The metal rafters were alive with twittering flocks of brown sparrows.

The floor held a bizarre collection of network access machines. The western end of Stuart's barn contained brand-new netlinks, many with the frazzled look of prototypes. The eastern end was jammed with collectors' items, specialized relics from the past hundred and twenty years of virtual space manipulation. Mr. Stuart had always specialized in media that were either dying or struggling to be born.

The walls were smorgasbords of crates and buckets of electronics parts. Stuart's creaky cleaning-robot was gamely wandering about, meticulously dusting the other machines. There was a requisite sandbox for the droppings of the domesticated birds. The lighting in the place was, as always, dreadful.

"I thought you were going to put in windows," Mia said.

"Real soon now," Stuart told her, slitting his eyes. "Who needs windows anyway? A netsite *is* a window."

"What are you running here that can handle a gestural pass-touch and get me into a memory palace set up back in the sixties?"

"That depends on your setup, but all life depends on the setup," Stuart said. Stuart had a pronounced taste for aphorisms. "Tell me about the initial parameters and the hardware it's on."

"I can't tell you anything about that."

Stuart shrugged gnomically. "You may be here quite a while, then. You want my advice, try it the simple way first. Plug a touchslate into one of those foveal curtain units and see if you can just bring up the palace right in front of you."

"You think that might work?"

"It might. You might try it out on spex if you want more . . ." Stuart paused portentously. "Discretion."

"Do you charge more for discretion, Mr. Stuart? I'm rather interested in discretion."

"I charge just to enter my building," Stuart said. "That's sufficiently outrageous for most folks." Someone yelled a long question at him from the new machines at the western end of the building—something about "naming trees" and "defuzzification." Stuart whipped his leathery neck around like an owl. "Read the manual!" he shouted. He turned to Mia again. "Kids . . . Where were we, ma'am?"

"Mia."

"What?"

"There *is* no manual!" the boy screamed in reply.

"Mia, M-I-A," Mia said patiently.

"Oh," Stuart said, tapping one hearing aid. "Nice to have you in the shop, Maya. Don't mind the kids here, they get a little rowdy sometimes."

"I'll try the curtain unit and the slate, please."

"I'll check you in," said Stuart.

Discretion was the sole advantage of obsolete hardware. Obsolete hardware was so bafflingly out-of-date as to be basically un-policeable. Modern virtuality standards were far tidier, sturdier, and more sensible than the primitive, frazzled, often dangerous junk from the rest of the century. Modern data archives were astonishingly free, accessible, and open. But there were hundreds of obsolescent formats, and vast backwaters of obsolescent data, that were accessible only on machines no longer manufactured or supported. Machines of this sort could only be used by hobbyist fanatics—or by people so old that they had learned to use these machines decades ago and had never abandoned them.

Stuart gave Mia a battered touchslate and a virtuality jewel case. Mia retired to the netsite's bathroom, with its pedestal sinks and mirrors. She washed her hands.

Mia clicked open the jewelry case, took its two featherlight earring phones, and cuffed them deftly onto her ears. She dabbed the little beauty-mark microphone to the corner of her upper lip. She carefully glued the false lashes to her eyelids. Each lash would monitor the shape of her eyeball, and therefore the direction of her gaze.

Mia opened the hinged lid of a glove font and dipped both her hands, up to the wrists, into a thick bath of hot adhesive plastic. She pulled her hands out, and waved them to cool and congeal.

The gloves crackled on her fingers as they cured and set. Mia worked her finger joints, then clenched her fists, methodically. The plastic surface of the gloves split like drying mud into hundreds of tiny platelets. She then dipped her gloves into a second tank, then pulled free. Thin, conductive veins of wetly glittering organic circuitry dried swiftly among the cracks.

When her gloves were nicely done, Mia pulled a wrist-fan from a slot below the basin. She cracked the fan against her forearm to activate it, then opened it around her left wrist and buttoned it shut. The rainbow-tinted fabric stiffened nicely. When she had opened and buttoned her second wrist-fan, she had two large visual membranes the size of dinner plates radiating from the ends of her arms.

The plastic gloves came alive as their circuitry met and meshed with the undersides of the wrist-fans. Mia worked her fingers again. The wrist-fans swiftly mapped out the shape of the gloves, making themselves thoroughly familiar with the size, shape, and movements of her hands.

The fans went opaque. Her hands vanished from sight. Then

the image of her hands reappeared, cleverly mapped and simulated onto the outer surfaces of the wrist-fans. Reality vanished at the rim of the fans, and Mia saw virtual images of both her hands extended into twin circles of blue void.

Tucking the touchslate under one arm, Mia left the bathroom and walked to her chosen curtain unit. She stepped inside and shut and sealed the curtain behind her. The fabric stiffened with a sudden top-to-bottom shudder, and the machine woke itself around her. The stiff curtain fabric turned a uniform shade of cerulean. Much more of reality vanished, and Mia stood suspended in a swimming sky blue virtuality. Immersive virtuality—except, of course, for the solid floor beneath her feet, and the ceiling overhead, an insect-elbowed mess of remote locators, tracking devices, and recording equipment.

The fabric curtain was woven from glass fiber, thousands of hair-thin multicolored fiber-optic scan-lines. Following the cues from her false eyelashes, the curtain wall lit up and displayed its imagery wherever Mia's eyesight happened to rest. Wherever her gaze moved and fell, the curtain was always ahead of her, instantly illuminated, rendering its imagery in a fraction of a second, so that the woven illusion looked seamless, and surrounded her.

Mia fumbled for a jack and plugged in the touchslate. The curtain unit recognized the smaller machine and immediately wrapped her in a three-hundred-and-sixty-degree touchplate display, a virtual abyss of smoky gray. Mia dabbled at the touchscreen with her gloved fingertips until a few useful displays tumbled up from its glassy depths: a cycle tachometer, a clock, a network chooser.

She picked one of San Francisco's bigger public net gates, held her breath, and traced in Martin Warshaw's passtouch. The wall faithfully sketched out the scrawling of her gloved fingertip, monster glyphs of vivid charcoal against the gray fabric.

The tracing faded. The curtain unit went sky blue again. Nothing much happened after that. Still, the little tachometer showed processing churning away, somewhere, somehow, out in the depths of the net. So Mia waited patiently.

After eight minutes, the tachometer vanished. The walls went stellar black, then leapt into a full-scale virtuality rendition.

Mia found herself in an architect's office. There was a big desk in simulated wood grain, and painfully gleaming brass lamps, and algorithmic swirls of simulated marble. The chairs were puffy, overstuffed, and swaddlingly comfortable. Old people's chairs. They were the kind of chairs that top-flight furniture designers had begun making back in the 2070s, when furniture designers suddenly realized that very old people possessed all the money in the world, and that from now on very old people were going to have all the money until the end of time.

The virtual office, with some fine display of irony, had been designed to resemble the office of a civil architect. Architects who designed actual buildings, as opposed to those who built virtual structures, tended to be rather snobbish and pushy about their intimate relation to tangible physicality. The walls around her were all corkboards, chalkboards, crayons, drafting paper, and string. All very analog and tactile. There wasn't a data screen anywhere in the place. Except, of course, that this entire virtual environment was itself a data screen.

There was a serious mismatch between Martin Warshaw's sophisticated memory palace and this randomly chosen and somewhat pokey little curtain unit. Against the rounded fabric walls, the corners of the virtual room looked quite nasty, with a stomach-churning visual warp. The simulation couldn't seem to decide where to put the floor. Rims of flooring slopped up on the lower edges of the screen, like a swamped rowboat slowly going under.

A simulated window in one wall showed an arty glimpse of a fake exterior garden, but the organic shapes within the garden were disastrous. The trees were jerky half-rendered blurs, a nightmare vision of x-rayed vegetation under alien sunlight as thick as cheese. The inside of the office boasted a virtual potted plant. Its big serrated leaves looked as stiff and lifeless as waffle irons.

Mia turned in place, gazing about the virtual office cautiously. A massive framed blueprint hung on the wall to her left. It showed a vast multistory edifice—the ground-floor plans of the memory palace itself, presumably. The blueprints were lavishly annotated, in horribly blurred and tiny print. The palace looked huge, elaborate, and quite intimidating. Mia felt as if she'd unwrapped a Christmas gift and found an entire steam locomotive crammed inside it. A multi-ton coal-fired virtual jack-in-the-box.

She turned toward the center of the room. The top of the wood-grain desk boasted a single framed photograph. Mia made stepping motions in place, and managed to reach the virtual desk without barging through it. She reached out one hand, fishing for the photo. The glove interface was hopelessly bad, full of stutter and overlap.

This was a very unhappy interface. And small wonder. No doubt this entire virtual environment was being encrypted, decrypted, reencrypted, anonymously routed through satellites and cables, emulated on alien machinery through ill-fitting, out-of-date protocols, then displayed through long-dead graphics standards. Dismembered, piped, compressed, packeted, unpacketed, decompressed, unpiped and re-membered. Worse yet, the place was old. Virtual buildings didn't age like physical ones, but they aged in subtle pathways of arcane decline, in much the way that their owners did. A little bijou table in the corner had a pronounced case of bit-rot: from a certain angle it lost all surface tint.

The place wasn't dead, though. A virtual gecko appeared and sneaked its way along the wall, a sure sign that little health-assuring subroutines were still working their way through the damper, darker spots in the palace's code.

Mia got a tentative grip on the photograph. She lifted it from the desktop, and the image burst free from the frame like a hemorrhage, and leapt up onto the fabric wall of the curtain unit, flinging itself all around her in a three-hundred-and-sixty-degree blast of bright red pixels the size of bloody thumbprints. Mia winced, put the photo back down, and peered at it sidelong through the membrane of her wrist-fan. Objects within hand's reach seemed a lot better realized graphically than the jittery mess up on the curtain walls.

The frame held another digital photograph of herself. A different picture this time: the very young Mia Ziemann was sitting on a threadbare red fabric couch in her red terry-cloth bathrobe, reading a paper magazine, her slim bare legs perched on a coffee table. Her hair was wet. The floor was littered with collegiate junk: fast-food packets, disks of recorded music, two unlaced walking shoes. The young Mia was unaware of the photographer. She looked relaxed and comfortable, yet deeply intent on her magazine.

Another little keepsake of Martin's. His posthumous message to the palace's chosen heiress.

Mia clawed open a drawer of the virtual desk. Empty. She knocked the photo into the empty drawer and shut it.

She opened another desk drawer. Scissors, paper, pens, tape, pins. She tried repeatedly, but failed to get a decent grip on the virtual scissors. She opened another drawer. A box of colored chalk.

Mia plucked a stick of pale green chalk from the box, and turned toward the chalkboard on the far wall. She marched in place toward the chalkboard—it reeled disturbingly as she grew nearer—and she reached out, her gloved fingers pinched and the virtual chalk outstretched.

Clearly this action called for much better gloves than the cheap peel-aways she was wearing. The chalk wobbled in and out of the surface of chalkboard like Dodgson's Alice having fits in a mirror. After prolonged struggle Mia managed to shakily scrawl a random message, the first thing that had come into her head:

MAYA WAS HERE

She added a potato-nosed Kilroy face, and, for good measure, scrawled some childish Miss Kilroy curls on Kilroy's domed noggin. She accidentally dropped the virtual chalk, which hit the floor with an audible click and vanished. After searching for it hopelessly with her wrist-fans, Mia found herself getting seriously seasick. She unplugged the touchscreen, threw open the wall of the curtain, and stepped outside.

Swallowing bile, she unstrapped the wrist-fans and put them away. She peeled off the gloves into shredded strips and dropped them into a recycler. That had been more than enough for a first try. If she ever entered Warshaw's palace again, she'd use top-of-the-line datagloves from work, and some decent spex. Mia felt nauseated. And obscurely disappointed. And deeply cheated. And desolately sad.

She walked down a crooked aisle among Stuart's phalanx of machines, breathing hard and trying to clear her head. She walked the length of the barn, down among the new machines. At the far end of the building she turned and headed back. She felt better now. Walking always helped her.

"Come with me to Europe," a woman said aloud. Mia stopped.

"We don't have time for Europe. Or the money," a man grumbled. The two of them were sitting together on a blanket on the floor, in an aisle among the machines. The man wore a big padded jacket and dirty leggings and big scuffed boots; he had a pair of glittering spex propped on his forehead. The woman wore a very peculiar garment, a tentlike brown poncho somehow suspender-strapped to a baggy pair of pleated harem pants. They'd been working together at a CAD rig. They'd stripped off their manipulation gauntlets and they were sprawling on their blanket and eating biscuits from a paper bag.

They looked rather dirty. They were talking too loud. Their faces were strange: unlined, lithe. Their gestures were sharp and abrupt. They seemed very upset about something.

They were young people.

"They could spin that polymer in six days in Stuttgart," said the girl. "Six hours, maybe."

"Stuttgart's not a real answer. At least here we've got some connections."

"That old man only keeps us here 'cause he likes to watch us play! We need some *vivid* people. People like us. In a place where it's happening. Not like this museum."

"We'll never get anywhere in Stuttgart. You know what the rents are like in Stuttgart? Anyway, are you saying we're not vivid?

You and me? We gotta be vivid in our own way, on our own ground! It doesn't mean anything, otherwise."

Mia walked past them, pretending not to eavesdrop. They paid her no attention. She sought out Mr. Stuart behind his counter. Stuart was digging with a multitool in the silvery innards of a broken helmet.

"I'm done, for now," Mia said.

"Great," Stuart said indifferently, tucking a spex monocle into one eye.

"Tell me about those two young people over there, the ones doing CAD work."

Stuart stared at her, his monocle gleaming. "Are you kidding? What business is that of yours?"

"I'm not asking you what networks they're accessing," Mia explained. "I just want to know a little about their personal lives."

"Oh, okay, no problem," Stuart said, relieved. "Those kids are in their twenties. Always got some little project going, you know how it is at that age. No sense of time scale, lots of energy to waste, head in the clouds. They make clothes. Try to."

"Really."

"Clothes for other kids. She designs them, and he instantiates them. They're a team. It's a kid romance. It's cute."

"What are their names?"

"I never asked."

"How do they pay you for the access time?"

Stuart said nothing. Pointedly.

"Thanks," Mia said. She went back to eavesdrop at greater length. The young people were gone. Mia quickly snagged her cashcard from the entranceway. There wasn't much left on the card, for Stuart's rates were very cruel to strangers. She hurried out of the building.

The boy and girl had backpacks slung over their shoulders and were walking uphill toward a bus stop.

When the bus arrived, Mia climbed aboard behind them. They sat in the back. Mia sat near them, across the aisle. They took no notice of her. Young people didn't like to notice old people.

"This town," the girl announced bitterly, "is boring me to death."

"Sure," the boy said, yawning.

"I'm bored *right now,*" the girl said.

"You're in a bus," the boy pointed out, with infinite tolerance. He began to root around in his pack.

Mia pulled her sunglasses from her purse, put them on, and pretended to gaze up the aisle of the bus. There were three dogs and a couple of cats aboard. Up near the front two well-dressed Asian men were eating from boxes with chopsticks.

The girl opened her backpack, fished out a rattlesnake, and hung it around her neck. The snake was beautiful. Its scaly skin looked like tesselated pavement as seen from a great height. The snake stirred a little at the contact with warm flesh.

"Don't get tight," the boy said.

"I won't get tight. Snakey's not loaded."

"Well, don't load him, then. You're always getting tight when we argue. As if that ever settles anything." The boy pulled an enameled comb from his bag, and ran it restlessly through his tousled hair. "Anyway, that snake would look stupid in Stuttgart. They just don't do rattlesnakes in Stuttgart."

"We could do Praha. We could do Milano." The girl toyed listlessly with the snake's rattle. "It's so slow here in the Bay. Nothing ever happens here. Darling, I'm miserable." She let go of the snake and tugged at a hank of greasy brunette hair. "I can't work if I'm miserable. You know I can't work if I'm miserable!"

"What am I going to do with you when you're miserable in Europe?"

"In Europe I'd never be miserable."

"Sure."

"You don't think I know my own mind," she said angrily. "That's always been your problem."

"You don't know your own mind, and you never have," he said bluntly. "Your mind is a pain in my neck."

"I hate you," the girl announced. She crammed the snake back into her backpack.

"You should go to Europe," Mia said aloud.

They looked up, startled. "What?" the girl said.

"You should go. You might as well go." Mia's heart skipped a beat, then started racing. "You're very young, but you have plenty of time. Go to Europe for five weeks. Five months. Five years. Five years is nothing. You should go to Europe together, and you can get it all out of your system."

"I beg your pardon?" said the boy. "Did we ask for this?"

Mia took off her sunglasses. She met their eyes.

"Let her alone," the girl said, quickly.

"It's no use going later," Mia said. "If you wait too long, then you'll know too much. Then it's always all the same, no matter where you go." She began to weep.

"Wonderful," the boy muttered. He stood up, grabbing the bus's bamboo pole. "Come on, we're leaving."

The girl didn't move. "Why?"

"Come on, she's having some kind of attack! That's not our problem. We've got problems enough."

"You're not old enough for real problems," Mia told him. "You can run a lot of risks now. You've got energy, and you're free. Go ahead and run a risk. Take her to Europe."

The boy stared at her. "Do I look like a man who takes career advice from strange old women who cry in public buses?"

"You look just like the kind of man . . . A man that I knew a long time ago," Mia said. Her voice was trembling. Her tear ducts ached dreadfully. They stung all the way down into her nose.

"You're very free with advice for other people. When was the last time *you* took any kind of risk?"

Mia wiped her burning eyes, and sniffed. "I'm taking a risk right now."

"Sure you are." The boy scoffed. "Like it's a big hazard for some gerontocrat to make fun of us! Look at you—you got your ambulances standing by for you around the clock! You got every advantage in the world! What have we got?"

He glared at her aggressively. "You know, ma'am, even though I'm only twenty-two years old, my life feels every bit as real and worthwhile as your life does! *More* real than your life! Do you think we're *stupid* just because we're young? You don't know half enough to offer us any advice—you don't know a thing about us, or our lives, or our situation, or anything else. You are condescending to us."

"No, she isn't," the girl said.

"You're patronizing us!"

"Oh, she is not! Look, she's crying, she really means it!"

"You are being profoundly impertinent!"

"Stop insulting this nice lady! She was completely right about every single thing she said!"

The bus stopped. "I'm leaving," the boy announced. "I resent it when old people deny the validity of my experience."

"Go ahead and run off, then," the girl told him, folding her arms and slumping back into the seat. The boy was startled. Slowly his face darkened. He slung his pack over one shoulder and stormed off, boots clomping down the stairs.

The bus started up again.

"I'm sorry," Mia said meekly.

"Don't be sorry," the girl said. "I hate him! He's holding me back! He thinks he can tell me what to do."

Mia said nothing.

The girl frowned. "I never slept with any man more than twice, without him thinking he could tell me what to do!"

Mia glanced up. "How old are you?"

The girl lifted her chin. "Nineteen."

"What's your name?"

"Brett," the girl announced. She was lying. "What's your name?"

"Maya."

Brett crossed the aisle and sat beside her. "It's nice to meet you, Maya."

"Likewise, Brett."

"I'm going to Europe," Brett announced. She began searching in her backpack again. "Stuttgart probably. That's the biggest city for the arts in the whole world. Have you ever been to Stuttgart?"

"I've been to Europe a few times. Not in many years."

"Have you been to Stuttgart since they rebuilt it?"

"No."

"Ever been to Indianapolis?"

"I did telepresence there once. Indianapolis seems a little scary nowadays."

Brett offered Mia a wadded paper tissue from the backpack. Mia accepted it gratefully, and blew her nose. Her tear ducts were all out of practice. They felt scorched and sore.

Brett gazed at her with frank curiosity. "You haven't been around very much lately, have you, Maya?"

"No. I don't suppose I have, really."

"You want to come around with me for a while? Maybe I could show you some things. Would that be all right?"

Mia was surprised and touched. The invitation was not entirely welcome, but the girl was trying to be sweet to her. "All right. Yes."

Brett led her off the bus at the next stop. They began walking together down Filmore. This street was rather heavily wooded. A giraffe was methodically cropping the trees. Mia was sure that the giraffe was perfectly harmless, but it was the largest urban animal she'd ever seen roaming loose in San Francisco. It was quite an exotic beast. Someone had been busy on the city council.

Brett merely ambled along at first, but then picked up her pace. "You can walk pretty fast," Brett said. "How old are you really?"

"I'm pushing a century."

"You don't look a hundred years old. You must be really smart."

"I'm just very careful."

"Do you have, like, osteoarthritis or incontinence or any really weird syndrome stuff?"

"I have a bad vagus nerve," Mia said. "I get attacks of night cramps. And I'm astigmatic." She smiled. It was an interesting topic. She could remember when strangers made polite chitchat about the weather.

"Do you have a boyfriend?"

"No."

"Why not?"

"I was married for a long time. When it was over, that part of life didn't seem very important anymore."

"What part *is* very important?"

"Responsibility."

"That doesn't sound very exciting."

"It's not exciting, but if you're not responsible, you can't take proper care of yourself. You get sick and fall apart." This truism sounded rather fatuous, pointless, and morbid, especially for a young person. "When you live a really long time," Mia offered carefully, "it changes everything. The whole structure of the world, politics, money, religion, culture, everything that used to be human. All those changes are your responsibility, they benefited you, they happened because of you. You have to work hard so that the polity can manage. Good citizenship is a lot of work. It needs a lot of self-sacrifice."

"Sure," said Brett, and laughed. "I forgot about those parts."

Brett led her into a mall—a nexus of junk shops near the Haight. There was a good crowd in the place, warming the benches, window-shopping, sipping tinctures in a café. A couple of cops in pink jackets sat on their bicycles, people-watching. For the first time in many years, Mia found herself catching a suspicious glance from a police officer. Because of the company she kept.

"Do you know this part of town?" Brett said.

"Sure. See that collectors' shop? They sell old media bric-a-brac, I buy paper-show things from them sometimes."

"Wow," Brett marveled, "I always wondered what kind of people went into that weird old place. . . ."

Brett ducked into a dark, tiny store, a redwood-fronted hole in the wall. It sold rugs, blankets, and cheap jewelry. Mia had never been inside the place in her life. It smelled strongly, almost chokingly, of air-sprayed vanilla. The walls were densely overgrown with deep green moss.

A tabby cat was asleep on the shop counter, sprawled lazily across the glass top. There were no human beings in sight. Brett made a beeline for a dress rack crammed in the corner. "Come see . . . see, this is all my stuff."

"All of this?"

"No, not everything on this rack," Brett said, sorting nimbly through the garment rack, "but this one is my design, and this one, and this one here. . . . I mean, I concepted these, it was Griff who instantiated them." Mia perceived from the sudden angry crease on Brett's smooth brow that Griff was the erring boyfriend. "This older guy, Mr. Quiroga, he's the owner. We kind of cut a deal with him to carry our stuff."

"They're very interesting designs," Mia said. They were very peculiar.

"You like them, really?"

"Of course I do." Mia pulled a red jacket from its hanger. It was made of a puffy spun plastic with tactile properties somewhere between leather, canvas, and some kind of chewable gelatin candy. Most of the jacket was candy-apple red, but there were large patches of murky blue on the elbows, neck, and hem. It had a lot of fat buttoned pockets, and a waterproof red rain hood crushed down inside a lumpy collar.

"See how well it holds its shape?" Brett boasted. "And it doesn't even have batteries. It's all in the cut and the weave. Plus the Young's modulus of the fiber."

"What's it made of?"

"Elastomers and polymers. A little woven ceramic for the high-wear spots. See, it's durable all-weather streetwear, just right for travel! Try it on!"

Mia slipped her arms through the padded sleeves. Brett busied herself tugging at the shoulders, then zipped it up to Mia's chin. "It fits great!" Brett declared. It did no such thing. Mia felt as if she'd been stuffed into a monstrous fruitcake.

Mia stepped before a narrow full-length mirror in another corner. There she saw a stranger improbably swaddled in a garish candied jacket. Maya the Gingerbread Girl. She put on her sunglasses. With the glasses, and with sufficiently bad light, she might almost look young—a very tired, puffy, sickly young woman in a kid's ridiculous jacket. Wearing improbably tidy, adult, and conservative slacks and shoes.

Mia jammed her fingers through her hair, shook her head, and destroyed her coiffure.

"That helps," she said, peering at the mirror.

Brett was surprised, and laughed.

"What a lovely jacket. What else could I ever need?"

"Better shoes," Brett told her very seriously. "A skirt. Long earrings. No purse, get a backpack. Real lipstick, not that medicated little-old-lady stuff. Nail polish. Barrettes. Necklaces. No girdle. No brassiere, if you can help it. Especially no *watch*." She paused. "And sway some more when you walk. Put some bounce in it."

"That seems like rather a lot."

Brett shrugged. "Looking vivid is mostly things you *don't* have to get and *don't* have to do."

"I don't have the cheekbones for that kind of life anymore," Mia said. "I talk too slowly. I don't wave my hands enough. I don't giggle. If I tried to dance, I'd ache for a week."

"You don't have to dance. I could make you look really vivid if you wanted me to. I'm pretty good at that. I have a talent. Everyone says so."

"I'm sure you could do that, Brett. But why would I want you to?"

Brett was bitterly crestfallen. Mia felt a sharp pang of guilt at having disappointed her. It was as if she'd deliberately slapped a small child in the street. "I do want the jacket," Mia said. "I'm fond of it, I want to buy it from you."

"You do, really?"

"Yes, really."

"Could you give me some grown-up money for it?"

"I beg your pardon?"

"I mean real money from a long-term investment account," Brett said. "Certified funds."

"But certified funds are only for special transactions. Life extension, stock ownership, pensions, that sort of thing."

"No, they're not. Certified money is the real money for the real economy. It's the kind of money that kids like Griff and me can never get our hands on." Brett's young-girl eyes—warm amber brown, with sclera so white and clear that they looked almost artificial—narrowed cagily. "You don't have to give me very much *real* money at all. I'd feel real happy with just a *little bit* of certified grown-up money."

"I'd like to give you some," Mia said, "but I don't have any way to do that. Of course I do have certified funds in my own name, but they're all tied up in long-term capital investments, like they're supposed to be. Nobody uses that kind of financial instrument for little everyday transactions like clothes or food. What's wrong with a nice cashcard?"

"You can't start a real business without certified funds," Brett said. "There's all kinds of awful tax problems and insurance problems and liability problems. It's all just part of the big conspiracy to hold young people back."

"No, it isn't," Mia said, "it's how we ensure financial stability and reduce liquidity in the capital markets. This is truly a dull and stuffy topic, Brett, but as it happens, I'm a medical economist, and I know quite a bit about this. If you could have seen what markets were like in the twenties, or the forties, or even the sixties, then you'd appreciate modern time-based restrictions on the movement of capital. They've helped a lot, life's a lot more predictable now. The whole structure of the medical-industrial complex is dependent on stable grant procedures and graduated reductions in liquidity."

Brett shrugged. "Oh, never mind, never mind. . . . I knew you'd never give me any, but I had to ask anyway. I hope you're not mad at me."

"No, it's all right. I'm not mad."

Brett gazed around the shop, her lips tightening in a glossy smirk. "Mr. Quiroga's not around. Probably doing civil support. He's supposed to run this place, but he's never in here when you want him. . . . Probably makes more treatment points from the government when he's out spying on us kids. . . . Can you give me fifteen marks for it? Cash?"

Mia took her minibank out of her purse, ratcheted fifteen market units onto a smartcard, and handed it over.

Brett carefully stuffed the card into a pocket of her backpack, and removed a scarcely visible tag from the puffy red sleeve of the merchandise. She tucked the tag under the sleeping cat, which meowed once, reflexively. "Well, thanks a lot, Maya. Griff'd be real glad to see me make a sale. That is, if I was ever gonna see Griff again."

"Will you see him?"

"Oh, he'll come looking for me. He's gonna sweet-talk me and apologize and all, but he's no good. He's smart but he's stupid, if you know what I mean. He's never gonna really do anything. He's never gonna really go anywhere." Brett was restless. "Let's go."

They exited the mall into Pierce Street. A Pekingese police dog with a pink collar came toddling down the hill. Brett stood perfectly still and stared at the tiny dog with blank and focused hostility. When the dog had passed them, she strode on.

"I could leave tonight," Brett declared, loosely swinging her young and perfect arms beneath the poncho. "Just step right onto a plane for Stuttgart. Well, not Stuttgart, because that would be a real crowded flight. But someplace else in Europe. Warszawa maybe. Airplanes are just like buses. They hardly ever really check to see if you've paid."

"That would be dishonest," Mia said gently.

"I'd get away with it! Hitching is easy if you have the nerve."

"What would your parents think?"

Brett laughed harshly. "I wouldn't get any medical checkups in Stuttgart. I'd just stay very underground in Europe, and I wouldn't get any checkups unless I came back here. I'd have no medical records in Europe. Nobody would ever catch me. I could hitch on a plane tonight. Nobody would care."

They were heading uphill and Mia's calves were beginning to burn. "You'd have a hard time getting anything done in Europe without appearing on official records."

"People travel like that all the time! You can get away with anything as long as you don't look important."

"What does Griff think about this?"

"Griff's got no imagination."

"Well, what if he comes looking for you?"

Brett's face clouded thoughtfully. "This man you knew. Your lover. Was he really a lot like Griff?"

"Maybe."

"What happened to him?"

"They buried him this morning."

"Ohhh," said Brett. "Comprehension dawns." Delicately she touched Mia's padded shoulder. "I get it all now. I'm sorry."

"It's all right."

They walked along for a while silently. Mia tried to catch her breath. Then Brett spoke up. "I bet you secretly loved him right up to the very end."

"No. Actually, it wasn't at all like that."

"But you went to his funeral today."

"Well, yes."

"So, I bet somewhere, deep inside, you really loved him the whole time."

"I know that would seem more romantic," Mia said, "but it just doesn't work that way. Not for me, anyway. I never loved him half as much as I loved a better man later, and now I scarcely even think about him, either. Even though I was his wife for fifty years."

"No, no, no," Brett insisted cheerily, "I bet anything that on New Year's Eve you take mnemonics and drink alcohol and think about your old boyfriends and cry."

"Alcohol's a poison," Mia said. "And mnemonics are more trouble than they're worth. Anyway, that's just the way young women think that old women act. Posthuman women aren't like that at all. We aren't all sad or nostalgic. Really old women, who are still healthy and strong—we're just very different. We just—we just get over all that." She paused. "Really old men, too, some of them . . ."

"Well, you can't have been all cold and indifferent to him, or otherwise you wouldn't have been crying about him on a bus."

"Oh, for heaven's sake," Mia said. "It wasn't him, it was the situation! It was the human condition! The posthuman condition . . . If I'd been crying because I regretted losing my love life, I'd have left with your boyfriend, not with you."

"Very funny," Brett said with an instant jealous scowl. Brett began walking faster, her elastic soles squeaking on the pavement.

"I never meant to suggest that I'd try to steal your boy-friend," Mia said with great care. "I'm sure he's very good-look-ing, but believe me, that's not high on my list of priorities."

They crossed Divisadero. "I know why you said all that just now," Brett declared sullenly, after half a block. "I bet you'd feel really good about it, if you could give me some nice grown-up advice, and maybe buy my jacket or something, and so I went back to Griff and we went together to Europe and acted just like you think young lovers ought to act."

"Why are you so suspicious?"

"I'm not suspicious. I'm just not naive. I know you think I'm like a little kid, that nineteen is a little kid. I'm not very ma-ture, but I'm a woman. In fact I'm kind of a dangerous woman."

"Really."

"Yes." Brett tossed her head. "You see, I have desires that don't accord with the status quo."

"That sounds pretty serious."

"And I don't mind hurting people if I have to. Sometimes it's good for them. To be hurt some. Shocked a little." Brett's sweet young face had a most peculiar cast. After a long moment Mia realized that Brett was trying to look wicked and seductive. She looked about as evil as a kitten in a basket.

"I see," Mia said.

"Are you rich, Maya?"

"In a way," Mia said. "Yes. I'm well-to-do."

"How'd you get that way?"

"Steady income, low expenditures, compound interest, and a long wait." Mia laughed. "Even inanimate objects can get rich that way."

"That's all you ever had to do?"

"It's not as easy as it sounds. The low expenditure is the hard part. It's pretty easy to make money, but it's hard not to spend money once you know that you have some."

"Do you have a big house, Maya?"

"I have an apartment on Parnassus. By the medical center. Not too far from here, actually."

"Is there a lot of room there?"

Mia paused. "You want to spend the night with me, is that what you're driving at?"

"Can I, Maya? Can you take me in? Just for a night. I'll sleep on the floor, I'm real used to it. See, I just don't want to stay in any place where Griff might find me tonight. I need a chance to think things out on my own. Please say yes, it would really help."

Mia thought it over. She could imagine a lot of possible harm in the situation, but the prospect somehow failed to deter her. She'd reached such an instant and intense rapport with the girl that she felt peculiar about breaking the connection, almost superstitious. She wasn't sure that she liked Brett, any more than she would have liked a chance encounter with her own nineteen-year-old self. But still: nineteen years old! It genuinely pained her to think of denying Brett anything. "Are you hungry, Brett?"

"I could eat." Brett was suddenly cheerful.

———

"It's so neat and clean here," Brett said, sweeping through Mia's front room almost on tiptoe. "Does it always look like this?"

Mia was busying herself in her kitchen. She had never been a tidy person by nature, but during her seventies, the habit of untidiness had left her. She'd simply grown out of messiness, the way a child might shed a tooth. After that, Mia always washed the dishes, always made her bed, always picked up loose objects and filed them away. Living that way was quicker and simpler and made every kind of sense to her. Litter and disorder no longer gave her any sense of relaxation or freedom or spontaneity. It had taken her seventy years to learn how to clean up after herself, but once she had learned the trick of it, it was impossible to go back.

She had no simple way to tell Brett about this. The profundity of this change in her personality would never seem natural to a nineteen-year-old. A half-truth was simpler. "I have a civil-support woman who comes in twice a week."

"Boy, that must be a real pain." Brett peered at a framed piece of paper ephemera. "What is *this* thing?"

"Part of my paper collection. It's the cover of a twentieth-century computer game."

"What, this giant silver thing with fangs and muscles and all these war machines and stuff?"

Mia nodded. "It was a kind of virtuality but it was flat and slow and it came in a glass box."

"Why do you collect stuff like that?"

"I just like it."

Brett was skeptical.

Mia smiled. "I do like it! I like the way it's hopelessly stuck between pretending to be high-tech ultra-advanced design, and actually being crude and violent and crass. It cost a lot to design and market, because people were very impressed when you spent a lot of money back then. But it still looks botched and clunky. There used to be thousands of copies of this game, but now they're forgotten. I like it, because not many people are interested in that kind of old-fashioned schlock, but I am. When I look at that picture and think about it—where it came from and what it means—well, it always makes me feel more like my real self, somehow."

"Is it worth a lot of money? It sure is ugly."

"That box top might be worth money if it still had the game inside. There's a few people still alive who used to play these games when they were kids. Some of them are museum fanatics, they own the antique computers, disks, cartridges, the cathode-ray tubes, everything. They all know each other through the net, and they sell each other copies of games that are still mint-in-the-box. For big-collector sums of money. But just the paper cover? No. The paper's not worth much to anybody."

"You don't play the games?"

"Oh, heavens no. It's really hard to get them to work, and besides the games are all awful."

They ate high-fiber fettucine with protein blocks in gravy, and flaked green carbohydrate. "This is really delicious," said Brett, shoveling it in. "I don't know why anybody ever complains about medical diets. The way you do it, it tastes really good. The flavors are so subtle. Lots better than plants and animals."

"Thanks."

"I ate nothing but infant formula until I was five," Brett bragged. "I was strong as a horse as a little kid, I was never sick a day in my life. I could do chin-ups, I could run all day, I could beat up all the kids who were still eating stuff like milk! And vegetables! Wow, that ought to be a crime, feeding little kids vegetables. Did you ever eat vegetables?"

"Not in about fifty years. I think it *is* a crime to feed vegetables to children now, actually. In California, anyway."

"They're really *nasty*. Especially spinach. And corn is disgusting. This big lumpy yellow cob with all these little *seeds* on it . . ." Brett shuddered.

"Do you ever eat eggs? Eggs are a good source of cholesterol."

"Really? I dunno, I might eat an egg if I found it in a nest somewhere." Brett smiled beatifically and shoved her empty plate aside. "You're a really good cook, Maya. I wish I could cook. I'm better at tinctures. You have a really big bathroom, right? Do you think I might take a bath? Would that be okay?"

"Why wouldn't it be?"

"You might have to disinfect afterward."

"Oh. Well, I'm very modern, Brett, I can manage that."

"Oh, good."

While Brett was bathing, Mia picked up Brett's shed clothes, microwaved them thoroughly for hygienic purposes, then washed and dried them. The elastic-soled shoes looked as though they would melt or burst if sterilized, so Mia didn't touch them. The shoes stank powerfully. It wasn't exactly an unpleasant smell, but there had been bare human feet in those shoes for a long time and some odd species of tame bacteria had been warmly and damply feasting inside them.

Brett came out of the bathroom in a towel. "You're probably gonna want to sterilize this towel," she said contritely, and handed it over. Brett was covered with hair. Armpits, pubes, nipples. Huge flourishing glossy patches of black human fur, almost like abbreviated lingerie. The effect of all this hair was surprisingly modest and practical. Brett sat down nude and hairy on the carpeted floor, just a little self-consciously, and started rooting in her backpack.

"That felt lovely," she said. "Plumbing is wonderful. I've been sleeping in a tent for four weeks."

"A tent, is it? How adventurous."

"Yeah, mostly up under the trees in Buena Vista Park. Up *in* the trees mostly, in hammocks. You get terrific views of the city up there. We use the public restrooms and eat out of cartons and it's a really cheap way to get by. It's getting too cold for that now, though."

"Is it safe?"

Brett shrugged. "This is San Francisco! Half the population is civil support. Nobody will bother you. What are they supposed to do to me, rob me? My clothes are all in stores and my designs are all in virtuality." She pulled a little plastic vial from a pocket of the bag, then produced her rattlesnake.

She opened the torpid animal's gaping cotton-white jaws and jabbed its fangs, one after another, through a pinhole in the elastic top of the vial. Then she pressed its dented, scaly head with the flat of her thumb. When the snake's fangs were loaded she stuffed it back in the bag. She took out a metal tube with a pull-off cap. She twisted a waxy taper from within the tube and began carefully anointing the spaces between her toes.

"This is footwax," she explained. "Live bacteria but they can't reproduce. They just eat up the jam and sweat and stuff so you don't get any wild flora living on you."

"That's clever."

"Well, you have to know how to squat, y'know! You can't just drop everything and start sleeping under trees and bridges. If you do it right, there's a lot of science to it. It's an artifice." Brett began working on her furry armpits with a roll-on.

"Where do you keep your spare clothes?"

Brett was surprised. "I'm a professional! If I need new clothes I just have them instanced out." She took out her cellular netlink and began plucking her brows in its mirrored flip-up screen.

Mia cleaned and put away the dishes. "How about dessert?"

"No, thanks."

"Something to wear? I'll loan you something."

"Oh, never mind, it's warm in here, I'm all right."

"A tincture, then?"

"Can you do hot chocolate?"

"Sure. Cacao is fun." Mia brought out her tincture set and began reconfiguring the catalyzers and synthesizers. Little tubes of amber polyvinyl and steel alloy. Gilded O-rings. Enameled pinch-clamps. Osmosis screens. Brewers and strainers and translucent hookah chambers. Step-by-step instructions. It was something to do with your hands while people talked.

Brett fished out her snake, and slapped it sharply on the back of the head. It recoiled at once and emitted an angry hissing rattle. Brett offered up her right forearm. The snake instantly lashed out and sank both fangs into her flesh.

Brett gently coaxed the snake loose and petted it soothingly. Then she dabbed an ointment on the twin puncture marks. A tiny rill of blood escaped. "Ouch," she remarked.

"What did you put in there?"

"Oh, the girl who gave me this stuff made me promise never to tell," Brett said smugly. "It makes me feel safe and warm whenever I sleep in strange places. . . . It does make me feel nice, but it's not really good for me. That's why I always let it hurt some. If you do unhealthy things and you don't let them hurt you first, then that's a good way to get into big trouble."

"An animal bite must be a big infection risk."

"What, nasty warm-blooded germs from a nice cold-blooded mouth? I don't think so. Snakey's really fast and clean. She's just my good friend in my backpack. . . . It's nice to have special things. And special friends." Brett blinked, heavy lidded. She smiled.

They had some cocoa. Brett fell asleep.

Mia tucked a blanket over Brett and retired to her narrow bed. She shoved the hyperbaric seal away and pulled the covers to her chin and fell into uneasy reverie. Her little bedroom chamber felt dead and empty, like the paper cell of an abandoned wasps' nest.

She had kept thoughts of the funeral at bay all day, but now in the dark and the silence the taste of mortality began, in its subtle limbic way, to prey upon her mind. Mia began to ponder, with pitiless clarity and accuracy, the endless list of syndromes in the aging process. The endless richness and natural variety of the pathways of organic decline.

Sutures knotting and calcifying. Cartilaginous membranes ossifying. Mineral deposits of stonelike hardness forming in the gall bladder, liver, the major arteries. Nails thickening, skin going scaly, hair thinning, graying, going all brittle. Nipples darkening, breasts sagging, ducts shrinking, glands puckering. The urogenital system, evolution's canny trade-off of fertility for mortality, permanently bewildered. Deposits of rich bloody marrow dying out in their bony nooks and crannies, replaced by thick yellow pockets of inert fat. Loss of acuity in the retinas and in the weirdly complex machineries of the inner ear. The ancient gland that was the brain, tirelessly shifting its hormonal sediments until its reptilian backwaters filled with toxic deposits as tough to clean out as a childhood neurosis.

Mia wasn't sick, and she certainly wasn't dying, but she was very far from young. She had kept her brain quite clean, but the repeated neural scrubbings had caused serious wear on certain peripheral nerves. In the lower spine, and in the long-stretched nerves of the legs. Her vagus nerve was especially bad. Her weak vagus was not a lethal threat, but the skipped heartbeats were far from pleasant.

Mia's lymph duct was an endless source of trouble, corroded and congealed with ancient bile. She had passing spasms of tinnitus in the left ear and had lost the higher pitches in the right. The synovial fluid in her knuckles and wrists had lost much of its viscosity. Cells in the human lenses didn't grow back, so there wasn't much to do about the loss of flexion and the resultant astigmatism.

And stress made everything worse. Stress made you grow when you were young, when you were young stress taught you lessons. But when you were old, then stress was the expressway to senility.

She could not sleep tonight. She wasn't young. Sharing her house with a young woman, however briefly, had brought that truth home to her. She could sense Brett's living presence in her house, Brett's vital heartbeat and her easy breathing, like the presence of a wild animal.

Mia rose and went in to look after the girl. In the tranquil grip of sleep the girl had slid from beneath her blanket and achieved some primal state of delicious repose. She sprawled there on the patterned carpet like an odalisque, wrapped in the kind of deeply languid erotic slumber that women achieved only in the Oriental genre paintings of nineteenth-century Frenchmen. Envy rose in Mia like poisoned smoke. She walked back to her bed and sat in it, and thought bitterly about the tissue of events that she called her life.

She fell into a doze. At three in the morning the night cramps hit her. Her left leg jerked as if gaffed, and her calf knotted in a rock-hard spasm beneath the sheets. After a dreadful moment a secondary but even more agonizing cramp bit the sole of her left foot. Her toes bent like fishhooks and locked into place.

Mia cried out in smothered anguish. She pounded at the cramp, knuckles smacking knotted flesh. The pain grew more severe, her body's living strength all short-circuited and turned against itself. It was potassium and it was catecholaminic pathways and it was a lot of other stupid terminologies and it was agony. She was having a cramp attack and she was in agony. She pounded on the treacherous muscle. With a sudden little spastic kick, her calf muscle went weak, all hot rubber and blood inside. She hastily massaged her pale and bloodless foot, whimpering to herself. The tendons creaked in her foot and ankle as the cramp fought back against her grip.

When she had tugged and eased her foot free of the evil seizure, Mia stood in her gown and limped methodically about the room. She leaned against the wall with both arms, propping herself at an angle, methodically stretching her Achilles tendons. Sleep was as far away as Stuttgart now. Her left leg felt like burnt rope.

There was nothing mysterious about these attacks. She knew their genesis exactly: potassium deficiencies, worn sheathing in the lower spine, diffusions of stress histamines through the somatic efferent fibers of a certain vertebra, a cellular metabolic cascade—but those words were just diagnosis. Stress brought the cramps on, or a little too much exercise, and every five weeks or so they would just spike right up on their own.

The truth was starker: she was old. Night cramps were a minor evil. People got very old, and strange new things went wrong with them, and they repaired what the racing and bursting technology allowed them to repair, and what they could not cure they endured. In certain ways, night cramps were even a good sign. She got leg cramps because she could still walk. It hurt her sometimes, but she had always been able to walk. She wasn't bedridden. She was lucky. She had to concentrate on that: on the luckiness.

Mia wiped her sweating forehead on her nightgown's sleeve. She limped into the front room. Brett was still asleep. She lay there undisturbed, head on one arm, utterly at peace. The sight of her lying there flooded Mia with déjà vu.

In a moment Mia had the memory in focus, beating at her heart like a moth in a net. Looking in one night at her sleeping daughter. Chloe at five, maybe six years old. Daniel with her, at her side. The child of their love asleep and safe, and happy in their care.

Human lives, her human life. A night not really different from a thousand other nights, but there had been a profound joy in that one moment, an emotion like holy fire. She had known without speaking that her husband felt it, too, and she had slipped her arm around him. It had been a moment beyond speech and out of time.

And now she was looking at a drugged and naked stranger on her carpet and that sacred moment had come back to her, still exactly what it was, what it had been, what it would always be. This stranger was not her daughter, and this moment of the century was not that other ticking moment, but none of that mattered. The holy fire was more real than time, more real than any such circumstance. She wasn't merely having a happy memory. She was having happiness. She had become happiness.

The hot glow of deep joy had shed its bed of ashes. Still just as full of mysterious numinous meaning. As rich and alive and authentic as any sensation she had ever had. Emotion that would last with her till death, emotion she would have to deal with in her final reckoning. A feeling bigger than her own identity. She felt the joy of it crackling and kindling inside her, and in its hot fitful glow she recognized the poverty of her life.

No matter how carefully she guarded herself, life was too short. Life would always be too short.

Mia heard her own voice in the silent air. When the sentence struck her ears, she felt the power of a terrible resolve. An instant decision, sudden, unconscious, unsought, but irrevocable: "I can't go on like this."

2

In volume, technical detail, and avuncular reassurance, the net's medical advice had no archival peer. A serious life-extension upgrade was a personal crisis to rank with puberty, building a mansion, or joining an army.

The medical-industrial complex dominated the planet's economy. Biomedicine had the highest investment rates and the highest rates of technical innovation of any industry in the world. Biomedicine was in a deliberate state of controlled frenzy, giving off enough heat to power the entire culture. In terms of government expenditure it outranked transportation, police, and what passed for defense. In what had once been called the private sector, biomedicine was bigger than chemisynthesis, almost as big as computation. Various aspects of the medical-industrial complex employed 15 percent of the planet's working populace. The scope of gerontological research alone was bigger than agriculture.

The prize was survival. Failure deterred no one. The spectrum of research was vast and multiplex. For every life-extension treatment that was accepted for human use, there were hundreds of schemes that had never moved beyond the enormous tormented ranks of the animal models. New upgrade methods were licensed by medical ethicists. Older and less successful techniques were allowed to lapse out of practice, taking their unlucky investors with them.

There were a hundred clever ways to judge a life-extension upgrade. Stay with the blue chips and you were practically guaranteed a steady rate of survival. Volunteer early for some brilliant new start-up, however, and you'd probably outlive the rest of your generation. Keep in mind, though, that novelty and technical sweetness were no guarantees of genuine long-term success. Many lines of medical advancement folded in a spindling crash of medical vaporware, leaving their survivors internally scarred and psychically wrecked.

Medical upgrades were always improving, never steadily, but with convulsive organic jumps. Any blue-chip upgrade licensed in the 2090s would be (very roughly speaking) about twice as effective as the best available in the 2080s. There had been limit-shattering paradigmatic breakthroughs in life extension during the 2060s and 2070s. As for the 2050s, the stunts they'd been calling "medicine" back then (which had seemed tremendously impressive at the time) scarcely qualified as life extension at all, by modern standards. The medical techniques of the 2050s barely qualified as common hygienic procedures. They were even cheap.

As for the traditional medical procedures that predated the 2050s, almost every one of them had been abandoned. They were dangerous, counterproductive, based in views of biological reality that were fundamentally mistaken.

Given these circumstances, it was wise to postpone your upgrade for as long as possible. The longer you waited, the better your choices would become. Unfortunately, the natural aging process never stopped in the meantime, so waiting too long made you subject to serious cumulative damage from natural metabolic decline. Sooner or later you had to hold your nose and make your choice. Since the outcome of leading-edge research was unknown by definition, the authorities could make no guarantees. Therefore, the pursuit of longevity was declared a fundamental freedom left to the choice of the individual. The polity offered its best advice, consensually derived in endless open meetings through vast thriving packs of experts, but advice was nothing better than advice.

If you were smart or lucky, you chose an upgrade path with excellent long-term potential. Your odds were good. You would be around for quite a while. Your choice would become and remain popular. The installed base of users would expand, and that would help you quite a lot. If anything went wrong with your upgrade, there'd be plenty of expertise in dealing with it.

If you were unlucky or foolish, your short-term gains would reveal serious long-term flaws. As the years ground on, you'd become isolated, freakish, obsolescent.

The truly bad techniques were the ones that complicated your transitions to another and better upgrade. Once your quality of life was irreparably degraded, you'd have no choice but to turn your attention to the quality of your death.

There were various methods of hedging your bets. You could, for instance, be conspicuously and repeatedly good. You always voted, you committed no crimes, you worked for charities, you looked after your fellow citizens with a smile on your face and a song in your heart. You joined civil support and served on net committees. You took a tangible wholehearted interest in the basic well-being of civilization. The community officially wanted you kept alive. You were probably old, probably well behaved, and probably a woman. You were awarded certain special considerations by a polity that appreciated your valuable public spirit. You were the exact sort of person who had basically seized power in modern society.

If you were responsible in your own daily health-care practices, the polity appreciated the way in which you eased the general strain on medical resources. You had objectively demonstrated your firm will to live. Your serious-minded, meticulous approach to longevity was easily verified by anyone, through your public medical records. You had discipline and forethought. You could be kept alive fairly cheaply, because you had been well maintained. You deserved to live.

Some people destroyed their health, yet they rarely did this through deliberate intention. They did it because they lacked foresight, because they were careless, impatient, and irresponsible. There were enormous numbers of medically careless people in the world. There had once been titanic, earth-shattering numbers of such people, but hygienically careless people had died in their billions during the plagues of the 2030s and 2040s. The survivors were a permanently cautious and foresightful lot. Careless people had become a declining interest group with a shrinking demographic share.

Once upon a time, having money had almost guaranteed good health, or at least good health care. Nowadays mere wealth guaranteed very little. People who publicly destroyed their own health had a rather hard time staying wealthy—not because it took good health to become wealthy, but because it took other people's confidence to make and keep money. If you were on a conspicuously public metabolic bender, then you weren't the kind of person that people trusted nowadays. You were a credit risk and a bad business partner. You had points demerits and got cheap medical care.

Even the cheap treatments were improving radically, so you were almost sure to do very well by historical standards. But those who destroyed their health still died young, by comparison with the elite. If you wanted to destroy your health, that was your individual prerogative. Once you were thoroughly wrecked, the polity would encourage you to die.

It was a ruthless system, but it had been invented by people who had survived two decades of devastating general plagues. After the plagues everything had become different, in much the way that everything was different after a world war. The experience of massive dieback, of septic terror and emptied cities, had permanently removed the culture's squeamishness. Some people died and some didn't. Those who took steps to fight death would be methodically rewarded, and those who acted like fools would be buried with the rest.

There were, of course, some people who morally disagreed with the entire idea of technologized life extension. Their moral decision was respected and they were perfectly free to drop dead.

Mia's choice of upgrade was known as Neo-Telomeric Dissipative Cellular Detoxification, or NTDCD. It was a very radical treatment that was very little tried and very expensive. Mia knew a great deal about NTDCD, because she was a professional medical economist. She qualified for it because she had been very careful. She chose to take it because it promised her the world, and she was in a mood to gamble.

Mia put 90 percent of her entire financial worth into a thirty-year hock to support continued research development and maintenance in NTDCD.

NTDCD was considered a particularly promising avenue of development. Medically speaking it was extremely difficult to perform. In medical upgrades, the promise and the difficulty were almost always tightly linked. Qualifying for such a lavish upgrade required an intimidating level of personal sacrifice. Patients qualifying for this treatment would have all their funds reinvested in maintenance and R&D. The funds would be returned handsomely if the avenue of upgrade paid off. If it didn't pay off, then the donor would probably be dead before the funds came back into liquidity.

Losing years of control over one's money was a very stiff price, but it was not the worst of it. The loss of money did not sting the way it once had stung. Money was no longer what money once had been. The polity had never been a free-market society. People dying of plague were not much impressed by free markets. The polity was a plague-panicked allocation society in which the whip hand of coercive power was held by smiling and stout-hearted medical rescue personnel. And by social workers. And by very nice old people.

––––––––––

Mia's forthcoming ordeal had been plotted in meticulous detail.

The first major trick was to stop eating. Her entire digestive tract would be clogged with a sterilizing putty.

The second trick was to stop breathing. Her lungs would

be filled with a sterilizing oxygenating silicone fluid. These two processes would immediately kill off most of the body's internal bacteria.

The third trick was to stop thinking. The blood-brain barrier would be scrubbed free from the capillaries of her skull and the cerebrospinal fluid would be replaced with a sterilizing saline fluid. Profound unconsciousness resulted.

The next trick, quite an advanced one, was to stop being quite so rigorously multicellular. Mia would be fetally submerged in a gelatinous tank of support fluids. Her internal metabolic needs would be supplied through a newly attached umbilical. The hair and the skin had to go. The bloodstream and lymphatic system would be opened to the support vat for the remaining course of the treatment. Red blood cell production would be shut down and the plasma replaced by a straw-colored fluid toxic to any cell which was not mammalian. All commensal organisms in the human body had to be destroyed.

Once the bacteria were thoroughly and utterly annihilated, the hunt would commence for the viruses and prions. It would take about a week to tag and destroy the genetic menagerie of imbedded human viruses. It would take about three weeks to destroy the vast metabolic cosmos of once-unsuspected human prions. These rogue proteins would mostly be shivered apart through magnetic resonance techniques.

Once this much had been accomplished, Mia would become an entirely antiseptic organism, a floating amniotic gel culture.

The DNA treatments could then commence. Intercellular repair required a radical loosening of the intracellular bonds so as to facilitate medical access through the cell surfaces of the corpus as a whole. The skinless body would partially melt into the permeating substance of the support gel. The fluidized body would puff up to two and a half times its original volume.

At this point, flexible plastic tubing could worm its way into the corpus. The skinless, bloated, and neotenically fetalized patient, riddled with piercings, would resemble an ivory Chinese doll depicting acupuncture sites.

Specific procedures would take place in the marrow of the

femurs, the spine, the ventricles of the brain, the sinuses, and other deeply interiorized spaces. Toxic buildups and precipitated mineralized bodies in the arteries, gall bladder, and lymphatic system—especially the metabolically crucial coacervate deposits in the pineal gland—would be reduced or eliminated.

On a genetic level, Mia's cells would be studied for cumulative replication errors. Precancerous and/or junk-burdened cells would be tagged with artificial antibodies and made the targets for programmed apoptosis. Some 15 percent of the body's cells would be killed during this period and removed by migratory artificial phagocytes. This process alone would require over a month.

The surviving cells would then be treated to a neo-telomeric extension. The telomeric ends of the chromosomes were a genetic clock, wearing thin as the human cell approached its Hayflick limit of allowable replications. New telomeric material would be spliced onto the chromosomes, tricking the aging cells into believing in the fiction of their own youth. The cells would then begin replicating furiously in the nutrient broth, and the wasted body would regain its 15 percent of lost body mass.

The extremely rapid growth within a buoyant support vat was closely akin to fetal growth. It was to be expected that there would be certain developmental abnormalities, especially in the adult joints and musculature. This was an expected price for marination in a fountain of youth.

The recovery process posed its own difficulties. The skin had to be regrown, commensal bacteria had to be gently reintroduced, the interior fluids had to be painstakingly replaced with natural substances. It was not entirely certain when the patient would regain consciousness, or what that state of consciousness might entail in the way of somatic sensation.

"I believe what you're trying to say is that this will be extremely painful," said Mia.

Her counselor was Dr. Rosenfeld, a sharp-faced, brilliantly preserved clinician with two dark wings of hair. Dr. Rosenfeld was a man of her own age. He had taken pains to inform Mia that he still considered himself fully bound by the Hippocratic oath he had taken some seventy years previously. In Dr. Rosenfeld's opinion, there were a few hundred million Johnny-come-lately medical technicians, and then there were actual doctors. Dr. Rosenfeld was a traditional, actual doctor. He would never allow any patient in his clinical charge to enter such a profoundly transformative state without a great deal of previous bedside manner.

"The term 'pain,' " said Dr. Rosenfeld, "is a relic of folk models of mental function. We have to draw a distinction between the higher-level subjective experience of pain, and the basal-level sequence of somatic nerve transmissions. All of these practices in NTDCD would be extremely painful to a fully operational brain, but your brain is going to be considerably less than operational. Have you heard of Korsakoff's syndrome?"

"Yes, I have."

"Of course, in modern practice we recognize thirty-one distinct substates of Korsakoff's. . . . You will be placed into one of those amnesiac modes during the procedure. It's like a virtuality, but it's a profound healing space. Extreme states of so-called pain may flash through certain preconscious processing centers involved in working memory, but those experiences will simply not be recorded through any normal channels. We'll be doing constant emission scanning, and I can guarantee you that whatever preconscious events may occur will never be consciously accessible, either during the time of treatment or afterward."

"So I'll feel it, but I won't feel it."

"That's semantics again. 'Feel' is a very broad and inexact folk term. So is the term 'I,' for that matter. Maybe we can say that there will be feelings, but there won't be any 'I' to have them." Dr. Rosenfeld smiled. "Ontology is fascinating, isn't it? I hope we can work through this discussion without invoking René Descartes."

"I've read René Descartes."

"The old fellow was remarkably prescient about the pineal gland." Dr. Rosenfeld spread his long-fingered, tapered, well-kept hands. "NTDCD is no mere maintenance procedure. This is the closest that humankind has yet come to genuine rejuvenation. This might be a treatment program that could put our patients on the path to immortality."

Mia only smiled. It was a claim that she had heard and read many times before. Medical entrepreneurs loved to claim that their particular line of life extension would carry patients all the way to a future transcendant medical breakthrough.

"It's a public-relations tactic that's been rather overblown," Dr. Rosenfeld admitted. "Still, look at the figures and trends. It's very clear that the speed of improvement in life extension is itself improving. Sooner or later we will hit the plateau. We'll reach a rate of life-span improvement of one year per year. At that point, the patients will become effectively immortal."

"*Some* patients," Mia said. "Maybe."

"I'm not saying that we're there yet, or even that we can see it. Obviously there are many hard decades of research ahead. But with NTDCD, some of our patients may, possibly, live to see that day."

"I didn't ask you for any such promises, Doctor. Anyway, I'll believe in immortality when I see it done for rats and dogs."

"We've done it already for fruit flies and nematodes," said Dr. Rosenfeld.

"I'm not a fruit fly," Mia said.

"Too true," said Dr. Rosenfeld. "I take your point. But you are a very special woman in a privileged position. Only forty human beings have gone through this treatment to date. Furthermore, none of them have had the exact clinical experience that you'll be undergoing. This treatment in its present form is only two years old. There is very little postoperational experience with patients. And that is a matter that concerns us both."

Mia nodded helpfully.

"Once you're out of the tank, you'll be consciously experiencing the end results of a very profound metabolic change. Once you enter your convalescence, you're not going to be the same woman who's sitting here in front of me right now. You'll discover that you're not even the mistress of your own body. You'll have lost a lot of nervous and muscular coordination."

Dr. Rosenfeld opened a notebook. "You're ninety-four years old. Your records tell me that you've lost about 12 percent of the neuronal and glial tissue that you had when you were, say, twenty.

That's perfectly normal and natural, but NTDCD is very, very far from normal and natural. You're going to get all that tissue back—not the original tissue, mind you, but a new infiltration of fresh brain tissue that is essentially unimprinted. And brain tissue is not something you can turn on and turn off, plug in or plug out. It's going to be part of you. The new you."

"How dangerous is that?"

"Let's just say you're going to require a lot of surveillance and counseling during the integrative process."

"What's the worst I can expect?"

"Very well . . . As you know, in the early days we had two fatalities. Catastrophic neural failure, cessation of higher functions, euthanasia. The customary ethical procedure—tragic, but customary. You could die in this treatment. That has happened."

"And?"

"And profound dissociation. What they used to call schizoid behavior, in the old days. Some preepileptic manifestations. We understand these mental processes fairly well these days, on a cellular level. Unless there is gross physical damage, strokes, infarcts, amyloid degeneration, then we simply don't allow our patients to enter states of dementia. We can interfere and avert most gross neuronal misbehavior."

He leaned back in the chair. "But there are other and subtler disturbances: culture shock, anomie, postoperation letdown, a few hints of bipolar disorder. Plus good old-fashioned human mulish impatience . . . Human consciousness is the highest and most complex metabolic function in all of nature. We can throw medical terms at the soul, but we can't box it up. We simply can't give people their identity the way we might give an injection; in the end, people have to find their own souls."

"Are you religious, Doctor?"

"Yes, I am, actually. I'm a Catholic lay brother."

"Really. How interesting."

"I wouldn't advise any use of entheogens under your medical circumstances, Mia. If you want to see your Savior face-to-face, then He will wait for you. You'll have plenty of time." Dr. Rosenfeld smiled.

Mia nodded and wisely said nothing.

Dr. Rosenfeld hesitated. "May I ask something? When was the last time you had an orgasm?"

Mia thought it over. "I'd have to say about twenty years."

"Very wise. I'm sure that has helped your metabolism. But you're going to become a sexual person again, with something very close to the full complement of metabolic drives. I won't say that's unpleasant, because of course sexuality is very pleasant, but it won't be easy for you. In fact, sexuality is generally the worst recuperative problem that our patients face."

"Really. How odd."

"People of our advanced years come to terms with a loss of libido. Our elderly patients often think they can repress sexual urges through a simple act of will. That's a canard. If human beings could control sexuality, the human race would have ceased to exist during the Pleistocene." He paused reflectively. "You're postmenopausal, of course. There's not much we can do about egg-cell lines. We wouldn't want to do egg-cell restoration anyway, because the ethicists don't approve. So you won't become fertile again."

Mia smiled. "Well, Doctor, I've been a young woman before. I've been married, I had a child. When I was young, people died from sexual diseases. Even contraception was troublesome. I've always been rather careful about that aspect of my life."

"Ah, but back then you had years to get accustomed to puberty. You didn't have a subjectively sudden dusting and cleaning of your entire limbic and hormonal systems. We're redoing your brain, and most of the brain doesn't think or reason. The human brain is a gland, it's not a computer."

Dr. Rosenfeld drummed his shining fingertips against the desktop. "People don't live because life is a rational decision. People don't get out of bed in the morning because of cost-benefit analysis. People don't get into bed together because they've decided on that course of action through logical deduction. Sexuality is an aspect of being, and you cannot stop your being through any mental act of will. You're going to be a ninety-four-year-old woman who can look, act, and feel like a twenty-year-old girl. Of course there will be complications."

"Can't I just take libido suppressants?"

"That's an option. Libido suppressants are very popular nowadays, but I wouldn't advise that you use them. Hormones have a strong function in physical development. Young people have a lot of hormones because young people really need those hormones, and you also need your hormones for the sake of proper development in your new brain tissue. My advice to you as your physician is that you are better off putting up with the troubles. Think of them as growing pains."

Mia smiled. "Are you advising me to take lovers?"

"Mia . . ." He patiently steepled his fingers. "Even if you can find lovers, and that's no small matter under your circumstances, taking lovers doesn't seem to help. It's not a simple matter. Our patients are elderly people, they've been through marriage, they've had children. They don't want to start flirting or courting. They don't want to commit to life partners, or start new families. They've already been through that aspect of human experience, they learned by it and they put it behind them. It's not that they're incapable of loving other people, but they've reached a state of deep maturity, of posthuman self-actualization. They just don't have it in themselves to maintain a committed and passionate sexual relationship. And yet after the treatment, the drives are very strong. Our patients tend to find it distressing. It's demeaning, and very difficult to integrate."

"I can see that this is a matter you take very seriously, Doctor."

"I do take it seriously. NTDCD is a very important technical development. I don't say that merely because I myself have been working in it. The experiences of the first NTDCD patients are of crucial interest to society and polity. Please have a look at this." Dr. Rosenfeld opened his notebook and showed her the screen.

An animation ran. A nude young man appeared. He was festooned from head to foot in what seemed to be junk jewelry. A plastic coronet. Earrings. False eyelashes. A little glued-on breastplate. Armlets. Bracelets. Ten identical finger rings. A dozen adhesive patches on his torso, groin, and thighs. Knee buckles, anklets, and shiny little toe rings. His hair was very short. He was strolling about an apartment, a bit clumsily and gawkily, and methodically petting a black cat.

"Those are positional tracking devices," Mia said.

"Yes. Also galvanic skin response, a tiara encephalometer, basal core temperatures, stool and urine samples, and a battery of comprehensive lab tests twice a week."

"I've never seen so many positional trackers on just one person. It's as if he were doing virtuality."

"Yes, rather. Muscular coordination is one of the critical factors in convalescence. We need complete and accurate readouts on the positioning of the limbs at all times. For tremor, palsy, cramping . . . Especially at night, because sleep disturbances seem to be one of our more prominent effects. The encephalometer you see him wearing is for possible strokes, infarcts, preseizure activity, neuronal or glial abnormalities. . . . This patient is Professor Oates, he's been one of our stars. He's a hundred and five."

"My goodness." She looked at him. He was a beautiful young man.

"He's been most cooperative. I'm sorry to say that cooperating with us is necessarily obtrusive and cumbersome. It very much hampers one's career and social life. Professor Oates is very kindly making the necessary sacrifices for the advancement of medical knowledge and the good of the polity."

Mia watched the screen. The nude Professor Oates did not look particularly happy about the situation. Mia spoke carefully. "I admire his courage in making such a brave act of self-abnegation."

"Professor Oates has always been very disciplined, very public-spirited. As you might expect of him, given the situation . . . He was a physicist, actually. Now he says he's giving up physics. Wants to take up architecture instead. He's very enthusiastic about architecture. As eager as a new student."

Mia closely studied the screen. In point of fact, although he was very attractive, Professor Oates did not look particularly human. He looked like a gifted professional actor posing for the cameras in the role of an ungainly nude undergraduate. "Would that be actual architecture, or virtual architecture?"

"I couldn't tell you," said Rosenfeld, surprised. "You could take that matter up with the professor. Naturally we have our own NTDCD civil-support group. It meets regularly on the net. Brilliant people, charming people. I must be frank, and tell you that you'll have your share of misery—but at least you'll be in very good company."

Mia sat back. "Well, Professor Oates is obviously a very accomplished young man. I beg your pardon—not young. A distinguished scholar."

"You aren't the first to make that mistake," said Dr. Rosenfeld, pleased. "People genuinely think they're young, these patients. People tend to believe what they see."

"That's lovely. I'm glad for him. It gives me a lot of hope."

"There is another matter. You remember the professor's cat?" Dr. Rosenfeld reached beneath his desk and pulled out a plastic lab cage. Inside there was paper litter and a small sleeping rodent. A hamster.

"Yes?" Mia said.

"We're going to do to this little animal what we're going to do to you. This hamster is five years old. That's very old for a hamster. Everything you go through, she's going to go through. Not in the same tank with you of course, but as part and parcel of the same procedure. You're about to become posthuman. And she's going to become postrodent. We want you to look after her for us, when she's done."

"I don't like pets."

"This isn't your 'pet,' Mia. This is a very valuable fellow entity which is about to share your unique state of being. Humor us in this, please. We know what we're doing." Dr. Rosenfeld tapped the cage with his thumbnail. The elderly hamster, in a doddering doze, showed no response. "There's a big difference between surviving this procedure and truly getting well. We do want you to get well, Mia, we truly want you to be all right, and we know that this will help your healing process. We can tell a great deal by the way you choose to treat a fellow creature who's been through your own brand of purgatory. It can be very lonely on the far side of humanity. Think of her as your lucky charm and your totem animal. Believe in her. And the best of luck to both of you."

***

Mia made her will. She fasted for three days. They shaved her, all over. They stripped her. They stuffed her with the paste. Then they started on the lung work, and they narcotized her utterly. All the rest of it went into the place where experiences that cannot be experienced must go.

***

When she awoke, it was January. She was very weak and tired and she had no hair. Her skin was blotchy and covered with lanugo, like an infant's skin. There were cold hard rings on her fingers and something nasty and tight around her head, but they made her keep everything on. She spent most of the first two days clenching her fists, raising the fingers into eyesight, slowly and deliciously stroking her face, and sometimes deliberately licking her fingers and the cold smooth rings.

She ate the mush that they gave her, because they complained if she didn't eat.

She had forgotten how to read.

On the third day she woke with a brisk new sense of intelligence and clarity and discovered that the little angular scrawls had become letters and words again. She opened her notebook and looked into it with a sense of absolute wonderment. It was full of the most abstruse and ridiculous economic and bureaucratic nonsense imaginable. She spent the day in gales of laughter, kicking her feet and looking at the screen and rubbing the itchy stubble on her head.

In the afternoon she climbed restlessly out of bed and began tottering about the hospital room. She put some chow and water in the hamster's cage, but the hamster was sleeping almost all the time, just lying there inert and pink and very slightly furry. One of the nurses asked if she had given a name to the hamster. She couldn't think of any names that would fit the circumstances, so she didn't call the hamster anything.

In the evening her daughter called from Djakarta, but she didn't want to speak to anyone from Djakarta. She told the nurses to say that she felt fine. She didn't say or do much during the rest of the evening. She'd come to realize that the room was saturated with machines that were always watching her, and some of the machines were so clever that they were practically invisible.

On the fourth day they gave her some new hard and chewy food and also some sweet things that were quite delightful. She asked for more, and pouted when they wouldn't give her any. Then they dressed her in very nicely double-stitched blue cotton overalls and took her into a room that they said was a children's room. There weren't any children in it, so she had it all to herself, and it was a very nice room. It had bright colors and the lighting was as clear and fresh as summer sunlight and it had machines to swing on and climb on. She worked herself into fits of laughter climbing and swinging and tumbling off onto the padded floor, until she had kind of an accident in the coveralls. Then she made them stop so she could clean herself up.

Then she went back to her room and watched some political news on her notebook. She had a long intense chat with Dr. Rosenfeld about American politics in the 2030s. She had been intensely interested in politics during the worldwide crisis of the 2030s, and when she thought about what had happened back then, it made her so mad she could scream. She talked a great deal about her favorite stupid policies and politicians of the thirties, and she got a lot of indignation off her chest. Dr. Rosenfeld said she was coming along very well. He asked her if she had named the hamster yet. She couldn't understand why they were getting so worked up about that topic. She didn't much like the hamster.

On the fifth day they introduced her to another NTDCD patient named Juliet Ramachandran, a very nice young woman who was one hundred thirteen. Juliet had been blind before the treatment because of retinal degeneration, and she had a postcanine Seeing Eye dog who could talk. Mrs. Ramachandran had been in civil support for many years and had a very polished manner. Mia and Juliet and the dog all got along together very well, and had a long talk about the treatment and other things. The dog had grown all its fur back, while Juliet had a lovely silk turban. The dog was a real chatterbox, but Juliet said that was a passing phase.

Juliet kept saying the words, "Mia Ziemann." This made her laugh.

"Do you know that your name is Mia Ziemann?"

She could tell that Juliet was getting agitated. "All right, have it your way, miazeeman, miazeeman, don't rub it in." Life wasn't easy for Juliet, recovering her sight and everything. Juliet was very frank about her troubles, and kept talking about the peculiar sensation of objects "touching the backs of my eyes." It was kinder to be gentle with poor Juliet. She decided that she would try very hard to answer whenever anyone said "Mia."

On the sixth day she made a point of responding to "Mia," and they began to treat her differently and better. When they asked if she had named the hamster, she said "Fred." When they said that that was a boy's name she said it was short for Frederika. She took the hamster out and dandled it and made sure it had its chow. They were very pleased with this behavior.

The hamster was a nasty little ratlike thing that waddled and had beady black eyes and shrunken jittery paws. It was growing some nice soft brown fur, though. One day the hamster had a kind of brief fit in its cage, but she decided not to tell anybody. It would only upset them.

On the seventh day, she realized that she had once truly been someone called Mia Ziemann, and that there was probably something pretty seriously wrong with her. She didn't feel at all sick, however. She felt terrific, wonderful. She felt very glad to have the privilege of being whoever she might be. When she thought seriously about really being Mia Ziemann, however, there was a taste in her mouth as if she had bitten her tongue. She felt a peculiar kind of dread, as if Mia Ziemann was hiding in the closet and waiting for dark. So that Mia Ziemann could come out and caper ghostfully around the hospital room.

In the afternoon she put on some of her Mia Ziemann clothes and went for a long walk, five or six times around the hospital grounds. The Mia clothes were very well made, but unfortunately they didn't fit. She was not only thinner and svelter but she had grown five centimeters taller. She was walking pretty well now, but there was a strange wobbling roll in her hips. During her walk, she saw quite a few people around the hospital who were truly and profoundly unhealthy. She realized how lucky she was.

In the evening she started reading net discussions from the NTDCD support group. It was very flattering to have her intelligence overestimated by such brilliant people. She felt that she ought to contribute, and that probably she had some worthwhile medical experiences to write about, but her typing had gotten all rusty somehow.

She was always very good and patient with the support people when they did the tests, even though the tests hurt her quite a bit. They had some other tests that were just puzzles: playing chess problems, doing crosswords, stacking oddly shaped blocks. The word tests were plenty tough, but when it came to stacking blocks she was a whiz. Apparently her geometric modeling skills had increased by about 15 percent. Much of this result was improved reaction time, but some of it seemed to be genuine neoneuronal integration, according to the emission results. When she'd paged through this medical prognosis, she grew very proud of her achievement, and firmly decided she would do less talking from now on and just look at pictures more. Play to her cognitive strengths. Maybe even draw some pictures, or take some photographs, or model in clay or virtuality. There were so many fabulous possibilities.

After they gave her some plasticine, she had a stroke of insight and did the hamster. She put a lot of cunning effort into the rodent's portrayal. When they saw the results, they were delighted with her, just as she had firmly suspected they would be. They said that it would soon be time for her to be released and continue the convalescence at her newly remodeled apartment.

She'd been suspecting the truth for quite a while, but she now fully realized that the people guarding her were as dumb as bricks. It would be fairly elementary to get out from under their thumbs and go someplace else where she could pursue other activities—something a lot more interesting than hanging around eating medicated mush with a hamster. This prospect was very enticing. Her only regret was that one of the male support people was really good-looking, and she had fallen for him a little bit. It was just as well, though. Even if she'd asked him to kiss her, it would only have been one of those severe medical ethical standards things. He'd never even make it to second base.

She was answering to "Mia" all the time now. She even did some of Mia's work. There was a trick to it, like throwing your eyes out of focus. She would relax deep inside and let the Mia feeling come up, and then she could do quite a few useful things, type a lot faster, enter passwords back in the LEL-SF Assessment Collaboratory, collate spreadsheets, examine her flowware, sign the Mia name even. She came to recognize that the Mia thing didn't want to hurt her. The Mia wasn't jealous, and didn't mean her any harm at all. The Mia thing was meek and obliging and accommodating, and not very interesting. The Mia seemed to be really tired and didn't care very much about anything. The Mia was nothing but a bundle of habits.

She'd learned to get along a lot better by talking less, just by listening and watching. It was amazing how much people revealed to you, if you carefully watched their faces and what they did with their hands. Most of the time what people were really thinking had nothing to do with the words coming out of their mouths. Men especially. All you had to do was just wriggle in the chair a little bit, and nod and smile nicely, and give them a kind of sidelong glitter of the eyes, and they just knew in their male heart of hearts that you must be perfectly okay.

Women weren't so easy to fool that way, but even women would get all impressed if you just seemed perfectly happy and confident. Most women were very far from perfectly happy and confident. Most women really needed to complain. If you just coaxed them to complain at you, and nodded a lot, and said Oh-poor-dear and I'd-have-done-just-the-same-thing, then they would unload all sorts of things on you. They'd become all emotionally close to you and grateful. The women would go away knowing that you must be perfectly okay.

They made a big deal about her going home for convalescence. There was even press coverage—a net reporter asked her questions. He was a good-looking guy, and she started flirting with him a little bit during the interview, and he got all flustered and touched. She took the hamster home to Parnassus Avenue with her, along with the reporter. She made the reporter a nice dinner. The reporter came along like a lamb. He was very taken with her.

She was glad to have a chance to cook and eat, because they'd told her at the hospital that she had problems with her appetite. It was very true, too—if food was put in front of her she'd be happy to eat it, but if food wasn't put in front of her then she wouldn't miss it. She'd hear her stomach rumble and she'd get weak and maybe a little dizzy, but there wasn't any real hunger. It seemed she'd gone a little bit food-blind somehow. She could smell food and she could taste it and she liked to eat it, but the tiara said there was some kind of glitch in her hypothalamus. They were hoping it would pass. If it didn't pass by itself, then they'd have to do something about it.

Cooking was great—she never had to think about cooking, she just relaxed and it flowed right out of her hands. She listened to the reporter brag for two hours about all his important contacts. She fed him and made him a tincture. He was just a kid, only forty. She was really tempted to start kissing him, but she knew that would be a critical error at this point. They'd outfitted her apartment like a telepresence site. She couldn't even scratch without every finger being instantly recorded in real time in some 3-D medical database.

When the reporter left, she hugged and kissed him at the door. Not much of a kiss, but it was the first kiss she'd had in absolutely forever. She couldn't believe she had gone so long without kissing anyone. It was unbelievably stupid, like trying to live without water.

Then she was alone in her apartment again. Alone, wonderfully, sweetly, and incredibly alone. Except for all her medical monitors. Just herself. And all the surveillance machines. She cleaned and washed everything and straightened it away.

When she was done with cleaning, she sat perfectly still in the apartment at the lacquered cardboard kitchen table. She had the oddest sensation. She could feel herself growing inside. Her self felt so big and free. Bigger than her body. Her self was bigger than the entire apartment. In the silence and the stillness she could feel her self pushing mutely at the windows.

She jumped up restlessly and put on a tab of Mia's music. It was that awful yard-goods background music that people listened to nowadays, twinkly discreet music that sounded like it was stapled together out of dust. The walls were covered with hideously offensive antique paper art. The drapes looked like they had died against the walls. Someone had shriveled up inside this apartment, it was like the shrunken insides of a dead walnut. A dead woman's wrinkly dry skin.

She tried to sleep in Mia's bed. It was a nasty little old person's bunk with a big ugly oxygen shroud. The mattress had been designed to do peculiar things in the way of firm spinal support. She didn't want her spine supported anymore, and in any case it was a very different kind of spine now. Plus her monitors itched and crunched against the sheets. She crawled out into the front room and wrapped up in a blanket on the floor.

The hamster, which was mostly nocturnal, had come awake and was gnawing vigorously on the bars of its cage. Gnaw, gnaw, gnaw. In the darkness. Scratch, scratch, scratch.

Around midnight, something snapped. She got up, put on her underwear, kicked on her Mia slacks. Too short, they showed her ankles. Put on a Mia brassiere. A total joke, this brassiere had no connection to reality. Put on a Mia pullover. Found a really nice red jacket in the closet. The jacket fit great. Found Mia shoes that pinched a little. Found a purse. Too small. Found a big bag. Put some underwear in the bag. Put in some lipstick. A comb, a brush, a razor. Sunglasses. A book to read on the way. Some socks. Some mascara, some eyeliner. A toothbrush.

Her netlink began ringing urgently. She'd had it with the netlink.

"They have got to be kidding," she announced to the empty room. "This is not my place. This is nowhere. I can't live like this. This isn't living. I am out of here." She walked out of her front door and slammed it.

She hesitated on the landing, then turned, opened the door, went back in. "Okay, okay," she said. "Come on, you stupid thing." She opened the cage, grabbed the hamster. "Come on, you can come, too."

She threw the tiara off just outside the apartment. A hospital van arrived, flashing its way up the street and parking outside her building. She ditched the earrings and all ten finger rings on her way up Parnassus Avenue. While she waited for a taxi she slipped out of her shoes and socks and got rid of the nasty toe gadgets. The skin under there was all pale and sticky.

The taxi arrived.

Once in the taxi she shimmied out of her slacks and ditched the knee buckles and a large gluey complement of obnoxious stick-on patches. Out the window with them. On the train on the way to the airport she went to the ladies' and shredded her way out of the breastplate, and about a dozen more patches. The patches were a big itchy pain and when they were gone her morale began to soar.

She arrived at the airport. The black tarmac was full of glowing airplanes. They had a lovely way of flexing their wings and simply jumping into the chill night air when they wanted to take off. You could see people moving inside the airplanes because the hulls were gossamer. Some people had clicked on their reading lights but a lot of the people onboard were just slouching back into their beanbags and enjoying the night sky through the fuselage. Or sleeping, because this was a red-eye flight to Europe. It was all very quiet and beautiful. There was nothing to it really.

She walked to a departure stairs and worked her way up. The stewardess spoke to her in Deutsch as she entered the aircraft. She opened her bag, pulled out the hamster, showed the hamster to the stewardess, put the hamster back in. Then she spun on her heel and walked with perfect joy and confidence right down the aisle. The stewardess didn't do a thing.

She chose a nice brown beanbag in business class and lay down. Then a steward brought her a nice hot frappé.

At three in the morning the aircraft took off and she finally fell asleep.

When she woke up again it was eight o'clock in the morning, February 10, 2096. She was in Frankfurt.

She deplaned and wandered around the Frankfurt airport, lost and sticky eyed and blissfully without plans. She didn't have any money. No cashcard, no credit. No ID. The civil-support people from the flight were deliberately checking in with the local authorities, but the Deutschland authorities didn't bother to go looking for you if you didn't go looking for them.

She had some water from a fountain and went to a bathroom and washed her face and hands and changed her underwear and her socks. Her face didn't seem to need much makeup anymore, but she direly missed her makeup. Walking around without makeup made her feel far more anxious than any mere lack of ID.

She emerged from the bathroom and walked along with the other people so that no one would notice her.

The crowd led her through about a million glass-fronted halls and kiosks, down escalators into an ivy-grown train station. It seemed that Deutschlanders were really fond of ivy, especially if the ivy was growing really deep underground where ivy basically had no business growing.

There was a young European girl down there with very short

hair and a bright red jacket. Since she also had very short hair and a bright red jacket, she thought it would be clever to follow this young girl and do as she did. This was a very wise plan, as the girl knew just where to go. The girl fetched biscuits in a paper bag from a Deutschlander civil-support kiosk. So she fetched a bag, too. She didn't have to pay. The biscuits were really good. She could feel the vitamin-stuffed government-subsidized nontoxic goodness racing through her grateful innards.

Once she'd wolfed down half a dozen biscuits and had some more water, she began to feel quite cozy and pleased with herself. She gave some crumbs to the hamster.

Inside the train station hall twelve guys in big woven ponchos and flat black hats were playing Andean folk music on pipes and guitars. These South American guys had set up a card-reader on a post, but you didn't have to pay them if you didn't want to. You could just sit and listen to their free music. There were plenty of free beanbags around to lie in, and there was free water, and plenty of free biscuits, and a very nice free ladies' room. As far as she could figure it, there was no reason why she couldn't just spend the rest of her life right here in the good old Frankfurt train station.

It was warm and cozy, and just watching all the different European people wander past with their luggage was endlessly fascinating. She felt a bit conspicuous sitting there in her public beanbag publicly nibbling her public biscuits, but she wasn't hurting anybody. In fact, everybody who looked at her obviously thought she was great. The Deutschland people smiled at her. Men especially smiled at her quite a lot. As she killed an hour, she saw ten or twelve little kids in the crowd. Even the little kids smiled at her.

Everybody thinking they had something important to do. How pathetically amusing. Why couldn't they just sit still and enjoy life? What was their big hurry? All this aimless running around . . . They were all gonna live a million years—wasn't that the point of everything? You could just lie still in a beanbag and be at peace with the universe, perfectly happy.

She enjoyed this thoroughly, for about an hour and a half.

Then she became indifferent. Openly bored. Restless. Agitated, and finally unable to sit still a moment longer. Besides, the guys from the Andes had begun to repeat the same songs again, and that whistle thing they were blowing was really irritating. She got up and chose herself a train like everybody else was doing.

Inside the train it was noisy. With talk. The train itself didn't make any noise at all, but the people aboard were chattering and eating noodles and drinking big malts. It was an extremely fast train and as silent as an eel. It ran on tracks but it didn't touch them. She put her bag under the seat and wished that she could understand Deutsch.

When she picked her bag up, she found the neck of the bag yawning open, and realized that her hamster had escaped. The nasty little hairbug had finally made a break for it, either inside the train, or back at the Frankfurt station. At first she was a little upset, but then she realized how funny it was. Hamster on the loose! Mass panic grips Europe! Well, good-bye, good riddance, and good luck, postrodent! No hard feelings, okay?

She got off the train at Munchen because she liked the name of the city. Once it had been Munich or Muenchen or Moenchen or even München, but the All-European Orthographic Reformation had made it into Munchen. Munchen, Munchen, Munchen. Somebody had said that Stuttgart was the greatest city for the arts in the whole world, but Stuttgart wasn't half so pretty a name as Munchen.

She knew she would love Munchen as soon as she discovered that they were giving away pretzels at the kiosks. Not little American dry stick pretzels with iodized salt either, but big warm bready pretzels that probably had traces of actual wheat and yeast in them. In the Munchen station there were about a hundred kids from all over Europe lined up laughing for these big bracelet-sized Munchen pretzels. The Bavarian civil-support bakery people had very smug looks about this situation. You could just tell they had some kind of ulterior motive.

She gleefully munched her two giant pretzels and drank more water and then she found another and even prettier girl, with long blond hair and a blue velvet coat, and followed her. And that was how she ended up in the Marienplatz.

There was a tubestation outlet in the platz, and a gushing fountain with a circular stone railing, and a big marble column with four bronze cherubs skewering devils. A gilded Virgin Mary stood at the column's top, doing a kind of civil reconnaissance check. There was a telepresence site in one corner, and a bunch of fashion stores with glowing and moving mannequin displays. Lots of spindly Euro pedal-bikes parked around. There were all kinds of people wandering the Marienplatz. Tourists from all over the world. Especially Indonesians.

She leaned against the edge of the fountain railing, like the other kids in the platz. The fountain had three muscular bronze statues pouring eternal streams of water from big bronze buckets. The sun was setting already, and it was plenty cold. All the kids had flushed cheeks and windblown hair and they were in jackets and colored neck wrappings and odd-looking Euro-kid boots.

Every once in a while a pair of big German-shepherd police dogs would trot by the platz, and the kids would stop talking and tighten up a little.

The Marienplatz was a beautiful plaza. She liked the way the Muncheners had taken good care of their church: peaked arches, balconies, fishy-looking stone Christian saints transcending the flesh. She especially liked the colorful medieval wooden robots up in the clock tower.

Up on the tower's steeple, dangling by their heels high above the platz, were three naked Catholics with their arms folded in prayer. They were doing a penitential performance ritual. Not calling any outrageous attention to themselves or anything, in fact it was pretty hard to notice the Catholics up there, dangling naked by the ridged teeth of the stone Gothic spire. They were exposing the flesh to the wind and the cold, very pious and dedicated, and obviously higher than kites.

Someone spoke to her, right at her elbow. She turned, looking away from the steeple penitents. "What?" she said.

And there stood a young good-looking guy in a sheepskin jacket and sheepskin pants—basically, in fact, the guy was wearing an entire sheep, included the tanned and eyeless head, which was part of his jacket lapel. He was white and woolly-curly all over. But he had black slicked-back hair, which went well with his rather slicked-back forehead and his sloping black eyebrows. "Ah, English," he said. "No problem, I speak English."

"You do? Good. Hi!"

"Hi. From where are you coming?"

"California."

"Just come to Munchen today?"

"*Ja.*"

He smiled. "What's your name?"

"Maya."

"I'm Ulrich. Welcome to my beautiful city. So you're all alone, no parents, no boyfriend? You are standing here in the Marienplatz two hours, you don't meet anybody, you don't do anything." He laughed. "Are you lost?"

"I don't have to go anywhere in particular, I'm just passing through."

"You *are* lost."

"Well," Maya said, "maybe I am a little lost. But at least I haven't been spying on other people for two whole hours, like you have."

Ulrich smiled slowly, swung a big brown backpack off his shoulders, and set it at his feet. "How could I help but to watch such a beautiful woman?"

Maya felt her eyes widen. "You really think so? Oh, dear . . ."

"Yes, yes! I can't be the first man to tell you this news! You're lovely. You're beautiful! You're cute like a big rabbit."

"I bet that sounds really nice in Deutsch, Ulrich, but . . ."

"I'm sure I can help you. Where's your hotel?"

"I don't have one."

"Well, where's your luggage, then?"

She lifted her handbag.

"No luggage. No hotel. No place to go. No parents, no boy-friend. You got any money?"

"No."

"How about an ID? I hope you have your ID."

"Especially no ID."

"So. Then you are a runaway." Ulrich thought this over, with evident glee. "Well, I have good news for you, Miss Maya the Runaway. You're not the only runaway to come to Mun-chen."

"I was kind of thinking of taking the train back to Frankfurt tonight, actually."

"Frankfurt! What a waste! Frankfurt is a tomb. A grave! Come with me and I'll take you to the most famous pub in the world!"

"Why should I go anywhere with some guy who's so terribly mean to sheep?"

Ulrich touched his sheepskin coat with a look of wounded shock. "You're making funny! I'm not mean! I killed this sheep myself in single combat. He wanted to take my life! Come with me and I'll take you to the famous Hofbrauhaus. They're eating meat! And drinking beer!"

"You've got to be kidding."

"It's not far." Ulrich crossed his fleecy white arms. "You want to see, or don't you?"

"Yeah. I do want to see. Okay."

He took her to the Hofbrauhaus, just as he had promised. There were massive stone arches outside and big brass-bound doors and uniformed civil-support people. Ulrich shrugged out of his coat, and quite neatly, in a matter of seconds, stepped deftly out of his pants. He stuffed the sheepskins into his capacious backpack. Beneath the skins he was wearing brightly patterned leotards.

Inside, the Hofbrauhaus had a vaulted ceiling with murals and ironwork and lanterns. It was wonderfully warm and smelled very powerfully of burning and stewing animal meat. A veteran brass band in odd hats and thick suspenders was playing two-hun-dred-and-fifty-year-old polkas, the kind of folk music that was so well worn that it slipped through your ears like pebbles down a stream. Strangers were crammed together at long polished wooden benches and tables, getting full of alcoholic bonhomie. Maya was relieved to see that most of them weren't actually drinking the alcohol. Instead, they were drinking big cold malts and inhaling the alcohol on the side through little lipid-tagged nose snifters. This much reduced the dosage and kept the poison away from the liver.

It was loud inside. "You want to eat something?" Ulrich shouted.

Maya looked at a passing platter. Chunks of animal flesh swimming in brown juices, shredded kraut, potato dumplings. "I'm not hungry!"

"You want to drink some beer?"

"Ick!"

"What do you want, then?"

"I dunno. Just to watch everybody act weird, I guess. Is there some quiet place here where we can sit down and talk?"

Ulrich's long brows knotted, in impatience with her, she thought, and then he methodically scanned the crowd. "Do something for me, all right? You see that old tourist lady there with the notebook?"

"Yes?"

"Go ask her if she has a tourist map. Talk to her for one minute, sixty seconds, nothing more. Ask her . . . ask if she can tell you where is the Chinese Tower. Then come outside the Hof-brauhaus and meet with me again. In the street."

"Why?" She looked searchingly into his face. "You want me to do something bad."

"A little bad maybe. But very useful for us. Go and talk to her. There's no harm in talking."

Maya went to stand by the old woman. The old woman was methodically and neatly eating noodles with a fork and a spoon. She was drinking a bottle of something called Fruchtlimo and was very nicely dressed. "Excuse me, ma'am, do you speak English?"

"Yes, I do, young lady."

"Do you have a map of Munchen? In English? I'm looking for a certain place."

"Of course I do. Glad to help." The woman opened her notebook and deftly shuffled screens. "What do they call this place you want to go?"

"The Chinese Tower."

"Oh, yes. I know that place. Here we go. . . ." She pointed. "It's located in the English Gardens. A park designed by Count von Rumford in the 1790s. The Count von Rumford was Benjamin Thompson, an American émigré." She looked up brightly. "Isn't it funny to think of a town this ancient being redesigned by one of our fellow Americans!"

"Almost as funny as Indianapolis being redesigned by an Indonesian."

"Well," said the woman, frowning, "that all happened long before you were born. But I happen to be from Indiana, and I was there when the Indonesians bought the city, and believe me, when that happened we didn't think it was very funny."

"Thanks a lot for your help, ma'am."

"Would you like me to print you a map? I have a scroller in my purse."

"That's okay. I have to meet someone, I have to go now."

"But it's quite a long way to the tower, you might get lost. Let me just . . ." She paused, surprised. "My purse is gone."

"You lost your purse?"

"No, I didn't lose it. It was right here, right below the bench." She glanced around, then up at Maya. She lowered her voice. "I'm afraid someone's taken my purse. Stolen it. Oh, dear. This is very sad."

"I'm sorry," Maya said, inadequately.

"Now I'm afraid I'll have to talk with the authorities." The old woman sighed. "This is very distressing. They'll be so embarrassed, poor things. . . . It's dreadful when things like this happen to guests."

"It's very nice of you to think of their feelings."

"Well, of course it's not my loss of a few possessions, it's the violation of civility that hurts."

"I know that," Maya said, "and I'm truly sorry. I wish you could take my purse instead." She put her own bag on the table. "There's not much in here, but I wish you could have it."

The old woman looked at her for the first time, directly, eye to eye. Something quite strange happened between them then. The woman's eyes widened and she turned pale. "Didn't you say that you had an appointment," she said at last in a tentative voice, "that you had an appointment, ma'am? Please don't let me keep you."

"Yes, okay," Maya said, "good-bye, *wiedersehen*." She left the Hofbrauhaus.

Ulrich was waiting for her outside in the street. He had put his woolly suit back on. "You take much too long," he chided, turning. "Come with me." He began walking up the street, to a tubestation.

On the way down the escalator Ulrich opened his brown backpack and began rooting in its depths. "Ah-hah! Yes, I knew it." He pulled up a little featherlight earclamp. "Here, wear this on."

Maya put the earclamp onto her right ear. Ulrich began speaking to her in Deutsch. A stream of Deutsch gibberish emerged from his lips, and the earclamp began translating on the fly.

"[This will be much better,]" the earclamp repeated, in dulcet mid-Atlantic English. "[Now we'll be able to converse in something like intellectual parity.]"

"What?" Maya said.

"The translator works, isn't it?" Ulrich spoke English and patted his ear anxiously.

"Oh." Maya touched the earclamp. "Yes, it's working."

Ulrich slipped happily back into Deutsch. "[Well, then! Now I can demonstrate to you that I'm rather a more clever and resourceful fellow than my limited skills in English irregular grammar might indicate.]"

"You just stole that woman's purse."

"[Yes, I did that. It was expedient. It was too frustrating to speak to you otherwise. I was sure that a woman of her age and class would have a tourist's translator. And who knows, perhaps there are other interesting things in the purse.]"

"What if they catch you? Catch us?"

"[They won't catch us. When I took the purse I was in my leotards, and there was no one in brightly colored leotards recorded entering or leaving the building. There are certain techniques by which one does these appropriations safely. The craft is difficult to explain to a neophyte.]" Ulrich brushed briskly at the woolly sleeves of his jacket. "[But back to the point. I'm rather good at understanding English, not so good at speaking it.]" Ulrich laughed. "[So you can speak to me in English, and I will speak to your earpiece in Deutsch, and we'll get on very well.]"

They reached the bottom of the escalator and began working their way through the maze of potted plants: cycads, ferns, gingkos. "[When someone speaks a pidgin version of your language,]" Ulrich told her, "[it's hard not to underestimate their intellect. They always seem like such a fool. I wouldn't care to have you underestimate me. That misapprehension would put us on entirely the wrong footing.]"

"Okay. I understand you. You can speak beautifully. But you're a thief."

"[Yes, we European purse-snatchers have traditionally benefited by an exquisite education.]" She could hear the tone of sarcasm in Ulrich's Deutsch even as she heard the running translation in English. The translator had a way of punching bits of English, with just the right pitch and timbre, through the blocky syllables inside the Deutsch. This was going to take some getting used to.

They stepped aboard a tube train, and sat together in the back of the car. Ulrich didn't bother to pay. "[It's better to leave the scene of the crime in short order,]" he murmured. He took her handbag from her, opened it, and emptied the entire contents of the stolen purse into it, deftly hiding the operation in the cavernous depths of his own backpack. "[Here,]" he said, giving her back her own handbag. "[That's all yours now. See what you can find that's of use to you.]"

"This is very dishonest."

"[Maya, you are dishonest. You are an illegal alien traveling without ID,]" Ulrich said. "[Are you ready to be honest and to go home? Do you want to honestly face the people that you ran away from?]"

"No. No, definitely, I don't want that."

"[Then you're breaking the rules already. You will have to break a lot more such silly rules. You can't get a real job without ID. You can't get health checks, you can't get insurance. If the police ever bother to formally question you, they will take one little sniff of your DNA and they will find out who you are. No matter where you came from in the whole wide world, no matter who you are. The polity's medical databanks are very good.]" Ulrich rubbed his chin. "[Maya, do you know what an 'Information Society' is?]"

"Sure. I guess so."

"[Europe is a true Information Society. A true Information Society is a society made of informers.]" Ulrich's dark eyes narrowed. "[A society of 'rats.' 'Sneaks.' 'Snitches.' 'Judases.' 'Stool pigeons.' Is my rhetorical point penetrating that translator?]"

"Yes, it is."

"[Then that's a fine translator! What an excellent grasp of the Deutsch vernacular!]" Ulrich laughed cheerfully, and lowered his voice. "[Munchen is a good place to hide, because the police here move slowly. If you're smart and you have good friends, then you can survive in Munchen as a runaway. But if they ever take real notice of you, then the bulls will come to arrest you. You can count on that.]"

"Are you an illegal, Ulrich?"

"[Not at all, I'm a legal Deutschlander. Twenty-three years old.]" He stretched, putting his arm behind her shoulders. "[I simply enjoy pursuing the life of a petty criminal for reasons of pleasure and ideology. Too much honesty is bad for people.]"

Maya looked inside her handbag. She felt a vague urge to complain further, but she decided to shut up when she saw what a fine haul he'd made. The minibank was useless away from its proper owner, of course, but there were a couple of cashcards in there with pin money already slotted in them. Also a Munchen tubeticket. Sunglasses. Brush and comb set. Hair lacquer. Lipstick (not her color), night cream (hydrolyzer compound), internal pH chalk (peppermint flavored). Mineral tabs for tinctures. A hypo set. Tissues. A handsome little netlink. A scroller. And a camera.

Maya fished out the camera. A little digital tourist job. It fit her hand with lovely smoothness. She peered experimentally through the lens, then turned and framed Ulrich's face. He flinched away, and quickly shook his head.

Maya examined the camera's readout and cleared the internal disk of photos. "You really want me to keep all this stuff?"

"I know you need it," Ulrich said in English.

"Great." She began carefully polishing the camera with a paper tissue.

"[I happened to look inside your bag,]" Ulrich confided, "[while you were staring up at the steeple at those crazy Catholics. I saw that there was nothing much in your bag except a half-eaten welfare pretzel and some panties spotted with rat dung. This made me very curious.]" Ulrich leaned closer. "[I declined to appropriate your useless purse. I thought it much better that I offer you my protection. I don't know who you are, little Californian. But you are very unworldly. You won't last long in Munchen without a friend.]"

She smiled at him sunnily. Perfectly happy and confident. "So you're my new friend?"

"[Certainly. I'm just the kind of bad company you need.]"

"You're very generous. With other people's property."

"[I'd be generous with my own property if I were allowed to have any.]" He took her hand and squeezed it, very gently. "[Don't you trust me? You might as well trust me. We'll have much more fun that way.]" He lifted her fingers, and lightly touched them to his lips.

She pulled her hand free, clapped her palm against the back of his neck, and leaned into him. Their faces collided. Their lips met.

Kissing him was absolute rapture. Heat rose from his sleek young neck inside the woolly collar. The smell of male human flesh in close proximity hit a core of memory within her that lit her up all over. She could feel her whole personality pucker and collapse as if her bare brain had bitten into a lemon. She began to kiss the stuffing out of him.

"[Be careful, little mouse,]" Ulrich said, tearing free with a happy gasp. "[People are watching.]"

"Can't I kiss a guy on a subway?" she said, wiping her mouth on her coatsleeve. "What's the harm?"

"[Not much for us,]" he agreed. "[But it might make these people remember us. That's not smart.]"

She looked up the length of the railway car. A dozen Muncheners were staring at them. Caught out, the Deutschlanders continued to stare, with deep and solemn interest and without one shred of inhibition. Maya frowned, and raised her camera to her face in self-defense. The Deutschlanders merely smiled and waved at her, clowning for the lens. Reluctantly, she put the camera back into her purse. "Where are we going, anyway?"

"[Where do you want to go?]"

"Where can we go lie down?"

Ulrich laughed delightedly. "[It's just as I thought. You're a madwoman.]"

She poked his ribs. "Don't tell me you didn't like that, you big faker."

"[Of course I liked it. You're the exact sort of madwoman I've been looking for all my life. You're very pretty, you know. It's very true. You should let your hair grow out.]"

"I'll get a wig."

"[I'll get you seven wigs,]" Ulrich promised. He'd gone all heavy lidded. "[One for every day of the week. And clothes. You like nice clothes, don't you? I can tell from that jacket that you're a girl who likes nice clothes.]"

"I like vivid clothes."

"[You ran away from home to be vivid, little mouse? Vivid people have a lot of fun.]" She'd taken his breath away for a moment, but all the kissing was having a delayed effect on Ulrich. He'd gotten his initiative back and he was having a hard time controlling his hands.

"[Necking always makes me stupid,]" Ulrich announced,

meditatively massaging her left thigh. "[I should take you to a cheap hotel, but I'm going to take you to my favorite criminal den.]"

"A criminal den? How lovely. What more could I need?"

"[Better shoes,]" he told her, very seriously. "[Contact lenses. Cashcards. Wigs. Skin tint. Some pidgin Deutsch, to get by. Maps. Food. Plumbing. A nice warm bed.]"

They left the train in Schwabing. Ulrich took her to a squat. It was a four-story twentieth-century apartment house, in cheap and hideous yellow brick. Someone had methodically ripped all the electrical wiring out of the building, reducing it to unrentable junk. Ulrich picked up a wire-handled oil lamp from the stoop by the front door.

"[You can't keep the health inspectors out of a squat,]" Ulrich warned her. They ignored the shattered elevator and headed up the first of several flights of darkened, reeking stairs. "[Civil-support people are stubborn pests, they are very brave. But Munchen police are very efficient and therefore lazy. They want machines to do their work, and it's hard to bug or tap a squat when it has no electricity.]"

"How many people live in this dump?"

"[They come and they go. About fifty people. We are anarchists.]"

"All young people?"

"The dead-at-forty," Ulrich said in English, and smiled. "[They call us young. . . . Old people don't like squats. They don't want freedom or privacy. They want their archives, cleaning machines, reclining chairs, real money, monitors and alarms everywhere, all the comforts. Truly old people never squat. They don't feel the need.]" Ulrich leered halfheartedly. "[One of many such needs that old people no longer feel. . . .]"

"Do you have parents, Ulrich?"

"[Everyone has parents. Sometimes we misplace them.]" They reached the landing on the third floor, and he lifted the hissing lamp to study her face. He looked very solemn. "[Don't ask about my parents, and I won't ask about yours.]"

"Mine are dead."

"[How lovely for you,]" Ulrich said, patiently climbing stairs. "[I'd be sorry for you, if I believed that.]"

They reached a top flight, puffing for breath. They walked down a chilly hall with bare, graffiti-tagged walls. The graffiti was very subversive, neatly stenciled, highly politicized. Much of it was in English. TO BUY A NEW CAR WOULD MAKE YOU SEXUALLY ATTRACTIVE, insinuated one graffito. CONSUME MORE RESOURCES TO GRATIFY SHORT-TERM DESIRES, another suggested darkly.

Ulrich opened an ancient padlock with a metal key. The door shuddered open with a scream of hinges. The room within was dark and icy, and it stank. The interior walls had mostly been kicked out and replaced with blankets on ropes. The place smelled of slow decay and wild mice.

Ulrich slammed the door and shot a bolt. "[Isn't this luxurious?]" he said, voice echoing in the fetid gloom. "[It's real privacy! I don't mean legal privacy, either. I mean that this area is physically inaccessible to surveillance.]"

"No wonder it smells like this, then."

"[I can repair the smell.]" Ulrich methodically lit half a dozen scented candles. The room began to fill with the piercing waxy reek of tropical fruits: pineapple, mango. She doubted that Ulrich had ever tasted a pineapple or mango. Presumably that lack of direct experience made the scents more appealingly exotic.

Maya examined the stinking dive in the romantic glow of the candlelight. "You sure have a lot of electronic gizmos in here, considering that you got no electricity."

"[Appropriated materials.]" Ulrich nodded. "[As it happens, I share this area with three other gentlemen with similar interests. We've found that pooling resources is a necessity for our life outside the law.]"

He hooked the lantern on a rope that dangled from the ceiling, and set it swaying gently. Shadows swam the walls. "[We don't live here. Under no circumstances would one keep appropriated materials in one's regular domicile. Any serious commercial fencing operation is also quite difficult, thanks to time-based currencies, the informant network, panoptic tracing measures, and other means of gerontocratic oppression. So my comrades and I use this area as our joint storeroom, and occasionally we sleep with women in it.]"

"It's a real mess. Fantastic. Can I take a picture of it?"

"No."

She gazed in wonder at the ugly clutter: bags, shoes, sporting goods, recorders, dismembered laptops, heaps of tourist clothes from raided luggage. "This place is a real archive. You got any touchscreens in here that can recognize a gestural passtouch and get me into a memory palace set up back in the sixties?"

"[I'm sorry, darling,]" said Ulrich, "[but I have no idea what you're talking about.]" He advanced on her, arms spread.

They began kissing feverishly. The room began warming up nicely, but not so warm as to make it fun to step out of your clothes. "Where can we do it?"

"[There's a sleeping bag over there. I stole it from a skier and it's very warm. Big enough for two.]"

"Okay," she said, pulling free from his insistent grip, "I want to do it, and you know that I want to do it. Right? But I know that you want to do it, worse than I want to do it. So that means I get to make the rules. Okay?"

Ulrich raised his sloping brows. "'Rules?'"

"That's right, Ulrich, rules. Rule number one, you don't know who I am, or where I came from. And you don't ever try to find out."

"Oh, I like your idea of rules, treasure. This could be fun."

"Rule two, you don't brag about me to any of your ratty friends. You don't ever say anything about me to anybody."

"That's very good, I am certainly no informer. That's two rules, but . . ." Ulrich paused. "[You are rapidly expanding the conceptual territory.]"

"Rule three, I get to stay in this squat until you get tired of me, and you have to make sure I don't freeze to death, and you have to watch me and make sure that I eat."

"[We'd better work on all those proposals later,]" Ulrich said. "[They sound ambitious. Anyway, I've never been able to obey more than two rules at a time even under the best of circumstances.]"

That seemed sensible, given the situation. She climbed into the sleeping bag with him. They shed their clothing and embraced. There was sweet delightful groping and stroking and some vigorous heaving. It seemed to take the usual nice long time, but in reality it took about eight minutes. Which was just as well.

When he was done, she sat up in the bag. The skier's stolen bag was lined with woven foil and by now it felt like a kitchen toaster. "That was lovely. I feel very happy now."

"[I'm also delighted,]" Ulrich declared gallantly. He was postcoitally morose, and visibly trying to assemble a state of consciousness that was not hormonally driven. It had been a long time since she had seen this happen to a man in her company, but in its own way it was a touchingly familiar sight. She'd come to terms with the realities of male physiology a very long time ago. It would have been lovely to kiss him some more, but if he ran true to form, he would want to either eat a sandwich or go right to sleep.

"I should get us some nice food to eat," Ulrich offered, with machinelike behavioral accuracy. "What do you like?"

"Oh, something colloidal. Something very cross-linked and tryptophan-ish."

"[I'm sorry, what?]"

"Anything but vegetables or dead animals."

"Okay." Ulrich climbed methodically into his clothing. He managed a cheery wink. "[I love it when a girl wears nothing but a translation earpiece. A sight like that makes life seem so full of promise.]" He left. She heard him padlocking the door shut behind him, heard his footsteps down the hall.

The thought of being locked within the criminal den did not disturb her in the least. She got up immediately and began compulsively to clean the room. The state of disorder had been driving her crazy.

She stopped her cleaning frenzy when she discovered a little stolen laptop television. Genuine televisions, with their broadcast datastream, lack of keyboards, and miserably unilateral interface, were real oddities. She'd spent years collecting kitschy oddities from the enormous freakish garbage heaps of twentieth-century television culture, before she'd discovered the even odder CD-ROM and software media niches.

She tried turning the television on. There was no battery inside it. She began searching, and quickly discovered that all the electronic devices in the room had been deprived of their batteries. Except, of course, for the newly stolen devices that were still in her bag. She eviscerated the netlink and transplanted its battery into the laptop television. She turned the television on.

A Deutschlander talk show appeared onscreen. The host was a St. Bernard dog. He had an actress with him. Maya methodically cleaned the room as she watched the show and listened through one ear.

"[My problem is with reading,]" the dog confessed in fluent Deutsch. The dog had shaggy St. Bernard genetics, but he was very well dressed. "[Mastering speech is one matter. Any dog can do that, with the proper wiring. But reading is an entirely different level of semantic cognition. The sponsors have done their best for me—you know that as well as I do, Nadja. But I have to admit it, right here, publicly—reading is a very serious challenge for any postcanine]."

"[Poor baby,]" the actress said with genuine sympathy. "[Why fight it? They say it's a postliterate epoch anyway.]"

"[Anyone who could say that is deeply out of touch,]" the dog said gravely and with dignity. "[Goethe. Rilke. Günter Grass. Heinrich Böll. That says it all.]"

Maya was fascinated by the actress's clothing. The actress was wearing diaphanous military gear, greenish see-through combat pajamas, and a paratrooper's sweater in satin. Her face was like something chiseled in cameo, and her hair was truly awe-inspiring. Her hair deserved a doctorate in fiber engineering.

"[We're all on our own in this epoch,]" the actress mourned. "[When you think what they can do to us on set nowadays—the weird mental spaces they're willing to put people into, in pursuit of a decent performance . . . And then there are the gutter net-freaks, those stinking paparazzi . . . But you know, Aquinas, and I mean this: You're a dog. I know you're a dog. It's not any secret. But truly—and I mean this from the bottom of my heart—I feel happier on your show than I would on anyone else's.]"

The audience applauded politely.

"[That's very sweet of you,]" the dog said, wagging his tail. "[I appreciate that more than I can say. Nadja, tell us a little about this business on-set with Christian Mancuso. What was that all about?]"

"[Well, Aquinas, just for you,]" the actress said. "[It's certainly not something I would tell to just anyone. . . . But it happened like this. Christian and I are both in our sixties, we're not young people. Of course. We'd been working together on this project for the company, Hermes Kino. We'd been within the set together for six weeks. We got along wonderfully—I was used to his company, you know, we'd emerge from the set, decompress, have dinner together, talk about the script. . . . Then one night, Christian took me in his arms and kissed me! I suppose we were both rather surprised by that. It seemed very sweet, though.]"

"*Natürlich,*" the dog agreed.

"[So we both agreed to go on the hormone course, I suppose it was his idea really.]"

The audience applauded politely.

"[So that was what we did. We took a thorough hormone course together. Sex made a lot of difference. Really, it was quite astonishing how intense the experience was. In the long run I have to say it was good for me. It did seem to open me up creatively. I enjoyed it. Quite a bit. I know Christian did, too.]"

"[How do you know that?]" the dog prompted.

"[A woman knows, that's all. . . . I suppose it was the most profound erotic experience of my whole life! I did things that I never would have done as a younger woman. When you are young, sex means so much to you. You get so serious and formal about it. . . .]"

"[Do tell us,]" the dog suggested. "[You might as well tell us now, while you're still in the mood.]"

"[Well, certain things like—well, we liked to play dress-up. Bed dress-up.]" She smiled radiantly. "[He enjoyed it, too, it was very delightful for both of us. A kind of drunkenness really. A hormonal bender. You can look at my medical records if you don't believe what I'm telling you.]"

"[Dress-up?]" said the dog skeptically. "[That's all? That seems very innocent.]"

"[Aquinas, listen. Christian and I are both professionals. You have no idea what professionals can do when we put our minds to dress-up.]"

The audience laughed, apparently on cue.

"[Then what happened?]" asked the dog.

"[Well,]" said the actress, "[after about eighteen months—I wouldn't say that we'd tired of it exactly, but we'd certainly settled down. Christian came back from a routine checkup, and he had these bladder cysts. The hormones were responsible. Christian decided that he had to back off. So of course, I did the same. And the moment that happened, all the energy went out of our relationship. We became . . . well . . . slightly embarrassed with one another. We no longer tried to live and sleep together.]"

"[That's a shame,]" the dog said, conventionally.

"[If you're thirty, maybe it is.]" The actress shrugged. "[Once you're sixty, you become accustomed to the facts of life.]" There was scattered applause.

The actress sat up briskly, excited. "[I'm still on very good terms with him! Truly! I would work together with Christian Mancuso at any time. Any project. He's a fine actor! A real professional! I feel no shame or embarrassment about our sordid little carnal tryst. It was helpful to both of us. Artistically.]"

"[Would you do it again?]"

"[Well . . . Yes! Maybe . . . Probably not. No, Aquinas. Let me be very frank with you here. No, I'll never do that again.]"

The door shrieked open. Ulrich appeared, and called out something in Deutsch. The translation earpiece was caught between the jabber of television and Ulrich's remark. The little machine could not decide where to direct the user's attention, so it fell into silence.

Maya turned the television off. The translator perked up again with a telltale little squeak.

"I hope you like Chinese food," Ulrich said.

"I love Chinese."

"[I thought you would. Little lumps of chopped-up dreck that don't look like anything. Perfect for a Californian.]" He gave her a carton and chopsticks.

They sat together on the chilly floor, and ate. He gazed about the room. "[You've been moving things around.]"

"I've been cleaning up the place."

"What a little treasure you are," Ulrich said, munching solemnly.

"Why do you keep all this junk anyway? You should have sold all this stuff a long time ago."

"[That's not so easy. You can sell the batteries. There's always a ready black market for batteries. The rest of this loot is all too dangerous. Better to wait for a good long while, to throw off the scent.]"

"You've been waiting a long time already. This junk's all covered with dust and there's mice living in it."

Ulrich shrugged. "[We meant to keep a cat, but we don't get up here often enough.]"

"Why do you rob people at all, if you're not going to sell what you steal?"

"Oh, we sell it, we sell it!" he insisted. "We do! A little extra cash is always nice." He poked at the air with his chopsticks. "[But that's not our premier motivation, you see. We simply do our part to outrage the gerontocratic haute bourgeoisie.]"

"Sure," she said skeptically.

"[Cash isn't everything in life. We just had sex,]" Ulrich informed her, triumphantly. "[Why didn't you ask me for money?]"

"I don't know, I just didn't feel like I had to."

"[Maybe you *should* have asked for cash. You're an illegal. But me, I'm a European citizen! They'll feed me, they'll shelter me, they'll educate me, they'll even entertain me, and it's all free! If I volunteer myself, they'll even find lovely useful things for me to do, like pulling up weeds and cleaning up forests and other healthy boring nonsense. I don't have to steal to survive. I'm a thief because I *think differently.*]"

"Why don't you resist them a bit more directly, if you're so wonderfully radical?"

"[I want to rebel in a way that causes them the maximum shame and embarrassment, for my minimum effort and risk! Robbing tourists is optimal.]"

Maya ate her shredded Chinese protein, and looked him over. "I don't think you really mean any of that, Ulrich. I think that you steal people's luggage because you're obsessive. And I think that you hoard all this junk because you can't bear to part with any of your lovely forbidden trophies."

Ulrich stabbed his chopsticks into the mix in his carton. A slow flush rose up the fine white milky column of his young male neck. "[That's very perceptive, darling. That's just the sort of thing that a motivational counselor in school would tell me. So, you've said it to me. So what?]"

"So, there may be some very nice things here, but they're not the sort of things that I need. That's what."

Ulrich crossed his arms. "What is it you think that you need, little mouse?"

" 'Better shoes,' " she quoted. " 'Contact lenses. Cashcards. Wigs. Skin tint. Some pidgin Deutsch, to get by. Maps. Food. Plumbing. A nice warm bed.' "

Ulrich winced. "You have a fine memory."

"In the short term," she said. "Also, some forged ID would be very nice."

"[You can forget forging ID,]" he grumbled. "[The bulls beat the forgery problem a long time ago. You'd have better luck forging the moon.]"

"But we could sell off this useless junk, and we could get all the rest of it."

"Maybe. Probably," he said in English. "But you are cheating me. You should have told me of your great ambitions. Before we became lovers."

She said nothing. She was touched that he'd described the two of them as "lovers." It showed such a sweetly adolescent will to immolation that she could scarcely bear to maneuver him, even though it was pathetically easy to do.

She ate methodically. Her judgmental silence etched its way into him like a slow-acting acid.

"[Well, I've been meaning to sell it all anyway,]" Ulrich told her at last, boasting, and lying. "[There are certain ways to do that. There are good ways. Interesting ways. But they're not easy. They're risky.]"

"Let me run all the risks," she told him at once, crushing him with a single blow. "Why should you run any risks? That's beneath your dignity. I see you in the starring role of the silent criminal mastermind. A European paranoiac criminal genius. Did you ever watch that old silent film, *Dr. Mabuse, Der Spieler?*"

"[What on earth are you babbling about?]"

"It's very simple, Ulrich. I like risks. I love risks. I live for risks."

"That's marvelous," Ulrich said. He had become very sad.

She spent two days in Munchen, running around on her stolen tubeticket, mostly favoring a place downtown called the Viktualienmarkt. This ancient shopping locale had been a food market in some preindustrial time, hence the Deutsch business about "viktuals," but it had long since turned into a dive for kids and tourists, where there was a lot of business transacted in cash. There was still a little food around, like those ubiquitous Munchener "white sausage" concoctions, but it was mostly tourist-trap kitsch and street couture.

The street couture enthralled her. She was dying for decent cosmetics. She'd been making do with the aging caked-up crud she'd found in Ulrich's stolen bags—there was even a bad wig in one of them—but she needed her own decisions, her own true colors, brighter, faster, looser, stranger. In the Viktualienmarkt there were whole open-air stalls of mysterious Deutschlander cosmetics. Cosmetics for cash. Lipstick—*mit lichtreflektierend Farbpigmente. Very modeanzeigen. O so frivol! Radikales Liftings und*

Intensivpeelings. Der Kampf mit dem Spiegel. O so feminin! Schönheits-cocktail, die beruhigende Feuchtigkeitscreme. Revitalisierende! Die Wissenschaft der Zukunft! Die Eleganze die neue Diva!

Für den Körper, for the body: *eau essentielle, le parfum.* The perfume was voodoo. She happened to sample a traditional Parisian scent that Mia had once used on a special night sixty years ago. The evocative reek struck her such a blow of rapturous déjà vu that she dropped her bag and almost fell down in the street. *Elixier des lebens!* Some of it she photographed. Some of it she stole.

On the third day Ulrich piled her and a fat duffel bag of carefully chosen loot into a stolen car. They wove their way out of the city and headed for the outskirts of Stuttgart. She was wearing her jacket and a pair of slightly-too-tight sporty thermal ski pants and chic little stolen hiking boots. She had a new wig, a big curly blond mess. With a nice vivid scarf. Sunglasses. Foundation, blusher, mascara, lashes, lipstick. Nail polish, toenail polish, foot-wax, nutrient lotion, and a scent that made her feel more like Mia. When she felt sufficiently like Mia she knew that she could work her way out of anything.

The day was chill and drizzly. "[A friend stole this car,]" Ulrich told her. "[He took certain steps with its brain. I could rent us a car legally, of course, but then I considered our destination and cargo. I'm a bit concerned about geographical backtracking should they happen to remotely search the machine's memory. A stolen and stupid car is safer for us.]"

"Natürlich." He was so funny. She'd gotten used to him in very short order. Having sex with Ulrich was just like losing her virginity. She'd felt just the same mild disdain for the man involved and the same triumphant secret sense of having finally annihilated her childhood. Sex was like sleeping, only better exercise and more fun. It was something you did when you felt like jumbled-up blocks inside. It obliterated loneliness and when you came to on the far side of the experience there was a new sense of ease. Every time they had sex together, she came out of it feeling that much more settled inside her own skin. They'd been together

three days so far and it had happened about ten times. Like ten pitons driven into a cliff, climbing high above everything that was old and Mia.

"[I wish I could strip this car completely and drive it with my own hands,]" mused Ulrich, watching Munchen's old suburban sprawl roll by. "[That must have been a thrilling experience.]"

"Manual driving killed more people than wars."

"[Oh, they're always fussing about mortality rates, as if mortality rates were the only thing that mattered in life. . . . You should find this event rather interesting. There will be real enemies of the polity there.]"

The car found an autobahn and tore down it almost silently, at an inhumanly high rate of speed. The other European cars were streamlined and blisteringly fast, with lines and colors like half-sucked candy lozenges. Quite often you could see their owners snoozing or reading inside. "Does the polity have real enemies?"

"[Of course! Many! Countless hordes! A vast spectrum of refuseniks and dissidents! Amish. Anarchists. Andaman Islanders. Australian aborigines. A certain number of tribal Afghanis. Certain American Indians. And that's just in the A's!]"

"*Prima,*" Maya offered, tentatively.

"[You mustn't think that every human being in the world has been bribed into submission and complacency, just because the polity can offer you a few rotten years of extra life.]"

"Fifty or sixty extra years. And counting."

"[It's a magnificent bribe,]" Ulrich admitted, "[but there are many people all over the world who refuse to be co-opted. They live outside the medical law. Outside of the polity.]"

"I know about the Amish. Amish aren't outlaws. People admire the Amish. They envy their sincerity and simplicity. Plus the Amish still practice real agriculture. People find that very touching."

Ulrich was wearing his sheepskin, as usual. He picked fretfully at a bare patch on the elbow. "[Yes, there's a cheap popular vogue for the Amish. The polity turned the Amish into pop stars. That's the polity's primary means of subversive integration. They'll make you a prized exhibit in their culture zoo. So they can boast of their so-called tolerance, while subverting the genuine cultural threat posed to their hegemony.]"

Maya tapped her ear. "I think my translator got all of that, but it didn't seem to mean much."

"[It's all about freedom! Ways to seize and keep your freedom, and your individual autonomy. The way to live outside the law is to be an outlaw.]"

She thought it over. "Maybe you can steal some autonomy for a few years. But the cautious people will outlive you in the long run."

"[That remains to be seen. The polity was created for old people, but the regime itself is not that old. At heart, they're a bunch of panic-stricken dodderers wrapping everything in knitting yarn. They think they've created a thousand-year regime. The Amish have been the Amish for four hundred years. Let's see these miserable grannies outlive the Amish.]"

The towers of Stuttgart rose over the horizon. They were four hundred stories tall and made of scaled gelatin and they looked like giant fish. Sweet little white pennants of the purest water vapor were being exhaled from the tops of the stacks. If you looked carefully you could see the walls of the towers gently breathing. Puckering and glistening, repeatedly.

"I had no idea Stuttgart looked so much like Indianapolis," Maya said.

"You have visited Indianapolis?"

"Telepresence."

"Oh, yes."

She looked at the distant towers and sighed. "They say Stuttgart is the greatest city for the arts in the whole world."

"Yes," Ulrich said meditatively, "Stuttgart is very artificial."

Large green hills surrounded the city. The hills were compacted rubble, from the former urban structure of Stuttgart. Stuttgart had suffered very harshly during the plagues of the forties. Most of the city had burned down after the panic-stricken population had abandoned town. The scorched infectious wreckage had been demolished by the returning survivors, and Stuttgart had been entirely rebuilt during the gaudy and visionary fifties and sixties. The architects of the new Stuttgart had had nothing left of their past to restrain them, so they'd rolled up their sleeves in a fine biomodernist frenzy and attempted to create compelling icons for their own cultural period. People often got a bit hysterical when they were trying to prove to themselves that they had some right to be survivors.

The car left the highway. The drizzle had cleared off and a pale winter sun emerged. The hillsides were very nicely wooded in leafless young chestnut trees. Occasional chunks of stained concrete rubble broke picturesquely through the topsoil.

They parked and climbed out. Ulrich set the car off to wander by itself, to come when he called for it. "[The car will be much safer out on the roads,]" he said, slipping the netlink inside his shirt on a cord. "[We don't want to park a car next to these people.]"

They headed uphill, through the young woods. They passed two men in patchwork brown leather coats, with dark beards, metal necklaces, earrings. The men sat under a large umbrella, on folding chairs beside a small wicker table. One of the men methodically photographed every passerby. The other was chatting into a cellphone in a language Maya couldn't recognize. As he talked and nodded and grinned, he deftly twirled a yard-long alpenstock. The stick was nicely polished, hefty, very solid. It looked as though it had seen a lot of nasty use against the sides of people's heads.

The two guards nodded minimally as Maya and Ulrich worked their way past them, up the slope. A trickle of Euro bourgeoisie were working their way through the trees, interspersed with big knotted crowds of the aliens, who greeted one another with uncanny whoops of laughter.

They emerged in a clearing on the far side of the hill. The far slope had been taken over by big sloping black tents, smoldering campfires, and folding tables heaped with merchandise and junk. Dozens of used cars sat in roped-off lots, where gangs of bearded, beaded men in spangled hats and silver necklaces were loudly bargaining. Dark-eyed women walked through camp with bright striped skirts and braids and earrings and silver anklets. Astonishing numbers of children raced underfoot.

Ulrich was ill at ease, face tight, smiling mechanically. A lot of Deutschlanders picked their way among the junk tables, mostly young people, but they were far outnumbered by the aliens.

These people were truly extraordinary. She was seeing a cast of features on people's faces like she hadn't seen on any human being in forty years. Faces from outside of time. Crow's-feet, age spotting, networks of crabbed lines. Women gone gray and sagging in ways in which women simply weren't supposed to sag anymore. Ferociously patriarchal old men in barbaric finery whose walk and gestures radiated pride and even menace.

And the children—entire packs of shrieking little children. To see so many little children in one place at one time was very strange. To see large packs of children all from a single narrow ethnic group was an experience beyond the pale.

"Who *are* these people?" Maya said.

"[They're *tsiganes*.]"

"Who?"

"[They call themselves Romany.]"

Maya tapped her ear. "My translator doesn't seem to understand that word, either."

Ulrich thought it over. "These people are gypsies," he said in English. "This is a big gathering camp for European gypsies."

"Wow. I've never seen so many people in one place who weren't on medical treatments. I had no idea there were this many gypsies left in the whole world."

Ulrich went back to Deutsch. "[Gypsies are not rare. They're just hard to notice. The Romany have their own ways of movement and they are good at hiding. These people have been Europe's outcasts for eight hundred years.]"

"Why aren't the gypsies just like everybody else by now?"

"[That's a very interesting question,]" Ulrich said, pleased to hear it brought up. "[I often wonder that myself. I might learn the truth if I became a gypsy, but they don't let *gajo* do that. We're both *gajo,* you know. You're American and I'm Deutschlander, but we're both just *gajo* to these people. These people are nomads, and outcasts, and thieves, and pickpockets, and swindlers, and anarchists, and dirty *lumpenproletariate* who don't use life extension or birth control!]" Ulrich looked them over with a certain proprietary joy, then his smile slowly faded to a deeply troubled look. "[Still, all those fine qualities don't prove that they're entirely romantic and wonderful]."

"Oh."

"[We're trying to sell these people some stolen property,]" Ulrich reminded her. "[They're going to try to cheat us.]"

Three Romany men passed them, carrying a lamb. A crowd of gawking *gajo* gathered quickly. She couldn't see over the shoulders of the jostling men, but she heard the lamb's last anguished bleat, and the crowd's eager gasp. Followed by delighted gasps and groans of shock and titillation.

"They're killing that animal over there," she said.

"[Yes, they are. And skinning it, and gutting it, and putting its carcass on a stick, and roasting it over a fire.]"

"Why?"

Ulrich smiled. "[Because roast mutton tastes lovely. A little bit of mutton can't hurt you.]" His eyes narrowed. "[Also, eating the animal makes you feel better about the dirty pleasure you took in seeing it killed. The bourgeoisie . . . they will pay well to eat a thing that they saw killed.]"

At the base of a nearby hill, a gypsy did public stunts on a motorcycle. His ancient and incredibly hazardous vehicle had no autopilot of any kind. The spitting, fluid-powered machine beat its combustive pistons with a bestial roar and spat blue clouds of toxic smoke.

The gypsy stood on the seat, did handstands on the handlebars, roared up the hill and down, zipped up a ramp and flew over an iron barrel. He wore boots and a spangled leather jacket and he had no helmet.

At last he leapt deftly from the machine and flung his arms wide and did a brisk little jig on the damp tire-torn earth. The *gajo* were stunned by the man's insane courage. They applauded wildly. Some few of them threw a thin scattering of little gleaming disks. A young Romany boy picked them eagerly from the dead winter grass as the hero wheeled his brutal machine away.

"What did they throw at him?"

"[Coins. Silver coins. The gypsies are silversmiths. You deal in old coins if you want to deal seriously with gypsies. Their use of coins deeply confuses all modern taxmen and auditors.]"

"A black market in old metal money," Maya said. "That's *klasse*." She tasted the word. "*Klasse. Super.*"

"[Yes, today we'll be bartering our tiresome bunch of stolen luggage for some silver coins. Coins are easier to hide and store and carry.]"

"Will they be genuine silver coins? I mean, genuine historical European currency?"

"[We'll see. If some gypsy tries to pick our pockets or break our heads, then yes, they're probably real coins. Otherwise, they're useless slugs. Lead. Fakes.]"

"You're making these Romany people sound really awful."

"Awful? What makes them awful?" Ulrich shrugged. "[They never declared a war. They never started a pogrom. They never enslaved another people. They have no God, no kings, no government. They are their own masters. So, they despise us and they rob us and flout our rules. They are an alien people, truly outside society. I'm a thief and you're an illegal, but compared to them, you and I are spoiled children of the polity, we are nothing but amateurs.]" He sighed. "[I like the Romany and I even admire them, but to them, I'll always be just another *gajo* fool.]"

The gypsies were selling paper flowers, clothespins, carpet beaters, brooms, coconut mats, quilts, old clothes, used tires, car upholstery. Some of the tables offered luck charms and herbal perfumes and various weird species of curdled tincture. The gypsies seemed fanatically attached to their aging cars and trucks, their bulging multicolored trailers all plated and enameled. There were even some sheep on exhibit, clipped and groomed like museum pieces, and some horses in jingling harness that looked as if they were meant to do actual horse work.

Spirited bargaining was going on, with a lot of arm waving and beard stroking, but not many goods were actually changing hands. What's more, the women posted at the tables didn't seem to be taking retail work to heart. "Ulrich, this is really interesting. But this isn't major economic activity."

"[What do you expect? There aren't any efficient, industrial gypsies. Gypsies who get efficient and industrial don't stay gypsies.]"

"I can't believe they're not on extension treatments. They don't get checkups or anything? Why not? Why do they want to live and die like this? What's really driving them?"

"You're very curious, treasure." Ulrich crossed his fleecy arms. "[All right, I'll tell you. Fifty years ago, there were gypsy pogroms all over Europe. People said that dirty gypsies carried plague. They said the gypsies broke the quarantines. And people, absolutely normal civilized European people, picked up hatchets and shovels and chains and iron bars and ran to Romany ghettos and Romany camps and they beat the Romanies and tortured them and raped them and set fire to their homes.]"

Maya felt stunned. She gaped at him. "Well, those were dreadful times. All kinds of aberrations . . ."

"No aberrations at all!" Ulrich declared cheerfully. "[Racism is very authentic. Despising other people and wanting them dead—that's a dear and precious thing to the human soul. It never has to be taught to anyone. People do it every single chance they get.]"

He shrugged. "[You want the real truth about gypsies? This is Europe, and it's the end of the twenty-first century. The people in power today were alive sixty years ago, during those plagues and those gypsy pogroms. Today, they don't kill gypsies. No, today, when they notice the gypsies at all, they act like superficial sentimentalists and genteel snobs who need a feudal relic to coddle and patronize. But another pogrom would happen tomorrow if there were another plague.]"

"That's a dreadful thing to say."

"[Dreadful, but it's very true. The Romany probably *were* carrying the plague, Maya, that's the funny part. And you know something even funnier? If the Romany weren't complete racial chauvinists themselves, then we'd have absorbed the last one of them centuries ago.]"

"You're being very nasty, Ulrich. Are you trying to shock me? There aren't going to be any more plagues. The plagues are all over. We exterminated every one of the plagues."

Ulrich snorted skeptically. "[Don't let me spoil your fun, treasure. You wanted to come here to do business, not me. You have the list of goods, don't you? Go see if you can sell something.]"

Maya left him. She gathered her courage and approached a gypsy woman at a table. The woman was wearing a patterned shawl and smoking a short clay pipe.

"Hello. Do you speak English?"

"A little English."

"I have some items that are useful to travelers. I want to sell them."

The woman thought this over. "Give me your hand." She leaned forward, minutely examined Maya's palm, then sat back down on her folding canvas seat. She puffed a blip of smoke. "You're a cop."

"I'm not a cop, ma'am."

She looked Maya up and down. "Okay, maybe you don't know you're a cop. But you're a cop."

"I'm not *polizei*."

The woman pulled the pipe from her mouth and pointed with the stem. "You are not a little girl. You dress like a little girl, but that's a lie. You can fool the little boy over there, but you don't fool me. Go away and don't come back."

Maya left in a hurry. She was badly shaken. She began to hunt for someone dealing at a table who wasn't a gypsy.

She found a young Deutschlander woman with styled reddish hair and bee-stung lips and a big consignment of used clothes. This situation looked a lot more promising.

"Hi. Do you speak English?"

"Okay, sure."

"I have some things I want to sell. Clothes, and some other things."

The woman nodded slowly. "That's a nice jacket. *Très chic.*"

"Thanks. *Danke.*"

The woman stared at her in forthright Deutschlander fashion. She had two precise arcs for brows and long crimped lashes. "You live in Munchen, yes? I saw that jacket at the Viktualienmarkt. You came to my shop twice, to look at clothes."

"Really?" Maya said, with a sinking feeling. "I'm staying in Munchen, but I'm just passing through."

"American?"

"Yes."

"Californian?"

"Yes."

"Los Angeles?"

"Bay Area."

"I could have guessed San Francisco. They do that work in polymer. You know, they could have done that jacket in Stuttgart in just a few hours. Better, too."

Ulrich came over. The woman glanced up at him. "Ciao Jimmy."

"Ciao Therese."

They began speaking in Deutsch. "[New girlfriend?]"

"[Yes.]"

"[She's very pretty.]"

"[I think so, too.]"

"[Trying to move some product?]"

"[Not to you, treasure,]" said Ulrich glibly and in haste. "[I'd never move product in Munchen, I don't burn people where I live. She doesn't know any better, so that's why I came over to stop this. No harm done. All right?]"

"She called you 'Jimmy,' " Maya realized.

"I answer to that name sometimes," Ulrich said in English.

Therese laughed. She spoke to Maya in English. "You poor little sausage! You love your new boyfriend? He's a real wonderboy, your Jimmy. He's all heart."

Ulrich frowned. "She made a little mistake, that's all."

"I don't love him," Maya said loudly. She took off her sunglasses. "I just need some things."

"What?"

"Contact lenses. Silver money. Wigs. Maps. Food. Plumbing. A nice warm bed. And I want to learn some Deutsch so I can stop being such an idiot."

"She's an illegal," Ulrich said, hand closing on Maya's upper arm. "The poor little thing is hot."

Therese looked at the pair of them. "What are you trying to sell?"

Ulrich hesitated. "Give her the list," he said at last.

Therese looked it over. "I can move this stuff. If it's in good condition. Where is it?"

"In the boot of my car."

She looked surprised. "[Jimmy, you've got a car?]"

"[It's on loan from Herr Shrottplatz.]"

"[You sure can pick nice friends.]"

Ulrich turned to Maya and smiled sourly. "[I forgot to mention junkies in my former list of interest groups opposed to the current order.]"

"[Twenty big dimes,]" Therese told him, bored.

"[Thirty dimes.]"

"[Twenty-five.]"

"[Twenty-seven.]"

"[Go and fetch it, then. Let's see the goods.]"

"Come on," Ulrich said, tugging at Maya's arm.

Therese spoke up. "Leave the Yankee for a minute. I want to practice my English."

Ulrich thought it over. "Don't do something stupid," he said to Maya, and left.

Therese looked her over, judgmental and cool. "You like nice boys?"

"They have their uses, I guess."

"Well, that one's not a nice boy."

Maya smiled. "Well, I know that."

"When did you get into Munchen? When did he pick you up?"

"Three days ago."

"What, three days and you're already here in a camp and dealing? You must really like clothes," Therese said. "What's your name?"

"Maya."

"What are you in Munchen for? Who's after you? Cops?"

"Maybe." She hesitated, then took the risk. "I think mostly it's medical people."

"*Medical* people? What about your parents?"

"No, not my parents, that's for sure."

"Well, then," said Therese, with an air of cosmopolitan assurance, "you can forget about the medical people. The medical people never do a thing to investigate, because they know that in the long run you'll have to come to them. And the cops—well, the cops in Munchen never do much about runaways unless they've got the parents behind them, pushing."

"That's nice to hear."

"Sleep under bridges. Eat pretzels. You'll get along. And you should dump the boyfriend there. That kid is ugly. One of these days, the bulls will break his head open and stir his brains like porridge. And I'm not going to shed one tear, either."

"He's been telling me about European radical politics."

"Munchen isn't a good town for that topic, darling," said Therese, wryly. "What's your hair look like when you're not wearing that wig?"

Maya pulled off her scarf and wig. After a moment, she dropped them on the table.

"Take off the jacket and turn around for me," Therese said.

Maya peeled off her jacket and turned slowly in place.

"You have truly interesting bone structure. You swim a lot?"

"Yes, that's right," Maya said, "I did a lot of swimming just lately."

"I think I could use a girl like you. I'm not so bad. You can ask around town about me, anyone will tell you that Therese is okay."

"Are you offering me a job?"

"You could call it a job," Therese said. "It's couture, it's apparel, it's the rag trade. You know the rag trade, don't you? It means you can have some rags and maybe a place to sleep."

"I really need a job," Maya said. Quite suddenly, she began

to cry. "Never mind me crying," she said, wiping her cheeks, "it's so funny, it comes so easily lately. But please let me have the job, I just need a place where I can be okay for a while and try to be more like myself."

Therese was touched. "Come over here around the table and sit down."

Maya walked around the table and sat obediently in Therese's folding fabric chair. "I'll be okay soon, really, I'm not as silly as this usually, I'll work really hard, truly."

"Calm down, girl, stop babbling. Tell me something. How old are you?"

"I think I'm about two weeks old."

Therese sighed. "When was the last time you ate a decent meal?"

"I don't remember."

Therese stooped and dug around under the table. She came up with a bag of government granola and a mineral water. "Here. Eat this. Drink that. And remember, you steal one pin from me and I kick you into the street." She looked downhill. "Joy of joys. Here comes your boyfriend."

Maya tasted the granola. The granola was fabulous. She jammed an entire handful into her mouth and munched like a hamster.

Ulrich, red-faced and puffing, dropped the duffel bag onto the tabletop. "Let's talk business."

"Prima," Therese said. "[By the way, I just hired your girlfriend for my shop.]"

"[What?]" Ulrich laughed. "[You're kidding, right? She can't even speak to the customers.]"

"[I don't need another salesgirl, I need a mannequin]."

"[Therese, this is really shortsighted and counterproductive of you. I have to say I'm disappointed. You're doing this just to spite me,]" Ulrich said. "[I thought you'd gotten over that little contretemps we had before.]"

"[Me? Spiteful? Never! This girl is pretty, she can't talk much, and she's got a real bird in her head. She's a perfect mannequin.]"

"You shouldn't trust this woman," Ulrich told Maya in English. "She says you're crazy."

"So did you," Maya said, munching. She glugged some mineral water. "It's a job and I'm an illegal. It's a really good break for me. Of course I'm gonna take it. What did you expect?"

Ulrich flushed, slowly. "I did everything you asked from me. I never broke even one of your rules. You're not being very grateful."

Maya shrugged. "Jimmy, there's a million girls in the Marienplatz. Go pick up some other girl. I'll be fine now."

Ulrich yanked the bag from the table and slung it over his shoulder. "[If you think you're moving up in society by going to work in this cow's stupid little shop, you'll soon learn differently. If you want to go, go! But don't think you can come crawling back to the life of freedom!]"

"Her shop's got heating," Maya pointed out.

Ulrich turned in fury and lurched away.

There was a long silence. "Girl, you are really cold," Therese said at last. Half-admiring.

3

Maya went to work for Therese in her shop in the Viktualienmarkt. The shop was glass-fronted brick, untidily crammed with clothes and shoes, with a tiny office in the back where Therese scraped out a narrow financial niche. Therese dealt mostly in cash, often in barter, sometimes in precious metals. Maya lived in the shop, wore her pick of the merchandise, and slept under Therese's desk. Therese slept in her parents' high-rise with a variety of scruffy, dangerous-looking, semiarticulate boyfriends.

It was a great comfort to be compelled to work and not have to spend so much time being perfectly free and happy and confident. All that freedom and happiness and confidence was terribly wearing.

One night at the shop in late February, Maya awoke to find herself sleepwalking, yet still compulsively putting the stock in order. That was Mia's doing. Mia was all right now. Mia liked this situation. Mia felt very safe and at ease now that she had duties.

Maya worked quite hard and without complaint and without much in the way of reward, and Therese appreciated this. Like most young people who had created careers for themselves in the contemporary economy, Therese was a great connoisseur of the gratuitous gesture. Still, Maya was dissatisfied. She couldn't read the tags in the clothing, and she couldn't discuss things properly with the customers. This would not do.

Maya begged some cash off Therese, went to a cut-rate language school in the Schwabing section of Munchen, and bought 500 cc's of education tinctures. These particular philters were said to convey a new plasticity for language, "giving the adult brain the eager syntactical receptiveness of a child of three." All the smart drugs in the world couldn't make the Deutsch language a cheap or easy accomplishment—but the "child of three" part certainly met its billing. The neural dope found her inbuilt mastery of English and put its pharmaceutical foot right through it, like a boot through a stained-glass window.

"You'd better ease off that cheap dope and try learning Deutsch the old-fashioned way," Therese said.

"Ist mein Deutsch so schlecht, Fräulein Obermufti?"

Therese sighed. "Maya, you try too hard. People enjoy having foreign girls in a couture shop. It's cute to be a young foreign girl. At least you can make correct change with silver money, and that's more than Klaudia has ever managed."

"Ich verstehe nur Wurstsalat. Am Montag muss ich wieder malochen."

"Would you *stop that*? It's eerie."

"I really need to do this so that, uhm, *können Sie mir das Dingsda da im Schaufenster zeigen?"*

"Listen, darling, you can't give anyone fashion advice. You don't have any proper sense of chic. You dress just like a little California magpie." Therese stood up. "I never dreamed you'd treat the shop like an adult's job. You need to relax. You're an illegal, remember? If you start fussing about making money, some cop is going to notice you."

Maya frowned. " 'Any job worth doing is worth doing well.' "

Therese thought this over. The tone and the sentiment didn't agree with her at all. "That's like something my grandmother would say. I think I know some people who can help you, darling. Let's stop this nonsense, it's a slow day anyway."

Therese made some net calls, and then shut up shop. They took the tube into Landsbergerstrasse and crossed the Hacker-Brucke. Maya saw the distant towers of the cathedral rising behind the train station. The ancient permanence of Munchen—combined with the seductive possibility of instant escape. The contrast gave her a deep moment of intense inexpressible pleasure.

All the young people in Munchen seemed to know Therese. Therese had a thousand vivid friends. Therese even personally knew some old people, and it was touching to see that they treated her almost as an equal. It often seemed that Therese's little clothing store scarcely existed as a shop per se. The shop was just the physical instantiation of her vast and tenuous gray-market web of tips, barters, bribes, pawns, trade-offs, swaps, hand-me-downs, subtle obligations, and frank kickbacks.

Today's particular friends of Therese had a production studio in the basement of a low-rise in Neuhausen. There were strict laws in central Munchen about obscuring the skyline with high-rises, so the local real-estate entrepreneurs had tried burrowing into the earth. The faddish subterranean buildings had a big overhead from ventilation and heat pollution, and they'd gone broke so repeatedly that they were forced to rent out to kids.

Therese's friends were sculptors. Their studio was down in the bowels of the place, oddly shaped and full of coughing lunglike racket from the ventilator next door. "Ciao Franz."

"Ciao Therese." Franz was a stout Deutschlander with a brown beard and a rumpled lab coat. He wore spex on a neck chain. "[So this is the new mannequin?]"

"Ja."

Franz fiddled with his spex, scanning Maya as she strolled into the studio. He smiled. "[Interesting bone structure.]"

"[What do you think?]" Therese said. "[Can you cast her for me? Maybe a nice porous plastic?]" They started bargaining, in a vivid Deutsch so thick with argot that Maya's translator choked.

Another guy showed up from the back of the lab. "Hey, hello, beautiful."

"*Ich heisse Maya.* And yes, I speak English." She shook the new guy's plastic-gloved hand.

"Ciao Maya. I'm Eugene." Eugene removed his spex, let them dangle on the neck chain, and looked her up and down bare eyed. "I like your color sense. You've got a lot of nerve."

"Are you American?"

"Toronto." Eugene looked pretty good without his spex on. A bit gawky and hawk faced, but with a lot of energy. Eugene hadn't bathed in a long time, but he was giving off an intriguing scent, like warm bananas. "You've never been in our studio before, right? Let me give you the tour of the works."

Eugene showed her a camera-crowded scanning pit and a pair of big, translucent assembler tanks. "We map out our various models here," said Eugene, "and this is how we do physical instantiation. This old classic," he patted the transparent wall of the tank, "is a laser-cured thermoplastic instantiator. Modern industrial standards passed her by some time ago. But we're not industrial people here in the lab. We do artifice. Franz has worked some intriguing culturotechnical variations."

"Really? *Wunderbar.*"

"You know how thermocuring works?"

"*Nein.*"

Eugene was very patient. He was obviously taken with her. "You fill this tank with a special liquid plastic. Then you fire lasers through the plastic, and the lasers cause the liquid plastic to cure into a durable solid object. The object's proportions are defined by the movements of the beam—sculpted from liquid into solid, at the focus of coherent light. Naturally the beam is an output from our design virtuality—so we can design physical objects from scratch inside a computational space. Or else we can photocopy Three-D actualities. Like, for instance, your body. Which is what we'll be doing today."

The technical English verbiage seemed to be driving the language tincture out of her head. "I think I understand. What you do is like photography."

"Right! Very much like photography! *Solid* photography. The plastic's expensive, but we can carbonate it. We can get cheap

Three-D foam objects that are mostly gas. The real fun is in whipping it all the way up to aerogel. That way, we can make a structure the size of an elephant that weighs about three kilos."

Maya gazed respectfully at the machine. "That's a big tank, but it's not big enough for an elephant."

"You make the elephant in pieces and then you laminate the sections together," Eugene explained, rolling his eyes slightly.

She spoke carefully. "I'm sorry. I'm not normally this stupid, but I'm on drugs."

Eugene burst into laughter. "You're a lot of fun."

"So you're a sculptor? An artist?"

"Artifice isn't art."

"Are you an engineer, then?"

"Artifice isn't engineering. Let me show you something else. You're a couture model, right? You ought to find this intriguing."

Eugene led her over to a life-sized plastic nude sprawling on the floor. The nude woman was lying on her back with her hands laced behind her head and a vague expression of animal bliss.

"Who's your model?"

"She's nobody. And everybody. See, Muncheners are very big on nude sunbathing. We just went down to the Flauchersteg one Sunday last summer, and we scanned a bunch of people with our spex. Then we did a physical composite of all the models, a collation in our virtuality. Then we output the collation in plastic, and we got her: The Average Nude Munchener Sunbathing Woman." Eugene looked at the statue with pride, then jerked his thumb over his lab-coated shoulder. "We got her husband, Mr. Nude Munchener, stashed over there in the corner; he's a little hard to see right now because his finish wore off and his substance is semitranslucent."

"Right."

"You can see that as a model she's not particularly compelling; I mean, entirely average people are unremarkable by definition, wouldn't you say? But creating this image was just the first step. My next concept was to get about a hundred men to look at her—while wearing spex, of course, so we could track the movement of their attention."

"How'd you get a hundred people to stare at a nude plastic statue?"

"Well, we just bicycled her down to the Marienplatz and made it a performance event. The tourists were real cooperative."

"Oh."

"Then we collated our attention statistics in an algorithm and plotted it in virtuality and fused it out. Come have a look."

He strolled over to a corner and whipped away a thin black sheet.

"Wait a minute," Maya said, "I . . . I *know* this thing. It's the . . ."

"The *Venus of Willendorf.*"

"That's it. That's *her.*"

"My original conjecture was that we were going to output the most beautiful woman in the world," Eugene said, "a feminine form that would absolutely compel male attention! But what we got here is basically a pretty good replica of something that a Paleolithic guy might have whittled out of mammoth tusk. You start messing with archetypal forms and this sort of thing turns up just like clockwork."

"What's the man look like?"

"The man as seen by men, or the man as seen by women?"

"The man as seen by women."

Eugene shrugged. "Somehow I knew you'd ask that. . . . Well, have a look." He crossed the floor of the studio and removed another sheet.

"What went wrong?" Maya said.

"Well, we're not quite sure. We think maybe it was our sampling procedure. I mean, you get these two rather odd artificer guys, me and Franz, asking total female strangers in the Marienplatz to put on spex and stare at a naked plastic guy. . . . We got a few volunteers, but it was kind of a small self-selected crowd of women, and this is what we ended up with."

The statue was a big angry-looking horned mask connected to a swollen bunch of bulging bubbles.

"It looks like they tried to boil him to death."

"You see those three, um, leglike appendages here? They're

supposed to float detached in midair, but we couldn't cast it that way. We still don't get what happened to his nose; it looks like they just sort of stared right through him."

Maya gazed meditatively at the statue. The initial impression of ugliness seemed to fade after a while. It was getting harder and harder to stop watching the thing. She felt a growing sense of excitement. It was as if they'd dragged the statue whole and true from some sticky crevice deep in her own brain. "Eugene, this artwork is doing something to me. This feels very . . . unreal."

"Thanks a lot." Eugene shrugged. "We lost interest in this one, we figured we had a flaw in our procedurals. I'm thinking now that maybe self-portraits are the next conceptual step. We scan you, we show you yourself, then we plot out your attention algorithm as you're looking at your own replicated body. That way we can cast your internal self-image in permanent plastic."

"I think this boiling-bubble guy would be a lot less scary if he were really small," Maya offered thoughtfully. "Like something I could wear on a charm bracelet, maybe."

"You'd have to take that up with Franz. Franz does our merchandising."

Therese came up. "Franz says he'll cut me a discount if we do six of you," she told Maya.

"I thought we were just going to do just one nice replica dummy of me for the store window."

"Sure, but if we do six dummies then I can retail you. Assuming the product would move, that is."

"Certainly this girl will sell," said Franz with confidence.

"The problem with couture mannequins is they're not very tactile," Eugene opined. "We've been doing some great work in surfaces. We got some new finishing techniques that feel just like wet sealskin."

Therese made a quick moue of distaste. "We don't want people feeling up the mannequins, Eugene. It wrinkles the clothes."

Eugene was crestfallen. He considered a further argument, then looked at his watch. "Well, I can't stay chatting, I gotta see a dog about a man. . . ." He looked at Maya. "Y'know, I enjoyed meeting you. You're a really fascinating conversationalist. If you're not too busy, why don't you drop by the Tête du Noyé in Praha next Tuesday? You know where that is?"

"No."

"It's in the Praha Old Town, the Staromestska. The Tête is a tincture joint for the artifice crowd. We got a crowd of very vivid people from the net, they meet there in Praha once a month. Someone like you—I think maybe you'd fit right in."

———

Franz and Eugene delivered six Mayas next Monday. Eugene had jointed their shoulders, knees, elbows, and hips on plastic swivels. He had trimmed their skulls inside the design virtuality, so the finished mannequins had no hair.

The shop was now in possession of six tall plastic nudes with slightly startled expressions. The mannequins weighed about five kilos each, so lightweight and breezy that it was a good idea to weight their feet lest they topple over.

Maya and Klaudia spent the day dressing the plastic mannequins, doing their wigs and makeup, and assembling them in action tableaus outside the shop.

Klaudia was surprisingly good at this. Klaudia was no genius at making change but she was great at deploying mannequins—mannequins clambering over café tables, mannequins brandishing tennis rackets, mannequins chewing enthusiastically on each other's feet. The outdoor orgy of well-dressed plastic Mayas was a powerful crowd draw. Maya would take her own place among the plastic stiffs and then suddenly move, on Klaudia's cue. The effect was profound.

Maya found it lovely to be publicly admired. So publicly, and with such intense repetition. The romantic ingenue Maya; the big floral pink powderpuff Maya; the Maya in gallopades with gleaming wads of costume jewelry and big kicky wings of eyeliner; the Maya in the white neon battery suit; the high-kicking hey-sailor Maya in red and white culottes; the sporty mountain-hiking Maya;

the cool and classic draperied Maya with a fluted frappé glass. The Maya multiplicity was grand fun, a pocket spectacle. Still, when the day was over, Maya felt peculiarly thin and stretched. Strangely and terribly weary.

It was Therese's biggest commercial day in months. They sold so much stock (including every last one of the Maya dolls) that Therese decided to leave town for an acquisition tour.

"You can run along and have some fun in Praha while I'm out of town," Therese said to Maya. "You'd better take Klaudia with you. I never knew Eugene to ask any girl for a date before. Taking Klaudia will widen your options."

"Eugene wasn't making a date with me, and I don't even like Eugene. Much. Besides, why should I go to Praha? There are plenty of vivid cafés here in Munchen."

"Don't be a mule, darling. Praha is a big fashion town. The Tête du Noyé is a scene. You're a model in the rag trade, so it's important for you to make scenes."

"That kind of fun sounds like a lot of work."

"Well, at least it's work of a different kind. Klaudia deserves time off from the store, and so do you. Anyway, if Klaudia runs off to party without you to look after her, she'll only get into trouble. Klaudia always does."

"That's all very clever and convenient, Therese. You're always so full of wiles and angles."

"I have to make arrangements. I can't do business from an empty shop, you know that as well as I do. Get Klaudia off my hands for a little while—and take your camera, too. There are big armies of vivid women in Praha." Therese narrowed her eyes. "Those Praha vivid girls . . . They have an iron grip on the fragile exotic look."

There was no resisting a determined Therese. Maya and Klaudia loaded their backpacks and their hangered garment bags, and caught the Praha train late Tuesday morning. Klaudia paid. Klaudia almost always paid; she had a little salary, plus a tidy allowance from her wealthy and influential Munchener parents.

They fell headlong into their beanbags. Maya felt cranky and exhausted. Klaudia was twenty-two; the previous day of excitement and frenzied labor had only improved her mood. Klaudia was ready for anything. "[You'd better eat something, Maya,]" she said in Deutsch. "[You never eat anything.]"

"I'm never hungry."

Klaudia adjusted her own earpiece translator. Despite weary years of the finest state-assisted classroom training, Klaudia's English was highly unstable. "[Well, you'll eat something today, or I'll sit on you. You look so pale. Look at that wig. Can't you even try?]" Klaudia deftly adjusted Maya's secondhand mop of blond curls. "[You have the strangest hair, girl, you know that? Your natural hair feels more like a wig than this wig does.]"

"That's from my shampoo."

"[What shampoo? Are you trying to kid me? You never shampoo. You should let me spritz you a nice protein strengthener. I know you're trying to grow your hair out, but you should let me trim it a little. Without that wig, you look like a big *ragazzina*.]"

"Ja, Klaudia, ich bin die grosse Ragazzina."

Klaudia gave her the look that locals always gave her when she tried her broken Deutsch—a look as if her intelligence had suddenly plummeted.

The train pulled out of the station with the ease and silence of a skate skimming ice. The car was three-quarters full. Klaudia examined every one of the passengers in their car with her forthright Deutschlander stare. She elbowed Maya suddenly. *"Na, Maya!"*

"What?"

"[See that old lady sitting back there with the police dog and the little kid? That's the president of the Magyar Koztarsasag.]"

"The president of *what?*"

"Hungary."

"Oh." Maya shook her head. "I know we're all supposed to call people by their own proper names nowadays, but speaking Hungarian, that's pushing it."

"[She's an important polity figure. You should go ask for the log-on address to her publicity palace.]"

"Me? I feel so sleepy," Maya said.

"[She's a big politician. She'll speak English to you. What a shame she's so badly dressed. I wish I could remember her name. You could take my picture with her.]"

"If she's really a politician, she'll appreciate it if we respect her privacy."

"[What?]" Klaudia demanded, skeptically. "[Statespeople *hate* privacy. Government people don't do that privacy nonsense.]"

Maya yawned. "I don't know what it is, but I feel so worn out today. I'm having a sinking spell. I think maybe a little nap . . ."

"[I'll get you something,]" volunteered Klaudia, squirming onto her high heels, eyes gleaming. "[A tincture. How about caffeine?]"

"Caffeine? That's addictive. And isn't it awfully strong?"

"[It's our day off! Let's be daring! Let's drink caffeine and get really *sternhagelvoll*! We'll run around Praha all day! Praha, the Golden City!]"

"Okay," Maya said, sinking into her pastel blue beanbag and fluttering one hand at the wrist. "Go, go. Bring me something. . . ."

Maya slumped bonelessly into the luscious depths of her beanbag and gazed up at the roof of the train car. A blank expanse of gleaming metal. This railcar was a real antique. It had been designed for advertisements, before advertising had been outlawed worldwide. Light flashed by through the bare limbs of the trackside arbors against the gleaming expanse of the roof. Flash, flash, flash.

She emerged from her daze with a piercing ache behind both eyes. Something was really hurting her ear. She pulled it off. An earcuff. The skin of her ear was all pinched beneath it, as if she'd been wearing it for weeks. She plucked the little device off her head, held it in her hand, gazed at it blankly, then let it drop on the floor. . . . What *was* she wearing?

She was wearing a red jacket over a long-sleeved low-cut

shirtdress, a slinky number that looked and clung like lace and snakeskin. The dress ended at midthigh. She wore spangled metallic hose and high-heeled ankle boots.

Mia got onto her feet, wobbling. She began walking unsteadily down the aisle of the train car, wobbling in the absurd boots. Her toes were pinched and her ankles ached. She felt very strange and weak—starved, headachy, shaky, really bad.

She was alone inside a train with twenty or thirty foreigners. An alien landscape was rushing at terrific speed by the window.

She had a very bad moment then, an all-over shudder of identity crisis and culture shock, so that she swayed where she stood and felt sweat break out all down her back. Then the nausea passed and she came out of it, and she felt extremely different.

She was Mia Ziemann. She was Mia Ziemann and she was having a very strange reaction to the treatment.

A dog was staring at her. It was the police dog belonging to the Magyar president. The dog was crouching on his beanbag at the edge of the aisle, looking very efficient in his strapped and buttoned police-dog uniform. His ears were cocked alertly and his eyes were fixed on Mia.

The president of Hungary sat next to the dog, together with a ten-year-old boy. She was showing the boy the screen of her notebook, pointing into its depths with a virtuality wand, a slim and elegant access device like an ivory chopstick. The boy was gazing into the woman's screen in primal trust and fascination, and the president was teaching him something, speaking gently in Magyar.

The old woman had the most astonishing hands. Hands that were wrinkled and deft and strong. A face supernaturally full of character, a postmortal face. The face you had when you were a very strong-willed, very healthy, very intelligent woman a hundred and twenty years old, and you had seen many sorrows and had made many painful decisions, and you had lost all illusion, but had never lost your self-respect, or your desire to help.

Of course this lady would speak English. She was a European intellectual, she would speak English, along with her consummate mastery of five or six other languages. She had authority—no, she *was* authority. So Mia would totter over to this saintly woman, and beg her help, and say, I'm sick, I'm hungry, I'm weak, I've lost my way, I've run away, I've broken my faith and abandoned all my duties and my obligations, I've done something bad, and I'm sorry. I'm very sorry, please help me.

And the president would look at her and she would master the situation in an instant. She would not be embarrassed or upset, she would be very wise, and she would know just what to do. The president would say, My dear, be calm, sit down, rest a moment, of course we can help you. There would be networking, and explanations, and advice and guidance and food, and a warm safe place to sleep. And the blasted tatters of her life would be stitched back around Mia Ziemann, like a big warm quilt of official forgiveness and grace.

She stumbled forward.

The dog said something in Deutsch.

"What?" Mia said.

The dog switched to English. "Are you all right, miss? Shall I call a steward? You smell a little upset."

The president looked up and smiled politely.

"No," Mia said, "no. I'm feeling much better now."

"What a lovely dress. What's your name?" asked the president.

"Maya."

"This fine young man is Laszlo Ferencsi," the president said, patting the shoulder of the boy.

"I won the school essay contest!" Laszlo piped up in English. "I get to stay with the president today!"

Maya swallowed hard. "That's great, kid. You must be really proud."

"I am the future," Laszlo confided shyly.

"I'm a big ragamuffin," Maya said. She tottered to the back of the cabin, found the ladies', knelt on the floor with a squeak of stockings, and had the dry heaves.

Klaudia found her in the ladies', hauled her out, and bullied her into eating. Once the nutrient broth had hit her system, Maya's morale began to soar.

Klaudia gently clipped the translator back onto Maya's head. "[I knew you were in trouble when you left your earpiece. . . . It's a good thing Therese sent me along to look after you! You don't have any more sense than a rabbit! Even a rabbit knows enough to eat.]"

Maya dabbed cooling sweat from her forehead. "Rabbits never have my problems unless they've done something really postlagomorphian."

"[No wonder Eugene likes you. You talk just as crazy as he does. You better stick close to me at this party tonight. These artifice characters are real stuck-up oddballs.]"

Maya gazed out the window and sipped pale broth from her spoon. It felt so good to be someone new. So good to be herself. So good to be alive. It was much, much more important to be alive than to be anyone in particular. Thick Bohemian forest outside the train window, the branches just beginning to leaf out for spring. Then they were silently sliding at very high velocity on skeletal arches over intensely cultivated green fields. Vast irrigated stands of tall and looming gasketfungus.

The giant fungi weren't plants. They'd been designed to transmute air, water, and light into fats, carbohydrates, and protein, with a bioengineered efficiency previously unknown to the world of nature. A field of engineered gasketfungus could feed a small town. The fungi were two stories tall: dense, green, leafless, square edged, and as riddled as a sponge. Once you got used to the monsters, they were rather pretty. And it was nice that they were pretty, because they covered most of rural Europe.

They spent the afternoon in the center of Praha. In Mala Strana. In the Old Town, Stare Mesto. Cobbled squares. Cathedrals. Spires and ancient brick and footworn stone. Gilded steeples, railings, bridges, damply gleaming statuary. The river Vltava. Architecture centuries old.

Klaudia shopped frenetically, and methodically stuffed Maya with fast food from the street stalls. The tasty nourishing grease hit Maya like a drug, and her world grew easy and comfortable. Everything was cheerful, everything was making sense.

They took their cameras to the Karel Bridge. This was not the peak of the tourist season, but Praha was always in vogue. Praha was an artifice town, a couture town. People came here to show off.

Of course most of the tourists were old people. Most of everyone was old people. And old women had never dressed so beautifully, never carried chic so well into such advanced years. The bridge was aswarm with older women, Europe's female gerontocrats, ladies who were poised, serene, deeply experienced, deliberate, and detached. Firm but gentle *femmes du monde,* who were all the more tolerant of human foibles since they were left with very few of their own. Gracious women who knew how to listen, distinguished women who could love their enemies until those enemies fell into little pieces. Beautiful, clever, accomplished women, gently quivering with the electricity of determined and long-tested ego.

Old women in winter glissade jackets, in porous-weave two-tone nattiere sweaters. Old women in smart, self-contained business suits of pinkish apricot, poilu blue, eucalyptus. Women in stylish padded winter pajamas of pale yellow and crepuscular blue. Hard sleek hairstyles without a trace of gray, bobbed and parted at the side, with capescarves flung over one shoulder and neatly pinned with seashell brooches. Surplice fronts and fringed lapels, mousselines, failles, polycarbon chiffons, marquisettes, matelassés, rich crepes, and restrained lamés. Sheath dresses over the sleek planar lines of unobtrusive medical cuirasses. A slender postsexual profile with a waistline that seemed to start at midthigh, breaking into smart flounces and chic little gouts of astrakhan and breitschwantz. Beautiful teeming masses of posthuman women.

The old men in the crowd dressed with columnar forbidding dignity in belted coats and dark medical vests and tailored jackets, as if they'd outgrown the prospect of intimate human contact. The old men looked suave and unearthly and critically detached, a race of scholarly ice kings who walked so slowly in their beautifully polished shoes that it seemed they were being paid by the step.

And then the vivid people. They were a minority of course, but they were less of a minority in Praha, and that made them bold and intense.

Young men. Lots of bold and intense young men, that surplus of men that every generation boasted before the male mortality rate kicked in. Swaggering young bravos with lucid unlined skin like angels, because acne was as dead as smallpox. They favored gleaming jackets and odd heavy boots and patterned neck-scarves. It was a generation of young men fed from birth on biochemical ambrosia, with perfect teeth and perfect eyesight and lithe, balletic posture. The real dandies among the boys wore decorative translator earcuffs, and didn't mind a dusting of blusher to accentuate the cheekbones.

Vivid women. Black-sleeved print dresses, garishly patterned fabric shawls, swirling postiche capes, gunmetal shoe-gloves with zesty little flip-up ankle collars. Patterned frocks, flirty short jackets, lots of lacquer red. Backpacks with little bells and clattering bangles, and very serious lipstick. Praha had a vogue for checkered winter gloves nicked off at the fingertips for the emergence of daggerlike lacquered nails. Big serious cinching waistline belts, belts that threw the hips out. And décolletage, whole hot hormonal acres of décolletage, even in winter. Big cushiony vivid cleavage that went beyond allure and became a political statement.

The young women were thrilled to be photographed. They laughed at her and clowned for the camera. Many people in Praha, even the kids, wore spex, but nobody wore glasses anymore. Corrective lenses were a prosthetic device as dead as the ivory pegleg.

Praha was giving her new insight.

She found herself suddenly understanding the profound alliance between old European city centers and young Europeans. All the world's real and serious business took place in the giant, sophisticated, intelligent high-rise rings around the downtowns—buildings with advanced infrastructure, buildings with the late twenty-first century embedded in their diamond bones and fiber-optic ligaments.

Still, those in power could not bring themselves to demolish their architectural heritage. To destroy their own cultural roots was to leave themselves without even the fiction of an alternative, marooned in a terrible vacuity of postindustrial pragmatism. They prized those aging bricks and those moldering walls and, for oddly similar reasons, Europe's young people were similarly prized, and similarly sidelined.

Young kids lurking in old cities. They formed an urban symbiosis of the profoundly noneconomic, a conjunction of the indestructible past with a future not yet allowed to be.

Maya and Klaudia dressed in a ladies' and left their bags in a public locker. The Tête de Noyé was in Opatovicka Street, a three-story building with a steeply pitched tiled roof. You entered it by walking up a short set of worn stone steps with ornate iron railings, and then directly down a rather longer set of wooden steps into the windowless basement, where they kept the bar. All this stepping up and down made very little architectural sense, but the building was at least five hundred years old. It had been through so many historic transitions that it had a patina like metamorphic rock.

Klaudia and Maya were met at the foot of the stairs by an elderly spotted bulldog in a tattered sweater and striped shorts, possibly the ugliest intelligent animal Maya had ever seen. "Who asked ya here?" demanded the dog in English, and he growled with unfeigned menace.

Maya looked quickly around the bar. The place was lit by a few twinkly bluish overheads and the pale glow of a rectangular wallscreen. The bar smelled like seaweed, like iodine. Maybe like blood. Twenty people scattered in it, dim hunched forms slumped in couches around low tables. Many of them were wearing spex. She could see faint pools of lit virtuality squeezing out around the rims of their lenses. There was no sign of Eugene.

"That guy over there invited us," Maya lied glibly, pointed, and waved. "Hey!" she shouted. "*Na mensch!* Ciao!"

Naturally some male stranger at a far table looked up and politely waved back at them. Maya breezed past the dog.

"*Na* Maya!" Klaudia whispered, sticking close. "[We are way overdressed for this. This place is a morgue.]"

"I love it here," said Maya, perfectly happy and confident. She went to the bar.

Faint analog instrumental music was playing, muted and squeaky. The bartender was studying an instruction screen and repairing a minor valve on an enormously ramified tincture set. The tincture set stretched the length of the mahogany bar, weighed four or five tons, and looked as if its refinery products could demolish a city block.

The bartender wore a thin, ductile, transparent decontamination suit. This was the kind of gear that courageous civil-support people had once used when cleaning out plague sites. The bartender was naked beneath his gleaming airtight veil. His unclothed body in the plastic suit was covered head to foot in thick gray fur. From a distance, his dense body hair looked very much like a gray wool sweater-trouser set.

The bartender, to their disquiet, now took notice of them. He slapped his notebook shut with a bang, and shuffled over. He was very old—or very sick—and walked as if his feet ached.

His face was a solid mass of gray beard—no eyebrows, no visible nose, no forehead, ears, or temples. The hairless membranes of his lips and eyelids were three pale patches in a face-smothering snarl of whiskers.

"You're new here," the bartender announced, through an external speaker on his suit.

"That's right. I'm Maya, and this is Klaudia. We do couture."

The bartender looked them over in the relatively lucid lighting directly over the mahogany bar. He had a small scabby bald patch on the crown of his head. "I like young girls in fine clothes," he said at last, blinking. "The dog gives you any trouble, you tell him to come to old Klaus."

Maya smiled at him sunnily. "Thank you so much. It's very

good of you to have us in to your famous establishment. We won't be any trouble, I promise. Can we take pictures?"

"No. What are you drinking?"

"Caffeine," Klaudia said bravely.

Klaus deftly served up two demitasses. "You want animal cream?"

"Nein danke," said Klaudia with a scarcely perceptible shudder.

"No charge, then," said Klaus, returning to his repair work.

Maya and Klaudia took their clattering cups and saucers to a couch-and-table set, and sat down together. Klaudia threw her ribbed cloak aside and shivered inside her pink ruffled top.

"[This sure isn't my kind of party,]" Klaudia moaned quietly. "[I was sure there would be dancing and music and public sex and maybe some anandamines. This bar is like a tomb or something. What's that awful music they're playing?]"

"That's antique acoustic analog music. There wasn't much vertical color to the sound back in those days. The instruments were made of wood and animal organs."

Klaudia sipped nervously at her demitasse. "[You know what the problem is, Maya? This is a party for intellectuals. It's really stupid to be an intellectual when you're young. You should be an intellectual when you're a hundred years old and can't feel anything anymore. Intellectuals are so pretentious! They don't know how to live!]"

"Klaudia, relax, okay? It's still early."

The wall mural was the most warm and inviting object in the Tête du Noyé. It was not glassy or screenlike at all, it was very painterly, very like a canvas. The screen had been broken up into hundreds of fragments, honeycombed cells, slowly wobbling and jostling. The moving cells swam among one another, and pulsed, and rotated, and mutated. A digital dance of the flowers.

Maya lifted her demitasse cup, formally touched it to her lower lip, and put it back on the table. She watched Klaudia fidget for a while, and then glanced at the mural again. The amber floral shapes were mostly gone, replaced by a growing majority of cool geometrical crystals.

She wasn't quite sure how she knew it, but she realized somehow that the mural was watching her. The mural had some way to monitor people—probably cameras, hidden behind the screen. Whenever anyone looked at the mural directly, its movement slowed drastically. It only really got going when no one was looking at it.

Maya opened her backpack, and slyly watched the mural in the mirror of her makeup case. The mural knew no better, and thought it had escaped her attention. The little cells became quite lively, flinging sparks of information at one another, blossoming, conjugating, spinning, kaleidoscoping. Maya snapped her case shut, and turned to face the screen directly. The cells froze guiltily in place and crept along on their best behavior.

Eugene ambled over. "Ciao Maya!"

"Ciao Eugene." She was glad to see him. Eugene had bathed. He'd combed his hair. He was looking very natty in a long brocade coat and stovepipe slacks.

Eugene smiled winningly. "*Was ist los,* Camilla?"

"Klaudia," Klaudia said, frowning and tucking in her legs on the couch.

Eugene sat down cheerfully. "You should have logged on at the bar! That's the custom here at the Tête. I didn't even know you'd arrived."

"There's a first time for everything, Eugene."

"Most people log on from home to say they're coming. This scene is very netted. The Tête is our meat rendezvous. I'm pleased that you've come. How do you like our host?"

"I don't much like him," Klaudia said primly in English.

"Amazing character, isn't he? He's a fascinating conversationalist. Got a million stories. He was a cosmonaut."

"Really?"

"Yeah, the only Czech in the lunar colony. Stayed up on the moon all during the plague years. That's why he wears the suit. They had those immune system problems with the long-term radiation. He tried to make it on Earth without his suit at first, but he caught the staph and it scarred him pretty bad. That's why he went for the heavy fur."

"I've never met a cosmonaut."

"Well, you've met one now. Klaus owns the Tête. I gotta warn you, Klaus doesn't much like to talk about his moon years. Most of his friends died during the blowouts and the coup and the purges. But he's really good to the local scene. He was the only Czech lunarian, a national hero. So the Praha city council lets him do anything he wants. Klaus is no stuffy gerontocrat, he's really been to the edge. *Mit ihm konnte man Pferde stehlen.*"

"You don't have to speak Deutsch just for me," Klaudia pouted.

"Deutsch is no problem! We got a Shqiperisan guy right over there trying to find someone here who can speak Geg. Geg, or maybe Tosk."

"Where's he from?"

"Tirana."

Reluctantly, Klaudia brightened. "[I love men from Shqiperise,]" she said in Deutsch. ["They're so industrial and romantic. What does he do?]"

"Virtualitat," Eugene said.

"Prima." Klaudia stood up and left.

Maya patted the couch seat next to her. "Come sit closer."

Eugene edged over cautiously.

"Tell me something about the woman who did that wall mural."

"How do you know a woman did it?"

"I can just tell, that's all."

Eugene watched the mural, which noticed his attention and slowed instantly. "It's a cellular automata display. From the fifties, to judge by the technique. I hope she built it solid, because you'd have a pretty hard time replacing the works-and-wares from a dead platform like that."

"It's beautiful, isn't it? That gimmick almost made me angry, before I realized what she meant to say."

Eugene scratched his head. "You got me. Not my variety of gimmick at all. Paul would know, Paul's a scholar."

"Who's Paul?"

Eugene smiled guardedly. "Paul pretty much lays down the

law in our little scene. Y'know, I don't like being told what to think. Because I'm not much for ideology. But I trust Paul. And I think that Paul trusts me."

"Is Paul here tonight? Introduce me, all right?"

"Sure."

Eugene led her across the bar. Half a dozen people were eagerly clustered around a muscular red-haired young man in a vivid display suit. His suit jacket showed a splendid satellite view of night-lit Praha, patterned streetlights sprawled across his black lapels and down both his glossy sleeves. He was telling some lively and elaborate anecdote in Français. His enthralled listeners laughed aloud, with the clubby sounds of friends absorbing in-jokes.

Maya waited patiently until the story was wound up in a torrent of alien wisecracks. Then she spoke quickly. "Ciao Paul! Do you mind English?"

The red-haired man scratched his beard. "I have great respect for the English language, but that's Paul there at the end of the table, darling."

"Oh."

"Don't do that, okay?" Eugene muttered. He led her past a clutter of legs and drinks.

Paul was dark and stocky and clean-shaven, wrapped in quiet conversation with a sharp-nosed woman with black bangs and no lipstick. Paul was groping with an oversized table napkin. The square decorative cloth had a life of its own. It flapped and wriggled and seemed determined to crawl up Paul's forearms.

Eugene whispered. "Let me get you something."

"A mineral water? Thanks." Maya perched on the edge of the couch and watched as Paul and the dark-haired woman discussed the glimmering, flopping cloth in rapid and fluent Italiano.

Paul wore gray fabric trousers and a buttoned fabric shirt in faded khaki; he'd thrown his coat over the back of the couch. The woman wore dark tights and boots and elbow-length white smartgloves. The woman was putting a lot of effort into ignoring her.

Paul deftly pinched a corner of the kerchief. The wriggling cloth went limp. He attached the kerchief to a slender cable, pulled a notebook from beneath the couch, and, still speaking nonstop Italiano, began pounding the keys and observing a readout in some grisly technical dialect of English.

Paul touched a final key and a process began execution. Then he turned alertly to Maya. "American?"

"Yes."

"Californian?"

"That's right."

"San Francisco."

"You're very clever."

"I'm Paul, from Stuttgart. I program. This is Benedetta, she's a coder from Bologna."

"Maya. From nowhere in particular, really. Don't do much of anything." She offered her hand to the woman across the table.

"You're a model," Benedetta said wearily.

"Yes. Sometimes. Barely."

"Ever had one real idea to trouble your pretty head?"

"Not really, but I can dust myself off if I trip over one."

Paul laughed. "Benedetta, don't be gauche."

Benedetta brushed at Maya's fingers with her smartglove, and slumped back into the couch. "I came a long way to talk to this man tonight. I hope you can wait to flirt with him until everyone gets very tight."

"Benedetta's a Catholic," Paul explained.

"I am *not* a Catholic! Bologna is the least Catholic city in Europe! I am an anarchist and an artificer and a programmer! I plan to hang the last gerontocrat with the guts of the last priest!"

"Benedetta is also a miracle of tact," Paul said.

"I only wanted to ask about the mural," Maya said.

"*The Garden of Eden,* Eva Maskova, 2053," Paul said.

Eugene had returned from the bar, but he was wrapped up in another story from the raconteur. Eugene was leaning on his elbows on the back of the couch, snorting with laughter, and sipping absently from Maya's mineral water.

"Tell me about this Eva person. Where is she now?"

"She took too many tinctures and fell off her bicycle, and she broke her neck," Benedetta said coolly. "But the medicals patched her back together. So she married a rich banker in España, and now she works for the polity in some stupid high-rise in Madrid."

Paul shook his head slightly. "You're very unforgiving. In her own day, Eva had the holy fire."

"That's for you to say, Paul. I met her. She's a perfect little middle-aged bourgeoise who keeps houseplants."

"She had the holy fire, nevertheless."

Maya spoke up. "Her mural. It's all about people like yourselves, isn't it? When they're left to themselves, they do miracles. But when they're scrutinized and analyzed from the outside, then they dry up."

Paul and Benedetta exchanged surprised glances, then turned to look at her.

"You're not an actress manqué, I hope," said Benedetta.

"No, not at all."

"You don't dance? You don't sing?"

Maya shook her head.

"You don't work in artifice at all?" Paul demanded.

"No. Well—sometimes I take photographs."

"It had to be something," Benedetta said triumphantly. "Show me your spex."

"Don't have any spex."

"Show me your camera, then."

Maya pulled the tourist camera from her woven purse. Benedetta gave a short bark of laughter. "Oh, that's hopeless! What a relief! For one terrible moment I thought I'd met an intelligent woman who liked to wear spangled tights."

A tall man in a long gray coat and mud-smeared work pants stumbled down the stairs. "Emil has come," said Paul, with pleasure. "Emil has remembered! How amazing! Just a moment." He rose and left them.

Benedetta watched Paul go, with deep irritation. "Now you've done it," she said. "Once Paul gets started with that holy fool, there'll be no end to it." She unplugged her writhing handkerchief and stood up.

It wouldn't do to be abandoned. Not when she was just getting through. "Benedetta, stay with me."

Benedetta was surprised. She looked at Maya forthrightly. "Why should I?"

Maya lowered her voice. "Can you keep a secret?"

Benedetta frowned. "What kind of secret?"

"A programmer's secret."

"What on earth do you know about programming?"

Maya leaned forward. "Not much. But I need a programmer. Because I own a memory palace."

Benedetta sat back down. "You do? A big one?"

"Yes, and yes."

Benedetta leaned forward. "Illegal?"

"Probably."

"How did someone like you acquire an illegal memory palace?"

"How do you think someone like me acquired an illegal memory palace?"

"I hate to speculate," Benedetta said, pursing her lips. "May I guess? You traded sexual favors for it."

"No, certainly not! Well . . . Yes, I did. Sort of. Actually."

"Let's pop your palazzo open and look about inside." Benedetta deftly wrapped the kerchief around her neck. The cloth twitched a bit, then flashed into a pattern of gold and paisley. Benedetta picked up her smooth and slender notebook and her metal-studded purse. "We'll go behind the bar where it's discreet."

"You've been so patient with me already, Benedetta. I hate to impose."

Benedetta stared at her for a long moment, then dropped her eyes. "All right. I was stupid. I'm sorry that I was stupid to you. I'll be better now. So can we go?"

"I accept your apology." Maya stood up. "Let's go."

Benedetta led her into an especially bluish and subterranean niche behind the long mahogany bar. Someone had been doing blood sampling on the tabletop. There was a litter of crumpled chromatographs and a diamond-beaked mosquito syringe.

Benedetta swept the litter aside, thumped her notebook down, and unreeled an antenna from its top. "So. What is required? Gloves? Spex?"

"I need a touchscreen for my password."

"A touchscreen! It must be fate that I brought my furoshiki." Benedetta whipped her kerchief off, set it on the table, and smoothed it flat. "This will work. It's from Nippon. The Nipponese love the obscure functionalities." She plugged the corner of the inert cloth into her notebook and the cloth flashed into vivid glowing eggshell white.

"I've never seen one of these furoshiki." Maya leaned over the table. "I've certainly heard of them. . . ." The intelligent cloth was woven from a dense matrix of fiber-optic threads, organic circuitry, and piezoelastic fiber. The hair-thin optical threads oozed miniscule screen-line pixels of colored light. A woven display screen. A flexible all-fabric computer.

Benedetta opened her purse, removed an exquisite pair of Italian designer spex, and slipped them on.

"Those are lovely," Maya said.

"You need spex and gloves? Well, you're in the right crowd. We'll ask Bouboule. We can trust Bouboule. All right?"

"I suppose so."

Benedetta tapped her spex and clawed at invisible midair commands. "You'll love Bouboule," she promised. "Everyone loves Bouboule. She's rich and generous and funny and promiscuous, and likes to punch cops in the face. She'll be dead at forty."

Benedetta stroked at her notebook keys. Then she aimed her spex across the table at Maya. Maya's face bloomed across the fabric kerchief in full color.

"The Miracle of Saint Veronica!" Benedetta said, and smirked. "Let me find the touch function."

"This is a big secret. I'm being very rash in trusting a stranger with this. I'm sure you realize that, Benedetta."

"You're very pretty," Benedetta said slowly, staring into her screen and typing. "You shouldn't be so pretty, and also push me so hard."

"Pretty is just a technique of mine. You're pretty. I could make you look really vivid if you wanted me to."

"I hate body artifice," Benedetta said, fingering keys with great expertise. "It's even worse now that women's bodies last forever. We women are so much of the female body it's fatal to us, we even have to die beautiful. Even Paul . . . he talks to me about theory. Like a colleague! Like a philosopher! Then the glamour girl appears in her wig and lipstick and it's like his little Muse just jumped off the train for him. Women never learn! Men contemplate beauty, but we have to *be* beauty. So the female is always the other, and we're never the center."

Maya blinked. "Men and women just think differently, that's all."

"Oh, that's so stupid! 'Anatomy is destiny.' That's all gone now, you understand? Anatomy is *industry* now! You want to do some terrifying male mathematics, little glamour girl? Put enough stickers on your head and I'll teach you calculus in a week!"

"You can break a blood vessel doing that sort of thing."

"Don't be a hypocrite, darling. I'm sure you've done things to your breasts that are a thousand times more radical than calculus. Wait a moment—here it comes."

Benedetta's eggshell white furoshiki turned a smoky slate gray. "That's good. Just a moment while I find a public netsite. . . . Here we have it."

Bouboule arrived at their table. Bouboule had a lacquered little cupid's-bow mouth, no chin, and large, luminescent brown eyes. She wore a narrow-brimmed domed hat, fancy spex on a neck chain, a woven sweater, a long scarf, and she carried a large yellow backpack. "Ciao Benedetta."

"Bouboule is from Stuttgart," Benedetta said. "What was your name again?"

"Maya."

"Maya is going to show us a secret, Bouboule."

"I adore secrets," said Bouboule, settling down with a wriggle. "How charming of you, Maya, to share your secrets with little nobodies like ourselves. Do you mind if my monkey sees?"

A golden marmoset crept up Bouboule's solid back and shoulder. The marmoset was fully clad in miniature evening dress, tie and tails. The monkey's eyes were two gleaming metallic domes. Implanted mirrorspex.

"Does your monkey talk?" Maya asked. The monkey had no shoes. Its furry little feet, protruding from the trouser's hems, seemed peculiarly ghastly.

"My monkey's a virtualist," Bouboule said airily. "Maya, where are your spex?"

"Don't have spex. Got no gloves either."

"*Quel dommage!*" said Bouboule, clearly very pleased. "My uncles manufacture spex in Stuttgart. I have four uncles. All brothers! Do you know how rare that is nowadays, to have four brother men, all from one family? Five childs! With my mother, all together. That never happens now! But things always happen to me that should never happen." Bouboule opened her pack and handed Maya a plastic-wrapped pair of wire-rimmed spex.

"Liquid film?" Maya said, examining the lenses.

"Disposables," shrugged Bouboule. "Take these smart-gloves—I don't say these are gloves of the mode. These are gloves to wear on party nights, when you might wake up who knows where. Don't break the fingers, stretch them out slowly . . . that's the way."

"You're very kind to loan me these," Maya said.

"No loan, keep them! My uncles like gifting toys to the childs, they have a very long-term view of the market."

"I have something for you, too, Maya," said Benedetta suddenly, apparently on impulse. Benedetta groped with two fingers beneath the high rolled collar of her blouse. She tugged out a diamond necklace, with a pendant on a thin golden chain. "Here. This is for you. Yours is the greater need."

"A diamond necklace?"

"Don't look so surprised, any idiot can make diamonds," Benedetta said. She handed it over. "Look at the pendant."

"A little nightingale in a golden nest! This is so lovely, Benedetta. I can't possibly accept this."

"Gold is dirt. Stop gaping, and pay attention. The bird nest goes inside your ear. It's a translator. All the diamonds are memory beads, they contain all the European languages. See the little numbers etched on the beads? The bird, she is hatching English, Italiano, and Français now. You don't need Italiano as your major language, so put in English, that's egg number one . . . put English in the center of the nest, and put Italiano back on one side. Italiano, that's egg number seventeen."

"Italiano is *seventeen?*" said Bouboule.

"It's a Swiss device. From Basel."

"What humorless people the Swiss are," said Bouboule. "Just because Milano bought Geneva . . . What a grudge."

Maya took the Italiano egg from the chain. Then she pried the English egg loose from the golden nest, and carefully popped the Italiano diamond egg beneath the bird's etched little circuitry feet. The tiny eggs snapped nicely into place with satisfying little clicks.

She gently tucked the little pendant into the hollow of her right ear. The pendant wriggled about like a metallic earwig. Something threadlike and waxy crept into her ear canal. She felt an instant violent urge to claw the device out of her head, but she accepted the tickling penetration, shivering on the spot.

"[It has no battery,]" Benedetta told her in Italiano. "[You have to keep the bird warmed by your skin at all times. If she ever gets cold, the bird will die.]"

The new translator had a wonderful flutelike resonance, a tiny piping right next to the surface of her right eardrum. "But it's so lovely! So clear!"

"Remember—no battery."

"No battery. Okay. But that seems like an odd oversight."

"That's not a bug, it's a feature," Benedetta said glumly. "That bird is a shareware device. The Swiss weren't missing any tricks when they built it."

Maya clipped the diamond chain around her neck, and tucked it beneath her blouse. She couldn't help but feel pleased. "You're very generous. Would you like my Deutsch translator?"

Benedetta looked it over. "Deutsch-to-English. I can't use this. It's tourist kitsch." She tossed it back. "[Now we can talk like civilized people. Show us your palazzo.]"

"I certainly hope this works." Maya traced her passtouch into the glossy surface of the woven computer. "Are my gloves turned on?"

"[Something is processing,]" Benedetta diagnosed skeptically.

Bouboule pulled on a pair of exquisitely tailored lemon yellow smartgloves and carefully adjusted her spex. "This is so exciting. Patapouff and I love memory palaces. Don't we, Pouffpouff?"

Maya tensed in expectation that the monkey would speak aloud. The monkey said nothing. Maya forced herself to relax. Talking dogs were okay. There was definitely something awful about monkeys.

A blurry test pattern appeared on Maya's spex. She ran her finger along the stem of the right eyepiece until the pattern focused and clarified. She pressed the nosebridge to bring the depth in. These were habitual gestures, little technical actions she'd been doing for decades, but she felt a sudden thrill. Her astigmatism was all gone. Her astigmatism was entirely cured, and until this instant she had never managed to miss it.

"[It's an office!]" Benedetta said triumphantly. "[Such a strange old office! I'll navigate, okay?]"

"A man's office," Bouboule said, bored.

"[Where does this man keep his pornography?]" Benedetta asked.

"What?" Maya said.

"[You never found his pornography? There's not a man alive who doesn't hide pornography in his memory palazzo.]"

"He's not alive," Maya said.

Bouboule said something wicked, and laughed. "A pun in Français," the bird translator fluted, in its sweet but peculiarly characterless English. "The context is not understood."

"[I see here the big blueprint,]" said Benedetta, examining one wall. "[The sixties, eh? They built like maniacs then. Library.

Gallery. Artificial Life Zoo—that sounds good! Business records. Health records. CAD-CAM pattern storage.] 'Movies.' Are there movies in this place?"

"What is that word, 'movies'?" Bouboule said.

"Cinématographique."

"Prima!"

"[Tailor's measurements . . . tincture recipes. House plans. Oh, that's very nice! To keep your physical house plans inside your palazzo. Three or four different houses! This man must have been quite rich.]"

"He was rich several different times," Maya said.

"[Oh, look at this thing! He had a ptydepe tracker.]"

"What's a ptydepe?" Maya said.

Benedetta, forced into technical definitions, switched to English again. "A Public Telepresence Point, a PTP. He has—he had—a scanner-collator that could sample public telepresence records. Good for tracking friends. Or enemies. The program will sample millions of public telepresence records for years, cataloging appearances of the target person. It's a dataminer. Industrial spyware."

"Illegal?" Bouboule asked with interest.

"Probably. Maybe not, when he had it built."

"Why do you call it a 'ptydepe'?" Maya said.

"Ptydepe, that's what they always call the PTPs here in Praha. . . . It's such a strange language, Czesky."

"Czesky is not the noun," said Bouboule helpfully. "Czesky is only the, what-you-call, adverb. The proper name of the language is Czestina."

"Czestina is egg number twelve, Maya."

"Thank you," Maya said.

She felt tiny paws stealthily creeping into her sleeve. Maya shrieked and yanked her spex off.

The monkey, alarmed, leapt back to the safety of Bouboule's shoulder, where it revealed a rack of needlelike teeth.

Bouboule, blinded to reality by her spex, groped gently in midair. "Bad tactility?"

"Bad old protocols," Benedetta said, similarly blinded.

Maya glared silently at the monkey's silver-capped eyeballs. "Touch me again and I'll whack you," she mouthed silently. The monkey adjusted its tuxedo lapels, flicked its prehensile tail, and jumped off the back of the couch.

"I found an access!" Benedetta said. "Let's go up to the roof!"

Maya put on her spex again. Doors shunted aside in the wall. They entered a virtual darkness. White rings ran past them downward, like galloping zebra stripes.

They emerged on a crenellated rooftop. Fake gravel underfoot.

And there were *other* memory palaces. Warshaw's partners in crime perhaps? She could not understand why people running memory palaces would want to make their premises visible to one another. Was it somehow reassuring to see that other people were hiding here as well? Rising in the horizon-warped virtual distance was a mist-shrouded Chinese crag, a towering digital stalagmite with the subtle monochromatics of sumi-e ink painting. Some spaceless and frankly noneuclidian distance from it, an enormous bubbled structure like a thunderhead, gleaming like veined black marble but conveying a weird impression of glassy gassiness, or maybe it was gassy glassiness . . . A smooth and elegantly gilled construction with a mushroom's sloping tip, fibrous at the bottom, columnar and veiny up the sides. Another palace like a honeycomb set on end, surrounded by hundreds of motes all slowly flying and detaching and absorbing, like a dovecote for virtual pterodactyls.

"What a strange metaphor," said Bouboule, thrilled. "I've never seen a virtuality this old that is still functional."

"I wonder where we are," Maya said. "I mean, I wonder where on earth all this is running."

"This might not represent real processing," Benedetta said. "This looks fantastic, but it could be the tripes of one little machine in a closet somewhere in Macau. You must never trust the presentation. Through another interface, this might look very quotidian and bourgeois."

"Don't be such a mule, Benedetta," said Bouboule, excited.

"Gerontocrats don't live that way! No man who owned a place like this would come here just to fool his own eyes. This is an old man's soulscape. An exclusive resort! A criminal enclave."

"I wonder if any of these strange places are still inhabited. Maybe they are all dead, and still running on automatic. They are haunted castles in virtual sand."

"Don't talk that way," Maya said tightly.

"Let's fly!" Benedetta leapt gracefully from the edge of the parapet.

The spex went dark.

Benedetta gasped. "Oh! Pity! That broke the contact."

They took their spex off, and gazed at one another silently.

"How did you come to own this place?" Bouboule said at last.

"Don't ask," said Benedetta.

"Oh." Bouboule smiled. "Did the old man leave you money, I hope?"

"If he did, I never found the treasure," Maya said, folding her spex. "Not yet, anyway." She tried to give the spex back.

"No, no," Bouboule insisted, " you keep them. I'll find you nicer ones. What's your address?"

"No fixed address. No net address. Really, I'm just passing through."

"Come and stay with me, if the wanderjahr takes you to Stuttgart. There's plenty of room at my uncles'."

"That's very sweet of you," said Maya. "You're both so kind and generous to me—I scarcely know what to say."

Benedetta and Bouboule exchanged the oddly guileless glances of young sophisticates. "Not at all," said Benedetta. "We have our own little ways. We can always tell when we discover a sister spirit."

"In the scene we are modern women," declared Bouboule somberly, "who have made the decision to live free! We all have desires that don't accord with the status quo. We are contemporary women! We gaze at the stars all together, or we die one by one in the gutter."

Bouboule bent over suddenly. "What's that? Oh, look, Patapouff found a nice mosquito! It's a lucky sign. Let's test our blood and do some stickers to celebrate. Something very warm and cozy."

"I don't know," Benedetta demurred, "my lipid levels are so low lately. . . . Maybe a mineral water."

"Me, too," Maya said.

"Let's get some nice boy to fetch us a drink," said Bouboule. She plucked up the inert fabric computer and flapped it over her head.

"Who's that guy that brought you?" Benedetta said to Maya. "Eugene?"

"I didn't come here with Eugene."

"Eugene is an idiot, isn't he? I hate people who confuse algorithms and archetypes. Besides, he's from Toronto."

"Est-il Québecois?" said Bouboule, with interest.

"Toronto's not in Quebec," Maya said.

"C'est triste. . . . Oh, ciao Paul."

"You've stolen the party, Benedetta," said Paul, smiling. "This is Emil, from Praha. He's a ceramicist. Emil, this is Maya, a model, and Benedetta, a programmer. And this is Bouboule. She's our industry patroness."

Emil bowed to Bouboule. "I'm told that we have met."

"In a way," said Bouboule, her face clouding. She rose, kissed Emil's cheek briefly, and walked away. The marmoset ran after her and bounded onto her shoulder.

"They were lovers once," Benedetta explained, wrinkling her nose.

Emil sat down mournfully. "Was I really that woman's lover?"

"Don't talk scandal, Benedetta," Paul chided. "Let me see the furoshiki." He set his notebook down. "Emil, this device is fascinating, you should watch this closely." He rolled up his sleeves.

Emil glanced at Maya. He had lovely dark eyes. "Were *we* once lovers?"

"Why do you ask?" Maya said.

Emil sighed bitterly. "Paul is so persuasive," he muttered.

"He always convinces me to attend these parties of his, and then I commit some terrible faux pas."

Paul glanced up from his screen. "Stop whining, Emil. You're doing fine tonight. Come look at this device, this will cheer you up. It's marvelous."

"I'm not a digital person, Paul. I like clay. Clay! The least digital substance on earth."

"You have really good English," Maya said, moving closer.

"Thank you, my dear. You're certain we've never met?"

"Never. I've never been to Praha."

"Then you should let me show you the city."

Maya glanced at Paul and Benedetta. They had launched into furious Italiano, enraptured by the fabric machine. "That might be very nice," she said slowly. "What are you doing after this party?"

"What am I doing at this moment?" countered Emil. "Embarrassing myself and everyone, that is what. Let's go for a walk. I need fresh air."

Maya gazed slowly around the subterranean bar. No one was watching them. No one cared what she did. She was perfectly free. She could do whatever she pleased. "All right," she said. "If you like."

She found her red jacket. Emil found a long dirty coat and a slouch hat. There was no sign of Klaudia. "I have a friend here at the Tête," she told Emil. "We'll have to come back for her. Just a little walk around the block, all right?"

Emil nodded absently. They left the Tête. Emil stuffed his large bony hands in his coat pockets. The night was clear and still, and growing colder steadily. He began walking up Opatovicka Street.

"Are you hungry?" Emil asked.

"No."

Emil walked on silently, staring at the pavement. They passed streets with utterly impossible names: Kremencova, Vjircharich, Ostrovni.

"Shouldn't we be going back?" Maya said.

"I'm having a crisis," Emil confessed wearily.

"What kind of crisis?"

"I shouldn't tell you. It's a complicated story."

Emil had a Czech British accent. She could scarcely believe she was walking through such a lovely city, on a cold clear night, hearing such a touchingly exotic version of her own language. "I don't mind. Everyone has troubles."

"I'm forty-five years old."

"Why is that a crisis?"

"It's not my age," said Emil, "it's the steps I took to evade my other difficulties. You see, I was a potter. I was a potter for twenty-five years."

"Yes?"

"I was a bad potter. A wheel kicker, a mud dauber. Technically adept, but lacking the holy fire. I couldn't commit myself wholly to the craft, and the better I became at technique, the less inspiration I felt. I was sickened by my own inadequacies."

"That sounds very serious."

"It's all right to be a happy amateur. And it's all right to be truly gifted. But to be competent and middling bad at an artifice that you care about—that's a nightmare."

"I wouldn't know," Maya said.

This remark seemed to crush Emil completely. He pulled the slouch hat down over his eyes and trudged.

"Emil," she said at last, "would it help you to talk in Czestina? I happen to have a Czech translation unit with me."

"Maybe you can't understand, but my life was untenable," Emil said. "I decided I had gone too far. I had to erase my mistakes, and try to start again. So, I talked to some friends. Tincture people. Very hard-case tincture people. I got them to give me a very strong broad-spectrum amnesiac."

"Oh, dear."

"I injected it. When I woke up next morning, I couldn't even talk. I didn't know who I was, or where I was, or even what I was. I didn't know what a potter's wheel was. All I saw was that I was in a studio and there was a wheel and a lump of damp mud in a bag. And broken pots. Of course I'd broken all my worthless ugly pots the night before, before," he smacked his skull with the flat of his hand, "before I broke my own head."

"Then what?"

"I put the mud on the wheel, I spun it, and I could work clay. It was a miracle. I could do clay without any thought, without any doubt. I knew nothing about clay and yet the skill came out of my hands. Clay was all I had—all that I was. Clay was all that was left of me. I was an animal that made pots."

Emil laughed. "I made pots for a year. They were very good pots. Everyone said so. I sold all of them. To big collectors. For big money. I had the gift now, you see. At last I was good."

"That's quite a story. What did you do then?"

"Oh, I took my money and learned again how to read and write. Also, I took English lessons. I never could learn English properly before, but, in the state I was in, English was easy. Bit by bit, some of my old memories came back. Most of my personality is gone forever. No great loss. I was never happy."

She thought this over. She felt glad she had come to Praha. Here of all places she'd somehow found someone who was truly her kind of guy.

"Let's go back to the party now."

"No, I can't bear to go back. My studio is just up this street." Emil shrugged. "He's a nice man, Paul, he means well. Some of his friends are all right. But they shouldn't admire people like me. I made a few good pots, but I'm not Paul's case study in the liberation of the holy fire. I'm a desperate man who destroyed himself for the sake of mud. Paul's people should admit this to themselves. I'm a monstrous fool. They should stop romanticizing posthuman extremities."

"You can't go home and brood, Emil. You said you'd show me the city."

"Did I tell you that?" said Emil politely. "I'm very sorry, my dear. You see, if I promise something early in the morning, then I can almost always fulfill it. But if it's late at night . . . well, it's something to do with my biorhythms. I grow forgetful."

"Well, then, at least show me your studio. Since we're so near."

Emil locked eyes with her. A very knowing look. "You're welcome to see where I live," he said, meaning nothing of the kind. "If you feel you must."

The building was dark and impossibly old. Emil's studio was on the second floor, up a creaking set of stairs. He unlocked the door with a metal pocket key. The floors were uneven wooden boards and the walls were lined in ancient flowered paper.

Most of the floor space was taken up with tall wooden racks of earthenware. There were two big mud-stained sinks, one of them dripping steadily. A white kiln, and stained pegboards hung with tools of wire and wood. A potter's wheel, a crowded work-table. Dusty sacks of glazing compound. A primitive kitchen full of handmade crockery in finger-grimed white cupboards. Old windows warped with damp, with lovely flowerpots sprouting the skeletal remains of houseplants. Crumpled sheets of canvas and paper everywhere. Sponges. Gloves. The sharp smell of clay. No shower, no toilet; the bath was down the hall. A sagging wooden bed with grime-smeared sheets.

"At least you have electricity. But no computer of any kind? No netlink? No screens?"

"I once had a notebook here," Emil said. "A very clever machine. My notebook had my schedules written in it, addresses, numbers, appointments. Many helpful hints for living from my former self. One morning I woke up with a bad headache. The notebook began to tell me what to do that day. So, I opened that window there"—he pointed—"and I dropped that machine onto the street. Now my life is simpler."

"Emil, why are you so sad? These pots are beautiful. You took a medically irrevocable step. So what? A lot of people have bad luck with their upgrades. There's nothing to be gained by fussing about that, once it happens. You just have to find a way to live on the far side of that event."

"If you must know," Emil grumbled. "Look at this." He put an urn into her hands. It was squat and round with a glaze in ocher, cream white, and jet black. The pattern was crazily energetic, like a chessboard struck by lightning, and yet there was enormous clarity and stillness to the piece. It was dense and heavy and sleek, like a fossil egg for some timeless state of mind.

"My latest work," he said bitterly.

"But Emil, this thing is wonderful. It's so beautiful I wish I could be buried in it."

He took the urn off her hands and shelved it. "Now look at this. A catalog of all my works since the change." He sighed. "How I wish I'd had the good sense to burn this stupid catalog. . . ."

Maya sat on Emil's workstool and leafed through the album. Print after print of Emil's ceramics, lit and recorded with loving care. "Who took these photographs?"

"Some woman. Two or three different women, I think . . . I've forgotten their names. Look at page seventy-four."

"Oh, I see. This one is very like your latest work. It's part of a series?"

"It's not *very like,* it's *identical.* But that piece was *spontaneous.* It came to me in a moment's inspiration. You see what that means? I've begun to repeat myself. I've run dry. I have hit my creative limits. My so-called creative freedom is only a cheap fraud."

"You've created the same pot twice?"

"Exactly! Exactly! Can you imagine the horror? When I saw that photograph—it was a knife in my heart." He collapsed on the bed and put his head in his hands.

"I can see that you regard this as something very dreadful."

Emil flinched and said nothing.

"You know, a lot of ceramics people create work with molds. They make hundreds of identical copies of a work. Why is this so much worse than that?"

Emil opened his eyes, hurt and bitter. "You've been discussing my case with Paul!"

"No, no, I haven't! But . . . You know, I take photographs. There's no such thing as an original digital photograph. Digital photography has always been an art without originals."

"I'm not a camera. I'm a human being."

"Well, then that must be the flaw in your thinking, Emil.

Instead of torturing yourself about originality, maybe you'd be happier if you just accepted the fact that you're posthuman. I mean, people don't remain human nowadays, do they? Everyone has to come to terms with that sooner or later."

"Don't do this to me," Emil moaned. "Don't talk that way. If you want to talk that way, go back to the party. You're wasting your time with me. Talk to Paul, he'll talk like that for as long as you like."

Emil kicked a wadded bathrobe from the edge of the bed. "I'm not posthuman. I'm just a foolish, very damaged man who had no real talent and made a very bad mistake. I can no longer remember things very well, but I know very well who I am. All the clever theories in the world make no difference to me."

"So? It seems like your mind's already made up. What's your solution for this so-called crisis?"

"What else?" said Emil. "What else is there to do? I can't spend my existence going round and round in circles. I'm going to throw myself out the window."

"Oh dear."

"Taking the amnesiac was only a cowardly compromise. A half measure. I'm not what I wanted to become. I never will be that person. I can't live being anything less."

"Well," Maya said, "of course I'm not one to talk against suicide. Suicide is very proper, it's always a perfectly honorable option. But . . ."

Emil put his hands over his ears.

Maya sat next to him on the bed, and sighed. "Emil, it's silly to die. You have such beautiful hands."

He said nothing.

"What a shame that such beautiful strong hands should be turning into clay. Deep under the cold, hard earth. When you could be slipping those hands under my shirt."

Emil sat up. His eyes gleamed. "Why do women do this to me?" he demanded at last. "Can't you see that I'm a shattered emotional wreck? I have nothing to give to you. In the morning, I won't even remember your name!"

"I know that you won't," Maya said. "Of course I realize

that about you. I never met anyone quite like you before. It's a very attractive quality. I don't know quite why, but truly, it's very tempting, it's terribly hard to resist." She kissed him. "I know that's an awful thing to say to you. So let's stop talking now."

———————

She woke in the middle of the night, in a strange bed in a strange city, to the soft rise and fall of another human breath. The structure of the universe had shifted again. She felt soft and sweetly wearied, deeply warmed by his sleeping presence. Having a lover was like having a second soul. She had enough spare souls for every man in the world.

———————

In the morning she made them breakfast. Emil, just as he had promised, did not remember her name. He was cheerfully embarrassed about this fact. A quick bed-wrestling match knocked their affair into order. Emil ate his breakfast, grinned triumphantly, and started working. Maya, unable to bear the disorder, started cleaning the studio.

To judge by the state of his catalog, Emil had been living alone for two, maybe three months. The documentation of his work was out of order and out of date. She would have to see to putting the record straight. This was clearly the open-ended legacy of being with Emil. To judge from the varying competence of the photographs, she was the fourth in a series.

Giving the place a good cleaning job was even more revelatory. Women had blown through Emil's studio like a series of storm fronts. Hairpins here. A single crumpled stocking there. Shoe liners. An empty lipstick. Pink feathers off some long-lost costume. Cheap sunglasses. Mismatched cooking utensils. Lubricants. Blood testers. And, of course, the photographs. The women doing the photographs had been the ones investing real effort.

"I feel good today," Emil declared, as well he should. "I'm going to create a new piece just for you, Maya. A piece to capture your unique qualities. Your generosity. Your goodness."

"I'm not your clay vessel, you know."

"Of course you are, my dear! We are all clay vessels. Why contradict Scripture?" Emil chuckled merrily and started pounding clay.

Maya found her way downtown and rescued her luggage from the storage locker. Klaudia's backpack and garment bag were gone. Klaudia had left her a note. In Deutsch. Maya couldn't read Deutsch, of course, but to judge by the angular scrawl and the forest of exclamation points, Klaudia had been furious.

Maya found a public netsite. She plugged in her camera and wired her photos to Therese at the shop. Then she had lunch.

When she had finished dutifully nourishing herself, she called the shop in Munchen.

"Where are you?" said Therese.

"I'm still in Praha. How is Klaudia?"

"She's back. Mad. Worried. Hung over. Humiliated. You're not being helpful, Maya."

"I picked up a guy."

"That's exactly what I thought. . . . When will you be back?"

Maya shook her head. "Therese, if I don't look after this one, he's going to throw himself out the window."

Therese laughed. "Have you lost your mind? That's the oldest art-boy scam in the book. Show some sense and get back right away. I've brought in a lot of new stock."

"Therese . . ." She sighed. "You were right. The Tête is a scene. I'm very taken with these artifice people. They're going to teach me to be vivid. I'm not coming back to Munchen."

Therese was silent.

"Therese, did you see my photos?"

"The photos are not bad," Therese said. "I think maybe I can use the photos."

"They're awful. But I'm going to take lessons. In photography, in spex work. I'm going to get better. I'm going to get better equipment and I'm going to really work in artifice. I'm going to make myself into one of these people."

"You're not happy here at the shop, darling?"

"I don't want to be happy, Therese. There's not enough of me to be happy. I'm not my own woman yet, I have to learn to be more like myself. These artifice people, I think they can help me. They have my kind of hunger."

"You sound very certain very suddenly. What changed your mind for you? One night in bed with some man? Why don't you get on the train and come back here? Trains are very easy."

"I can send you lots of photos, if you want them. But I can't go back to the shop."

"If you don't come back to Munchen, I'll have to get someone else. There won't be a welcome for you anymore."

"Get someone else, Therese."

"My poor little Maya! Always so ambitious. And artifice people are so chic." Therese sighed. "Cleverness doesn't make them nice people, you know. You're very innocent, and they could hurt you."

"If I wanted safe and nice, I'd have stayed in California. My life is risk. I'm an illegal. I'm on the drift, the wanderjahr. You were very good to me, but Munchen's not my home. I have to leave sometime. You knew that."

"I knew that," Therese acknowledged. She lowered her voice. "But still: you owe me. Don't you owe me?"

"That's true. I owe you."

"I fed you, and I clothed you, and I sheltered you, and I never turned you in. That was a lot, wasn't it?"

"Yes. It was a lot."

"I'm going to ask you for a big favor in return, darling. Someday."

"Anything."

"You'll have to be very discreet for me."

"I can be discreet," she promised. "I can specialize in discreet."

"When the time comes, you'll know. Just remember that you owe me. And try to be careful. *Wiedersehen,* darling." Therese hung up.

––––––––––––

Though he couldn't be bothered to feed himself properly, Emil very much liked to eat. With a woman in reach, he complained bitterly if not methodically fed, as if this were some fracture in the bedrock of the universe.

Emil had a little money. He was too confused to properly manage the funds he had acquired; there were half-drained little cashcards stuffed in nooks and crannies all over his studio. So Maya went shopping for them, and began eating with more regularity and determination than she ever had before. Czech medical chow, such as noki. Chutovky. Knedliky. Kasha, and goulash. It was solid and enticing food and it made her cheerful and energetic.

Once Emil was properly fed, he generally became lively. It was sweet to be Emil's lover, because he was never blasé. Whenever he ran his agile and dexterous hands across her flesh, there was always an element of shocked discovery to his caress. Sex made him all surprised and pleased and reverent and grateful.

Emil became very productive under this hearty regimen. He kept firing up his kiln. The kiln wasn't a microwave exactly, it was a specialized potter's resonator. Like most modern gadgetry, Emil's kiln was foolproof, very clean, extremely quick, and altogether eerie. He'd pull out a freshly zapped pot with a monster pair of padded tongs. The irradiated clay would give a ghastly crystalline shriek as it hit the air and began to cool. The pot would gush heat like a fireplace brick. The whole studio would steam up and get very cozy. Maya would saunter around in slippers and an untied bathrobe, naked under her diamond necklace. Hair almost long enough to fuss with now. It was rather stiff and scruffy hair, but the speed of its growth was impressive.

If he liked the way the work had turned out, he would throw her on the bed to celebrate. If he didn't like it, she would throw him on the bed to console him. Then they would tiptoe down the hall and wedge into a hot bath together. When they were clean they would eat something. They spoke English together, and a little guttural Czestina in Emil's more intimate moments. Life was very simple and direct.

Emil hated time stolen from his work. From Emil's subjective point of view, any day spent in keeping up life's little infrastructures was a small eternity lost forever. With a permanent magic supply of groceries and electric power, Emil would have slumped into solipsism.

It was impossible to manage Emil in the morning, because he was always so startled and intrigued by her unexpected presence in his household. However, after a week, a certain visceral familiarity with her seemed to be seeping into Emil below the level of his conscious awareness. He seemed less surprised by her intimate knowledge of his desires and routines, and he became more trusting, more amenable to suggestion.

One evening she sent him out to buy new underwear and get himself a proper haircut, carefully noting the shops to be visited and the exact items and services to be purchased. She wrote them down on a cashcard and strung the card on a little chain around his neck.

"Why not tattoo it on my arm?"

"That's very funny, Emil. Get going."

She felt much better without him underfoot. Maybe it was that steady and nourishing diet, maybe it was the unceasing intensity of their relationship, but she was very restless today. Irritable, almost ready to come out of her skin. She felt as if she needed to be contained somehow, and dressed in tights and a sweater.

There was a knock at the door. She assumed it was Emil's dealer, an obscure gallery owner named Schwartz who dropped by every couple of days looking for product, but it wasn't. It was a portly Czech woman in a powder blue civil-support uniform. She carried a valise.

"Dobry vecer."

Maya quickly tucked the bird-nest translator into her ear, a reflexive habit by now. "How do you do. Do you speak English?"

"Yes, a little English. I am the landwoman here. This is my building."

"I see. I'm pleased to meet you. May I help you with something?"

"Yes, please. Open the door."

Maya stepped aside. The landlady bustled in and looked the studio over sharply. Slowly, a pair of the lighter stress marks disappeared from between her much-furrowed brows. Maya took her for seventy-five, maybe eighty. Very sturdy. Very well preserved.

"You go in and out for days now," the landlady said briskly. "You're the new girlfriend."

"I guess so. Uhm . . . *jmenuji se* Maya." She smiled.

"My name is Mrs. Najadova. You are much *cleaner* than his last girl. You are Deutschlander?"

"Well, I came here from Munchen. But really, I'm just passing through."

"Welcome to Praha." Mrs. Najadova opened her valise and thumbed through a series of accordion folders. She produced a fat sheaf of laminated papers in English. "This are your support documents. All for you. Read them. Safe places to eat. Safe places to sleep. This is important medical service. Maps of Praha. Cultural events. Here is coupons for shops. Schedule of train and bus. Here is police advice." Mrs. Najadova shuffled the documents and a little stack of cheap smartcards into Maya's hands. Then she looked her in the eye. "Many young people come to Praha. Young people are reckless. Some people are bad. The wanderjahr girl must be careful. Read all of the official counsel. Read everything."

"You're very kind. Really, this is enormously helpful. *Dekuji.*"

Mrs. Najadova removed a gilt-embossed gilt smartcard from her jacket pocket. "These are church services. You're a religious girl?"

"Well, no, not actually. I'm always pretty careful about drugs."

"Poor girl, you are missing the true fine part of life." Mrs. Najadova shook her head mournfully. She set her valise down, and deftly removed a telescoping dust-mop handle and a sterile packet of adhesive sponges. "I must sample the room now. You understand?"

Maya put the documents on the new bedspread. "You mean for contagion sampling. Yes, I've been wondering about that. Do you have some tailored subtilis or maybe some coli? Something I can spread around to knock back any pathogens. That corner under the sink smells kind of yeasty."

"From the medical support," said Mrs. Najadova, visibly pleased. "You report for official checkup. They will give you what you need to keep good house."

"Isn't there another way to get those microbe cultures? I'm not really due for a checkup just yet."

"But it's free checkup! Gift by the city! It's all written on the documents. Where to go. How to report."

"I see. Okay. Thanks a lot."

Mrs. Najadova assembled her mop and began methodically creeping about the studio, scraping and dabbing. "The potter has wild mouses."

"Mm-hmm."

"He has bad hygiene. He leaves food and insects come."

"I'll watch for that."

Mrs. Najadova, having reached a decision, looked up. "Girl, you must know this. The girlfriends of this crazy man, they are not happy. Maybe at first a few days. In the end they always cry."

"It's very sweet of you to be so considerate. Please don't worry, I promise you I'm not going to marry him."

The door opened. A neatly hair-cut Emil came in with a shopping bag. A violent argument erupted at once, in blistering Czestina. There was shouting and stomping and vile condemnation, charge and countercharge. It seemed to last forever. At last Mrs. Najadova retreated from the studio, with a shake of her mop and a final volley of vitriolic threats. Emil slammed the door.

"Emil, really. Was all that necessary?"

"That woman is a cow!"

"I'm surprised you could even remember her name."

Emil glowered. "To forget a lover is very sad. A tragedy. But to forget an enemy is fatal stupidity! She is a *cop*! And a *spy*! And a health inspector! And a gerontocrat! She is a bourgeoise, a philistine! A fat rich rentier! And on top of all that she is my landlord! How could she be worse?"

"It's true that combining landlady with all those other social functions does seem excessive."

"She spies on me! She reports me to hygiene authorities. She poisons the minds of my friends against me." His brows knotted. "Did she talk to you? What did she say?"

"We didn't really talk. She just gave me all these free coupons. Look, I can rent a bicycle with this one. And this chipcard here has a Praha net directory in English. I wonder what it says about photography studios."

"It's all rubbish. Worthless! A commercial snare!"

"When was the last time you actually paid the rent here? I mean, how do you *remember* to pay the rent?"

"Oh, I pay. Of course I pay! You think Najadova runs a charity? I'm sure she reminds me."

She cooked. They ate. Emil was upset. The loss of his morning and the quarrel with the landlady had put him off his feed. His hair looked much nicer now, but Emil was a congenital challenge to grooming. He spent the evening paging through his catalog of works. This was not a good sign.

She seemed unable to shrug off the argument—the fight had shredded her nerves. As the night advanced she grew ever more irritable. She was jumpy, short-tempered. She felt bad—a strange internal tightness.

Her breasts grew swollen and achy. Then she realized the truth. It had been such a long time that it almost felt like an illness. But it was womanhood. She was about to have her first period in forty years.

They went to bed. Sex chased his bad mood away, but left her feeling as if she'd been sandpapered. The night wore on. She began to realize that she was in for a very hard time. No mere lighthearted hiatus in the month's erotic festivities. The event stealing over her body was something vengeful and postwomanly and medical. Her eyelids were swollen, her face felt waxed and puffy, and an ominous intimate ache was building deep within the pelvic girdle. Her mood was profoundly unstable. It seemed to rocket up and crash down with every other breath.

Emil tumbled into sleep. After an hour she began to quietly weep with bewilderment and pain. Crying usually helped her a lot nowadays, it came easily and would wash any sadness away like clear water over clean sand. But weeping wasn't working that way tonight. When the tears gave out, she felt very sane, and very lucid, and very, very low.

She shook Emil awake as he lay peacefully slumbering.

"Darling, wake up, I have to tell you something."

Emil woke up, coughed, sat up in bed, and visibly reassembled his command of English. "What is it? It's late."

"You remember who I am, don't you?"

"You're Maya, but if you tell me anything this late at night, I won't remember tomorrow."

"I don't want you to remember it, Emil. I just want to tell it to you. I have to tell it to you. Now."

Emil grew alert. He tucked the heavy curtain behind the headboard of the bed and a turbid mix of moonlight and streetlight entered the studio. He looked into her eyes. "You've been crying."

"Yes . . ."

"And you have to confess something? Yes, I can see. . . . I already know it. I can see the truth there in your eyes. . . . You've been unfaithful to me!"

Amazed, she shook her head.

"No, no," he insisted, raising one hand. "You don't have to tell me a word! It's all too obvious! A beautiful young girl, with a poor shattered crackpot—no man in the world could be easier to deceive! I know—I offer nothing to command a woman's loyalty. My arms, my lips—what do those matter? When Emil himself is a ghost! A man who scarcely exists!"

"Emil, listen to me now."

"Did I ever *ask* you to be faithful to me? I never asked for that! All I asked was that you not *humiliate* me. I gave you freedom to do as you please—take a dozen lovers, take a hundred! Just don't let me know. And yet you *have* to let me know, don't you? You have to shatter my illusions with this . . . this last vile confidence."

"Emil, stop it! You're acting like a child."

"Don't call me your child, you tramp! I'm twice your age!"

"No, you're not, Emil. Be quiet now. I am much, much older than you. I'm not a young girl named Maya. I'm old, I'm an old woman. My name is Mia Ziemann and I'm almost a hundred years old." She began to weep.

Emil was stunned. A ghastly silence passed. Slowly, Emil withdrew by inches to his edge of the bed.

"You're not joking?"

"No, I'm not joking. I'm ninety-four—ninety-five, something like that—and in my own way, I'm a lot like you. I underwent a very powerful upgrade. Just a few months ago. It made me this way, and it broke me into pieces, it put me on the far side of everything."

"You weren't unfaithful to me?"

"No! Emil, no, that has nothing to do with reality! I'm telling you the truth here. Get it through your head."

"You're telling me you're a hundred years old. Even though you're very obviously about twenty."

"Yes."

"Well, you're not an old woman. I know old women. I've even *had* old women. You may be a lot of things, my dear, but you're not an old woman." He sighed. "You've taken something. You're tight."

"The only thing I'm tight on is Neo-Telomeric Dissipative Cellular Detoxification, and believe me, compared to the harmless tincture dope you little kids like to mess with, this stuff is voodoo."

"You're telling me you're a female gerontocrat? Why aren't you snug in your penthouse with a hundred monitors on you?"

"Because I tore them all off and I skipped town, that's why. I signed all their papers for very advanced treatment and then I broke every law in the book. I hitched a plane to Europe. I'm on the lam. I'm an illegal alien and a fugitive from a research program.

And Emil, someday they're going to catch me. I don't know why I did it. I don't know what's going to happen to me." She began sobbing bitterly.

He waited a while, and when he spoke again his voice had changed. Bewildered, quizzical. "*Why* are you telling me this?"

She choked on her tears, too wracked with anguish to go on.

He waited another while, and then spoke in yet another tone. Speculative, stunned. "What am I supposed to do with you now?"

She wailed aloud.

"I think I understand now," Emil concluded at last, loudly and finally. "You're something truly *freakish,* aren't you? You're like a little *vampire!* Feeding on me! Feeding on my life and my youth! You're like a little lamia from the storybooks. A little . . . bloodsucking . . . posthuman . . . demon-lover . . . incubus!"

"Stop! Stop it! Don't go on, I'm going to kill myself!"

"Something like this could only happen in Praha," Emil declared slowly, and with increasingly obvious satisfaction. "Only here in the Golden City. The City of Alchemists. That's a very, very odd story that you just told me. It's almost too odd to think about! To have heard such a story! In a very strange way, it makes me feel very proud to be Czech."

She wiped her streaming eyes with the edge of the sheet. "What's all that?"

"I'm the *victim* in this tale, aren't I? I'm the sacrificial victim. I'm the toy for a sexual golem. Why, it's the most amazing thing . . . the most amazing, mystical . . . It's so dark and strange and erotic." He looked at her. "Why did you ever choose *me?*"

"I just . . . I just really liked your hands."

"It's too astonishing." Emil adjusted his pillow. "You can stop crying now. Go ahead, stop it." He leaned back and interlaced his fingers on his hairy chest. "I won't tell a soul. Your terrible secrets are completely safe with me. No one would believe me anyway."

The extent of his egotism stunned her so much that she almost forgot her despair. "You don't think I should . . . kill myself?" she said in a small voice.

"My goodness, woman, what's the point? There's nothing wrong with *you*. You're no criminal, you just defrauded the gerontocrats of a few of their lab-rat studies. What are they supposed to do to you—make you *old* again? Shrivel you up in daylight like an apple in a cellar? They can't do that. They think they rule the world, but they're all doomed, a gang of sick centenarians with their ridiculous technologies. . . . Trifling and tinkering with human flesh, when they have no concept of the power of imagination . . . And all to send me *you*! You! Like a little pink beach crab just pulled out of her shell!"

"I'm not a little beach crab. And I'm not an incubus." She drew a harsh breath. "I'm an outlaw."

He laughed.

"I am! I used to pretend that I was someone else, really someone else, so that I didn't have to face up to what I really wanted. But I was lying, because I was Mia all along, I've always been Mia, and I'm Mia right now, and I *hate* them! They don't want me to *live*! They only want me to exist and wear out the days and the years, just like they do! I could walk into the street right now— well, if I put on some clothes—and I could call the lab in the Bay, and I could say, 'Hello everybody in California, it's me, it's Mia Ziemann, I just had a bad reaction to the treatment, I'm sorry, I'm in Europe, I lost my head for a while, please take me back, put all your things inside me and up me and on me, I'm all right now, I'll be really good.' And they *would*! They'd send a plane and probably a reporter, and they'd give me my job back and put a cold towel on my forehead. They're so *stupid,* they should all die! I'll never go back to that life, I'd rather be killed, I'd rather jump out the window." She was trembling.

Emil touched her hand, and said nothing for a long time. Finally he got up and fetched her a glass of water. She drank it thirstily, and wiped at her eyes.

"That's what you had to tell me, is it?"

"Yes."

"That's all of it?"

"Well, yes."

"Did you ever tell it to me before?"

"No, Emil, never. I've never told it to you or to anyone else. You're the first one, truly."

"Do you think you'll have to tell it to me again?"

She paused, considering. "Do you think that you'll remember it?"

"I don't know. I might remember it. I don't often remember things that I'm told this late at night. I might not remember it with some other woman, either, but there's something very deep about the two of us. You and me. I think . . . I think we were fated to meet."

"Well . . . Maybe we . . . No. No, I can't believe that, Emil. I'm not religious, I'm not superstitious, I'm not even mystical, I'm just posthuman. I'm posthuman, I made a moral choice to go beyond the limits. I made that choice with my eyes open, and now I have to learn how to survive in my own private nightmare."

"I know a way out for you."

"What's that?"

"You'll have to be brave. But I can mold you all into one piece. No doubts, no secrets, no pains, just one whole new woman. If you wanted me to."

"Oh, Emil . . ." She stared at him. "Not the amnesiac."

"Of course the amnesiac. You wouldn't think I could misplace a valuable thing like that, I hope. This Ziemann person you talk about, this old woman, this incubus that you have . . . We could brush her away from you. Clean away, just like a witch's broom."

"How would that help us? I'd still be an illegal alien."

"No you wouldn't. We'd brush that away too. You'd be my wife. You'd be young. And new. And fresh. And you'd love me. And I'd love you." He sat up in bed, waving his hands. "We'd write it all down tonight. We'd explain to ourselves just how to go about it, so we could see it together in the morning. We'd get Paul to help us. Paul is good, he's clever, he has friends and influence, he likes me. We'll marry, we'll leave the city, we'll go into Bohemia. We'll plant a garden and work clay. We'll be two new creatures together in the countryside, and we'll live outside bourgeois reality, forever!"

He was full of passionate excited inspiration and conviction, and she was trying to respond to him, when the black lightning of suspicion hit her and she knew, with a deep uneasy lurch, that he had made this offer to other women before.

————————

When she woke in the morning there was no sign of Emil. The room reeked of blood. She'd bled all over the sheets. She crawled out of bed, stuffed a makeshift pad into her underwear, put on a robe, and made herself a pain tincture. She drank it, she stripped the sheets, she turned over the stained mattress, and then collapsed into bed exhausted.

Around noon there was a knock on the door. "Go away," she moaned.

A key rattled in the lock and the door opened. It was Paul.

"Oh it's you," she blurted. "Ciao Paul."

"Good afternoon. May I come in?" Paul stepped into the studio. "I see that you're alive. That's excellent news. Are you ill?"

"No. Yes. No. How can I put this delicately? I'm not at my feminine best."

"And that's all? That's it? Well." Paul smiled briefly. "I understand."

"Where is Emil?"

"Yes," Paul hedged. "Let's discuss that, shall we? Your name is Maya, am I right? We met very briefly at last month's session at the Tête. Your friend was the couturiere who got very tight and had the shoving match with Niko."

"I'm sorry to hear about that."

"Have you eaten?" said Paul, slinging his backpack onto the floor beside the kiln. He smoothed his dark hair back with both hands. "I haven't eaten today. Let me make us something. This kitchen seems nicely stocked. How about a goulash?"

"Oh goodness no."

"A little kasha. Something very light and restorative." Paul began running water. "How long have you known our good friend Emil?"

"I've been living with him ever since that night at the Tête."

"Three weeks with Emil! You're a brave woman."

"I'm not the first."

"You've made changes here," Paul said, gazing alertly about the studio. "I admire your sense of devotion. Emil requires a lot of looking after. He called me this morning. Very agitated. I took the express from Stuttgart."

"I see." She found the bedspread and pulled it up over her knees. "He said you were close friends. He always speaks very highly of you."

"Does he? That's touching. Of course, it was natural of Emil to call me. I have my net-address tattooed onto his forearm."

She blinked. "I never noticed any such tattoo."

"It's rather subtle. The tattoo only becomes visible on his skin when he is very upset."

"Was Emil very upset this morning?"

Paul sifted yellow powder into a saucepan. "He woke me this morning and told me that a strange woman was dying in his bed. Dying, or possibly dead. An incubus. A golem. He was very confused."

"Where is he now?"

"He's relaxing, he's having a sauna. Schwartz is looking after him. I'll have to call them now. Just a moment." Paul unclipped the netlink from his collar and began speaking in Deutsch as he delicately stirred the pan. Paul was soothing, then funny, then authoritative, then lightly satirical. When Paul had restored sense and order to the universe, he clipped the phone back to his shirt collar.

"You should keep your fluids up," he said. "How about a nice mineralka? With maybe two hundred micrograms targeted enkephalin and a bit of diuretic and relaxant. That should put you to rights." He fetched his backpack, opened it, and pulled out a clear zippered bag. It held an arsenal of stickered foils and airtight capsules.

"Did you think I'd be dead when you walked in here, Paul?"

"The world is full of possibilities." Paul opened a cabinet, retrieving spoons and bowls. "I thought it best to be here first, that's all."

"To put the proper cast on the situation before the authorities showed up?"

"If you like." He brought her a fine ceramic bowl of steaming mush and a tapered china vase of mineral water. "You'll feel less distraught if you eat this." He went back and fetched his own bowl.

She sipped at her fizzing mineralka. *"Merci beaucoup."*

"English is fine, Maya. I'm a programmer, I'm a conquered subject of the global argot of technique. We might as well collaborate with English. It's silly to fight it now."

They sliced a yellow stick of lipid and stirred white cubes of sucrose into their kasha, and they ate together on the bed. The cozy little ritual made her feel five years old. She was very weak and had a viperish temper. It was not a good idea to fight with Paul.

"I'm not easy to get along with when I'm this way," she said. "We had an argument last night and I upset him. It's not good to tell him things late at night, it affects his sleep." She sighed. "Besides, this morning I do look half-dead."

"Not at all," said Paul. "In your own hair and without cosmetics your face has great character. Less conventionally pretty perhaps, but far more compelling. There's an element of melancholy remoteness, a weltschmerz. It's a face that is almost iconic."

"You're very tactful and galante."

"No, I'm speaking as an aesthetician."

"What do you do in Stuttgart, Paul? I'm very sorry that I took you from that work today, whatever it was."

"I program. And I teach at the university."

"How old are you?"

"Twenty-eight."

"They let you teach at that age?"

"The European university system is very ancient, and convoluted, and bureaucratic, but yes, if you have publications, and sponsors, and a concerted demand from the students, yes, you can teach. Even at twenty-eight." He smiled. *"C'est possible."*

"What do you teach?"

"I teach artifice."

"Oh. Of course." She nodded repeatedly. "You know, I need to find someone who can teach me photography."

"Josef Novak."

"What?"

"Josef Novak, he lives here in Praha. I don't suppose you know his work. But he was a great master. A pioneer of early virtuality. I'm not sure that Novak still takes students, but of course his name leapt to mind."

"He's a gerontocrat?"

" 'Gerontocrat'? A good teacher should never be scorned. Of course, Novak is not an easy man to know. The very old are rarely easy people to know."

"Josef Novak . . . wait, did he do a desktop environment called *Glass Labyrinth* back in the teens?"

"That's far before my time." Paul smiled. "Novak was very prolific in his youth. All lost works now, of course. The tragic loss of all those early digital standards and platforms . . . it was a great cultural disaster."

"Sure, *Glass Labyrinth, The Sculpture Gardens, Vanished Statues,* Josef Novak did all of those. Those were big hits then! They were wonderful! I had no idea he was still alive."

"He lives about a block from here."

She sat up. "He does? Then let's go see him! Introduce me, all right?"

Paul glanced at his wrist. "I have a class in Stuttgart this afternoon . . . I'm a bit pressed for time today, I'm afraid."

"Oh, of course. I'm sorry."

"But I'm glad to see that you're feeling so much better."

"Those painkillers kicked in. Thanks a lot. Anyway, I'm always much better after I eat."

"So you're familiar with Josef Novak's early work. You're an antiquarian, Maya. That's very interesting. It's remarkable. How old are you?"

"Paul, maybe it would be a good idea if I didn't see Emil for a few days. It might be better for Emil if I just cleared out of his life for a little while. I mean, considering. What do you advise?"

"I'm sure Emil will recover by tomorrow morning. Emil almost always does. But I can imagine that course of action might be wise. Considering."

"Maybe I'll just wanderjahr for a few days. Do you mind if I take the train back with you to Stuttgart? Just to talk along the way. If that's not an imposition."

"No, not at all, I'd be delighted with your company."

"I'll dress. All right?"

There was no place in the studio to dress in privacy. The young were not much concerned with privacy. Maya tunneled awkwardly into tights and a sweater. Paul, with perfect indifference, did the washing up.

She glanced into her pocket mirror and was horrified. The truth could not have been more obvious if it were flashing on her brow in neon. This face was not the face of a young woman. It was a posthuman face, pale and pinched and brimful of exotic forms of anguish it was not fully allowed to experience. The sculptured, waxy face of some outmoded plastic mannequin.

She rushed to the kitchen sink and set to work with cleansing gel. Toning lotion. Pore reliner. Epidermal matrix. Foundation. Blusher brushes. Mascara. Eyeliner. Gloss. Eyelash curler. Scleral brightener. Brow pencil. She'd forgotten to brush her teeth. The teeth would have to do.

The mirror showed her that she'd beaten the truth into submission. Smothered it in cosmetics. The hair was still awful but the natural hair was always pretty bad.

She found a bright Czech shawl, her kick-on shoes, her big warm gray beret. She slipped a couple of semidepleted cashcards into her backpack. Somehow she'd be all right now. Wrapped up, warm, contained. Perfectly happy and confident.

Paul, all patience and indifference, had been studying Emil's more recent works. He'd found a wooden box and opened it. "Did he ever show you this?"

"I don't think so."

"It's my favorite." Paul reached with exaggerated care into the shredded lining of the box and retrieved a delicate white cup and saucer. He set them on Emil's worktable. "He did this piece just after the change. He was thrashing at reality like a drowning man."

"A cup-and-saucer set," Maya said.

"Touch them. Pick them up."

She reached for the cup. The cup sizzled under her fingertips, and she jerked her hand back. Paul chuckled.

She reached out again with one forefinger and gently touched the saucer. There was a faint electrical tingling, the feeling of something soft yet spiky brushing back at her skin. A crackly sandpaper creeping.

Paul laughed.

She gripped the cup with determination. Without moving, it seemed to buzz and writhe within her fingers. She set it back down. "Is there a battery inside it? Is that the trick?"

"It's not ceramic," Paul said.

"What is it, then?"

"I don't know. It resembles ceramic, and it gleams like ceramic, but I believe it's piezoelectric foamed glass. Once I saw him pour a tincture into that cup. The liquid slowly seeped through both the cup and the saucer. Some quality—the porosity, or the fractal dimension, or maybe a van der Waals charge—it reacts very oddly when it contacts the fingertips."

"But *why?*"

"It is an *objet gratuit.* A work of artifice that demonstrates the bankruptcy of the quotidian."

"Is it a joke?"

"Is Emil a joke?" Paul said somberly. "Is it a joke to be no longer human? Of course it is. What is a joke? A joke is a violation of the conceptual framework."

"But that's not all there is to it."

"Of course not."

"So tell me the rest of it."

Paul restored the cup and saucer to its box, and put the box back on its shelf, with reverent care. "Are you ready to go? Then we should go." He picked up his backpack, opened the door for her, ushered her through, locked it carefully behind him.

They walked loudly down the creaking stairs. Outside, the

day was overcast and windy. They headed toward the Narodni tubestation. She walked at his shoulder. In her flats, she was as tall as he was. "Paul, please forgive me if I'm too direct. I come from very far away, and I'm a naif. I hope you can forgive me that. You're a teacher, I know that you can tell me the truth."

"I'm touched by your optimism," Paul said.

"Please don't be that way. What do I have to do—to convince you to tell me the truth?"

"Consider that object," Paul told her very politely. "It destroys the quotidian swindle. It confronts us with a tactile violation of conventional cognition."

"Yes?"

"The destruction of the human condition offers us an avalanche of novel creative approaches. Those possibilities must be assimilated and systematically deployed by the heirs of humanity. Artifice is *not* Art. Although it deploys the imagination of the preconscious, it recognizes that the imagination of the unconscious is impoverished. We honor the irrationality of the creative impulse, but we deny the primacy or even the relevancy of hallucination. We harness the full power of conscious rationality and the scientific method in pursuit of the voluntary destruction and supercession of human culture."

They walked down the stairs of the tubestation. Paul discreetly produced a laminated travel pass from an inner jacket pocket. "The human condition is over. Nature is over. Art is over. Consciousness is ductile. Science is an infinite powder keg. We confront a new reality formerly obscured by the inbuilt limits of mammalian primates. We must create work which brings this new reality to the surface, a sequence of seemingly gratuitous gestures which will form in their aggregate the consciousness of posthumanity." Paul's limpid gaze grew more intense. "At the same time, politically, we must not shatter the fragile surface tension of an aging human civilization which pretends to utopian tranquillity but is secretly traumatized beyond all possibility of healing. Beneath the repellent husk of the dying humanist agenda, we must systematically alter the physiological basis of cognition and the state of culture, and bear an honest, objective, and unpretentious witness to the results. That is the basic nature of our program as artificers."

"I see. Can you buy me a ticket?"

"A ticket to the train station, or a ticket all the way to Stuttgart?"

"Actually, could you buy me both of those tickets? Including a round-trip ticket."

"Why don't you just take my Europass? It lasts till May."

"Could I do that, Paul? That's too generous."

He handed her the laminated pass. "No no, I can get another smartcard from the university. Europe is full of situational perquisites." He approached a machine and did business with it.

They boarded the Praha tube and clung to the hand straps. She looked at him. She loved the way he swept his hair back behind his ears. She admired the fine sweep of his dark mobile eyebrows, the line of his hooded eyelids. It was a comfort to be in his physical presence. He was so young.

"Tell me something else, Paul. Go on."

"We must prepare to take creative possession of the coming epoch. An epoch so poetically rich, so boundlessly victorious, so charged with meaning, that only those prepared to bathe in cataclysm will transcend the singularity. Someday, we will render powerless all hatred of the marvelous. The admirable thing about the fantastic is that the contained is becoming the container; the fantastic irresistibly infiltrates the quotidian. It is only a matter of time, and time is our one inexhaustible resource. There is no more strength left in normality; there are only routines."

"What you just said. It's so beautiful."

He smiled. "I like to think so, too."

"I wish I were that beautiful."

"I think you're making a category error, my dear."

"All right—then I wish I could *do something* that beautiful."

"Perhaps you already have." He paused. "It's a truly interesting concept, 'beauty.' An intersection of three worlds . . ."

The tubetrain pulled into a stop in the Muzeum station and an absolute horde of tourists piled in, a jostling mess of backpacks and bags and alien chatter. They stood amid the crowd, swaying on their hand straps. He'd tried to convince her that he could disturb the universe and the two of them were standing packed amid a horde of indifferent strangers like animals in a cattle car.

It began to get very hot within the train. A muted series of cramps gnawed away deep inside her and when she had come sweating out of the far side of the pain she realized that this was a day when she could do something truly crazy. Something mad and spontaneous and psychically automatic. Levitate. Leap off a building. Throw herself on her aching belly and kiss the feet of a policeman. Fly to the moon and dig into its white chalky soil and absolutely *grope for Luna* . . . Paul looked at her with undisguised concern. She gave him her brightest smile.

At the central train station she limped off to the ladies'. She did business with hygienic machines, drank two cups of water, and departed in better order. The pretty face in the mirror, with its dilated eyes and a little dotting of sweat beneath its layered treatments, seemed to blaze with the holy fire.

Paul was being very considerate. He got them beanbags in first class with a nice fold-down table. The Stuttgart express was a very rapid train.

"I love European trains," she babbled, her scalp glowing beneath her beret. "Even the really fast ones that spend most of their time underground."

"Maybe you should wanderjahr to Vladivostok," Paul said.

"Why would I want to do that?"

"It's a tradition in our group. Vladivostok, the far edge of the Eurasian continent. You have a Eurocard now, and you said that you wanted to drift. Why not drift to Vladivostok? You'll be alone quite a while. You can relax and marshal your thoughts. You can reach the far rim of Asia and return in about four days."

"What do you do once you reach the Pacific Rim?"

"Well, if you're one of us, then you go to a certain obscure Vladivostok ptydepe—sorry, I mean Public Telepresence Point— and you perform a gratuitous act. Our group maintains a constant scan on this particular Vladivostok PTP through a conceptual sieve. Any gesture sufficiently remarkable to attract the attention of the scanner will be automatically mailed to everyone in our netlist."

"How will I know if my gesture is sufficiently gratuitous?"

"By intuition, Maya. It helps if you've seen other performances. It's not a matter of merely human judgment—our sieve program has its own evolving standards. That's the beauty of the beauty in it." Paul smiled. "How does anyone truly know how anything is out of the ordinary? What is ordinariness? What makes the quotidian so seemingly frail and yet so totipresent? The membrane between the bizarre and the tedious is inherently ductile."

"I guess I'm missing a lot, not being in your network."

"Without a doubt."

"Why does your group even meet physically at that bar in Praha, if you're so thoroughly netted?"

Paul considered this. "Do you have your translator? Is it working?"

"Yes. Benedetta gave me a translator at the Tête." She showed Paul her diamond necklace.

"How very good of my valued colleague Benedetta. Any machine of Benedetta's would translate Français, I imagine. Put it on." Paul clipped a sleek little pad to his own ear.

Maya worked her diamond beads and tucked the golden bird's nest in her ear. Paul began speaking Français. "[You can still understand me, I presume.]"

"Yes, my machine is working fine."

"[There are millions of earpiece translators in circulation. They're a modern commonplace. You speak English, I speak Français as I am doing now, and the machines interpret for us. And if the background noise is low . . . and our speech is not too infested with jargon or argot . . . and if not too many people are speaking all at once . . . and if we are not referring to some context beyond the comprehension of small-scale machine processing . . . and if we don't complicate our exchange with too many nonverbal interactions such as human gestures and expressions—well then, we understand one another.]" He gestured broadly. "[That is to say, despite all the odds, we force some modicum of human meaning through this terribly intimate ear-mounted membrane of computation.]"

"Yes, that's it exactly! That's just exactly how it works."

"[Look at my face at this very moment, as I speak. A certain set of musculatures being put into play, a certain state of tensility that holds the face in readiness for a characteristic physical sequence of verbal movements—Français. Consciously, I'm not aware of shaping my face. Consciously, you're not aware of noticing it. Nevertheless big wedges of our human brains are dedicated to the study of faces—and to the perception of language as well. Studies prove that we can recognize one another as aliens, not because of posture, genetics, or dress, but because our languages have physically shaped our faces. That's a preconscious human perception. A translator doesn't do that. A network doesn't convey that. Networks and translators don't have thought. They have only processing.]"

"Yes?"

"[So now you see me through your eyes, and hear Français through one ear, and receive machine-enunciated data through your machine-assisted ear. Something is missing. Something is also superfluous. Parts of you that you don't comprehend can sense that it's all a muddle.]"

He reached across the table and took her hand. "[Now I'm holding your hand while speaking to you in Français. Look, I'll hold your hand in both of mine. I'll gently stroke your hand. How does that feel?]"

"It feels just fine, Paul."

"And how does it feel now that I'm speaking to you in English?"

Surprised, she pulled her hand away.

He laughed. "There. You see? Your reaction demonstrates the truth. It's the same with networks. We meet physically because we have to supplement the networks. It's not that networks lack intimacy. On the contrary, networks are too precisely intimate, in too narrow a channel. We have to meet in a way that feeds the gray meat."

"That's very clever. But tell me—what would have happened if I hadn't pulled my hand away?"

"[Then,]" said Paul with great rationality and delicacy, "[you would have been a woman of blunted perceptions. Which you are not.]" And that seemed to be pretty much the end of that.

She noticed for the first time that his right hand had a ring on the third finger. It looked like a dark engraved band—but it was not a ring at all. It was a little strip of dark fur. Thick-clustered brown fur rooted in a ring-shaped circlet of Paul's flesh.

They were sliding with enormous magnetic levitational speed through the diamond-drilled depths of the European earth. She was taking enormous pleasure in his company and she felt absolutely no desire to flirt with him. It would be like trying to throw a come-hither at a limestone stalactite. Intimacy was not a prospect that appealed. It would take a woman of enormous self-abnegation and tolerance to endure the torment of that much clarity on a day-by-day basis. If he had a girlfriend she would sit across the breakfast table from him with fork in hand, and every day she would be impaled on the four steel tines of his intelligence and his perception and his ambition and his self-regard.

Paul was gazing at her silently, clearly undergoing some very similar line of assessment. She could almost hear the high-speed crackle of neurochemical cognition seething through the wettest glandular depths of his beautiful leonine head.

She was insanely close to confessing everything. It was an extremely stupid thing to do, especially twice in a row, but she was feeling incredibly reckless today and she wanted risk in the way that one might want oxygen and, most of all, she just really, really felt like it. She didn't want to ever touch Paul, hold him or caress him, but she direly wanted to confess to him. To immolate herself, to force him to take real notice.

But it wouldn't be like confessing to Emil. Poor Emil, in his own peculiar animal fashion, was outside time, unwoundable, indestructible. Paul was very actual. Paul talked about cosmic transgressions but Paul was not beyond the pale. Paul was young, he was just a young man. A young man who didn't need her troubles.

Their eyes met. There was a sudden terrific tension between them. It would have felt like sexual attraction with anyone else. With Paul it felt like an attack of telepathy.

He stared at her. Surprise struck him visibly. His fine brows arched and his eyes widened.

"What are you thinking, Paul?"

"Sincerely?"

"Yes. Of course."

"I'm wondering why I see this frivolous young beauty. Here, across this table from me."

"Why shouldn't I be here?" she said.

"Because it's a facade. Isn't it? You're not frivolous. And I feel quite certain suddenly that you're not young."

"Why do you say that?"

"You're very beautiful. But it's not a young woman's beauty. You're terribly beautiful. There is an element of terror to your presence."

"Thanks very much."

"Now that I recognize that fact, it makes me wonder. What do you want from us? Are you a police spy? Are you civil support?"

"No. I'm not. I promise."

"I was civil support once," Paul said calmly. "Youth-league civil support, in Avignon. I was quite ambitious about the work, and I learned about interesting aspects of life. But I quit, I gave it up. Because they want to make the world a better place. And I knew that I didn't want the world to be any better. I want the world to become more interesting. Do you think that's a crime, Maya?"

"I hadn't thought of it in that way before. It doesn't seem very much like a crime."

"I know a police spy rather well. She reminds me of you very much. She has your strange self-possession, your peculiarly intense presence as a woman. I was looking at you just now, and I realized that you look like the Widow. So it all became clear to me suddenly."

"I'm not a widow."

"She's an astonishing woman. Enormously beautiful, sublime. She's like a sphinx. Like some untouchable creature from myth. She takes a deep interest in artifice. You'll likely meet the Widow someday. If you stay in our company."

"This Widow person—she's an artifice cop? I had no idea there was any such thing as a police force for artifice. What's her name?"

"Her name is Helene Vauxcelles-Serusier."

"Helene Vauxcelles-Serusier . . . My goodness, what a wonderful name she has!"

"If you don't know Helene already, then you might not want to meet her."

"I'm certain I don't want to meet her. Because I'm not an informer. Actually, I'm a criminal fugitive."

"Informer, criminal . . ." He shook his head. "There's far less distinction there than one might think."

"You're very right as usual, Paul. It's rather like that blurry distinction between terror and beauty. Or youth and age. Or artifice and crime."

He stared at her in surprise. "Well put," he said at last. "That's just what Helene would say. She's quite the devotee of blurry distinctions."

"I promise that I'm not a police agent. I'd prove it to you, if I could."

"Maybe you're not. It's not that civil-support people can't be pretty, but they usually consider your kind of glamour to be suspect."

"I'm not suspect. Why should I be suspect?"

"I suspect you because I have to protect my friends," Paul said. "Our lives are our lives, they're not a theoretical exercise. We're a much put-upon generation. We have to treasure our vitality, because our vitality is methodically stifled. Other generations never faced that dilemma. Their parents fell into their graves and power fell into their laps. But we've never been a natural generation. We're the first truly native posthumans."

"And you have desires that don't accord with the status quo."

"Mais oui."

"Well, so do I. I have a whole lot of them."

"No one asked you to become one of us."

It was a terribly wounding thing to say. She felt as if she'd been stabbed. He stared at her in direct challenge and she was suddenly too tired to go on fencing with him. He was too young and strong and quick, and she was too upset and broken up to push him into a corner. She began to cry. "What happens now?" she asked. "Should I beg for your permission to live? I'll beg if you want me to. Just tell me that's what you want."

Paul glanced anxiously around the train car. "Please don't make a scene."

"I have to cry! I want to cry, I deserve it! I'm not all right. I don't have any pride, I don't have any dignity—I don't have anything. I'm hurt in ways you can't even imagine. What else should I do but cry? You've caught me out. I'm at your mercy. You can destroy me now."

"You could destroy us. Maybe that's what you want."

"I won't do that. Give me a chance! I can be vivid. I can even be beautiful. You should let me try. Let me try, Paul—I can be an interesting case study for you."

"I'd love to let you try," he said. "I like to feast with panthers. But why play games with my friends' safety? I know nothing about you, except that you seem very pretty and very posthuman. Why should I trust you? Why don't you simply go home?"

"Because I can't go home. They'll make me be old again."

Paul's eyes widened. She'd struck through to him, she'd touched him. Finally he handed her a kerchief. She glanced at the kerchief, felt it carefully to make sure it wasn't computational, then wiped her eyes and blew her nose.

Paul pressed a button on the rim of the table.

"You let Emil stay with your group," she offered at last, "and Emil's worse than I am."

"I'm responsible for Emil," he said gloomily.

"What do you mean?"

"I let him take the amnesiac. I made arrangements."

"You did? Do the others know?"

"It was a good idea. You didn't know Emil earlier."

A giant crab came picking its way along the ceiling of the train car. It was made of bone and chitin and peacock feathers and gut and piano wire. It had ten very long multijointed legs and little rubber-ball feet on hooked steel ankles. A serving platter was attached with suckers to the top of its flat freckled carapace.

It picked its way through barely perceptible niches in the ceiling, stopped, and dropped beside their beanbags. It surveyed them with a circlet of baby blue eyes like a giant clam's. *"Oui monsieur?"*

"[The mademoiselle will be having a bottle of *eau minerale* and two hundred micrograms of alcionage,]" said Paul. "[I'll have a *limoncello* and . . . oh, bring us half a dozen croissants.]"

"Très bien." It stalked away.

"What *was* that thing?" Maya said.

"That's the steward."

"I can guess that much, but what *is* it? Is it alive? Is it a robot? Is it some kind of lobster? It sounded like it was talking with real lips and a tongue!"

Paul looked exasperated. "Do you mind? This *is* the Stuttgart express, you know."

"Oh. Okay. Sorry."

Paul gazed at her silently, meditatively. "Poor Emil," he said at last.

"Don't tell me that! You have no right to tell me that! I'm good for him. I know I'm good for him. You don't know anything about it."

"*Are* you good for Emil?"

"Look, what can I do to make you trust me? You can't just write me off, you can't just push me out. You say you want something really strange to happen in the world. Well, I'm really strange, all right? And I'm happening."

Paul thought this over, tapping the edge of the table with his fingertips. "Let me test your blood," he said.

"All right. Sure." She pulled up the sleeve of her sweater.

He stood up, retrieved his backpack from the overhead compartment, opened it, rummaged about methodically and removed a blood-test mosquito. He placed the little device on the center of her forearm. It sniffed about, squatted, inserted its hair-thin beak. There was no pain at all. Maybe a tiny itch.

Paul retrieved the blood-glutted device. It bent down and unfolded its wings, which formed a display screen the width of a pair of thumbnails. Paul bent down close and stared.

"So," he said at last. "If you want to keep your secret, you'd better not let anyone else try a blood test."

"Okay."

"You're very anemic. In fact, there's a lot of fluid inside you that isn't even blood."

"Yeah, those would be cellular detox detergents and some catalyzed oxygen transports."

"I see. But there's more than enough DNA in here for me to establish your identity. And to turn you in to civil support. If that ever should prove necessary."

"Look, Paul, you don't have to take the trouble to trace my medical records. We've come this far—I'll just *tell* you who I am."

Paul forced the mosquito to disgorge on a slip of chromatograph and folded the stained paper neatly. "No," he said, "that's not necessary. In fact, I don't even think it's wise. I don't want to know who you are. That's not my responsibility. And that's certainly not what I want from you."

"What do you want from me?"

He looked her in the eye. "I want you to prove to me that you're not human yet still an artist."

———

Stuttgart was a big loud town. Big, loud, sticky, and green. A city of gasps, grunts, wheezes, complex organic gurglings. People liked to shout at each other in Stuttgart. People emerged in sudden pedestrian torrents from sphinctering holes in the walls.

The famous towers were frankly cyclopean but their rhythmic billowing made them seem soothingly oceanic, rather than mountainous. She could hear the monster towers breathing with a viscous, tubercular rasping. Their breath galed above the furry streets and smelled of steam and lemons.

"My family helped to build this city," Paul volunteered, neatly skirting around a large splattered puddle of a substance much like muesli. "My parents were garbage miners."

"Were?'"

"They gave it up. Garbage was like any other extractive industry. The best and richest landfills played out early. Nowadays garbage mining is mostly left to wildcatters, methane drillers, small-timers. The great garbage fortunes are gone."

"I see."

"No need to fret, my mother did very well by her career. I'm a child of privilege." Paul smiled cheerfully. He was relaxed, he was glad to be home.

"Your parents are Français?"

"Yes. We're from Avignon originally. Half the population of Stuttgart are Français."

"Why is that?"

"Because Paris has become a museum." The lighting changed over the street. An enormous ribbed membrane peeled from the side of a tower and deployed itself over the neighborhood. A flock of white cranes wheeled in beneath it, landed in the streets like so many white-feathered commuters. The birds began to peck at the sidewalk, hard enough to break it into chunks.

"The finest extracts from the dumps," Paul said, "iron, aluminum, copper, and such—their market value crashed once modern materials came into production. Cheap diamond of course, cheap diamond beats anything. But sugarglass, optical plastics, fullerenes, and aerogels"—he gestured at the cityscape around them. A small deft man with a proprietarial interest in structures four hundred stories tall. "The carbon-based products drove construction metals off the market. People in Stuttgart are progressives, they despise the shibboleths."

"This place is a lot like Indianapolis."

"Not at all! Nothing like it!" Paul protested. "Indianapolis was a political act, a freak by revanchist Asians. Stuttgart is serious! Stuttgart is meaningful! It is the only truly modern city in Europe!

The only city whose builders truly believed in a future—rather than some endless recycling of the past."

"I'm not sure I'd be real happy if the future looked like this."

"It won't. Any more than the world came to look like New York City a century ago. It was enough that for a certain period of time the world *wanted* to look like New York City. Stuttgart is that kind of urban cynosure. It's the only city in the world where modern society was allowed to speak with an authentic architectural voice."

"You use the past tense, I see."

"There won't be many other Stuttgarts. Gerontocratic society lacks the will and energy to innovate on the grand scale. Unless, as with Stuttgart, some large city is leveled by a cataclysm and the survivors have no choice." Paul shrugged. "Not a pleasant prospect! There may be some fanatics who consider holocaust an acceptable price for change, but I've studied holocaust, and holocaust is vile. The change we face has its own inexorability. There's much to be said for survival. Live long enough, and reality will melt beneath your feet." He paused, considering. "I'm very fond of Praha. That city surely has lessons for the world as profound as Stuttgart's. Praha outlasted its own epoch and became a beautiful freak, a charming atavism. Praha found a second chance. Now Praha is the chrysalis for a larval form of posthumanity."

They walked on. The skies of Stuttgart were full of aerial transports that uncoiled like butterfly tongues, adhered to a distant tower, and then rolled up neatly to the other side. These reeling walkways carried sliding capsules within their flaccid bulk. They were grotesquely efficient, like ductile pedestrian boas.

Paul led her down a long flight of stairs and beneath a solemn stone arch with a series of thick beaded curtains. The sky vanished. The air warmed. They emerged under a coarse mossy roof with humps like fabric but the apparent rigidity of concrete. The walls grew spongy and disturbed, under long brilliantly glowing strands of sun-bright optical fiber. It was hot and damp, a stony greenhouse. The air reeked of vanilla and bananas. "This is my favorite quarter of town," said Paul. "I lived here for years before I took my teaching post. This quarter was planned and built by theorists of the edible cityscape."

"Theorists of the what?"

"The walls here are gasketfungus. You can eat the city raw. The walls are quite nutritious." It didn't seem a particularly good idea to eat the fungal walls. The locals had been carving graffiti into them with some kind of herbicide. Patchy letters of wilted yellow. BENEATH THE BEACH—THE PAVEMENT. Curls of Arabic. A Kilroy face with a mess of loopy curls.

They walked beside a brilliantly lit multistory building. The open floors were marked in numbered slots. People were lying in cavities in these numbered areas, under searing artificial sunlight. The people wore spex and were covered from head to foot in big gray-green wads of dense organic fiber.

"What's this place? A morgue?"

"It's a public bathhouse."

"Where's the water?"

"It's not water bathing, it's exfoliation. You're dipped in jelly and you lie under the lights. They dust you in spores and those filaments of mold take root in your skin. When the mold stops growing the machines scrape you clean with strigils. The mold peels off in sheets. All the body dirt and skin flora come away with the web. It's very exhilarating."

"It's a bath in living mold?"

"Yes, an exacting process. They offer a little virtuality to pass the time in the tank, as you see. It's an amenity, especially for those who live rough in the edible quarter. It's a public service. When you're done they paint you with the local blend of human microbes."

"Yes, but it's *mold*."

"A very tame and pleasant mold. There's no harm in it." He paused. "I hope you're not shocked by something as harmless as public nudity. That's very common in Stuttgart."

"Of course I'm not shocked by nudity, but it's mold!"

"Such provincialism," Paul said, half smiling. He was clearly piqued. "This was designed to be the friendliest city in Europe.

Not that the citizens are particularly friendly—they're like people in big cities anywhere. Rather, the city's structure is uniquely friendly to its users."

Paul pointed across the street, where a swarm of gnats was congregating in midair with a collective basso hum. "If you were lucky enough to acquire a room in that exclusive hostel over there—why, it's all lattice. You can eat the walls. You can carry out any human excretory function wherever you please. Wherever you sleep, a bed of moss grows beneath you to cushion you. It's always warm and damp. Very tactile, very epidermal, very sensual, extremely civilized. Here, the microbes are all domesticated. Life is recycled, but morbid decay has been beaten. Decay is gone like a bad dream."

"Hmmm." She studied the side of the hostel, a shaggy damp cascade of multicolored mosses. "When you put it that way, it doesn't sound half bad."

They ducked together into a doorway as a truck passed, soaking the environment with a dense yellow fog.

"It was a visionary scheme. A city to free its users of material bioconstraint. A source of shelter, nourishment, inspiration, and, of course, permanent safety from the terrors of plague. Perhaps this final result wasn't intended, but the city itself is so generous that it annihilates economics. It requires a peculiarly nonpossessive nature to live here in the long term. Rebels, dreamers, philosophers . . . The mentally retarded also find this quarter very convenient and popular. . . . Over the years, the quarter has become infested with mystics."

"Penitentes?"

"Yes, Catholic extremists of all sorts, but also many Submissionaries. Ecstatic Submissionaries, and Charismatic Submissionares. Mohammed's disciples. Unfortunately the Ecstatics and Charismatics are intense rivals and bitterly hate one another."

"Isn't that always the way." They stepped aside as three nude women shot by on bicycles, their swollen, bricklike calves pumping furiously.

"Fanatics always hate and fear their own dissidents far more than they loathe the bourgeoisie. By that symptom shall you know them. . . . That failing is what cripples the fanatics. There has been violence here in Stuttgart, street brawls, even a few killings. . . . Did you ever take an entheogen, Maya?"

"Never, no."

"I did. I took it here."

She looked around. Shaggy walls, greenness, hot misty light, an urban universe of little crawling things. "What happened?"

"I saw God. God was very warm and caring and wise. I felt enormous gratitude and love for Him. It was clear strong Platonic reality, totally authentic, the light of the cosmos. It was reality as God sees it, not the fragmentary halting rationality of a human mind. It was raw mystical insight, beyond all argument. I was in the living presence of my Maker."

"Why did you do that? Were your parents religious?"

"No, not at all. I did it because I had seen religion consume other people. I wanted to see if I would be strong enough to come out of the far side of it."

"And?"

"And yes, I was strong enough." Paul's eyes grew distant. "Ah, there's a packet tube. I have a class to teach soon. I'm sorry, but I have to leave you now."

"You do? Oh dear."

Paul walked to the front of the packet tube and entered an address on a keypad. A vault door shunted open. He tossed his backpack into the padded capsule. "I'm leaving you because I must," he said patiently, "but I'm leaving you in lovely Stuttgart. I hope you'll put your time here to good use." The capsule vanished. Another capsule instantly took its place. Paul hit a repeat key, crawled deftly into the padded interior, and doubled his arms around his knees. "Until we meet in Praha, Maya."

"*Au revoir,* Paul." She waved at him, and the door shunted with a brisk pneumatic pop.

She spent three strange aching days in Stuttgart, ghosting the honeycombed plazas and haunting the city's peculiarly liberal apothecary malls. On the evening train back to Praha she collapsed into her beanbag and was left in silence and solitude. It felt so lovely to be within the familiar confines of a moving train again. She was vibrating with hormones and culture shock, and she hadn't been eating properly. Every passing hour carried her further into new realms of experience, strange deep somatic spaces that words such as "hunger" and "weariness" scarcely seemed to describe.

Sleep beckoned. But then the translator, which was still tucked into her ear, began to sing inside her ear. Very gently at first, a distant musical warbling. The music grew louder. She'd never known the device to malfunction, so she was ready when it made a kind of musical throat-clearing tone, and addressed her directly. "[Hello, user Maya.]"

"Hello?" she said.

"[This is an interactive message for you from Ohrschmuck Enterprises of Basel. We are the inventors and manufacturers of this translation necklace. Do you understand us? Please signify by orally responding 'Yes, I understand' in your favorite language, English.]"

" 'Yes, I understand.' "

She looked around the train car. She was speaking aloud to thin air, but no one considered this unusual behavior. They naturally assumed she was using a netlink.

"[User Maya, you've been in possession of the necklace for two weeks. You have already used its functionalities in English, Italiano, Czestina, Deutsch, and Français. We hope you'll agree that the translation service has been prompt and accurate.]"

"Yes, it certainly has."

"[Did you notice the fine physical workmanship of our necklace? It would have been simple to do a cheap knockoff in copper and silicon, but we prefer the classic chic of real jewels. We at Ohrschmuck take pride in our traditional European craftsmanship, and your use of our shareware proves that you're a discerning woman of taste. Any fly-by-night company can supply a working tourist translator nowadays. We at Ohrschmuck supply an entire library of modern European languages, including proprietary vocabulary segments featuring modern slang and argot. It's no simple matter to provide our level of linguistic service.]"

"I suppose not."

"[If you agree that our shareware necklace meets your exacting personal standards, then we think our efforts to please you should be rewarded. Doesn't that seem just and fair, user Maya?]"

"What is it that you want from me, exactly?"

"[If you'll simply wire us seven hundred marks, we can see to it that your translator is supplied with the very latest vocabulary updates. We also register you with our company, supply service referrals, and answer user questions.]"

"I'll certainly send you that money if I ever come across that large a sum."

"[We feel that we're worth our price, user Maya. We'll trust you to pay us. Our business is based on mutual trust. We know that you trust us. After all, you've been trusting our machine with the tympanum of your own right ear, a very tender and personal membrane. We feel sure that mutual respect will lead us to a long relationship. Our net-address will work from any net location in the world, and it takes cash. We look forward to hearing from you soon.]"

She was back in Praha by midnight, with her backpack and a shopping bag, giddy, exhausted, footsore, and in pain. But Praha looked so lovely. So solid, so inorganic, so actual, so wonderfully old. Bartolomejska Street looked lovely. The building looked lovely. She paused at Emil's door, then went upstairs and knocked at the door of Mrs. Najadova.

"What is it?" Mrs. Najadova paused, looked Maya up and down. "What has he done to you?"

"There are certain days in a month when a woman needs time to herself. But he doesn't understand."

"Oh, that dirty, thoughtless brute. That's so like him. Come in. I'm only watching television." Mrs. Najadova put her on the couch. She found Maya a blanket and a heating pad and made her a frappé. Then she sat in a rocker fiddling contentedly with her notebook, as the television muttered aloud in Czestina.

Mrs. Najadova's room was full of wicker baskets, jugs, bottles, driftwood, bird eggs, bric-a-brac. A blue glass vase with a bouquet of greenhouse lilies. And intensely nostalgic memorabilia of the former Mr. Najad, a great strapping fellow with a ready grin, who seemed to dote on skiing and fishing. To judge by the style of his sportswear he had been either dead or gone for at least twenty years.

Seeing the photos Maya felt a great leaping pang of pathos for all the women of the world who had married for a human lifetime, lived and loved faithfully through a human lifetime, and then outlived their humanity. All the actual widows, and the virtual widows, and those who sought widowhood, and those who had widowhood thrust upon them. You could outlive sexuality, but you never truly got over it—any more than you got over childhood.

Maya's golden bird chimed on her breast. It had begun to chime the hours lately, with small but piercing cuckoo sounds, a tactful referral, apparently, to the time elapsing without a payoff. She tucked the bird into her ear. It began at once to translate the mutter of the television.

"[It's a species of ontological limbo, really,]" said the television. It was Aquinas, the dog with the Deutsch talk show. The dog had been dubbed into Czestina. "[What I call my intelligence has its source in three worlds. My own innate canine cognition. The artificial intelligence network outside my skull. And the internal wiring that has grown among the interstices of my canine brain, programmed with human language. Among this tripartite intelligence, where does my identity reside? Am I a computer's peripheral, or a dog with a cybernetic unconscious? Furthermore, how much of what I call 'thought' is actually mere facility with language?]"

"[I suppose that's a problem for any talk-show host,]" agreed the guest.

"[I have remarkable cognitive abilities. For instance, I can do mathematical problems of almost any level of complexity. Yet my canine brain is almost entirely innumerate. I solve these problems without understanding them.]"

"[Comprehending mathematics is one of the greatest of intellectual pleasures. I'm sorry to hear that you miss that mental experience, Aquinas.]"

The dog nodded knowingly. It was very peculiar to see a dog nod in a conversation, no matter how well he was dressed. "[That assessment means even more, coming from yourself, Professor Harald. With your many scientific honors.]"

"[We have more in common than the layman might think,]" said the professor graciously. "[After all, any mammalian brain, including the natural human brain, has multiple functional sections, each with its own cognitive agenda. I have to confess something to you, Aquinas. Modern mathematics is impossible without machine aid. I had a simulator entirely interiorized]"—the guest, tactfully, tapped his wrinkled forehead—"[and yet I've never been able to fully *feel* those results, even when I can speak the results aloud and even somehow intuitively sense their rightness.]"

"[Tell me, do you ever do math in your sleep, Professor?]"

"[Constantly. I get many of my best results that way.]"

"[Myself as well. In sleep—perhaps that's where we mammals find our primal unity.]"

Slowly Professor Harald shook the dog's elegant prehensile paw. The audience applauded politely.

4

Maya woke at five in the morning. Her fingernails itched. They no longer seemed to fit her hands. The hormones surging through her made her nails grow like tropical bamboo. The cuticles were ragged, the keratin gone strangely flimsy. They felt very much like false nails.

She left the couch of Mrs. Najadova, fetched her backpack, crept silently out the door and down the stairs, and let herself into Emil's studio. Emil slept heavily, alone. She felt a strong temptation to crawl in next to him, to try to recapture sleep, but she resisted it. She wasn't fitting properly inside her own skin. There would hardly be comfort now in anyone else's.

She quietly found her red jacket. She poured water, then sorted nimbly through her happy little galaxy of analgesics. She decided not to take any more of the pills. She might need them badly next time, and she might not be in a place so understanding as Stuttgart.

Emil woke, and sat up in his bed. He looked at her with polite incomprehension, then pulled the bedspread over his face and went back to sleep. Maya methodically stuffed her backpack. Then she walked out his door. She did not know if she would ever be back. There was nothing there she wasn't willing to abandon.

She walked into the starlit street, entered a gently glowing net booth, and called for net help. The net's guidance was, as always, excellent. She linked to the netsite in San Francisco and connected synchronously to Mr. Stuart.

"What can I do for you this fine evening?" said Stuart, with a two-hundred-fifty-millisecond lag time but total vocal clarity.

"Mr. Stuart, I've been a longtime customer of yours and I need access to an old virtuality with defunct protocols."

"Well, ma'am, if they're in stock, we got 'em. Come on down to the barn."

"I happen to be in Praha at the moment."

"Praha, real nice town," remarked Stuart, deeply unsurprised. "I can link you through if the price is right, no problem on this end if you don't mind the lag. Why don't you hang up and virch in through our primary server?"

"No no—that's very generous of you, but I wondered if you had a colleague here in Praha who would understand my need for discretion. Someone in Praha that you could recommend to me. I trust your judgment in these matters. Implicitly."

"You trust my judgment, eh? Implicitly and everything, huh?"

"Yes."

"That's really nice. Personal trust is the core global infrastructure. You wouldn't care to tell me who you are?"

"No. I'd love to tell you, of course. But, well, you understand."

"All righty, then. Let me consult this handy trade reference. I'll be right with you."

Maya fidgeted with her tender fingertips.

"Try a place called the Access Bureau on Narodni Obrany in Praha Six. Ask for Bozhena."

"Okay, I got it. Thanks a lot." She hung up.

She found the address on a Praha civil-support map, and she

began to walk. It was a very long hike in the dark and the cold. Silent cobbled streets. Closed shops. Solitude. High clouds, and moonlight on the river. The otherworldly glow of the Hradcany, the castle dominating the old town as an ancient aristocracy had once loomed over Europe. All the variant spires of sleeping Praha. Iron lanterns, statuary, tiled roofing, dark arches and secretive passageways, wandering moon-eyed cats. Such a city—even its most ancient fantasies were far more real than herself.

Her feet on the cobbles grew hot with incipient blisters. The backpack dug into her shoulders. Pain and weariness pushed her into deep lucidity. She paused periodically, framing bits of the city with her camera, but could not bring herself to take a photo. Once the machine had touched her face, the viewfinder showed her only lies. It struck her then that the problem was simple: the lens was mounted backward. All camera lenses were mounted backward. She was trying so hard to engage the world, but her subject was behind her eyelids.

Just after dawn, she found the Praha street address. It was a stone-faced official-looking building, its rotten Communist-era concrete long since gnawed out and replaced with a jolly modern greenish foam. The building was still closed and locked for the night. There were discreet blue-and-white Czesky placards on the doors, but she couldn't read Czestina.

She found a breakfast café, warmed up, had something to eat, repaired her damaged makeup, saw life return to the city in a languid rattle of bicycles. When the building's front door opened with a programmed click of the clock, she was the first to slip inside.

She discovered the netsite on the building's fourth floor, at the head of the stairs. The netsite was closed and locked. She retreated, winded and footsore, to the ladies', where she sat in a booth with her eyes closed, and dozed a bit.

On her next attempt she found the door ajar. Inside, the netsite was a fabulous mess of vaulted ceilings, brass-knobbed doors, plastic-spined reference manuals, dying wire-festooned machinery. The windows had been bricked up. There were odd stains on the plaster walls, and cobwebs in the corners.

Bozhena was brushing her hair, eating breakfast rolls, and

drinking from a bottle of animal milk. Bozhena had very luxuriant hair for a woman of such advanced age. Her teeth were also impressive: big as tombstones, perfectly preserved, and with a very high albedo.

"You're Bozhena, right? Good morning."

"Good morning and welcome to the Coordinated Access Bureau." Bozhena seemed proud of her brisk technician's English. "What are your requirements?"

"I need a touchscreen to access a memory palace set up in the sixties. A contact of mine in San Francisco said you could supply the necessary discretion."

"Oh yes, we're very discreet here at Access Bureau," Bozhena assured her. "Also, completely out of date! Old palaces, old castles, all manner of labyrinths and dungeons! That is our local specialty." Without warning, Bozhena touched her earpiece and suddenly left the counter. She retired into a cloistered back room of the office.

Time passed very slowly. Dust motes floated in the glare of a few paraboloid overheads. The net machines sat there as inert as long-abandoned fireplugs.

Four elderly Czech women, bureaucratic functionaries, filtered one by one into the office. They were carrying breakfast and their knitting. One of them had brought her cat.

After some time, one of the women, yawning, arrived with a touchscreen, set it on the counter, checked it off on a notepad, and wandered off without a word. Maya picked the touchscreen from its grainy plastic box and blew dust from it. It was covered with peeling official stickers in unreadable Czestina. Ancient pre-electronic text, the old-style Czesky orthography from before the European orthographic reformations. Little circles, peculiar caret marks, a thicket of acutes and circumflexes and accent marks, so that the words looked wrapped in barbed wire.

Bozhena languidly reemerged, carefully tucked in her shin-length gray skirt, and sat at her magisterial plastic desk. She searched methodically through six drawers. Finally she found a lovely cast-glass paperweight. She set it on her tabletop and began toying with it.

"Excuse me," Maya said. "Do you happen to have any material on Josef Novak?"

Bozhena's face froze. She rose from her desk and came to the counter. "Why would you want to investigate Mr. Novak? Who told you we had Josef Novak in our archives here?"

"I'm Mr. Novak's new pupil," Maya lied cheerfully. "He's teaching me photography."

Bozhena's face fell into deep confusion. "You? Why? Novak's student? But you're a foreigner. What's he done this time, poor fellow?" Bozhena found her purse and began brushing her hair with redoubled vigor.

The door opened and two Czech cops in pink uniforms came in. They sat at a wooden table, booted up a screen, and sipped hot tinctures from cartons.

It struck Maya suddenly that the trusted Mr. Stuart had sent her directly to a Praha police bureau. These people were all cops. This was a cops' research establishment. She was surrounded by Czech virtuality cops. This was an antiquarian netsite, all right—but only because the Czech police had some of the worst equipment in the world.

"Do you know Helene?" Maya said casually, leaning on the countertop. "Helene Vauxcelles-Serusier?"

"The Widow's in and out," shrugged Bozhena, examining her nails. "All the time. Why, I don't know. She never has a good word for us."

"I need to call her this morning and clear a few little things. Do you happen to have Helene's net-address handy?"

"This is a netsite, not a reference service," Bozhena said tartly. "We love to help in Access Bureau, we are so very open and friendly in Praha with nothing to hide! But the Widow's not based in Praha so that's not my department."

"Look," Maya said, "if you're not going to help me on the Novak case, just say so straight out."

"I never said that," Bozhena parried.

"I've got other methods, and other contacts, and other ways to go about my job, you know."

"I'm sure you do, Miss Amerika," Bozhena said, with an acid scowl.

Maya rubbed her bloodshot eyes. "Look, let's make this real simple and easy for both of us," she said. "I'll just elbow my way through your dense crowd of eager clients here, and I'll scare up some action on that old magnetic tracker set. Don't think you have to help me, or anything. You don't bother me, and I won't bother you. We'll both just pretend this isn't really happening. Okay?"

Bozhena said nothing. She retreated back to her desk.

Fear and adrenaline had made Maya invincible. She found goggles and gloves. It struck her that no one ever bothered or interrupted people who were busy in goggles and gloves. Goggles and gloves would make her invisible.

She bullied the ancient machine into operation and she stroked in the passtouch. She conjured up the memory palace seemingly through sheer force of will.

The familiar architect's office appeared all around her, plating the screens a finger's width from the damp surfaces of her eyeballs. Someone had tampered with the blackboard. Along with the curly Kilroy and the greenish scrawl MAYA WAS HERE, the blackboard now had a neatly printed MAYA PRESS HERE and a button drawn in multicolored chalk.

Maya thought it over, then pressed the colored button on the chalkboard. The gloves felt good and solid, but nothing happened.

She looked around the virtual office. The place was aswarm with geckos. There were repair geckos all over the place, some as big as bread loaves and others milling like ants. The broken table had been removed. The plants in the garden outside were much better rendered now. They closely resembled real vegetation.

One of the armchairs suffered a sudden identity crisis and morphed itself into Benedetta. The virtual Benedetta was in a black hourglass cocktail dress and a cropped pink jacket with black piping. She had the unnaturally elongated legs of a fashion sketch, with highly improbable stiletto heels. Benedetta's face was an excellent likeness, but the virtual hair was bad. Virtual hair almost always looked phony, either like a rubber casting or some hyperactive Medusa subroutine. Benedetta had unwisely gone for an arty Medusa gambit, which rather overloaded the local data flow. When she moved too quickly, big shining wads of coiffure flickered violently in and out of existence.

The virtual model's lips moved soundlessly. "Ciao Maya."

Maya found a dangling plug on the spex and tucked it into her ear. "Ciao Benedetta."

Benedetta made a little curtsy. "Are you surprised?"

"I'm a little disappointed," Maya said. "Is my vocal level coming across okay?"

"Yes, I hear you fine."

"I never dreamed you'd steal my passtouch and take advantage of my act of trust. Really, Benedetta, how childish of you."

"I didn't mean any harm," Benedetta said contritely. "I wanted to admire the palazzo architecture and the period detail. And all the lovely antique coding structures."

"Of course you did, darling. And did you find the pornography, too?"

"Yes, of course I found the pornography. But I left this call button for you"—Benedetta gestured at the chalkboard—"because we have a little problem now. A little problem in the palazzo."

"We do, do we?"

"Something is loose in here. Something alive."

"Something you *let* loose, or something you *found* loose?"

"I can't tell you, because I don't know," Benedetta said. "I tried to find out, but I can't. Neither can anyone else."

"I see. How many 'anyone elses' have you let through here, exactly?"

"Maya, this old palazzo is very big. Wonderfully big. There's a lot of space. No one was using it, and it's wonderful that there are no network cops here. Please don't be jealous. Believe me, you never would have noticed us. If not for this little trouble."

"This isn't good news."

"But there is very good news. There's money inside this

place. Did you know that? Real money! Old people's certified money!"

"How nice. Did you and the gang leave any money for me?"

"Listen, I so much want to talk to you," said Benedetta. "About everything. But this truly is not a good time. I'm playing cards with my father right now. I don't like to do this kind of talk from my father's house. Can you come to Bologna and see me? I have a lot I can offer to you. I want to be your friend."

"Maybe I can come. Exactly how much money did you find? Do I have enough to pay off these Swiss shareware pests for this diamond necklace you gave me?"

"Don't worry about the necklace," Benedetta said. "The Ohrschmuck company went broke. They asked too much, so no one ever paid them. Just give the necklace to some other woman. She can use it free for a month before it starts to complain in the ear."

"You're such a treasure, darling."

"Let me call you later, Maya. I've been bad, I admit it. I will do for you so much better if you only give me a chance! Just for one thing, I can give you much better on-line presence—do you know that you look like a big ugly blue block to me? Where are you now?"

"I'm nowhere that you need to know about. Leave me a message with Paul."

Benedetta's virtual mouth stretched in surprise. "You didn't tell Paul about your palace, I hope."

"Why shouldn't I tell Paul?"

"Darling, Paul is only a theorist. But I am an activist."

"Maybe I'm a theorist, too."

"I don't think that you are," Benedetta said. "I don't think that at all. Am I wrong?"

Maya considered this. "All right, if we can't tell Paul, then leave a message for me at the Tête. I go there almost every day. I'm on pretty good terms with Klaus."

"All right. At the Tête. That's a good idea. Klaus is a good man, he is so discreet. Now I truly must go." Benedetta morphed. The chair recovered and lay sideways on the floor.

Maya tried to set the toppled chair upright. Her gloved hands plunged through it repeatedly, with the deep ontological uselessness of dysfunctional software. She struggled with the chair for quite some time, her back bent, wrestling air at various experimental angles.

She then became aware of another presence in the virtual room. She gazed about herself cautiously, not moving. The virtual presence oozed through the wall, moved through her presence like a crawling wind, exited through the far wall. A fractured glaze creeping through the fabric of computation.

Maya yanked her head from the spex and earphones. She stripped the gloves away from her swollen fingertips. She shut the machine down. Then she examined the sweat-smeared gear, regretting the vilely incriminating cloud of human DNA she had just deposited on Czech police equipment. She scrubbed at the spex a bit with her sleeve, just as if that token gesture would help anything. DNA was microscopic. Evidence was everywhere. Evidence was totipresent, the truth seething below awareness, just like germs.

But crime could not become a crime unless somebody, somehow, cared enough to notice.

She decided not to steal the handy touchscreen.

She was tired now, so she got onto a train and slept for two hours as it ran back and forth below the city. Then she walked into a netsite at the Malostranska tubestation and asked the net to find her Josef Novak. The net offered his address in a split second. Maya took the tube back to Karlovo Namesti and walked, footsore and limping, to Josef Novak's home. The place did not look promising. She examined her civil-support map, cross-checked it twice, and then pushed on the doorbell. No response. She pushed harder and the defunct doorbell cracked inside its plastic case.

She pounded on the iron-bound wooden door with the side

of her fist. There were muffled noises from the interior, but no-body bothered to answer. She banged again, harder.

An elderly Czech woman opened the door, which was se-cured on a short brass chain. She wore a head-scarf and spex. "[What do you want?]"

"I want Josef Novak. I need to speak to him."

"[I don't speak English. Josef isn't taking any visitors. Espe-cially not tourists. Go away.]" The door slammed shut.

Maya went out and had some chutovky with a side of knedliky. These little setbacks were very useful. If she remembered to eat every time she was locked out, shut out, or thrown out, it would keep her fit and healthy. After a final carton of tasty govern-ment-issue blancmange she returned to Novak's place and knocked again.

The same woman answered, this time in a thick winter night-robe. "[You again! The girl who smells like Stuttgart. Don't bother us, it's very rude and it's useless!]" Slam.

Another good reminder. Maya walked down the block and let herself into Emil's studio. Emil wasn't there. Emil's absence might have been worrisome, but she deduced from the state of his kitchen that he'd had to leave the place to eat. She scrubbed and mopped for a long time, and inoculated the studio with certain handy packets she'd acquired in Stuttgart. The studio began to reek of fresh bananas. This solid victory over the unseen world of the microbial gave Maya a great sense of accomplishment. She walked back to Novak's in the cold and darkness, and knocked again.

A bent white-haired man opened the door. He had a black jacket with one sleeve. The old man had only one arm. "[What do you want?]"

"Do you speak English, Mr. Novak?"

"If I must."

"I'm your new pupil. My name is Maya."

"I don't take pupils," Novak said politely, "and I'm leaving for Roma tomorrow."

"Then I'm also leaving for Roma tomorrow."

Novak stared at her through the wedge of light in his chained door.

"*Glass Labyrinth,*" Maya said. "*The Sculpture Gardens. The Water Anima. Vanished Statues.*"

Novak sighed. "Those titles sound so very bad in English. . . . Well, I suppose you had better come in."

The walls on the ground floor of Novak's home were a wooden honeycomb: a phantasmagoria of hexagonal storage racks. Jointed wooden puppets. Glassware. Etching tools. Feathers. Wicker. Postage stamps. Stone eggs. Children's marbles. Fountain pens and paper clips. Eyeglasses. Relief masks. Compasses and hourglasses. Medals. Belt buckles. Pennywhistles and windup toys. Some of the cubbyholes were stuffed to bursting. Others spare, a very few entirely empty. Like a wooden hive infested by some sentient race of time-traveling bees.

There were study tables, but no place to sit. The bare floor was waxed and glossy.

A sleepy female voice called down from the stairs. "[What is it?]"

"[A guest has come,]" Novak said. He reached into his baggy trouser pocket and pulled out an enameled lighter.

"[Is it that stupid American girl with short hair?]"

"[Exactly, the very same.]" Novak thumb-clicked a muddy flame and methodically lit a candelabrum. Six candle flames waxed. The overhead lights blinked out. The room was immersed in deep yellow. "[Darling, send down a beanbag, won't you?]"

"[It's late. Tell her to go away.]"

"[She's very pretty,]" said Novak. "[There are sometimes uses for someone very pretty.]"

There was silence. Then a pair of black beanbags came slithering down the candlelit stairs like a pair of undulant blood puddings.

Novak sat in his bag and gestured one-armed at Maya. His right arm was gone at the shoulder. He seemed very much at ease with his loss, as if a single arm were perfectly adequate and other people were merely being excessive.

Maya heaved her backpack onto the wooden floor. She sat in her beanbag. "I want to learn photography."

"Photography." Novak nodded. "It's wonderful! So very real, so much like life. If you are a Cyclops. Nailed in one spot. For one five-thousandth of a second."

"I know you can teach me."

"I have taught photography," Novak admitted like a man under torture. "I have taught human beings to see like a camera. What a fine accomplishment! Look at this poor little house of mine. I've been a photographer for ninety years, ninety! What do we have for all that hard work, the old woman and I? Nothing. All the terrible market crashes! Devaluations! Confiscatory taxes! Abolitions and eliminations! Political troubles. Plagues! Bank crashes! Nothing solid, nothing that lasts."

Novak glared at her with resigned suspicion, gone all peasant shrewdness suddenly, protuberant ears, bristling eyebrows, a swollen old-man's nose like a potato. "We have no property, we have no assets. We are very old people, but we have nothing for you, girl. You should go, and save everyone trouble."

"But you're famous."

"I outlived my fame, I am forgotten. I only go on because I cannot help myself."

Maya gazed around the sitting room. A unique mélange of eclectic clutter and utter cleanliness. A thousand little objects on the razor's edge of art and junk. A library of gimmickry rocket-blasted from the grip of time. Yet there was not a speck of dust in the place. Those who worship the Muses end up running a museum.

The burning candles gnawed their white cores of string inside their waxy sheaths. The white-haired Novak seemed perfectly at ease with an extended silence.

Maya pointed to the top of the honeycomb of wooden shelving. "That crystal vase," she said, "that decanter up there."

"Old Bohemian glass," said Novak.

"It's very beautiful."

Novak whistled softly. A trapdoor opened in the wall beside the kitchen and a human arm flopped out.

The arm landed on the wooden floor with a meaty slap of five outstretched fingers. Its naked shoulder had a feathery clump like the curled marine feet of a barnacle.

The arm flexed and leapt, flexed and leapt, pogoing deftly across the gleaming candlelit floorboards. It twisted and ducked, and then tunneled with unearthly speed into a scarcely visible slit in the empty shoulder of Novak's jacket.

Novak squinted, winced a bit, then lifted his artificial hand and flexed it gently.

He then shifted casually onto his left elbow in the beanbag and reached far across the room. The right arm stretched out, its hairless skin gone all bubbled and granular, his forearm shrinking to the width of bird bone. His distant hand grasped the decanter. He fetched it back, his arm reassuming normal size with a quiet internal rasp, like ashes crunching underfoot.

He gave Maya the decanter. She studied it in the candlelight.

"I've seen this before," she said. "I lived inside it for a little while. It was a universe."

Novak shrugged. With his new arm and shoulder attached, he shrugged in remarkable fashion. "Poets have said the same for a single grain of sand."

She looked up. "This glass is made of sand, isn't it? A camera's lens is made from sand. A data bit is like a single grain of sand."

Slowly, Novak smiled. "There's good news," he said. "I like you."

"It's such a wonder to hold the glass labyrinth," she said, turning the decanter in her hands. "It seemed so much more real when it was virtual." She gave it back to him.

Novak examined his decanter idly, stroking it with the left hand, the right one like a glove-shaped set of rubber forceps. "Well, it's very old. A little shape from culture's attic. Oh attic shape!" He began to recite aloud, in Czestina. " '[Designed with marble men and marble women, and forest branches, and weeds crushed by the feet. You silent formation. You twist our minds as if you were eternity. You poem of ice! When old age kills this generation, you will remain in the thick of other people's troubles.

A friend to humanity. You say to us, "Beauty is truth and truth is beauty." We know nothing else and we need to know no more.]' "

"Was that poetry?"

"An old English poem."

"Why not recite the poem in English, then?"

"There is no poetry left in English. When they stretched that language to cover the whole earth, all the poetry fell out of it."

Maya thought this over. It sounded very plausible, and seemed to explain a lot. "Does the poem still sound all right in Czestina, though?"

"Czestina is an obsolescent platform," Novak said. He stood up, stretched his arm like plasticine, and put his decanter in place.

"When do we leave for Roma?" Maya said.

"In the morning. Early."

"May I sit here and wait for you, then?"

"If you promise to blow out the candles," Novak said. And he trudged upstairs. After ten minutes his arm hopped down and deftly put itself away.

———————

They left for Roma in the morning. Mrs. Novakova had packed her husband an enormous shoulder-slung case. Novak didn't bother to take his prosthetic arm.

Maya shouldered her backpack. Bravely she offered to carry Novak's case. Novak handed it over at once. It weighed half a ton. Novak collected himself with a sigh of discontent, opened his front door with deep reluctance, and took three short steps across the ancient sidewalk into a very new and very polished limousine.

Maya put the case and her backpack in the trunk and climbed into the limo, which departed with silent efficiency. "Why won't your wife come with us to Roma?"

"Oh, these business events, they are tiresomeness itself, they are completely obligatory. They bore her."

"How long have you and Milena been married?"

"Since 1994," Novak grunted. "A marriage in name only now. We live like brother and sister." He stroked his chin. "No, that doesn't put it correctly. We're past any burden of gender. We live like commensal animals."

"It's very rare to be married for an entire century. You must be very proud."

"It can be done. If you forgive one another that awesome vulgarity of intimate desire—well, Milena and I are both collectors, we hate to throw things away." Novak reached one-handed to his collar and detached his netlink. He thumbed a net-address.

"Hello?" he barked. "Oh, voice mail, eh?" Novak slipped into angry Czestina. "[Still avoiding me? Well, listen to this, you drone! It's unthinkable—it's impossible!—that an aged invalid, missing his right arm, forgotten by the world, with no proper studio, and no professional help, could have a turnover of thirty thousand marks in a year! That assessment is preposterous! Especially for the year 2095, a year very poor in commissions! And what's this needless claptrap about the '92 extensions? Still demanding your late fees? And even penalties? After you bled us dry? An Artist of Merit of the Czech Republic! A five-time winner of the Praha Municipal Prize! Brought to his knees through your crazy persecutions! It's an open scandal! You haven't heard the last from me, you shiftless dodger.]" He shut the link.

"You tell them again and again," he mourned. "You pile up attestations, applications, documents, years and years of legal correspondence! Oh, they're senseless. They're like Capek's robots." He shook his head, then smiled grimly. "But I don't worry! Because I am very patient, so I will outlast them."

A private business plane was waiting for them at the Praha tarmac, a vision of aviation elegance in white, silver, and peacock blue. "Look at this," Novak fretted, at the foot of the hinged and perforated entry stairs. "Giancarlo should have sent a steward for me. He knows my grave state of decline."

"I'm here, Josef, I'll be your steward." She opened the trunk and gathered their luggage.

"He's such a creature *di moda,* Giancarlo. You should see his château in Gstaad, it's infested with those Stuttgart lobsters. You know, if they go haywire those crazy machines can murder you. Clip your throat clean through with pincers while you sleep." Novak stepped aside as Maya lugged the heavy baggage into the plane. Then he hopped spryly up the steps.

There were no beanbags. Maya paused, puzzled. Novak crouched where he stood, and a chair leapt into existence beneath him with silent blinding speed. The plane's flooring resembled fine Italian marble, but when presented with a lowering human rump its tricky surface puffed up a translucent airtight chair like a supersonic blister. Maya sat at random and a new chair leapt up instantly and caught her. "What a lovely plane this is," Maya said, patting the ductile arms of her chair.

"Thank you, madame," said the plane. "Are we ready for departure?"

"I suppose we are," Novak grumbled. The long slender wings underwent a silent high-speed vibration. The plane ascended vertically.

Novak gazed out the window with silent concentration until the last of his beloved Praha was out of sight. Then he turned to her.

"Do you model? Surely you must," he said.

"Sometimes."

"Do you have an agency?"

"No. I've never modeled for real money." She paused. "I don't *want* to do it for money. But I'll model for you, if you want me to."

"Can you show clothes? Do you know how to walk?"

"I've seen models walking. . . . But no, I don't know how."

"Then I'll teach you," Novak said. "Watch carefully, and see how I place my feet." They stood and their chairs vanished instantly, like silent burst balloons. Without the clutter of chairs around, there was lots of room to learn.

In 2065, Innocent XIV had become the first pope to undergo life extension. The exact nature of the pope's treatment was shrouded in mystery, a rare and very diplomatic exception to the usual political practice of full medical disclosure. The pope's decision, with its profound violation of the natural God-given life span and its grave challenge to the normal processes of papal succession, had caused a crisis in the Church.

The College of Cardinals, meeting in council to discuss the implications of the pope's action, had experienced an episode of divine possession. Their frenzied spiritual exaltation, ecstatic dancing, and babbling in tongues had looked to skeptics like chemically propelled hallucination. But those who had directly experienced the descent of holy fire had no doubt of its sacred origin. The Church had always survived the uncharitable speculations of skeptics.

After this divine intervention, formal Church approval of certain processes of posthumanization had swiftly followed. The Church now recommended its own designated series of life-extension techniques. These approved medical procedures, along with modern entheogenic tincture communions and various spiritual disciplines, were formally known as the "New Emulation of Christ."

The humble and metabolically tireless Holy Father, with his long white beard now grown out black for half its length, had become a central, iconic figure of European modernity. Many had once considered Innocent a mere careerist, the genial caretaker of an ancient faith in decline. After the holy fire, it became clear to all that the reborn pope possessed genuinely superhuman qualities. The pope's astonishing eloquence, his sincerity and his manifest goodwill, shook even the most cynical.

As his chemically amplified Church reconquered the lost ground of ancient Christendom, the vicar of Christ began to manifest miracles unknown since the days of the apostles. The pope had cured the lame and the halt with a word and a touch. He had cast out devils from the minds of the mentally ill. Furthermore, their recovery was often permanent.

He could also prophesy—in detail, and often rather accurately. Many people believed that the pope could read minds. This paranormal claim was attested not merely by credulous Catholics, but by diplomats and statespeople, scientists and lawyers. His uncanny insight into the souls of others had often been demonstrated on the world political stage. Hardened warlords and career criminals, brought into private audience with the pontiff, had emerged as shattered men, confessing their sins to the world in an agony of regret.

Pope Innocent had succored the poor, sheltered the homeless, shamed recalcitrant governments into new and more humane social policies. He had founded mighty hospitals and teaching orders, libraries, netsites, museums, and universities. He had dotted Europe with shelters and amenities for the mendicant and pilgrim. He had rebuilt the Vatican, and had turned ancient cathedrals and churches worldwide into ecstatic centers of Christian spirituality, vibrant with the awesome celestial virtualities of the modern Mass. He was certainly the greatest pope of the twenty-first century, probably the greatest pope of the last ten centuries, perhaps the greatest pope of all time. His sainthood was a certainty, if he could ever find the time and opportunity to die.

Maya found Roma a mess. There had been a miracle the day before. Miracles had become relative commonplaces since the advent of entheogens; it now took very unusual circumstances to attract public attention to sightings of supernatural entities. This latest miracle had raised the ante on the supernatural: the Virgin Mary had manifested herself to two children, a dog, and a Public Telepresence Point.

Children did not normally take entheogens. Even postcanine dogs were rarely given to spiritual revelations. And the recordings in Public Telepresence Points were supposed to be beyond alteration; they were certainly not supposed to show pillowcaselike glowing blurs levitating over the Viale Guglielmo Marconi.

The Romans were not particularly impressed by miracles. Goings-on at the Vatican rarely impressed native Romans. Nevertheless, the devout had poured into Roma from all over Europe to pray, do penance, to seek out relics, to enjoy the media coverage. The traffic—buses, bikes, trailers, sacred tourist groups in the robes of Franciscan mendicants—was dense, loud, incredible, festive, beyond sane management, primal Italian. It was also raining.

Maya gazed through the rain-streaked window of their latest limo. "Josef, are you religious?"

"There are many worlds. There is a world here which perceives in darkness," said Novak, tapping his wrinkled forehead. "There is a material world, the world lit by the sun. There is also virtuality, our modern immateriality pretending to exist. Religion is a virtuality of sorts. A very old one."

"But are you a believer?"

"I believe a few very modest things. I believe that if you take an object, and make it come to life through light, and carry that perception of life into a virtual representation, then you have achieved what they call 'lyricism.' Some people have a great irrational need for religion. I have a great irrational need for lyricism. I can't help myself, and I'm not interested in debate about it. So I won't trouble the faithful, if they don't trouble me."

"But there must be half a million people here today! All because of some dog and a computer and a couple of kids. What do you think about that?"

"I think Giancarlo will be piqued to be upstaged."

The limo, sparring gamely with the Roman traffic, carried them to their hotel, which, of course, was badly overbooked. Novak engaged in a vicious multilingual fight with the concierge, and won them separate rooms, to the considerable discomfiture of everyone in the lobby. Maya bathed and sent her clothes out.

When her clothes returned, an evening gown came with them. Novak's idea of feminine formal wear looked touchingly old-fashioned, but it was freshly instantiated and it seemed to fit very well, a credit to Novak's photographic eye for proportion.

Giancarlo Vietti, the master couturier of Emporio Vietti, was presenting his seventy-fifth spring collection. An event of this magnitude required a proper setting. Vietti had hired the Kio Amphitheater, an arched colossus in exquisite pastiche, built by an eccentric Nipponese billionaire after an earthquake had devastated much of Roma's Flaminio district.

They pulled up in front of the roseate columnar Kio and departed their taxi amid a sidewalk jostle of spex-clad Roman paparazzi. Novak did not seem particularly well known in Roma, but with his single arm he was certainly easy to spot. He ignored the clamoring paparazzi, but he ignored them very slowly.

They worked their way up the stairs. Novak examined the towering faux-marble facade with a feral eye. "Living proof that the past is a finite resource," he muttered. "It would have been better to mimic Indianapolis than to try to out-fascist Mussolini— with cheap materials."

Maya found herself admiring the place. It lacked the weed-eaten stony authenticity of Roma's many actual ruins, but it seemed transcendantly functional and had all the unconscious grace of a well-designed photocopier.

They entered the building, logged in, and discovered three hundred people preparing to eat, attended by crabs.

So many old people. She was struck by their corporate air of monumental gravity, by the striking fact that this chattering tonnage of well-manicured and brilliantly dressed flesh was so much older than the building that housed it.

These were Europe's shiny set. A people who had beaten time into submission, and with their spex-hooded, prescient eyes they looked as though they could stare through solid rock. Veterans of European couture, they had taken the essence of neophiliac evanescence and had frozen it around themselves like a shroud. They were as glamorous as pharaonic tomb paintings.

Novak slipped on his own pair of spex, then made his way deftly to his appointed place, following some social cue narrowcast to the lenses. Novak and Maya sat together at a small round table set with silver, draped in cream-colored linen, and surrounded by upholstered stools. "Good evening, Josef," said the man across the table.

"Hello, Daizaburo, dear old colleague. It's been a long time."

Daizaburo examined Maya over the rim of his elaborate spex with the remote and chilly interest of a lepidopterist. "She's lovely. Where on earth did you find that gown?"

"The first Vietti original I ever shot," said Novak.

"I'm astonished that particular Vietti is still on file."

"Giancarlo may have purged it from his own files. Mine are high capacity."

"Giancarlo was so young then," Daizaburo said. "Juvenilia suits your little friend so well. We're taking waters. Would you like a water?"

"Why not?" said Novak.

Daizaburo signaled a crab. It began speaking Nihongo. "English, please," said Daizaburo.

"Antarctic glacier water," offered the crab. "A deep core from Pleistocene deposits. Entirely unpolluted, undisturbed since the dawn of humanity. Profoundly pure."

"What a delightful conceit," said Novak. "Very Vietti."

"We have lunar water," said the crab. "Very interesting isotopic properties."

"Did you ever drink water from the moon, my dear?" Novak asked her.

Maya shook her head.

"We'll have the lunar water," Novak ordered.

A second crab arrived with a vacuum-sealed vial. Using shining forceps, it dropped two dainty cubes of smoking blue ice into a pair of brandy glasses.

"Water is the perfect social pleasure," said Daizaburo as the crabs stalked off to answer fresh demands. "We can't all share the brute act of liquid consumption, but we surely can all share the ineffable pleasure of watching ice melt."

The other woman at their little table leaned forward. She was small and shrunken and almost hairless, a person of profoundly indefinite ethnic origin who was wearing an enormous black chapeau. "It rode a comet from the rim of universe," she lisped alertly. "Frozen six billion year. Never know the heat of life—until we drink it."

Novak lifted his glass one-handed and swirled it, his craggy peasant face alight with anticipation. "I'm surprised there are still enough lunarians around to mine lunar ice."

"There are seventeen survivors up there. Such a pity they all hate each other." Daizaburo offered a brief and steely smile.

"Cosmic rebels, cosmic visionaries," said Novak, carefully sniffing his glass. "Poor fellows, they discovered the existential difficulties of life without tradition."

Maya looked at the people clustered at the other little tables and knowledge clicked within her like a light switch. She began cataloging treatments in her head. All these old people and all their old techniques. Wrinkle removal, hair growth, skin transplants. Blood filtration. Synthetic lymph. Nerve and muscle growth factor. Meiotic acceleration. Intracellular Antioxidant Enzymation: rejuvenant witches' brews of arginines, ornithines and cysteines, glutathiones and catalases. Intestinal Villi Lamination (IVL). Affective Circadian Adjustment (ACA). Bone augmentation. Ceramic joint prostheses. Targeted aminoguanidines. Targeted dehydroepiandrosterone. Autoimmune Reprogramming Systematics (ARS). Atherosclerotic Microbial Scrubbing (AMS). Glial-Neural Dissipative Defibrillation (GNDD). Broad-Spectrum Kinetic Metabolic Acceleration (BSKMA). Those were old-fashioned techniques. After that they had begun getting ambitious.

A bronze gong sounded. The three hundred diners rose from their little tables in unison, walked or limped or shuffled or rolled, and engaged in a huge and extremely well-ordered session of musical chairs. There was no fuss and no confusion. When they were done, everybody found themselves in the intimate company of new friends, with every appearance of spontaneous delight. Scurrying robots brought everyone fresh utensils and the soup course.

Josef's new tablemates—he seemed to know them well, or perhaps they were broadcasting biographies to be picked up by his spex—were speaking Deutsch. Maya had set her translator for Czestina and Italiano. She could have inserted the little diamond egg for Deutsch, but whenever she fussed with the necklace nowadays, it infallibly stopped and scolded her about how much she owed.

She felt ashamed of her necklace. The cheap gold and diamonds sparkled like so much radioactive junk on the exposed slope of her décolletage. She remained deaf to the Deutsch and said nothing, and her lack of contribution was not noticed in the slightest. She was young. She had nothing of interest to say.

The robots took the zuppa away and everyone moved again. A visually perfect, utterly bland, and intensely digestible cannelloni was served. Some guests chose to eat it, others merely beat it into submission. Then they moved again into fresh company for the delightfully molded and quite taste-free little gnocchi. Then again for gleaming rippled yellow wedges of a scent-free cheeselike substance. Then again for the fluted conical molds of the dolce. It was an intensely elaborate repast, none of it requiring much use of teeth.

The crowd adjourned to the gloomy grandeur of the Kio's display suite. There were booths here and there against the walls, very daring booths that almost looked as if they were engaging in advertising. This tweaking of the rules was mere bravado on Vietti's part, for blatant commerciality was not required in haute couture. True haute couture, the pursuit of genuine excellence in dress, required mostly patience. Patience was something that society's glitterati had a very great deal of, these days. Couture was a game of prestige, and the money that supported it came partly from the wealthy, and mostly from Vietti's licensing: spexware, scents, bath accoutrements, private spas, medicated cosmetics. An arsenal of intellectual property for a couturier who did not so much make clothing as tailor modes of living.

Here at last the lucky attendees, bones aching from the ascetic stools, found decent chairs in which to sit. They broke up into pew-like rows of competing subclasses. Various Indonesian, Nipponese, and American politicians and financiers who were considered peacocks of the shiny set invested the front row in determined effort to impress one another. They were backed by layers of net-editors, store buyers, photographers, actors, actresses, common or garden millionaires, and hommes and femmes du monde.

There were not quite enough chairs for everyone: a deliberate and very traditional oversight. Novak took her backstage through a milling crowd of socialites, junior designers, and minor celebrities.

The area backstage was full of European storks, African secretary birds, and American whooping cranes. These tall and solemn feathered bipeds awaited their cue with impressive single-minded dignity, deftly sidestepping the anxious humans.

The legendary couturier was the nucleus of a buzzing and highly motivated crowd of atelier subordinates. Vietti wore his version of working clothes: a seal black, vaguely furry, multipocketed getup that would have looked splendid with aqualungs. He tracked events for the show on a rainbow pair of fluttering wrist-mounted display fans.

"Josef, so good of you to come," said Vietti in English. He was tall and broad shouldered and square chinned and one of the very few people at the event who did not deign to wear spex. It was clear that Vietti had once been very beautiful. Many years and many pains had been at him. Now he had the slightly sinister ruinous dignity of the Roman Colosseum—although in point of fact Giancarlo Vietti was not Roman but Milanese.

Vietti glanced at Maya with the same absently indulgent gaze he'd been giving his obedient storks. His faded blue eyes widened suddenly. Finally he revealed a sparkling rack of ceramic teeth. "Oh, but Josef. But she's so cute! You rascal. Really, you shouldn't have."

"So you do remember."

"You thought I'd forget my first collection? It's like forgetting your first time under the knife." Vietti gazed at Maya, deeply intrigued. "Where did you find her?"

"She's my new student."

Vietti very gently touched Maya's jawline with one black-gloved fingertip. He plucked once at the end of a trailing length of her wig, and gave a quick adjusting tug at her shoulder seam. He laughed delightedly.

After ten seconds or so of hearty laughter, Vietti's cheeks flushed patchily and there were odd aquatic gurglings beneath the suit. Vietti put his left hand to his midriff, winced, wriggled a bit on the deep internal hooks of his life support. Then he examined a wrist-fan and sketched at the membrane with his forefinger.

"Let's put her on the catwalk tonight," he said. "A show in Roma is always such chaos anyway. And really, this is too cute."

"You mustn't, Giancarlo. That's costume plastic, it's a knockoff."

"I know this garment is your little joke on me, but we can get that fixed. Can she walk?"

"She can walk a little."

"She's very young, they'll forgive her if she can't walk." Vietti looked at her, expectantly. "The name?"

"Maya."

"Little Maya, I have a very good crew here. Let me put you in their hands. Can you walk in front of all these shiny people? They are terribly old, and they all have silly spex and too much money." Vietti winked at her, a leaden pretense of camaraderie across the awful gulf of a century.

"Sure I can." Perfectly happy and confident.

Vietti gazed at Novak limpidly. "And Josef—a few little pictures for me. For my little corner of the net."

"Oh, I couldn't," said Novak. "I haven't brought the proper gear."

"Josef, for old times' sake. You can use Madracki's gear, Madracki's a poseur, he's an idiot, he owes me the favor anyway."

"I'm all out of practice with couture. Really, it takes everything I have these days just to photograph an eggshell, a spiderweb. . . ."

"Josef, after you took the trouble to dress her! Don't be coy. The face is awful, it's true, that's little-girl makeup, vivid kitsch for kids, but we can see to the face. And the wig's a disaster. . . . But she's so sexy, Josef! Everyone was so very sexy in the twenties. Even I was sexy then." Vietti sighed nostalgically. "You remember how sexy I was?"

"When you're young, even the moon and stars are sexy."

"Ah, but people died so young in the twenties, so everyone was sexy then, everything was always so sexy. Even AIDS was sexy in the twenties. I don't have a single sexy thing in this collection, your little girl can be my sexy thing tonight, it'll be fun. Barbara will see to it." Vietti flapped his wrist-fans shut and clapped his hands. "Barbara!"

"You're very lucky," Novak told Maya, very quietly. "He wants to like you. Don't disappoint us."

She whispered back. "He's not going to pay me, is he? I can do this as long as I don't get paid."

"I'll look after that," Novak assured her. "Be brave."

Barbara was a senior Vietti assistant. Barbara had the accent of West End London, and the broad features and kinked black hair of a West Indian, combined with the painterly peaches-and-cream complexion of a Pre-Raphaelite lass on a canvas. Barbara was sober and efficient and dressed as beautifully as a ranking diplomat. Barbara was eighty years old.

Barbara took Maya into the cosmetic studio, which was crowded with male models. Ten or so stunningly beautiful men, in various states of partial dress, sat before brilliantly lit videomirrors, chattering, flexing biceps and quadriceps, methodically primping.

"This is Philippe, he'll look after you now," said Barbara, and she put Maya into a red support chair at the elbow of the cosmetician. Philippe was a small man with a tiny pinched mouth and brilliantined blond hair and enormous spex. Philippe took one look at her, blurted a horrified, "Oh dear no," and sent off for spatulas and cleansing cream and adhesive towels and power-brushes and a red alert for the hairdresser.

The two nearest models were having a chat. "Have you seen Tomi tonight? He's bulked. He's really bulked."

"It's the grandkid thing," said a second model. "I mean, you get over having the kid, but when the kid has a kid, I dunno."

"How's your new house, Brandon?"

"So far so good, but we shouldn't have drilled that deep in a seismic area. It's got me all worried."

"No, you got it made now, you and Bobby can seal it off, set up some hermetic germware, some very sweet discretion way down deep there, really, I'm green with envy." The model examined his videomirror. The screen showed him an image without reversal. "Do my eyelids look okay?"

"You had them tucked again?"

"No, something new this time."

"Adrian, the eyelids never looked better. Seriously."

"Thanks. Did I tell you I enlisted in the army?"

"You're kidding." Effortlessly Brandon bent double and placed his palms flat on the floor. He went into a handstand, then flexed his elbows methodically. His muscular legs, toes pointed at the ceiling like a high-diver's, looked as solid as cast bronze.

"Well," said Adrian, "my medical's running pretty high, and civil support, well, they're a bunch of dirty finks. Aren't they? But the armed forces! I mean, modern society—seriously—there has to be real authority! Somewhere on the far side of all these civilian broads, there have to be some serious guys willing to kick butts and take names. Capisci?"

Brandon curled into an effortless backflip. He examined his washboard abdomen in the mirror, frowned, and found a reactive girdle. "How long are you in for?"

"Five years."

"No problem, you could do a five-year enlistment on your head." Brandon adjusted the girdle, which sealed tight with a violent sucking sound. "You got through the army physical and everything?"

"Sure, they love me. They put me in the officer corps."

"They didn't mind the prostate thing?"

"The prostate thing is history, the prostate's very fresh and crunchy now. I'm doing weekends at a guard base in Cairo." Adrian stopped suddenly. "Philippe, what are you doing to that poor kid's eyebrows?"

"I'm in a hurry," Philippe complained.

"That's a period dress. You gotta do period eyebrows for this little girl, twenties eyebrows. You can't just pluck her out like she was Veruzhina on the rampage or something, this is an ingenue look." Adrian patted Maya's forearm with fatherly aplomb. "Haven't seen you around, kid. First time with Giancarlo?"

"Yes, it is. First time ever with anybody."

"Oh Brandon, listen to that, she's American."

"Are you guys American, too?" she said.

"Sure," smiled Adrian, "Europeans love the primal American male, big shoulders, upholstered, dumb as rocks, can't hardly talk, what's not to like?"

"They like us virile," said Brandon. "They pay real well for virile. You gotta pay for virile, because the upkeep on virile is murder." He laughed.

"You have very acid pores, sweetie," Philippe told her with deep concern. "Have you been bathing in mold?"

"Just once."

"You should. You really should! I've got a strain of cultured aspergillus that would do wonders for you. I need to move your hairline and depilate your upper lip. This may hurt a little."

Tweezers plucked, brushes whirred, greases soaked, powders reacted and settled. In thirty minutes all the men were meticulously dressed. Some of them were taking their turns outside.

Philippe showed her the new face.

She had been through many facials before, all kinds of facials, decades of facials. Most had been entirely cosmetic, pleasant but essentially worthless. Some had been functional, high-tech, genuinely restorative facials that left one's face raw and unsettled, the kind of face that wanted to be left alone in a warm dark room to collect itself. But Philippe's work was artifice. Still a Maya face—but a composed, radiant, flawless Maya face. Curled and slightly tinted lashes. Smoky eyelids. Brows like wings. Skin to shame damask. Pellucid irises and eyewhites as glossy as china. Lips like two poppy petals. A finished face. Human perfection.

Then they put the new wig on and she left human perfection for a higher realm. It was a very smart wig. This wig could have leapt from her scalp like a supersonic octopus and flung its piercing tendrils right through a plaster wall. But it was the tool of a major couture house, so it would never do anything half so gauche. It was merely a staggeringly pretty wig, a wig in rich, solid, deeply convincing, faintly luminescent auburn, a wig as expensive, as cozy, and as well designed as a limousine.

The wig settled to her scalp with an intimate grip rather more convincing than the grip of her own hair. When it curled lustrously about her neck and shoulders it behaved the way a woman's hair behaved in daydreams.

A gonging alarm sounded. The last men cleared out of the room. Four female models sauntered in. The women were tall and slender and fully dressed except for shoes. The shoes were being a lot of trouble, and anxious runners kept hauling new pairs in and out. The models, bored and patient, sipped tinctures and puffed at inhalants and ate little white sticks of calorie-free finger food. They nibbled and dabbed at their hors d'oeuvres, and their preternatural arms moved with perfect eerie grace, from painted plate to painted lip.

The models were old women, and they looked the way that modern old women looked when they were in truly superb condition: they looked like amenorrheic female athletes. Like pubescent female gymnasts who'd been bleached completely free of any youthful brio. They showed none of the natural signs of human aging, but they were just a little crispy, a little taut. The models were solemn and sloe-eyed and dainty and extremely strong. They looked as if they could leap headlong through plate glass without turning a hair.

Their clothes were decorative and columnar and slender hipped and without much in the way of bustline. To see these clothes was to realize just how garments could be beautiful, impressive, even feminine, while being almost entirely free of sexual allure. The clothes were splendidly cut and defined. Rather ecclesiastical, rather bankerly, rather like the court dress of high-powered palace eunuchs from the Manchu Forbidden City. Some of the clothes showed skin, but it was the kind of skin a woman might reveal as she conquered the English Channel.

The clothes were very rich in feathering. Not frail or showy feathers, but feathers in gleaming businesslike array, feathers in swathes like chain mail. Giancarlo had been very reliant on feathers this spring season. It was mostly the detail work with feathers that had sent these garments soaring into the unearthly realm of luxe.

"[It's not just the risk reduction,]" said the nearest model, in Italiano. "[You get a six-point-five percent rate of return.]"

"[I'm not sure the time is right for medical mutual funds,]" said a second model. "[Besides, I'm Catholic.]"

"[No one says you have to take a treatment on the banned list, you just invest in them,]" said the first model patiently. She was deeply, spiritually, untouchably beautiful; she looked like a bit player in Botticelli's *Primavera*. "[Talk to any Vatican banker sometime, darling. They're very simpatico and very up to speed about this.]"

The second model looked at Maya in surprise, and then at her wristwatch. "[When do you go on?]"

Maya touched her necklace and her ear. "I'm sorry, I don't speak Italiano."

"Your diamonds are so true to the past life, I love the diamonds," said the second model in halting but sympathetic English. "The hair, though—not so very good. That's very smart hair, that's not twenties hair."

"You're very sexy," the first model told her politely.

"Molte grazie," Maya said tentatively.

"There should be more couture for sexy women now, such a pity sexy women don't have proper money," the first model said. "When I was young and sexy they paid me so much money. It's so hard for young girls now, it's so hard to sell sexy. Really, it's not fair one bit, not at all."

The show was warming up outside; she could hear periodic bursts of applause. They brought her Vietti's gown, still warm from the instantiator. This gown fit at least as well as the cheaper version Novak had given her, but Vietti's stylists did not consider this a proper fit at all. Maya found herself naked and shivering beneath the impassive eyes and knowing hands of two men and three women. They slashed quickly at the gown with razorlike ceramic scissors and painted her goose-bumped flesh with quick-setting adhesive. In a fury of efficiency they squeezed and waxed her into the gown, then jammed her feet into pumps two sizes too small. Then, out the door in a bustle of anxious minders. Philippe hurried alongside her, retouching her face as she waited to take her cue.

When her cue came she left the curtain and walked as she had been taught. The catwalk's floods were as bright as double-ranked full moons and the audience beyond their arc was a gleaming mass of spex, nocturnal eyes in a gilded swamp. They were playing a twenties pop song, a theme she actually recognized, a song she'd once thought was slick. Now the ancient pop song sounded lost and primitive, almost feral. Theme music for the triumphal march of the living fossils.

They'd dressed her as a glamorous young woman from the 2020s. A joke, a little shattering blast at the conceptual framework. Because, in stark actuality, she'd been a young woman during the 2020s. She had never been glamorous then, not a bit like this, not even for a moment, because she had been far too busy and far too careful. And now through some astounding fluke of chic she had avenged herself. The joy of it was both nostalgic and immediate, melding in her head in a fabulous jouissance.

White laserflashes puffed from cameras in the audience, growing into a crescendo as she walked. She felt so radiant. She was stunning people. She was whirling past their machine-shrouded eyes like nostalgic vertigo. She was the cynosure, the belle, the vamp, the femme fatale. Lost love beyond mortal attainment, dressed to kill, dressed to bury, dressed to rise again and walk among mortals. She had crushed them with stolen charisma. They had dressed a risen ghost in a Milanese couture gown and let her trample time underfoot. She was making them love her.

She took the little pirouette at the end of the walkway, kicked back a bit with a crack of heels, sneered at them happily. She was so high above them and so wrapped in lunar brightness, and they were such low fetid dark creatures that not a one of them could ever touch her. The walk was taking forever. She had forgotten how to breathe. The sense of constriction made her frantic with excitement. A white crane leapt onto the catwalk, immediately recognized that it had done something rash, and hopped off into the crowd with a jostle of pipestem legs and a snowy flap of wings. She hesitated just before the curtain, then whirled and blew the crowd a kiss. They responded with a cataclysm of photographic flash shots.

Behind the curtain she found herself tingling, trembling. She found a stool in a corner and sat and fought for proper breath. The crowd was still applauding. Then the music changed and another model slid past her like an angel on casters.

Novak found her. He was laughing.

"What a brave girl. You don't give two pins, do you?"

"Was I all right?"

"Better than that! You looked so very pleased and wicked, like a little spoilt child. It was so pretty of you, so apropos."

"Will Giancarlo be happy with me?"

"I have no idea. He probably thinks you're a terrible brat to ham it up that way. But don't worry, it made the night for the rest of us." Novak chuckled. She hadn't seen Novak truly pleased before; he was like a man who'd just pulled off a trick billiard shot with a rubber cue. "Giancarlo will come around, once he hears them talk about you. Giancarlo's very clever in that way. He never judges anything until he sees what it's done to his public."

Maya tumbled hard from her crest of elation. The real world felt so deflated suddenly. Quotidian, wearied, flat. "I did the best that I could."

"Of course you did, of course you did," he soothed. "You mustn't cry, darling, it's all right now. It was very nice for us, it was different. They hire the pros to walk properly for them, and you were very sincere, they can't buy that." Novak took her elbow and led her backstage to a watercooler.

He deftly filled a cup with pristine distillate and gave it to her, one-handed. "It's so remarkable," he mused. "You can't show a garment to advantage, of course, because you're only a little beginner. But you truly have that look! Seeing you there, it was like archival video. Some Yankee girl from the twenties, in her too-tight shoes, so touchingly proud of her wonderful gown. What déjà vu, what *mono no aware*! It was uncanny."

Maya wiped at her tears, and tried to smile. "Oh, I'm so bad, I've ruined that wonderful job Philippe did on my eyes."

"No, no, don't fret now." Novak stroked his chin thoughtfully. "Maya, we're going to do a proper photo shoot. You and I. We can bring your Philippe in on the job, we can bill for him. When you are working on assignment for Giancarlo, it's very nice to have some good expensive people you can bill for. . . ."

"I should go thank Giancarlo. Shouldn't I? He really did me a huge favor, letting me go on. I mean, compared to all these professionals . . . And they were so kind to me, they weren't jealous at all."

"They are veterans. You're far too young to make them jealous. You can thank your friend Giancarlo on the net. It's better for us to leave now." Novak smiled. "You've beaten them, darling, you beat them like sick old dogs. We'll go now. It's always best to leave them wanting more."

"Well, I'll get dressed, then."

"Wear that gown. You can keep it. They had to hurry, so they had to ruin it."

"Well, I'd better return this incredible wig at least."

"Take the wig with us, we'll hold the wig. Just to make sure they call."

She managed to get rid of the pinching shoes. When she emerged from the dressing room she found Novak clawing one-handed at the air in the corridor, as if fighting off a phantom horde of gnats. He hadn't gone mad, he was only using the menus on his spex. He was calling them a taxi.

Novak led her deftly past half a dozen random well-wishers backstage. The professionals all seemed quite pleased and amused with her, in their rigid and terrifying fashion. They escaped the amphitheater by a stage exit. It was cold outside, cold enough to frost the breath. The sweat leapt off her bare neck and shoulders into the Roman night. She shivered violently.

When they rounded the corner of the Kio, the paparazzi spotted them. A dozen of them dashed up, yelling at her in Italiano. They were the youngest of the paparazzi, which accounted for the fact that they were willing to dash. Some of them held up ragged halos of fiber-optic flash wire, drowning the damp pavement in sudden gouts of light. Maya smiled at them, flattered. When they saw this response they yelled more loudly and with greater enthusiasm.

"Does anyone here speak English?" Maya said.

The paparazzi, circling them and staring through their

gleaming lenses, held a quick shouted consultation. A young woman hurriedly shoved her way through from the back. "I do, I speak English! Will you really talk to us?"

"Sure."

"Great! We all want to know how you pulled that off."

"What do you mean?"

"Like, how did you get your big break?" said the girl, hastily plucking the translation cuff from her ear. She was American. "Did you do it yourself?"

"No, of course not."

"Oh, so you owe it to your escort here? Does he sponsor you? What's your relationship with this guy exactly? And what's your name, and who is he, anyway?"

"I'm Maya and this is Mr. Josef Novak. There's certainly nothing illicit about our relationship."

Novak laughed. "Don't tell them that! I'm deeply touched to be a source of scandal."

"How do you know Giancarlo Vietti? How old are you? Where are you from?"

"Don't tell them anything," Novak advised, "let the poor creatures feed on mystery."

"Don't be that way," begged the young paparazza. She forced a business card on Maya. The flimsy card showed nothing but a name and a net-address. "Can I interview you later, Signorina Maya? Where are you from?"

"Where are *you* from?" Maya said.

"California."

"What city?"

"The Bay."

Maya stared at her. "Wait a minute! I can't believe this! I *know* you! You're Brett!"

Brett laughed. "Sorry, that's not my name."

"But it is! Your name is Brett and you had a boyfriend named Griff and I bought one of your jackets once."

"Well, my name's not Brett, and if anybody had one of my jackets it sure wouldn't be a runway model for Giancarlo Vietti."

"You *are* Brett, you had a rattlesnake! What on earth are you doing here in Roma, Brett? And what have you done to your hair?"

"Look, my name's Natalie, okay? And what does it look like I'm doing here? I'm hanging around on a cold pavement outside a couture show trying to pick up scraps, that's what." Brett pulled off her spex and stared at Maya in pained surprise. "How come you know so much about me? Do I really know you? How? Why?"

"But it's me, Brett! It's me, Maya," Maya said, and she shuddered from head to foot. A finger's width of glue popped loose on her back. She was freezing. And she suddenly felt very bad. Nauseated, dizzy.

"You don't know me," Brett insisted. "I never saw you before in my life! What's going on in there? Why are you trying to fool me?"

"The cab's here," Novak said.

"Don't go now!" Brett grabbed her arm. "D'you know there's a million girls who'd *kill* to do what you just did? How'd you do that? What do I have to do, to get that lucky? Tell me!"

"Don't touch her!" Novak barked. Brett jumped back as if shot.

"If you knew what it was like in there," Novak told her, "you'd go home tomorrow! Go lie on the beach, be a young woman, live, breathe! There's nothing for you there. They made sure of that long before you were born."

"I feel so bad, Josef," Maya wailed.

"Get in the taxi." Novak shoveled her inside. The doors shut. Brett stood stunned on the pavement, then jumped out and hammered at the window, shouting silently. The taxi pulled away.

———

Next morning she found she'd gotten write-ups on the net. There were white tuberoses from Vietti and eight calls from industry journalists. One of the journalists had called from the hotel lobby. He was camping out there.

They had breakfast smuggled into Novak's room. "You're not at the point where you can talk to real journalists," Novak told her. "Journalists are the class enemies of celebrity models. They become hormonally excited when they discover any fact that will cause you deep personal pain."

"I'm not a celebrity model." She certainly didn't feel the part. She'd had to shred the couture gown. It had required cleansing cream, a long-handled loofah, and half an hour to scrub the glue from her skin. She hadn't dared to sleep in the intelligent wig, and in the morning she discovered it limp and dead. She couldn't even manage to boot its software.

"That's true enough, but a pile of sand is not yet Bohemian crystal, my dear."

"I want to be a photographer, not a model."

"Don't be hasty. You should learn how to work to the camera before you torment other people with a lens. A few location shots will teach you proper sympathy for all your future victims." Novak patted his grizzled lips with a napkin, stood, and began emptying his travel case on the bed.

The false bottom of his case held two deep layers of gray equipment foam. Four sets of highly specialized spex. Lenses in 35 mm, 105, 200, 250. Two ductile fisheyes and a photogrammeter. A tripod. Filters. Two camera bodies. Sync cording. Ten meters of tunable laser fiber-optic lighting cord. Gaffer tape. A fat graphics notebook with a high-powered touch-up wand and backup storage. Multihead photofloods, roll-up reflector cards, filter frames, adapter rings, matte foil, a pocket superconductor.

Maya blinked. "I thought you said you hadn't brought proper equipment."

"I said I hadn't brought equipment to the *show*," Novak said. "Anyway, this gear is nothing much. Since I was forced to come here, I thought I might shoot—I don't know—a few of those lovely Roman manhole covers. . . . But a couture shoot! Oh, what a challenge."

"Won't Vietti help us? He's got a million flunkies on staff, he ought to give us anything we want."

"Darling, Giancarlo and I are professionals. The game between the two of us has rules. When I win, I give Giancarlo exactly what I want to give Giancarlo. He shuts up and pays me. When I lose, Giancarlo offers me the full and terrible burden of his tactful advice and help."

"Oh."

Novak examined his bedspread arsenal of digital photonbenders and tugged thoughtfully at the bulbous end of his large, aged, cartilaginous male nose. "A couture session is no mere still life, it truly needs a team. You don't take couture shots, you *make* them. The stylist for the clothing, the set dresser . . . a decent studio service is invaluable for props. A location scout . . . Hair designer, cosmetician very certainly . . ."

"How do we get all these people?"

"We hire them. After that, we bill Giancarlo for their services. That's the good part. The bad part is I have no decent contacts in Roma. And, of course, since I am devastated by business failure, I have no capital."

She gazed at him thoughtfully. She knew with deep cellular certainty that Novak had plenty of money, but extracting it from him would be like drawing ten liters of blood. "I think I have a little money," she said tentatively.

"You do? That's exciting news, my dear."

"I have a contact in Bologna who might help us. She has a lot of friends in virtuality and artifice."

"Young people? Amateurs."

"Yes, Josef, young people. You know what that means, don't you? It means they'll work for us for nothing, and then we can bill for whatever we like."

"Well," Novak allowed thoughtfully, "they're still amateurs, but it never hurts to ask."

"I can ask. I'm pretty sure I can ask. Before I can ask, though, I'm going to need some equipment for asking. Do you happen to know a nice discreet netsite in Roma that runs defunct protocols?"

That question was no challenge for Josef Novak. "The Villa Curonia," Novak said at once. "Of course, the old and wicked Villa Curonia. What a lovely atmosphere for a location shoot."

The Villa Curonia was a former private residence in Roma's Monteverde Nuovo. The shaggy green heads of indiscreet palm trees loomed behind its glass-topped brick walls. A certain eccentricity in the facade suggested that its builder had been some opium-smoking D'Annunzio aesthete with aristo relations in the highest and creepiest circles of the early twentieth-century Curia.

Inside, the villa had an arch-heavy interior courtyard with a dry fountain and pedestaled statue of Hermes, perfect for the midnight meetings of bagmen. The three-story east wing was riddled like cheesecloth with power leads and fiber optics, all scuffed parquet flooring and silent ivory corridors and monster antique virch-sets squatting like toads behind the locked doors of servants' cubbyholes. Two comically sinister brothers named Khornak were running the place, for heaven only knew what sub-rosa cabal of backers, and under their aegis the ancient building had achieved the silk-padded atmosphere of a digital bordello. A Roman house of assignation for man-machine liaisons.

Novak was busy and methodical, Maya busy and nearly manic. Benedetta proved very helpful. Benedetta was tireless once she perceived a link to her own ambitions.

Brett arrived on a rented bicycle around three in the afternoon. Maya ushered her past the sidewalk guard post and the glowering Khornak brothers.

"This place is so amazing, it's so refined," Brett marveled. "It was so nice of you to ask me here."

"You can stop gushing at me just any time now, Brett. Tell me something—tell me how you got to Roma."

"You really want to know? Well, my first stop in Europe was Stuttgart, but the rents are so high there and the people are so snobby and full of themselves, so I just started doing a kind of wanderjahr, and, well, all roads lead to Roma, don't they? And nobody was interested in what I could do with clothes, so I kept asking around and I got this kind of piecework spex job with this

tabloid net, and I hang around on the shows and cafés and sometimes I get lucky and spot somebody who ranks."

"That's about what I imagined. You must know a lot of
secondhand shops around here, right?"

"You mean clothing stores? Sure. This is Roma, there's zil-
lions. The Via del Corso, the Via Condotti, you can get all kinds
of stuff for cash in Trastevere. . . ."

"Josef is upstairs, running through his files in Praha. He's
going to instantiate me some clothes from his files, some clothes
from the twenties. That's the theme of the shoot. You know the
style of that period?"

"Well, sure I do, sort of. In the twenties they were real big
on, like, camisades and aubades with lastex and tulle and lots of
optical fringe ribbon."

Maya paused. The camisades sounded plausible, but she
couldn't recall having ever worn so much as a centimeter of optical fringe ribbon. "Brett, we're going to need some props for the
session. Something to inspire Josef. He hasn't worked this way in
a long time, so we need something very atmospheric, something
very . . . well, very *Glass Labyrinth,* very early-Novak. Josef Novak
was always very big on the inherent poetry in things . . . on that
very strange intense poetic thingness that certain, uhm, things possess. . . . You have any real idea what I'm talking about here?"

"I guess so."

Maya handed her a fat cashcard. Brett checked the register
band and her eyes widened.

"Old playing cards," Maya told her. "Crescent moons. La-
dies' gloves. Colored yarn. Netting. Weird twentieth-century sci-
entific instruments. Obsolete prosthetics. Driftwood. Prisms.
Compasses. Brass-tipped walking sticks. Some ratty stuffed animals
with scary glass eyes, like minks or weasels or, you know, ermines.
Broken windup toys. Do you know what a phonograph was?
Well, never mind the phonographs, then. Do you get my general
Novak-ish drift here?"

Brett nodded uncertainly.

"Okay, then take that money I just gave you, scout out some
junk shops, tell them you're my stylist. You're working on my

photo shoot for Giancarlo Vietti. Try to borrow whatever you can, rent what you can't borrow, and don't buy anything unless you're willing to keep it yourself. We're in a big hurry here, so round up any vivid friends that can help you. Bring it all back here to the villa. Travel quick. Forget the bike, use taxis. If you get in trouble, call me. Time is of the essence, and money is basically no object. Understand all that? Okay, get going."

Brett stood blinking.

"What are you waiting for?"

"Nothing," she said. "It's just that it's so exciting. I'm just so glad to be really doing this."

"Well, do it quick."

Brett scampered off. Josef's first instantiations arrived by courier. They were costumery. They weren't about comfort or wearability. They were camera props, they were about photons.

Back in the twenties, they had still been very big on natural fibers, but there was no fabric in these costumes. They were all microscopic shirrings and shrinkings and tiny little squirms of extruded plastic. The costumes didn't breathe well and they rustled loudly when they moved, but they looked angelic. When you pinched or tucked them into place they stayed that way and laughed mockingly at gravity.

"Looks like you got us our money's worth."

"The Khornak brothers are robbing us," groaned Novak. "Sixteen percent transaction fees! Can you believe that?"

Maya peeled a tangerine cape-dress from the top of the heap and held it to herself. "That won't be a problem as long as they're discreet."

"Maya, before we begin this, give me an answer. Why is this being financed through the defunct production company of a dead Hollywood film director?"

"Is it?" Maya said, examining the printed sleeves. "It was supposed to be financed through the student activities budget of a Bolognese technical college."

"That childish dodge might fool a very impatient tax accountant. It won't fool me, or these miserable little fences either."

Maya sighed. "Josef, I happen to have a little grown-up

money. A certain grown-up gave it to me, and he really shouldn't have done that. That money is no good for me, and I have to get rid of it. This villa is a very good place to do that. Isn't it? This is a black-market underwire netsite. This is Roma, a very old and very wicked town. And this is the fashion industry, where people always spend absurd amounts of money for really silly reasons. If I can't launder hot money under these circumstances, I'll never be able to do it."

"It's risky."

"My life is risk. Never mind the stupid money. Show me what beauty is."

Novak sighed. "This isn't going to be beauty, darling. I'm very sorry, but it will only be chic."

"All right, then maybe I'll settle for glamour. I'm a woman in a hurry. I want it so much, Josef. I just have to have it now."

Slowly Novak nodded. "Yes. I can see that quality about you. That's just where your allure lies, darling . . . that's it, that's you, and that is this moment, exactly."

Philippe arrived at half past three to do her face. Philippe brought along a gift: a couture wig from the Emporio Vietti. This new wig boasted a built-in translation unit doing forty-seven major global languages through a translucent cord that snaked to the wearer's right ear. It was, said Novak, "very Vietti" to point-edly ignore their purloining of the other wig and then double the ante by sending along a much nicer one.

The wig came preprogrammed with a set of three twenties hairstyles, Vietti's tactful method of elbowing his way into the shot. It would have been crass to turn down such a handsome gift, and one that she needed so much. But Novak was angered by this little jab from his old patron. The irritation sent Novak into a frenzy of spontaneous invention.

"This I want from you, darling," Novak muttered. "Let me tell you what is happening tonight. The thrill of the uncanny lies in the piquancy of oxymoron. You remember what life was like in the twenties? Well, of course you don't. You can't, but you must pretend that you do, just for me. . . . When Giancarlo and I were young in the twenties, anything seemed possible. Now it's the nineties, and anything truly *is* possible—but if you're young, you're not allowed to do anything about those possibilities. You understand me?"

She nodded, stone-faced, careful not to damage her cosmetics. "Yes, Josef, I do understand. I understand perfectly."

"The uncanny is beauty *macchiato,* darling, beauty just a little spotted—with the guilty, with the monstrous. That's what Vietti really saw in you, when he said that he saw something cute. You see, my darling, in order to make this world very safe for the very old, we have changed life for the young in ways that are truly evil."

"Is that really fair, Josef? You're being very harsh."

"Don't interrupt me. Vietti cannot recognize that truth without recognizing his own complicity. That was why he was intrigued." Novak waved his single arm. "Tonight, you become the long-dead youth of the gerontocracy, in a dangerous liaison with the crushed youth of modernity. An impossible conspiracy, a dreamlike violation. Something that plays at sentiment and nostalgia, but conceals a core that is a little dangerous, a little perverse. I'm going to push that old man's face into it. He won't see all of it, because he can't allow himself to see the full truth; but what he can see of it, he will be forced to love."

They set to work. Maya lurking in svelte black by a half-dead antique virtuality engine. Maya passing a stuffed weasel and a stuffed envelope to a sullen half-naked errand boy (played by one of Brett's Roman acquaintances). Maya in a set of virching goggles like a domino mask, letting her signet ring be kissed by the Khornaks' burly security guard. (The glamour-struck guard was especially good in his role.) Maya spurning a packet of dope stickers and pretending to smoke a cigarette. A pensive Maya in candlelight, crouching in her high heels over a little playing-card castle of Roman bus tickets.

Ten, then a dozen, then a score of kids showed up at the villa netsite, in their street couture. Novak fed them into the shot. Faceless and crawling at her feet, their cheap and vivid gear gone half-grotesque in shadows.

When Maya saw the raw shots on Novak's notebook screen,

she was elated and appalled. Elated because he had made her so lovely. Appalled because Novak's fantasy was so revelatory. He'd made her a bewitching atavism, a subterranean queen of illicit chic for a mob of half-monstrous children. Novak's glamour was a lie that told the truth.

———————

Novak took a cab back to the hotel at half past one in the morning. The old man had not given so much of himself in a long time. He was palsied with an exhaustion that only a man in his one hundred twenties could manifest.

With Novak's departure, the Khornak brothers, who had been growing very nervous about the vivid kids, threw everyone out in a scattered welter of props and equipment.

The kids drifted off with cheery good-byes, rattling off on bicycles, or cramming half a dozen into a cab. When Brett and Maya inventoried the borrowed props they discovered that the extras had magpied off with a dozen or so small but valuable articles. Brett was reduced to tears by this discovery. "That's so typical," she said. "Really, you give people a chance, a real chance for once, and what do they do with it. They just slap you in the face."

"They wanted souvenirs, Brett. They gave us their time and we didn't pay them a thing, so I don't mind. Really, a stuffed weasel can't be worth all that much."

"But I promised the store people I'd take good care of everything. And I let the kids in on something really special, and they robbed me." Brett shook her head and sniffled. "They just don't get it here, Maya. These Roman kids, they're not like us. It's like all the life has been squeezed out of them. They don't do anything, they don't even try, they just hang out on the Spanish Steps and drink frappés and *read*. Good heavens, these Roman kids read. You just give them some fat paper book and they'll sit there and nod out for hours and hours."

"Roman kids read?" Maya encouraged, sorting shoes. "Gosh, how classical of them."

"It's awful, a terrible habit! In virtuality at least you get to interact! Even with television you at least have to use visual processing centers and parse real dialogue with your ears! Really, reading is so bad for you, it destroys your eyes and hurts your posture and makes you fat."

"Don't you think reading can be useful sometimes?"

"Sure, that's what they all say. You get some of these guys and they take lexic tinctures and they can read like a thousand words a minute! But still, they don't ever *do* anything! They just read about doing things. It's a disease."

Maya stood up reluctantly. All the standing and all the fittings had made her legs ache and her feet swell. Striking and holding poses was more physically grueling than she had ever imagined. "Well, it's too late to return any of this stuff tonight. You know any safe place we can store this junk overnight? Where do you live?"

"I don't think my place will do."

"You living up a tree again or something?"

Brett frowned, wounded. "No! I just don't think my place will do, that's all."

"Well, I can't carry all this weird stuff into that pricey hotel that I'm in, I'll never even get it past the doordog." Maya tossed her ringlets. She loved the new dark wig. It was infinitely better than hair. "Where can we squat with a closetful of prop junk at two in the morning?"

"Well, I know a really perfect place," said Brett, "but I probably shouldn't take you there."

Brett's friends were up at three in the morning, because they were hard and heavy tincture people. There were six of them and they lived in a damp cellar in the Trastevere that looked as if it had harbored thirty consecutive generations of drug addicts.

Drug addicts in the 2090s had entire new labyrinths of gleaming pathways to the artificial paradise. The polity would not allow any conventional marketing of illicit drugs, but with a properly kitted-out tincture set, and the right series of biochemical recipes, you could make almost any drug you pleased, in quantity sufficient to kill you and a whole tea party full of friends. The polity recognized that drug manufacture and possession were unpoliceable. So they contented themselves with denying medical services to people who were wrecking their health.

The situation, like all dodgy situations in the polity, had been worked out in enormous detail. Crude compounds that could stop your heart or scar your liver clearly damaged life expectancy, so their use drew stiff medical penalties. Drugs that warped cognitive processes in tiny microgram quantities did very little metabolic damage, so they were mostly tolerated. The polity was a medical-industrial complex, a drug-soaked society. The polity saw no appeal whatever in any primitive mythos of a natural drug-free existence. The neurochemical battle with senility had placed large and powerful segments of the voting populace into permanently altered states.

Maya—or rather Mia—had met junkies before. She was always impressed by how polite junkies were. Junkies had the innate unworldly gentility that came with total indifference to conventional needs and ambitions. She'd never met a junkie who wasn't politely eager to introduce others to the plangent transcendalities of the junkie lifestyle. Junkies would share anything: mosquitos, pills, beds, forks, combs, toothbrushes, food, and of course their drugs. Junkies were all knitted into a loose global macrame, the intercontinental freemasonry of narcotics.

Since they were allowed hearty supplies of any drug they could cook up, modern junkies were rarely violent. They rarely allowed themselves to be truly miserable. Still, they were all more or less suicidal.

Many junkies could talk with surprising poetic eloquence about the joys of internal chemistry. The most fluent and intellectualized junkies were generally the people who were most visibly falling apart. Junkies were just about the only people in the modern world who looked really sick. Junkies had boils and caries and stiff lifeless hair; junky squats had fleas and lice and sometimes that endangered species, the human pubic louse. Junkies had feet that peeled with hot itchy fungus, and noses that ran. Junkies coughed and scratched and had gummy bloodshot eyes. There were millions of people in the world who were elderly and in advanced decline, but only junkies had backslid to a twentieth-century standard of personal hygiene.

The junkies—a man and two women—made them welcome. There were two other men in the cellar as well, but they were peacefully unconscious in hammocks. The junkies were very tolerant of Brett's heap of stuff and, with a touching investment of effort, they somehow found a threadbare blanket to cover the goods. Then the male junkie went back to his disturbed routine. He was reading aloud from an Italiano translation of the *Tibetan Book of the Dead,* and had reached page 212. The two women, who were higher than kites, gave occasional bursts of rich, appreciative laughter and meditatively picked at their toenails.

Maya and Brett hoisted themselves into a double hammock. There were bloodstains in it here and there, and it smelled bad, but it had been a nicely woven hammock once and it was a lot cleaner than the floor. "Brett, how did you come to know these people?"

"Maya, can I ask you something? Just as a personal favor? My name's really not Brett. My name's Natalie."

"Sorry."

"There are two kinds of life, you know," said Natalie, spreading herself in the swaying hammock with great expertise. "There's the kind where you just grind on being very bourgeois. And there's the kind of life where you really try to become aware."

"That isn't news to me, I'm from San Francisco. So, what kind of crowbar are you using on the doors of perception, exactly?"

"Well, I'm kind of fond of lacrimogen."

"Oh, no. Couldn't you stick with something harmless like heroin?"

"Heroin shows up in your blood and your hair and they mark it down against you. But hey, everybody's brain has some lacrimogen. Lacrimogen's a natural neurochemical. It's a very vivid drug because it's surveillance-proof. Sure, if you use too much lacrimogen, it's a big problem, you get clinically depressed. But if you use just the right amount, lacrimogen really makes you a lot more aware."

"Oh, dear."

"Look, I'm a kid, all right?" Brett announced. "I mean, we both are, but I can admit that to myself, I really know just how bad that really is. You know why young people have it so hard today? It's not just that we're a tiny minority. Our real problem is that kids are so stoked on hormones that we live in a fantasy world. But that's not good enough for me; I can't live on empty hopes. I need a clear assessment of my situation."

"Brett, I mean Natalie, it takes a lot of maturity to live with genuine disillusionment."

"Well, I'll settle for artificial disillusionment. I know it's doing me a lot of good."

"I hardly see how that can be true."

"Then I'll show you why it's true. I'll make you a bet," Natalie declared. "We'll both do one hundred mikes of lacrimogen, okay? If that doesn't make you recognize at least one terrible lie about your life, I promise I'll give up lacrimogen forever."

"Really? I can hardly believe you'd keep that promise."

"Lacrimogen's not addictive, you know. You don't get the sweats or withdrawals or any of that nonsense. So of course I'd give it up, if I didn't know it was helping me."

"Listen, there's a monster suicide rate with lacrimogen. Old people take lacrimogen to work up the nerve to kill themselves."

"No, they don't, they take it so that they can put their lives into retrospective order. You can't blame the drug for that. If you need to work up the nerve to kill yourself, then it's pretty likely that you ought to go ahead and do it. People need to kill themselves nowadays, it's a social necessity. If lacrimogen lets you see that truth, and gets you past the scared feeling and the confusion, then more power to lacrimogen."

"Lacrimogen is dangerous."

"I hate safety. I hate everything about safety. They kill the spirit with safety. I'd rather be dead than safe."

"But you'd really give it up? If I took it with you, and then I told you to give it up?"

Natalie nodded confidently. "That's what I said. If you're too scared to do it with me, that's fine, I can understand that. But you've got no right to lecture me about it. Because you don't know what you're talking about."

Maya looked around the cellar. She knew she was in genuine danger now, and the threat had made the room become intensely real. The peeling walls, the cracked ceilings, and the huge and antiquated tincture set. The scattered books, the tincture bottles, the damp pillows, the broken bicycle, the underwear, the dripping tap, the rich, fruity, occluded tracheal snore from one of the unconscious junkies. Hairnets and locked shutters and the hissing rumble of a passing Roman trolley. A Brett place. She had followed Brett to this place, to this situation. She had followed Brett all the way.

"All right, I'll do it."

"Hey," Brett called out. "Antonio."

Antonio stopped his measured recitation and looked up politely.

"I'm running out of lacrimogen. I got only two doses left. Do you know where I can get some more?"

"Sure," Antonio said. "I can make lacrimogen. You want me to make it? For your beautiful friend? I can do it." He put his book aside and spoke to the women in rapid Italiano. The prospect of work seemed to please them all. Naturally, the first course of action was to do some stimulants.

"Please don't cry too loud," one of the women urged, rolling up her sleeves. She was very thin. "Kurt will wake up. Kurt hates it when people cry."

Brett produced the tag end of a roll of stickers from a glassine bag. She peeled off four ludicrously tiny adhesive dots. She attached two dots to the pulse point at her wrist, and another pair of dots to Maya's.

Nothing happened.

"Don't expect any rush of sensation," Brett said. "This isn't a mood-altering substance. This is a mood."

"Well, it's sure not doing much for me," Maya said with relief. "All I feel is tired and sleepy. I could use a bath."

"No bath here. They got a toilet. Behind that door. You don't mind paying for this, do you, Maya? Five marks? Just to keep them in feedstocks?"

It was technically illegal to sell drugs. You could barter them, you could give them away, you could make them yourself. Selling them was an offense. "If it will help."

Brett smiled, relieved. "I don't know why Novak wanted to make you look so weird and sinister. You're very sweet, you're really nice."

"Well, I have desires that don't accord with the status quo." She'd said that many times, and now, for the first time, she began to sense what the slogan really meant. Why vivid people had made those words their slogan, why they would say such an apparently silly thing and say it without a smile. The status quo was the sine qua non of denied desire. Desire was irrational and juicy and transgressive. To accept desire, to surrender yourself to desire . . . to explore desire, to seek out gratification. It was the polar opposite of wisdom and discretion.

And it was the core of junkie romance. Gratification as naked as geometry—the euclidean pleasures of the central nervous system, a pure form of carnality for the gray meat of the brain. An ultimate form of desire—not love, not greed, not hunger for power, just purified little molecular venoms that did marvelous intimate cellular things to gray meat. Insight swept over her in a wave. She hadn't seen the truth of the junkie life before because she'd been so busy despising them. Now she understood them better and she pitied them. The truth and the sadness were deeply and intimately linked. It was a truth that could not be grasped unless you were sad enough to let yourself understand.

Antonio and his two friends were busily working their tincture set. The proper use of a tincture set was something of a social art, it required composure and grace and foresight and attention to detail. The junkies had none of these qualities. They were awkward and rather clumsy and yet terribly determined. They were deeply intoxicated, so they made many small mistakes. Whenever they made a mistake they would retreat and try to think about it, and then they would mentally circle back to poke and prod and jiggle. It was like watching three little spiders gently preparing to eat a trapped and kicking insect.

She shuddered violently, and Brett gently stroked her arm. "Don't be afraid."

There hadn't been any fear at all until Brett unleashed the word. Then of course there was fear. A cold gush of nasty fear from a brimming reservoir like a vast black ocean. What had she to fear? Why get panicky all of a sudden? There was nothing to fear. Nothing, of course, except that she had surrendered herself to desire. Desire had grown in her aging brain in gray wedges of new neural flesh. Her youthful joie de vivre was every bit as counterfeit as the arachnid twitchings of a junkie. They dreamed of the artificial paradise, but she had become the artificial paradise.

She was blundering through Europe as if no one would ever guess the truth, but how could they fail to guess? She'd brazened her way through three months of outlaw existence with nothing to guard her but a mad veneer of perfect happiness and confidence. The eggshell surface of a crazy confidence trick. She'd been walking a suspension bridge of other people's disbelief. Only someone blind with manic exultation could believe that such a situation would last.

Of course they were going to catch her. Of course she would trip up eventually. Stark reality could shove its rhinoceros horn through the tissue of her fantasy at any moment. Denunciation and betrayal could come from any point of the compass. From Paul, who knew too much. From Josef, if he ever thought to bother. From Benedetta, who would turn on her in vengeful fury if she knew the ugly truth. What if Emil missed her and thought to ask a policeman for help?

The surge of terrible insight was enough to make her scramble headlong from the building, but the cruelly revelatory power of the drug froze her in place. Suppose she did run away again.

Suppose she jumped a train for Vladivostok or Ulan Bator or Johannesburg—what would happen if she ever got sick? Or if the treatment began to manifest side effects? How could she, a professional medical economist, have been so stupid? Of course a treatment as radical as NTDCD would manifest side effects—that was why they'd been wise enough to want to watch her closely in the first place. So that they could trace and study unexpected reactions. Especially in fast-growing tissue, like hair and nails . . .

Maya looked at her ragged fingertips and a whimper of anguish escaped her. How could she have done this to herself? She was a monster. She was a monster escaped from a cage and it was in the interests of everyone she knew, and everyone she met, to lock her up. She began to shake in abject terror.

"Maybe I shouldn't have given you so much," Brett said with concern. "But I didn't want you to take just a little lacrimogen, and ride it out all smug, and then make me give it up."

"I'm a monster," Maya said. Her lips began to tremble.

Brett put her arm around Maya's shoulders. "It's all right, sweetheart," she murmured. "You're not a monster. Everyone knows that you're very beautiful. You'd better cry some. With lacrimogen that always helps."

"I'm a monster," Maya insisted, and began obediently to cry.

"I never met a beautiful woman who wasn't deeply insecure," said Brett.

Antonio shuffled over and looked into the hammock. "Is she all right? Is she handling it?"

"She's not too great," Brett said. "What's that smell?"

"We overcooked the batch," Antonio said. "We have to flush and start over."

"What do you mean, flush?" Brett said tensely.

Antonio gestured at the bathroom door.

Brett sat up in the hammock, sending it swaying sickeningly. "Look, you can't flush a bad tincture down the commode! Are you crazy? You have to decompose a bad tincture inside the set. Man, they've got monitors in the sewer system! You can't just spew some bad chemical process into a city sewer. It might be toxic or carcinogenic! That makes environmental monitors go crazy!"

"We flushed bad batches before," Antonio said patiently. "We do it all the time."

"A bad lacrimogen run?"

"No, entheogens. But no problem."

"You are an irresponsible sociopath with no consideration for innocent people," Brett said mordantly, bitterly, and with complete accuracy.

Antonio grinned, maybe a little angry now, but too polite to show it. "You're always so nasty on lacrimogens, Natalie. If you want to be so nasty, get a boyfriend. You can feel just as bad from a love affair."

One of the women shuffled up. She was not Italian. Maybe Swiss. "Natalie, this isn't San Francisco," she said. "These are Roman sewers, the oldest sewers in the world. All catacombs and buried villas down there, dead temples of the virgins, drowned mosaics, Christian bones . . ." She blinked, and swayed a little. "Bad lacrimogen can't make old Roman ghosts any sorrier."

Brett shook her head. "You need to clean that tincture set, run a diagnostic, and then decompose the bad production. That's the proper method, that's all!"

"We're too tired," said Antonio. "Do you want some more or don't you?"

"I don't want anything out of that set," Brett said. "Do you think I'm crazy? That could poison me!" She burst into tears.

A sleeping junkie spoke up from his hammock. He was large and bulky, with heavy, threatening brows and four days of beard. "Do you mind?" he said in Irish-tinged English. "Do read aloud, my dears, converse, enjoy yourselves. But don't squabble and fuss. And especially, don't weep."

"Sorry, Kurt, very sorry," said Antonio. He carried a plastic-sealed pannikin behind the bathroom door. An ancient chain rattled, and water gurgled.

Kurt sat up. "My, our new guest is very lovely."

"She's on lacrimogen," Brett said defensively.

"Women need a man when they're on lacrimogen," rumbled Kurt. "Come cuddle up with me, darling. Cry yourself to sleep."

"I'd never sleep with anyone so dirty," Maya blurted.

"Women on lacrimogen are also very tactless," Kurt remarked. He turned away onto his side with a hammocky squeak.

There was silence for a while. Finally, Antonio picked up his book again and began to read aloud again.

"I'll tell you a secret," Brett whispered to Maya.

"What's that?"

"Let's lie down."

They lay down together in the hammock. Brett put both her arms around Maya's neck and looked into her eyes. They were both feeling so much pain that there was nothing but deep solace in the gesture. They were like two women who had crawled together from a burning car.

"I'm never going to make it," Brett said. A tear rolled slowly down her nose and fell onto Maya's cheek. "I want to do clothes, that's all I want. But I'll never make it. I'll never be as good as Giancarlo Vietti. He's a hundred and twelve years old. He has every file ever posted on couture, every book ever written. He's had his own couture house for seventy-five years. He's a multimillionaire with an enormous staff of people. He has everything, and he's going to keep it forever. There's just no way to challenge him."

"He'll have to die someday," Maya said.

"Sure. Maybe. But by that time I'll be ninety. I'll never get a chance to really live until I'm ninety. Vietti got to start young, he got to have experience, he got to be king of the world through this whole century. I'll never have that experience. By the time I'm ninety, I'll be turned to a stone."

"If he won't let you play in his world, then you'll have to make your own world."

"That's what all the vivid people say, but the old people won't let us. They won't give us anything but a sandbox. They won't give us real money or real power or any real chances." She drew a ragged breath. "And this is the very worst. Even if we had those things, we'd never be as good as they are. Compared to the gerontocrats, we're trash, we're kitsch, we're stupid little amateurs. I could be the most vivid girl in the world and I'd still be just a little girl. The gerontocrats, they're like ice on a pond. We're so deep down we'll never see the honest light of day. By the time our turn comes around, we'll be so old that we'll be cold blind fish, worse than Vietti is, a hundred times worse. And then the whole world will turn to ice."

She burst into wracking sobs.

Kurt sat up again. He was angry this time. "Do you mind? Who asked you here? If you can't get a grip, get out!"

"That's why I love junkies!" Brett shouted shrilly, sitting up red-faced and weeping. "Because they go where gerontocrats never go. To wrap up in a fantasy and die. Look at this place! This is what the whole world looks like when you're not allowed to live!"

"Yeah, okay, that's enough," agreed Antonio, carefully putting down his book. "Kurt, throw the little idiot out. Kick her hard into the street, Kurt."

"You kick her out," Kurt said, "you let her in."

There was a sudden violent burst from the bathroom. A blast of explosive compression. The door flew open and banged the wall hard enough to break a hinge.

Everyone stared in amazement. There were gurglings, then a sudden violent burst. Sewage jetted obliquely from the toilet and splattered the ceiling. Then rusty bolts snapped and the commode itself jumped from its concrete moorings and tumbled into the cellar.

A gleaming machine with a hundred thrashing legs came convulsing from the sewer. It was as narrow as a drainpipe and its thick metal head was a sewage-stained mass of bristles and chemical sensors. It grabbed at the doorframe with thick bristle-footed feet, and its hindquarters gouted spastic jets of white chemical foam.

It arched its plated sinuous back and howled like a banshee.

"Don't run, don't run," Kurt shouted, "they punish you more if you run," but of course everyone ran. They all leapt to their feet and scrambled up the stairs and out the door like a pack of panicked baboons.

Maya ran as well, dashing out into the damp and chilly Roman street. Then she turned and ran back into the squat.

She snatched up her backpack. The sewer guardian was sitting half-buried in an enormous wad of foaming sealant. It turned at her, aimed camera eyes at her, lifted two flanges on its neck, and began flashing red alarm lights. It then said something very ominous in Italiano. Maya turned and fled.

She reached the hotel at five in the morning. It had begun to rain a little, misting and damp.

She tottered into the hotel bar, knees buckling. It would have been lovely to go anywhere else, but she was tired of having no place to go. At least the walk and the lonely ride on an empty Roman trolley had given her something like a plan.

She would wait until Novak woke up, and then she would confess everything to him. Maybe, somehow, he would conquer his disgust and anger and take pity on her. Maybe he would even intercede somehow. And if he didn't, well, he deserved the chance to turn her in. The chance to avenge himself properly.

The cops in Praha seemed a little odd, so maybe they would be gentler about it than cops in Roma, or cops in Munchen, or cops in San Francisco. And she owed Novak that much; she owed him the truth. She owed the old man the truth after throwing her worthless self into his life.

She sat at a barstool, which whirled beneath her. The world went black for a moment and spun like a carousel. The dull realization struck her that she hadn't eaten all day. It had never once occurred to her to eat.

The bar was deserted. A bartender emerged from a staff door behind the bar. It was five in the morning, but maybe the doordog had tipped him off. The bartender strode over, a picture of solicitous concern. He was handsome and dapper and an infinitely better human being than she was. The hotel had very nice staffers, Roman people in their forties, kids who made it their business to serve the rich. "Signorina?"

"I need a drink," Maya groaned.

The bartender smiled gallantly. "A long night, signorina? An unlucky night? May I suggest a triacylglycerol frappé?"

"Great. Make that a double. And don't spare the saturated fats."

He brought her a tall frappé and a squat little clear protein chaser and a fluted bowl of Roman finger snacks. The first cold mouthful hit her such a metabolic shock that she almost passed out. But then it warmed inside her and began to seep into her famished bloodstream.

By the time the frappé was half gone, the panic had left her. She was able to sit up straight on the barstool. She stopped trembling, and kicked off her shoes. The bartender wandered tactfully to the end of the bar and engaged in some menu-pecking ritual with a partially disassembled house robot.

She opened her backpack and fetched out her compact and looked at her face and shuddered. She scraped the worst of the damage off with a cream-wipe and touched fresh lipstick on.

A Roman in elegant evening dress wandered into the bar from the direction of the house casino. He tapped on the bar with the edge of a poker chip and ordered caffeine macchiato. She could tell from the brittle look on his powdered and aquiline face that the tables had been cruel to him tonight.

The Roman took his demitasse, sat on a barstool two seats away, and glanced at her in the mirror behind the bar. Then he turned and looked at her directly. He looked at her legs, her bare arms, her bare feet. He judged her bustline and approved wholeheartedly. He deeply and sincerely admired the intimate contact of her hips with the barstool. It was a gaze of direct and total male sexual interest. A look that could not have cared less that her mind was a shredded mess of anguish. A warm and scratchy look that wrapped around her flesh like a Mediterranean sun.

He shot two inches of cream-colored tailored cuff and put his elbow on the bar and propped his sleek dark head on his hand. Then he smiled.

"Ciao," she said.

"Ciao *bella*."

"You speak English?"

He shook his head mournfully and made a little moue of disappointment.

"Never mind then," she said, and beckoned with one finger. "This is your lucky night, handsome."

5

ovak found her a place in Praha. She got a job cat-sitting. There wasn't any money in it, but the cats were lonely.

The place belonged to a former actress named Olga Jeskova. Miss Jeskova had appeared in several of Novak's early virtualities, among other thespian efforts. She had salted her money away in Czech real estate speculation, and now, seventy years later, she was quite well-to-do. Miss Jeskova usually spent Praha's foggy winters somewhere in the chic and sunny Sinai, doing unlikely medical spa things.

Miss Jeskova's Praha flat was on the fifteenth floor of a seventy-story high-rise in the edge-city ring. It was a twenty-minute tube ride to the Old Town, but that was a small price to pay for the space and the luxury. The actress's cats were two white furry Persians. The cats seemed to have been integrated in some biocybernetic fashion into the texture of the flat. The predominant note in the flat was white fur: white fur bed, white fur toilet, white fur massage lounger, white fur hassock, white fur net terminal. At night two very odd devices like walking nutcrackers came out and groomed everything with their teeth.

On April 20, Maya took her equipment and went to Emil's flat. Emil was up and working. He answered the door in his mud-smeared apron.

"Ciao Emil," Maya said.

"Ciao," Emil said, and smiled guardedly.

"I'm the photographer," she told him.

"Oh. How nice." Emil opened his door.

There was a girl in the apartment. She had waist-length hair and a black cowboy hat and a fur-trimmed coat and slacks. She was eating a goulash. She was Nipponese. She was lovely.

"I'm the photographer," Maya said. "I'm here to document Emil's latest work."

The girl nodded. "I am Hitomi."

"Ciao Hitomi, *jmenuji se* Maya."

"He is forgetful," said Hitomi, apologetically. "We weren't expecting. You want some goulash?"

"No thank you," Maya said. "Hitomi, do you photograph?"

"Oh no," said Hitomi emphatically, "I do wanderjahr from Nippon, we hate cameras."

Maya cleared the worktable, set out a rippling sheet of chameleon photoplastic, and set up her tripod. White against white would work best for the china. Diagonal lighting to reveal the hollowed shape of cups and saucers. The pots and urns were all about shape and tactility. She had been thinking about this project every day. She had mapped it all out in her head.

She was beginning to appreciate the lovely qualities of optic fibercord. You could do almost anything with optic fibercord, tune it to any color in the spectrum, bend it into any shape, and it would glow in any brightness along any section of its length. Soft, even shadows. Or strong, sculptural shadows. The deep shadows of backlighting. Or you could kick it way up and get very contrasty.

Novak said that if you exposed for the shadows the rest would come by itself. Novak said that all mystery was in the shadows. Novak said that he had truly never mastered shadows in ninety years. Novak said a great many things and she listened as she'd never listened to anyone before. She went home at night and took notes and fed the actress's cats and thought and dreamed photography for days and days.

"It's good you know your job so well," said Emil cordially. "I haven't looked at some of these pieces in . . . oh, such a long time."

"Don't let me take you from your work, Emil."

"Oh no my dear, it's a pleasure." Emil fetched equipment and moved the pots a bit and was very helpful.

She would have liked to take the raw shots back to the cats' apartment and touch them up with her wand, but the wand was terribly addictive. Once you got down to pixel level there was no end to all that gripping and blurring and twisting and mixing. . . . Knowing when to stop, what to omit, was every bit as important as any postproduction craftwork. Elegance was restraint. So she printed the photos out on the spot on Novak's borrowed scroller. Then she blew a bit of dust from the photo album and slipped the photos neatly into place.

"These are fine," Emil said sincerely. "I'd never seen such justice done to my work. I think you should sign these."

"No, I don't think that will be necessary."

"It was so good of you to come. What do I owe you?"

"No charge, Emil, it's just apprentice work. I was glad to have the experience."

"No one so determined should be called a mere apprentice," said Emil gallantly. "I hope you'll come again. Have we worked together before? It seems to me that I know you."

"It does? You do?"

Hitomi sidled over rhythmically and slipped her slender arm over Emil's shoulders.

"It wasn't you," Emil said, leafing through his album. "Your photos are much better than these others."

"We might have met at the Tête du Noyé," Maya suggested,

unable to resist. "I go there rather often. Are you going there later? There's a meeting soon."

Emil looked up at Hitomi adoringly, and caught her slender hand. "Oh, no," he said, "we've given up that little place."

———

"[It will be good to see my old friend Klaus,]" said Novak in Czestina as they walked together down Mikulandska Street. "[Klaus used to come to my Tuesdays.]"

"*Opravdu?*" said Maya.

"[They were Milena's Tuesdays, to tell the truth. Our friends always pretended they were my little meetings, but of course without Milena no one would have come.]"

"This was before Klaus went to the moon?"

"Oh, yes . . . [Good old Klaus was quite hairless in those days. . . . He was a microbiologist at Charles University. Klaus and I, we did a series of experimental landscapes, using photoabsorbent bacteria. . . . The light shone on his gel plate of inoculant. The exposure would last many days. Germs grew only where the light fed them. Those images had the quality of an organic daguerreotype. Then, over the weeks that followed, we would watch those plates slowly rot. Sometimes . . . quite often, really . . . that rot produced fantastic beauty.]"

"I'm so glad you're coming with me to meet my friends tonight, Josef. It means so much to me, truly."

Novak smiled briefly. "[These little émigré communities in Praha, they may love the local architecture, but they never pay proper attention to us Czechs. Perhaps if we catch the children young enough, we can teach them better habits.]"

Novak spoke lightly, but he had combed his hair, he had dressed, he had taken the trouble to wear his artificial arm. He was coming with her because she had earned a little measure of his respect.

She had come to know her teacher a little. There were veins of deceit and venality and temper in him, like the bluish veins in an old cheese. But it was not wickedness. It was stubbornness, the measure of a crabbed, perverse integrity. Josef Novak was entirely his own man. He had lived for decades, openly and flagrantly, in a way that she had dared to live only deep inside. Though he never seemed happy, and he had probably never been a happy man, he was in some deep sense entirely imperturbable. He was utterly and entirely Josef Novak. He would be Josef Novak until the day he died.

He would be dead within five years—or so she judged. He was frail, and had been very badly injured once. There were steps he might have taken toward increased longevity, but he seemed to consider this struggle to be vulgar. Josef Novak was one hundred twenty-one years old, far older than the people of his generation had ever expected to become. He was a relic, but Maya still felt a bitter sense of injustice at the thought of Novak's mortality. Novak often spoke of his own death, and clearly felt no fear of passing, but it seemed to her that a just universe would have let a creature like Josef Novak live, somehow, forever. He was her teacher, and she had come to love him very much.

The Tête was lively tonight. The crowd was much larger than she had expected and there was a tension and a vibrancy she hadn't sensed before. She and Novak logged in at the bar. Novak reached out about four meters and gently finger-tapped Klaus's helmet. Klaus turned, startled, then grinned bearishly. The two old men began to chat in Czestina.

"Ciao Maya."

"Ciao Marcel." She had come to know Marcel on the net—to the extent that anybody knew Marcel. The red-haired and loquacious Marcel never stopped talking, but he was not a revelatory or confiding man. He was twenty-seven years old and had already circled the world, by his own estimation, some three hundred and fourteen times. Marcel had no fixed address. He had not had a fixed address since the age of two. Marcel basically lived in trains.

Benedetta, who loved to talk scandal, claimed that Marcel had Williams syndrome. In his case, it was a deliberate derangement, an abnormal enlargement of Heschl's gyrus in the primary

auditory cortex. Marcel had hyperacusis and absolute pitch; he was
a musician, and a sonic artificer for virtualities. The syndrome had
also drastically boosted Marcel's verbal skills, which made him an
endless source of anecdotes, speculation, brilliant chatter, unlikely
linkages, and endless magnetic trains of thought that would hit a
mental switch somewhere and simply . . .

Benedetta claimed that the pope also had Williams syndrome. Supposedly this was the secret of the pope's brilliant ser-
monizing. Benedetta believed that she had the dirt on everybody.

"How chic you look, Maya. How lovely to physically witness you." Marcel's coat was a patchwork of urban mapping. Marcel lived in that coat, and slept in it, and used it as a navigation aid.
Now that she knew that Marcel's jacket was so plonkingly useful,
it somehow seemed rather less vivid. Paul would have described
that perception as a category error.

She kissed Marcel's bearded cheek. "You, too."

"Congratulations on your Italian venture. They say Vietti's
dying for another session."

"Giancarlo's not dying, darling, you mustn't get your hopes
up."

"I see you brought your sponsor. Your photographer. He
must be your man of the hour."

"He's my teacher, Marcel. Don't be gauche."

"I have my net set to read your posts in Français," said Marcel. "I wish you would post more often. In Français, your commentary is remarkable. Aspects of wit emerge that one simply can't
find in English anymore."

"Well, there's a quality in a good translation that you can
never capture with the original."

"There's another one, that's it exactly. How is it that you do
that? Is it deliberate?"

"You're very perceptive, darling. If you don't get me a frappé
I'm afraid I'll kiss you."

Marcel weighed these possibilities and got her the frappé. She
sipped it and gazed about the bar, leaning on one elbow. "Why
do things seem so *très* vivid tonight?"

"Do they? Paul has plans for a spring outing. A major immersion. I hope you'll come."

"Oh, I wouldn't miss a major immersion for anything." She had no idea what Marcel was talking about. "Where is Paul?"

Paul was sitting among a group of perhaps a dozen people. He had them spellbound.

Paul opened a small metal shipping canister and removed a life-size carving of a garden toad. The squat and polished toad appeared to be chiseled from a solid ruby.

"Is this one beautiful?" Paul said. "You tell me, Sergei."

"Well," said Sergei, "if it's a product of the Fabergé workshop as you tell us it is, then of course it's beautiful. Look at that exquisite workmanship."

"It's a toad, Sergei. Are toads beautiful?"

"Of course toads can be beautiful. Here is your proof."

"If someone said you were as beautiful as a toad, would you be pleased?"

"You are changing the context," Sergei said sulkily.

"But isn't that what the piece itself is doing? The shock of disbelief is the core of its aesthetic. Imagine people in the year 1912, taking a rare jewel and spending months of dedicated hand labor turning it into a toad. Isn't that perverse? It's that very perversity which gives the piece its trophy meaning. This is a Fabergé original, designed for a Czarist aristocrat. Czarist society was a culture generating jeweled toads."

Paul's little crowd exchanged uneasy glances. They scarcely dared to interrupt him.

"Still—are we to imagine that Czarist aristocrats believed that toads are beautiful? Does anyone here imagine that some Czarist aristocrat *asked* the Fabergé atelier to make her a beautiful toad?" Paul gazed about the circle. "But don't you imagine she was pleased with the result? Once she possessed it, she surely found it beautiful."

"I love the toad," Maya volunteered. "I wouldn't mind owning that toad myself."

"What would you do with it, Maya?"

"I'd keep it on my bureau and admire it every day."

"Then take it," Paul said. He handed it to her. It was surprisingly heavy; it felt just like a red stone toad.

"Of course that's not really a valuable Fabergé heirloom," Paul told them all, casually. "It's an identical museum replica. The Fabergé original was laser scanned to an accuracy of a few microns, and then instantiated in modern vapor deposition. Oddly, there were even a few flaws introduced, so that the artificial ruby is indistinguishable from the genuine corundum that forms a natural ruby. About a hundred toads were made in all."

"Oh, well, of course," said Maya. She looked at the little red toad. It was somewhat less beautiful now, but it was still a remarkable likeness of a toad.

"Actually, there were over ten thousand made. It's not artificial ruby, either. I lied about that. It's only plastic."

"Oh."

"It wasn't even fresh plastic," Paul said relentlessly. "It was recycled garbage plastic, mined from a twentieth-century dump. I just pretended it was the Fabergé original, in order to make my point."

"Oh, no," Maya mourned. People began laughing.

"I'm joking, of course," Paul said cheerily. "In point of fact, that truly is a Fabergé original. It was made in Moskva in 1912. The labor took fourteen skilled artisans a full five months to complete. It's one of a kind, completely irreplaceable. I've borrowed it from the Antikensammlungen in Munchen. For heaven's sake, don't drop it."

"You'd better have it back, then," Maya said.

"No, you hold it for a while, my dear."

"I don't think so. It wears me out when it keeps mutating like this."

"What if I told you that it wasn't even made by Fabergé? That in fact, it was an actual toad? Not human workmanship mimicking a toad, but an actual scanned garden toad. Cast in—well, you can choose the material."

Maya looked at the sculpture. It was a sweet thing to hold, and there was something about it that she truly did like, but it was making her brain hurt. "You're really asking me if a photograph of a toad can have the same beauty as a painting of a toad."

"Can it?"

"Maybe they're beautiful in different categories." She looked around. "Would someone else hold this, please?"

Sergei took it off her hands with a show of bravado and pretended to smack the toad against the table. "Don't," Paul said patiently. "Just a moment ago you admired it. What changed your mind?"

Maya left to look for Benedetta. She found her in a little crowd behind the bar. "Ciao Benedetta."

Benedetta rose and embraced her. "[This is Maya, everyone.]"

Benedetta had brought four of her Italian friends. They were polite and sober and steady eyed and in ominous control of themselves. They looked very intelligent. They looked very self-possessed and rather well dressed. They looked about as dangerous as any kids she had seen in a long time. Of course they were all women.

Benedetta wedged her into a place at the table. "I'm sorry that I have no Italiano," Maya said, sitting. "I have a translator, but I have to speak in English."

"We want to know, what is your relationship with Vietti?" said one of the young women quietly.

Maya shrugged. "He thinks I'm cute. That's all."

"What's your relationship with Martin Warshaw?"

Maya glanced at Benedetta, startled and hurt. "Well, if you have to know, it was his palazzo. You know about the palazzo?"

"We know all about the palazzo. What is your relationship with Mia Ziemann?"

"Who's that?" Maya said.

The interrogator shrugged and sat back with a dismissive flutter of her hand. "Well, we're fools to trust this person."

"[Of course we're fools,]" said Benedetta heatedly. "[We're fools to trust one another. We're fools to trust anyone. So now tell me of a better place where we can install those machineries.]"

"Benedetta, who are these people?"

"They are mathematicians," Benedetta said. "Programmers. Rebels. And visionaries. And they are very good friends of mine."

Radical students, Maya thought. Aflame with imagination because they were so wonderfully free of actual knowledge. "Who's the oldest person here?" she asked guardedly.

"You are, of course," said Benedetta, blinking.

"Well, never mind that question then. What's all this have to do with me anyway?"

"I'll draw you a little picture," Benedetta said. She spread out her furoshiki and pulled a stylus from behind her ear. "Let me tell you an interesting fact of life. About the medical–industrial complex." She drew an x-y graph with two swift strokes. "This bottom axis is the passage of time. And this is the increase in life expectancy. For every year that passes, posthuman life expectancy increases by about a month."

"So?"

"The curve is not strictly linear. The rate of increase is itself increasing. Eventually the rate of increase will reach the speed of one year per year. At that point, the survivors become effectively immortal."

"Sure they do. Maybe."

"Well, of course it's not true 'immortality.' There is still a mortality rate from accident and misadventure. At the singularity"—Benedetta drew a little black X—"the average human life span, with accident included, becomes about fourteen hundred and fifty years."

"How lovely for that generation."

"The first generation to reach the singularity will become the first truly genuine gerontocracy. It will be a generation which does not die out. A generation that can dominate culture indefinitely."

"Well, I've heard that sort of speculation before, darling. It's a nice line of hype and it always struck me as an interesting theory."

"Once it was theory. For you, it's theory. For us, it's reality. Maya, we *are* those people. We're the lovely generation. We are the first people who were born just in time. We are the first true immortals."

"You're the first *immortals?*" Maya said slowly.

"Yes, we are; and what is more, we know that we are." Benedetta sat back and tucked her stylus in her hair.

"So why are you meeting in a sleazy art bar in some little political cabal?"

"We have to meet somewhere," Benedetta said, and smiled.

"It had to be some generation," said another woman peevishly. "We are the someones. We don't impress you much. Well, no one ever said we would impress you."

"So you really believe you're immortals." Maya looked at the scrawl on the furoshiki. "What if there's a hitch in your calculations? Maybe the rate will slow."

"That could be quite serious," Benedetta said. She pulled her stylus and carefully redrew the slope of the curve. "See? Very bad. We get only nine hundred years."

Maya looked at the base of the fatal little curve. For her, it climbed. For them, it rocketed. "This curve means I'll never make it," she realized sadly. "This curve proves that I'm doomed."

Benedetta nodded, delighted to see her catching on. "Yes, darling, we know that. But we don't hold that fact against you, truly."

"We still need the palazzo," said another woman.

"Why do you need a palazzo?"

"We plan to install some things in it," Benedetta said.

Maya frowned. "Isn't there trouble enough inside that place, for heaven's sake? What kind of things?"

"Cognition things. Perception things. Software factories for the holy fire."

Maya thought about it. The prospect sounded very far-fetched. "What's that supposed to get you?"

"It gets us a way to change ourselves. A chance to make our own mistakes, instead of repeating the mistakes of others. We hope it will make us artificers who deserve our immortality."

"You really think you can do—what?—really radical cognitive transforms of some kind? And just with a virtuality?"

"Not with the kind of virtuality protocols they allow us nowadays. Of course you can't do any such thing where civil support is watching, because they designed the public networks to be perfectly safe and reliable. But with the kind of protocols they don't imagine yet—well, yes. Yes, Maya. That's exactly what we think we can do with a virtuality."

Maya sighed. "Let me get this straight. You're going to open up my palace, and install some kind of brand-new, illegal, mutant, brain-damaging virtuality system?"

" 'Cognitive enhancement' is a much better term," Benedetta said.

"That is truly crazy talk, Benedetta. I can't believe you mean that. That sounds just like some kind of junkie drug scheme."

"Gerontocrats are always making that category error," Benedetta said dismissively. "Software isn't neurochemistry! We—our generation—we *know* virtuality! We grew up with it! It's a world that today's old people will never truly understand."

"You certainly are terribly serious about this," Maya said, looking slowly around the table. "If what you tell me is true . . . well, you've got it made. Don't you? Someday, you'll run the whole world. More or less forever, right? So why make trouble now? Why don't you just wait a while? Wait until you reach that little black X on the graph."

"Because when we reach the singularity, we must be prepared for it. Worthy of it. Otherwise we will become even more stale and stupid than the ruling class is now. They're only mortals, and they are nice enough to die eventually, but we're not mortals and we won't die. If we obey their rules when we take power, we'll bore the world to death. Once we repeat their mistakes, our generation will repeat them forever. Their padded little nurse's paradise will become our permanent tyranny."

"Look, you'll never manage this," Maya said bluntly. "It's dangerous. It's a reckless, silly, extravagant gesture that can only get you in trouble. They'll surely find out what you're doing in there, and they'll jump on you. You can't keep any major secrets from the polity for eighty years. Come on, you're just a bunch of kids. I'm a gerontocrat myself, and I can't keep my precious secrets for three lousy months!"

Another woman—she hadn't been saying much—spoke up suddenly. Very diplomatically. "Mrs. Ziemann, we're truly sorry that we had to discover your secrets. We never wanted to spoil your secret life."

"You're not half as sorry as I am, darling."

The speaker pulled off her spex. "We'll never tell. We have learned what you are, Mrs. Ziemann, but we were forced to do that investigation. We are not a bit shocked by our findings. Truly. Are we?"

She looked around the table. All the others gamely pretended not to be shocked.

"We are modern young people," said the little diplomat. "We are free of old-fashioned prejudices. We admire you. We applaud you. You encourage us by your personal example. We think you are a fine posthuman being."

"That's so lovely," Maya said. "I'm really moved by that sentiment. I'd be even more touched if I didn't know you were flattering me. For your own purposes."

"Please try to understand us. We're not reckless. This is an act of deep foresight on our part. We do this because we believe in the cause of our generation. We are prepared to face the consequences. We are young and inexperienced, that is true. But we have to act. Even if they arrest us. Even if they punish us very severely. Even if they send us all the way to the moon."

"Why? Why are you risking this? You never cleared this through proper channels, you never asked anyone's permission. What gives you any right to change the way the world works?"

"Because we are scientists."

"You never put this question to a vote, that I ever heard of. This proposal hasn't been properly discussed. It's not democratic. You don't have the informed consent of the people you are going to affect. What gives you any right to change the way people think?"

"Because we are artists."

Another woman spoke up suddenly in Italiano. "[Look, I can barely understand all this stupid English. And politics in English are the worst. But that woman is not a hundred years old. This has got to be a scam.]"

"[She is a hundred years old,]" Benedetta insisted calmly, "[and what's more, she has the holy fire.]"

"[I don't believe it. I bet her photographs stink of death, just like Novak's. She's very pretty I suppose, but for heaven's sake, any idiot can look pretty.]"

"Do it," Maya said.

Benedetta brightened. "Truly? You mean it?"

"Do it. Of course I mean it. I don't care what happens to me. If it works—if it even looks like it works—if they even *think* it looks like it works—then they'll smother me alive. But that doesn't matter, because they're going to get me anyway. I'm doomed. I know that. I'm a freakish creature. If you really knew or cared about me or my precious life, you'd know all that already. You had better do whatever you have to do. Do it quick."

She knocked the chair back and walked away.

Back to Paul's table. She was in anguish, but sitting in the gaseous aura of Paul's charisma was much, much better than sitting alone. Paul sipped his *limoncello* and smiled. He had a new furoshiki spread before him on the table, with a lovely tapestrylike pointillistic photo of a desert sunset. "Isn't this sunset beautiful?"

"Sometimes," someone offered guardedly.

"I didn't tell you that I changed the color registers." Paul tapped the furoshiki with his fingernail. The sunset altered drastically. "This was the actual, original sunset. Is this sunset more beautiful than my altered version?"

No one answered.

"Suppose you could manipulate a real sunset—manipulate the atmosphere at will. Suppose you could turn up the red and turn down the yellow, as you pleased. Could you make a sunset more beautiful?"

"Yes," said a listener. "No," insisted another.

"Let's consider a martian sunset, from one of the martian telepresence sites. Another planet's sunset, one we can't experience directly with human flesh. Are the sunsets on Mars less beautiful because of machine intermediation?"

Silent pain.

A woman appeared at the head of the stairs in a heavy lined cape and gray velvet gloves. She wore a tricorn hat, glittering spex, an open-collared white blouse, a necklace of dark carved wood. She had a profile of classical perfection: straight nose, full lips, broad brow; the haute couture sister of the Statue of Liberty. She proceeded down the stairs of the bar with the stagy precision of a prima ballerina. She walked with more than grace. She walked with martial authority. She had two small white dogs in tow.

Silence spread over the Tête du Noyé.

"Bonsoir à tout le monde," the stranger proclaimed at the foot of the stairs, and she smiled like a sphinx.

Paul stood quickly, with something between a half bow and a reluctant beckoning. When they saw that he truly meant to speak to her, his little circle of listeners vacated his table with haste.

Paul offered his new guest a chair.

"How well you look, Helene. What are you drinking tonight?"

The policewoman sat with an elegant little whirl of her cape. "I'll have what the gentleman in the spacesuit is having," she said in English. She detached the dogs from their narrow gleaming leashes—just as if dogs of that sort needed leashes.

Paul hastily signaled the bar. "We were just having a small debate on aesthetics."

Helene Vauxcelles-Serusier removed her spex, folded them, made them vanish into a slit in the cape. Maya stared in astonishment. Helene's natural eyes, slate gray, astoundingly beautiful, tremendously remote, were far more intimidating than any computer-assisted perception set. "What charming preoccupations you have, Paul."

"Helene, do you think a mechanically assisted sunset can be more beautiful than a natural sunset?"

"Darling, there hasn't been a natural sunset since the dawn of the Industrial Revolution." Helene glanced briefly at Maya, then pinned her with the focused shaft of her attention like a moth in a cigar box. "Please don't stand there, my child. Do have a seat with us. Have we met?"

"Ciao Helene. I'm Maya."

"Oh, yes! Vietti's girl, on the net. I knew that I'd seen you. But you're lovely."

"Thank you very much." Maya sat. Helene studied her with grave interest and deep benevolence. It felt exactly like being x-rayed.

"You're charming, my dear. You don't seem one bit as sinister as you do in that terrible old man's photographs."

"The terrible old man is standing right over there at the bar, Helene."

"Oh dear," said Helene, deeply unmoved. "I'll never learn tact, will I? Really, that was so bad of me. I must go see your friend Josef and apologize from the bottom of my heart." She rose and left for the bar.

"Good heavens, Paul," Maya said slowly, watching Helene glide away. "I've never, ever seen such a—"

Paul made the slightest possible throat-cutting gesture and gazed at his feet. Maya shut up and looked down. One of Helene's tiny white dogs looked up at her with the chilly big-science intensity of an interplanetary probe.

Bouboule appeared. Sober and anxious. "Ciao Maya."

"Ciao Bouboule."

"Some of the girls are going for the breathe of air. Will you come with us? For a moment?"

"Certainly, darling." Maya gave Paul a silent look full of meaning, and Paul looked back, with a gaze of such masculine trench-warfare gallantry that she wanted to tie a silken banner to him.

She followed Bouboule through an unmarked door at the back of the bar, then up four flights of steep, switchback, iron-railed stairs. Bouboule had her marmoset with her. Maya had never felt so glad to see a monkey.

Bouboule led her through the junk-cluttered attic, and then up a black iron ladder. Bouboule threw back a heavy wooden trapdoor and they emerged on the slope of the ancient tiled roof of the Tête du Noyé. Now that it was spring, Praha's winter overcast had finally been chased away. The night was full of young stars.

Bouboule closed the trapdoor with a clunk and spoke for the first time. "Now I think it's safe to talk."

"Why is that cop here?"

"Sometimes she comes, sometimes she doesn't," Bouboule said dourly. "There's nothing we can do."

It was a sharp night. Cold and still. The marmoset chattered in distress. "[Be good, my Patapouff,]" Bouboule chided in Français. "[Tonight you must guard me.]" The marmoset seemed to understand this. He adjusted his tiny top hat and looked about as fierce as a yellow two-kilo primate could manage.

Maya scrambled with Bouboule to the peak of the roof, where they sat without a trace of comfort on the narrow ridgeline of arched greenish tiles.

The trapdoor opened again. Benedetta and Niko emerged.

"Is she onto us tonight?" Benedetta said anxiously.

Bouboule shrugged, and sniffed. "[I didn't tell. You and your little politicals, you are so secret with me that I couldn't tell if I wanted.]"

"Ciao Niko," Maya said. She reached down and helped Niko to the peak of the roof.

"We didn't meet in flesh before," said Niko, "but what you say on the net, it's very funny."

"You're very sweet to say that."

"I heal from that black eye your little friend Klaudia gave me, so I decide, I like you anyway."

"That's very good of you, Niko, dear. Considering."

"It's so cold," complained Bouboule, hugging her arms. "It's so stupid that the Widow can drive us to this. For two marks I'd run down there and slap her face."

"Why do they call her the Widow?" Maya said. The four of them were now squatting like four vivid magpies on the peak of the roof. The question seemed ideal for the circumstances.

"Well," said Bouboule, "most women get over sex in later life. But not the Widow. She keeps marrying."

"She always marries men of a certain type," said Benedetta. "Artists. Very self-destructive artists."

"She marries the dead-at-forty," said Niko. "Every time."

"She tries to save the poor gifted boys from themselves," said Benedetta.

"Had any luck?" Maya asked.

"So far, six dead ones," Bouboule said.

"That's got to hurt," Maya said.

"I grant her this much," said Benedetta. "She never marries them until they are really far gone. And I think she does keep them alive and working a little extra while."

"Any boy in her bed is too afraid to die," Niko said sweetly.

Bouboule nodded. "When she sells their work later, she always holds out for top mark! She makes their reputation in the art world! Such a lovely trick! Don't you know."

"I see," said Maya. "It's a coup de grâce, then. It's a charity."

Benedetta sneezed, then waved her hand. "You must be wondering why I called you here tonight."

"Do tell us," urged Maya, cupping her chin.

"Darling, we want to make you one of us tonight."

"Really?"

"But we have a little test for you first."

"A little test. But of course."

Benedetta pointed down the length of the roof. The roofline stretched for the length of the bar. At the roof's far edge rose the broad metal post of a shallow celestial bowl. Klaus's satellite antenna. Maybe twenty meters away.

"Yes?" Maya said.

Benedetta plucked the stylus from her hair. She adjusted a tiny knob, then bent over carefully and touched the stylus to a ceramic tile. Sparks flew. Blackness etched its way into the tile.

"Sign our membership list," Benedetta said. She handed Maya the stylus.

"Wonderful. Good idea. Where do I sign?"

"You sign on that post." Benedetta pointed at the satellite dish.

"You walk," Niko said.

"You mean I walk from here to there, along the peak of this roof."

"She's so clever," said Bouboule to Niko. Niko nodded smugly.

"So I just walk twenty meters in the dark along the peak of a slippery tile roof with a four-story drop on both sides," Maya said. "That's what you want from me. Right?"

"Do you remember," said Benedetta, quietly, "that vivid friend of yours in Roma? Little Natalie?"

"Natalie. Sure. What about her?"

"You asked me to look after your friend Natalie a little."

"Yes, I did."

"I did that for you," Benedetta said. "Now I know your Natalie. She could never pass this test. You know why? Because she'll stop in the middle, and she'll know that she can't win. Then the fear will kill her. The blackness and the badness will take her by her little beating heart, and she'll slip. Down she goes. Off the edge, darling. Bang, bang, bang, down the tiles. And then hard onto the cold old streets of Praha. If she's lucky, she'll land on her head."

"But since you are one of us," Bouboule said, "it's not risky."

"It only *looks* risky," offered Niko brightly.

"If these tiles were on the ground in the old town square, any fool could walk them," said Benedetta. "No one would ever slip or fall. The tiles are not dangerous. The danger is inside you. In your head, in your heart. It's your self that is the danger. If you can possess your self, then you go sign your name on the post and you walk back to us. It is safe as a pillow, safe as a bed; no, darling, it's safer than that, because there are men in the world. But to walk beneath the stars—well, it's in you, or it isn't in you."

"Go sign your name for us, darling," said Bouboule.

"Then come back to us and be our sister," said Niko.

Maya looked at them. They were perfectly serious. They meant it. This was how they lived.

"Well, I'm not gonna do it in heels," she said. She pulled off her shoes and stood up. It was good that Novak had taught her to walk a little. She fixed her eyes on the distant glow of the dish and she walked the spine of the roof. Nothing could stop her. She was perfectly happy and confident. Then she wrote:

MIA ZIEMANN WAS HERE

In a blast of sparks. It looked very nice there on the post with all the other names. So she did a little drawing, too.

The way back was harder because her bare feet were so cold. The tiles hurt her, and she picked her way more slowly, and this gave her more time to think. She would not fall, but it occurred to her in a cold black flash that she might deliberately throw herself from the roof. There was bittersweet appeal in the idea. If she was Mia Ziemann, as she had just proclaimed herself to be, then there was part of Mia Ziemann she had not yet made her peace with. This was the large and deeply human part of Mia Ziemann that was truly tired of life and genuinely anxious to be dead.

But she was so much stronger than that now.

"We hoped you would blow us a kiss," Benedetta said, scooting over to make room.

"I save that for gerontocrats," Maya said. She gave Benedetta the stylus.

The trapdoor opened a bit. One of Helene's dogs squirmed out. A little white dog had no business on a steep tile roof, but the dog walked like no dog had any business walking. It crept like a gecko, like a salamander. It saw them and it skidded a bit on the tile in surprise and it whimpered.

"*Voici un raton!*" Bouboule shouted. "Patapouff, *defends-moi!*"

A screech, a catapulting flash of golden fur. Primates were smarter than canines. Primates could climb like anything. The dog yelped in terror and tumbled from the edge of the roof with a howl of despair.

"Oh, poor baby," said Bouboule, hugging her shivering marmoset, "you have lost your fine chapeau."

"No, I see it," said Niko. "It's in the gutter." She scrambled down and fetched the tiny hat and brought it back.

They were silent for a moment, weighing the consequences.

"We'd better not go back down. You know another way out?" Maya said to Benedetta.

"I specialize in other ways out," said Benedetta.

───────────

The four of them caught the tube and split up. It seemed wisest. Maya took Benedetta home with her. She and Benedetta had a lot to discuss. Two in the morning found them nibbling canapés in the actress's white furry apartment. Then Novak called her on the actress's netlink. The screen was blank, a voice call. Novak hated synchronous video.

"You don't meet in the Tête again," he told her somberly.

"No?"

"She wept for her little dog. Klaus won't have that. It was cruel and stupid."

"I'm sorry for the accident, Josef. It was very sudden."

"You're a bad and destructive girl."

"I don't mean to be. Truly."

"Helene understands you far, far better than you will ever understand Helene. She means so well and has no malice, but how she suffers! She won't allow herself any luck." Novak sighed. "Helene was rude to me tonight. Can you believe that, girl? It's a tragedy to see a grande dame being crass. And in public! It means she is afraid, you see."

"I'm sorry that she was rude."

"If you could have known her, Maya, when she was young. A great patroness of the arts. A woman of taste and discernment. She asked for nothing but to help us. But the parasites crowded around her, taking advantage of her. Feeding on her, for decades. Never forgiving her anything. They have embittered her. She's defending you, you should know that. She defends you from far worse things than Helene Vauxcelles-Serusier. She guards the young people in artifice. Helene still believes."

"Josef," she said, "are you calling me from your house?"

"Yes."

"Don't you think this line might be tapped?"

"Helene has that capacity," Novak said, his voice tightening. "That doesn't mean that she will bother to listen."

"I'm sorry I made this night such a debacle. Do you hate me now, Josef? Please don't hate me. Because I'm afraid that worse is coming."

"Darling, I don't hate you. I'm sorry that I must tell you this, but there's nothing you can do to make me hate you. I am a very old man. There's nothing left of me but irony and pride, and a little muddy benevolence. I'm afraid perhaps you are becoming evil. But I can't find it in myself to hate that, or to hate you. You will always be my favorite little monster."

She had nothing to say to that, so she hung up.

"He really hurt me when he said that," she said to Benedetta, and began to cry.

"You should leave that old fool," Benedetta said, munching a fresh canapé. "You should come with me to Bologna. Come tonight. We'll catch a train. It's the finest city in Europe. There are colonnades and communards and blimps. You should see the arcades, they're so beautiful. And we have wonderful plans in Bologna. Come with us to the Istituto di Estetica. You can watch us as we work."

"Can I take photos of what you're up to?"

"Well . . ."

"I take such bad photos," she mourned. "Josef Novak doesn't take bad photographs. Sometimes they're wonderful. Sometimes they're just odd, but he never takes a bad one. Never, he just doesn't make mistakes. And me, I never take good ones. It's not that I have bad technique. I can learn the technique, but I still don't see."

Benedetta sipped her tincture.

"There's no one me inside to see with, Benedetta. I can be beautiful, because there is no great beauty without some strangeness in the proportion, and I am all a strangeness. But being beautiful doesn't make me all right. I'm not at one with myself. I am in fragments, and I'm starting to think that I'll always be in fragments. I'm a broken mirror inside, and so my work in artifice is always a blur. Art is long and life just isn't short anymore." Maya hid her face in her hands.

"You're a good friend, Maya. I don't have many true friends, but you're a true friend of mine. The years don't matter like you think they matter. They matter but they matter differently. Please don't be so sad." Benedetta began to search in her jacket pockets. "I brought you a gift from Bologna. To celebrate. Because we truly are sisters now."

Maya looked up. "You did?"

Benedetta searched through her pockets. She pulled out a suckered barnacle.

Maya stared. "That really looks like something I ought not to be messing with."

"Do you know what a cerebrospinal decantation is?"

"Unfortunately, yes, I do."

"Let me give this to you, Maya. Let me put it on your head."

"Benedetta, I really shouldn't. You know I'm not young. This could really hurt me."

"Of course it hurts. It took me a year to prepare this decantation. It hurt me every time. Whenever I felt a certain way—the way that was really me . . . I put this thing on my head. And it sucked me out, and it stored me. I thought I would use it sometime much later, to remember myself if I ever got lost somehow. But I want you to have it now. I want you to know who I am."

Maya sighed. "Life is risk." She took off her wig.

The barnacle went in through the back of her skull. It hurt quite a bit, and it was good that it hurt, because otherwise it would have come too easily. Perfusions oozed and she went very calm and supernaturally lucid.

She felt the mind of another woman. Not her thoughts. Her life. The unearthly sweetness of human identity. Loneliness, and a little bitterness for strength, and a bright plateau of single-minded youthful self-possession. The ghostly glaze of another soul.

She closed her eyes. It was deep, it was deep posthuman rapture. Awareness stole across her mind like black light from another world. And then the gray meat slowly ate that other soul. Sucked it hungrily into a million little crevices.

When she came to, the barnacle was gone. She was flat on the floor, and Benedetta was gently wiping her face with a damp towel. "Can you speak?" Benedetta said.

She worked her jaws, forced her tongue to move. "Yes, I think so."

"You know who you are?" Benedetta was anxious. "Tell me."

"That was truly holy," she said. "It's sacred. You have to hide that in some sacred place. Never let anyone touch that, or defile that. It would be too awful, and too terrible, if that were ever touched."

Benedetta embraced her. "I'm sorry, darling. I know how to do it. I know how it works. I even know how to give it to you. But I don't know how to hide from what I am, and what I know."

Three weeks passed. Spring had come and Praha was in bloom. She was still working with Novak, but it was not the same. He treated her like an assistant now, instead of a magical waif or a stranded elf. Milena could sense that there was trouble in the wind. Milena hated cops, but Milena was nevertheless making life hard, because Milena hated a disruption in the ancient Novak household even more than Milena hated cops.

Maya took a train to Milano and did a very boring shoot with some of Vietti's very boring staffers. Because it was a working engagement, she saw almost nothing at all of Milano, and precious little of the Emporio Vietti. Vietti himself didn't bother to show; the great man was off in Gstaad boiling his crabs.

The results of the shoot were perfect and glossy and awful, because it wasn't Josef Novak. She learned quite a bit during the shoot, but mostly she hated it. Nevertheless, she thought it was a smart thing to do. People had been fussing entirely too much about the Novak photographs. They were all over the net and they were rather too beautiful and they were much, much too true. It seemed to her that people would be happier if she proved she could be boring. Just another silly model, on just another couture shoot. And besides, there was money in it.

She persuaded Benedetta to come to Milano to handle the money for her. Benedetta didn't handle the funds herself, but she knew people, who knew people, who knew people who could handle money. Benedetta bought her a Milanese designer furoshiki, which was beautiful and useful, and a big Indonesian network server, which was useful and beautiful. Maya returned to Praha and the actress's apartment, wearing the furoshiki and carrying the server in its shatterproof case.

The Indonesian server came with an elaborate set of installation procedures in sadly mangled English. Maya booted the server, failed, wiped it, rebooted it, failed again. So she fed the actress's cats. Then she wiggled all the loose connections, booted the server, failed much worse than before, and had a frappé to calm down. She booted it again, achieved partial functionality, searched the processing crystal for internal conflicts, eliminated three little nasty ones. The system crashed. She ran a diagnostic test, cleaned out a set of wonky buffers, picked the main processor up and dropped it. After that, it seemed to work. She installed a network identity. Finally she plugged into the net.

The server rang immediately. It was a voice call from Therese.

"How did you know I was on-line?" Maya said.

"I have my ways," said Therese. "Did they really throw you out of the Tête because you killed a cop's dog?"

"Word gets around in a hurry, and no, I didn't do that, I swear it was somebody else."

"If word travels any slower than the speed of light now, it only means we're not paying attention," Therese said. "I was paying plenty of attention. Because I need a big favor from you."

"Is it *the* favor, Therese?"

"It is *the* favor, Maya, if you are discreet."

"Therese, I'm in so much trouble of my own now that I don't think yours can possibly affect me. What is it that you need?"

"I need a very private room in Praha," Therese said somberly. "It has to be a nice room with a very nice bed. Not a hotel, because they keep records. And I need a car. It doesn't have to be a very nice car, but it has to be very private. Not a rented car, because they keep records. I need the room for one night and I need the car for two days. After that, I don't need any questions, from anybody, ever."

"No questions and no records. Right. When do you need these things?"

"Tuesday."

"Let me call you back."

The actress's room was out of the question. Novak? She couldn't. Paul? Maybe, but, well, certainly not. Klaus? Since she'd become a regular at the Tête, she'd come to realize that Klaus was a very interesting man. Klaus had many resources through every level of Praha society. Klaus was a genuine doyen. Klaus was universally known and respected in Praha, and yet Klaus seemed to owe nothing to anyone; Klaus belonged to nobody at all. Klaus even liked her, but . . .

Emil. Perfect.

———————

She did what she could for Therese. The arrangements required a serious investment of time, energy, and wiles, but they seemed to work well enough.

At two in the morning on Tuesday she got a priority call from Therese. "Are you awake?"

"I am now, darling."

"Can you come and have a drink with me? I'm in the Café Chyba on the forty-seventh floor of this big rabbit nest you found for me."

"Are you all right, Therese?"

"No, I'm not all right," said Therese meekly, "and I need you to come and have a little drink with me."

Maya dressed in a hurry and went to the café. It took her forty minutes. When she arrived at the Café Chyba she found it deserted. It was a perfectly clean and perfectly soulless little bar, entirely automated, just the sort of place where one would end up at three in the morning when one was having an emotional crisis in an eighty-story modern Czech high-rise. Emotional crises seemed to be pretty rare in the high-rise, to judge by the lack of customers. This high-rise was inhabited by Emil's parents, who were, conveniently, in Finland for a month. In Suomen Tasavalta, rather.

Maya ordered a mineralka from a disgustingly cute little novelty robot. She sipped it and waited.

Therese appeared around half past three. She perched on the edge of a barstool and tried to smile. She had been weeping.

"Maya," she said, and took her hand. "You've grown up so much."

"This wig makes me look a lot more mature," Maya lied cheerfully.

"You're so chic! You're so . . . Well, I wouldn't have known you. I wouldn't, truly. Can I still trust you?"

"Why don't you just tell me what kind of trouble you're in, Therese. I'll see if I can figure out the rest of that later."

"He beat me."

"He did? Let's go and kill him."

"He's doing that already," Therese said, and began to cry.

Therese's boyfriend had never beaten her before, but since he was on the point of suicide, he seemed to feel a need to put a sharper point to their relationship. He'd whipped her on the back and bottom with a leather belt. Therese's boyfriend was a Corsican gangster.

Therese's boyfriend wasn't a cute gangster. There was nothing cute about him. He was a career criminal, a *consigliore* in the Black Hand organization; protection racketeers, pimps, hardcase tincture people. Major-league money launderers. Influence peddlers. Bribers of judges, suborners of police. Murderers. Men who put people's feet in buckets of cement. He was sixty years old and he called himself Bruno when he wasn't calling himself something else.

"How'd you come to know this character?"

"How do you think? I run a gray-market shop in the rag trade. I got mixed up with the rackets. Mafiosi dress very flash, and sometimes they steal clothes and sell them. The rag trade is very old. You know? It's very old and it has some strange things in its closets. I do little illegal things. Mafiosi do big illegal things. They counterfeit couture sometimes, they give people protection sometimes. It happens. It just happens." Therese shrugged.

Maya drummed her fingers slowly on the top of the bar.

"He likes the apartment you found for us," Therese offered. "It's funny to steal a last night from bourgeois people."

"I can't believe this," Maya said.

"Bruno's a real man," Therese said slowly. "I love real men. I like it when they can't be polite about it. I like it when men really . . ." She thought about it. "When they really *come unwound.*"

"That's not a healthy hobby, darling."

"Life is a risk. I like it when they're truly men. When nothing else matters to them but being a man. It's exciting. It really feels like living. I didn't think he'd beat me. But I was doing anything he wanted tonight. So he wanted to beat me. It's his last night on earth. I shouldn't have cried so much. I shouldn't have called you. I'm being a big baby."

"Therese, this is really sick."

"No, it's not," Therese said, wounded. "It's just old-fashioned."

"How do you know he's not going to *murder* you?"

"He's a man of honor," Therese said. "Anyway, I'm doing him a big favor tomorrow."

Bruno was dying. Therese's best guess was liver cancer. It was impossible to tell for certain, because Bruno hadn't been near official diagnostic machinery in forty years. First his rap sheet had caught up with him, and denied him access to life-extension treatments. Then he'd begun to do a number of extremely interesting and highly illegal things to himself through the medical black market. The extra testicle, apparently, was just the least of it.

Bruno was determined to die outside the reach of the polity. Should the authorities happen to render his corpse in one of those necropolitan emulsifiers, then alarm bells would ring from Dublin to Vladivostok. The Black Hand had been founded on the ancient tradition of *omertà,* silence until death. Nowadays, silence after death was just as necessary.

The romance between Bruno and Therese had been very simple. He'd met her in Marseilles when she was twenty. Bruno was always beautifully dressed, reeking of mystery, and entirely menacing. For Therese this combination was catnip. Bruno liked her because she was young, and cute, and no trouble for him, and pretty much ready for anything, and grateful for favors. Sometimes he bought her nice presents: shoes, gowns, sexy underwear, little holidays on the Côte d'Azur. He gave her contact with a very, very vivid side of life.

Once she had gone into the rag trade, Bruno became even more useful. Sometimes she had trouble from buyers and suppliers. If he happened to feel like it, Bruno would show up from out of town and have a little word with the offending parties. This never failed to effect radical improvement.

Sometimes Bruno would slap her around a little. This was only to be expected from a man who was perfectly capable of putting her enemies into cement. Not that Bruno had actually murdered anyone for Therese. If he had, he wouldn't have told her about it anyway. "It isn't that he hits you," Therese explained. "He hits you so you do what he wants. He's the man, he's the boss, he's the top. Sometimes he *makes* you do what he wants. That's what he is."

"This is seriously bad," Maya said.

Therese tossed her head irritably. "Did you think every criminal in Europe was like your loser boyfriend Jimmy the pickpocket? Bruno is a soldier! He's a boss."

"What happened to Jimmy?" Maya said. "I haven't thought about him in such a long time."

"Oh, they caught him," Therese said. "Jimmy was always stupid. They arrested him. They did a laundry job on his head."

"Oh, no," Maya said. "Poor Ulrich. Did it change his behavior much?"

"Totally," Therese said gloomily. "He used to steal purses from tourist women. Now he fills purses with useful goods and gives them to tourist women when they're not looking."

"Well, it's a good sign that they let him keep his anarchist political convictions."

"Oh, the polity, they fuss so much about behavior mod," said Therese. "They catch some nasty creep like Jimmy who ought to be dropped off a bridge, and every civil libertarian in the world starts whining on the net. Really, bourgeois people have no sense at all."

"So what's the plan with Bruno?"

"We're going to drive into the Black Forest tomorrow. He's going to kill himself. I'm going to bury him in a secret place where no one will ever know. That's our bargain. That's our secret and private arrangement."

"Young lady, you're not supposed to bury any lovers until you are very, very old."

"I've always been so precocious, it always gets me into trouble." Therese sighed. "Will you come with me tomorrow? Please?"

"Look, you can't ask that of me. If you think I can handle a sick and desperate man who's bent on suicide, well—" She hesitated. "Well, actually, I'd probably be better at that than anyone else you know."

"You're so good to me, Maya. I knew you would help me. I knew somehow, the moment that I saw you, that you were someone very special." Therese stood up. She was much happier now. "I have to go back and sleep with Bruno now. I promised I'd stay all night."

"A promise is a promise, I guess."

Therese looked around the deserted bar. "It's late, it's so strange and lonely here. . . . Do you want to come in and sleep with him with me?"

"I might not mind it all that much really," Maya said, "but I hardly see how that's going to help."

She met Bruno for the first time at ten in the morning. She was astonished by Bruno's uncanny resemblance to a twentieth-century matinee idol. The twentieth-century look mostly came from his bad health and the crudity of his makeup. Bruno had a broad wavy-haired rock-solid head with the greasy pores typical of heavy male steroid treatment. He wore a lacquered straw hat and a thin-lapelled dark suit and crisply creased tailored slacks and a shirt without a cellphone.

Bruno didn't bluster or threaten. He swaggered a bit, but he lacked the smooth enormous muscle of people truly devoted to muscle. Bruno was terrifying because he truly looked willing and able to kill people, without hesitation and without regret afterward. Bruno looked truly feral. He looked old and beaten, too, like a very sick wolf. He looked as if he had chewed off his own leg and eaten it and enjoyed the flavor.

For a man driving to his own execution, Bruno was remarkably cheerful and philosophical. She'd never met anyone bent on death who seemed so truly pleased about the prospect. He kept making little wisecracks to Therese, in some criminal south-of-France argot that baffled Maya's wig translator. Quite often he used obscenities. This was the sort of language no one used nowadays. Obscenity had simply gone out of use, vanished from human intercourse, gone like the common cold. But Bruno spoke obscenely and with relish. This verbal transgression would always upset Therese no end. She never failed to scold Bruno while showing unmistakable signs of arousal. It was like a table-tennis game between the two of them, and appeared to be their version of courting behavior.

The three of them ate in the car. The condemned man ate a hearty lunch. They finally drove up into some dense patch of forest north of the Czech border. This didn't seem to be the actual

Black Forest, but this seemed to matter not at all. The trees were leafing out and there was a warm spring breeze. The car—it belonged to Emil's ex-wife—protested bitterly at being ordered into the shrubbery at the side of the road. But there they left it.

Bruno retrieved a folding shovel and a heavy valise from the boot of the car. Then they set out on foot. Bruno knew very well where he was going.

They emerged in a small hillside meadow. Bruno opened the sharp ceramic shovel, hung his hat and jacket neatly from a branch, and began digging. He removed a wide circle of sod and carefully set it aside. As he dug, he began reminiscing.

"He says this is an old secret resting place," Therese translated. "Romany people used it a long time ago. Later, some other people put some troublemakers here."

Bruno wiped sweat from his brow. Suddenly he spoke up in English. "A man," he pronounced, "does his own work in this life." He looked at Maya and smiled winningly.

Bruno dug until he hurt too much to dig anymore. He sat down ashen faced and puffed at a gunmetal inhaler. Therese dug for him. When she got too tired, Maya had a turn. She'd dressed in flats and pants and a light sweater, not too bad for gravedigging. The only fashion touch was the furoshiki. She'd set it for olive and khaki. Something not too alluring.

They followed Bruno's direction. The result was not a normal grave. It was a conical pit with a round rim the size of a manhole cover. Bruno tossed out a few final wedges of dirt, and then explained to them the theory and craft of concealed burials.

The crux of the matter was rapid and complete decomposition. Truly high-speed decomposition caused the corpse to bloat rapidly. This side effect would disturb the surface of the grave. Therefore it was necessary to saw through the ribs up both sides, and to ventilate the intestines.

Bruno opened his valise. He had thoughtfully brought all the proper equipment. It had seen plenty of use. He had an old-fashioned ceramic bone saw, battery driven. He also had some kind of horse-doctoring veterinary hypodermic, with a great spike of a steel needle that could have stitched sheet aluminum.

Bruno now disrobed. He was covered from neck to groin in tattoos. Snakes. Roses. Handguns. Mottos in gutter Français. At least Therese had never lacked for things to read.

Bruno heartily pinched his own goosefleshed hide to show where the needle should go in. Into the thighbones. Into the meat of the calves. Into the biceps. Into the buttocks. Into the skull. He had a little canister of some highly carnivorous rot bacterium. Eating its way out from the injection sites, the decomposer would cook him down like tallow.

After he was settled nicely into the pit, they would have to shovel the dirt around him and carefully replace the lid of sod. It was best to leave a dome of extra dirt below the lid. This looked suspicious at first, but it would look much better in the long run because of the settling. The leftover dirt had to be scattered in the forest. And of course they must remove his clothes and the tools. Nothing metal to be left around the site. Nothing to attract attention.

"Ask him if he has any metal inside of him," Maya said. "Dental work, anything like that?"

"He says he's not old enough to have dental work made of metal," Therese translated. "He says the only thing on him made of solid iron is his manhood." She began to cry.

Bruno took two canisters the size of his thumbs from the pockets of his discarded pants. He then climbed, naked and peaceable, into his grave.

He stood there, leaned back casually, and shook the first of the thumb-sized objects in his fist. He sprayed a fine layer of black paint over his right hand. He beckoned to Therese, calling out something in the argot. She came over, trudging, reluctant, afraid. He gripped her hand gently with the black-painted hand, shook her hand firmly, pulled her close, whispered, kissed her.

Then he called Maya over. He kissed her as well. A long and deep and contemplative and very bitter kiss. He trapped the nape of her neck with his left hand. He didn't touch her with the painted black hand.

At last he released her. Maya gasped for breath, stumbled back, and almost slid into the pit with him. Bruno watched Therese for a moment. He seemed to be fighting tears. Therese was sprawled on the ground, watching him, sobbing bitterly.

He then picked up the second object, an inhaler. He stuck the muzzle into his mouth, squeezed the trigger, and sucked in a breath. He tossed the thing aside like a dead cigar, and went into instant convulsions. He was dead in five seconds.

"Get it off!" Therese screamed. "Get it off me, get it off!" She was waving her black-stained hand, clamping her wrist left-handed.

Maya began scrubbing the painted hand with Bruno's discarded jacket. "What is it?"

"Lacrimogen!"

"Oh my goodness." She scrubbed harder, but rather more carefully.

"Oh, I loved him so much," Therese howled, rocketing into hysterical grief. "Oh, I thought he'd beat me again and have sex with me in the grave. I never thought he'd give me the black hand. I wish I was dead." She broke into frantic Deutsch. "[Where is the poison? Spray it in my mouth. No, let me kiss him, there must be poison on his tongue to kill a hundred women.]"

She began crawling toward the lip of the grave, exploding with drug-propelled grief. Maya caught her by the ankle, and hauled her back. "Stay away from him, I mean it. Get away from him, and keep away. I'm going to cut him up now."

"[Maya, how can you! How can you saw him up and make him rot? It's not some piece of meat, it's Bruno!]"

"I'm sorry, darling, but once you've lived through the great plagues like I have, you really do learn that when people are dead, they're just plain dead." She could have bitten her tongue for that confession, but it didn't matter; Therese was too far gone, beyond listening. Therese began to howl till the woods rang, great horrid wails of primal bereavement and anguish.

Maya found a sheet of alcionage in Therese's backpack. It was pretty mild stuff, alcionage, so she reeled off six of them. Therese made no resistance when Maya stickered her neck. The impetus of her grief kept her rocking and moaning in a fetal position, clutching her tainted hand. Then the tranquilizer sandbagged her.

Maya fetched out the last of a mineralka and gave Therese's hand a thorough wet scrubbing. It was nasty stuff, that spray-on lacrimogen. You could murder somebody with it easily. She could hardly imagine a defter way to kill.

She walked over to the lip of the grave. Bruno was still dead. A little more dead, if anything. She closed his eyes for him. Then she filled the hypodermic.

"Well, big guy," she told him, "rest easy. You've found yourself a little girl who is truly happy to do this."

It was dark by the time she was done. It had been a very nasty job. It was like some macabre parody of medical practice. But it was enough like medical practice that it felt like honest work.

Therese had recovered. Therese was young and strong. Young people could whip their way through more moods in a day than old people managed in a month. Therese tottered back with Maya to the car.

"Where's his suitcase?" Therese said, red-eyed and trembling.

"I put it in the boot with all the clothes and tools."

"Get it out for me."

Therese searched through Bruno's case with frantic eagerness. She came up with a long rectangular tray of gray metalglass alloy. She opened it.

"I can't believe it," she said, looking into it with awestruck joy. "I was sure he was going to cheat me."

"I think he meant to kill you."

"No, he didn't. That was only a little bit of spray. He just wanted a woman to cry for him. I feel better now that I cried so much. I feel all right. I'll never cry for him anymore ever again. Look, Maya, look what he gave me. Look at my wonderful heirloom from my dead old man." She showed her the little hinged tray.

It was lined in black velvet and held two dozen little spotted seashells.

"Seashells?" Maya said.

"Cowries," Therese said. "I'm rich!" She carefully shut the

tray, then slammed the suitcase shut and kicked it into the boot. "Let's go now," she said, clutching the tray with both hands. "Let's go get a drink. I cried so much, and I'm so thirsty. Oh, I can't believe I've really done this." She opened the door and climbed inside.

They drove away with a rattle and crunch of brush. Suddenly Therese gazed over her shoulder, and laughed. "I can't believe it, but I won. I'm getting away with it. Now life will be so different for me."

"A box of little seashells," Maya mused. The car threaded its way through the darkened woodlands, heading for an autobahn.

"It's something that's not trash. The world is full of trash now," Therese said, settling back into her seat. "Virtualities and fakes. We've turned everything into trash. Diamonds and jewels are cheap. Coins, anyone can forge coins now. Stamps, they're so easy to forge, it's a laugh. Money is nothing but ones and zeroes. But Maya—*seashells*! Nobody can forge seashells."

"Maybe those are just cheap fake trashy seashells."

Therese opened the tray again, stabbed with anxiety. Then she smiled. "No, no. Look at these growth marks, look at this mottling. Only years and years of organic process can create a real seashell. Cowries are much too complex to be faked. These are *real*. Extinct species! So very rare! There will never be any more, ever. They're worth a fortune! So much—so much that I can do everything now."

"So what are you going to do with them, exactly?"

"I'm going to grow up, of course! I can leave that little dump in the Viktualienmarkt. I can start a real store. In a real building, a high-rise! For real customers who will pay me real money. I'm very young to be a store owner, but with this in my hands, I can do it. I can get old people to work for me. I'll hire my own accountant, and my own business lawyer. I'll start over legally. Everything aboveboard. Real business books, and I'll pay taxes!"

"Gosh, that sounds lovely."

"It's my dream come true. Real couture people will pay attention to me now. I'll carry real lines of clothing from professional designers. No more of this kid stuff. Kid stuff, kid stuff, kid stuff, oh, truly I'm so, so sick of the vivid life."

"I hope you'll stay out of trouble with Bruno's friends from now on."

"Of course I will," Therese said. "No matter what you think about the polity, well . . . they are making the world *better.* They really are! Bruno's gangsters—well, the police have got them. It's the medical thing, and the money, and the surveillance. . . . It's working. The bad boys are dying from it. Every year, less and less of them. The criminal classes are dying. They're very old and they were very strong for a long time but they are going away now, like a disease. There is something tragic there, but . . . but it's a great political accomplishment."

Maya sighed wearily. "Maybe I shouldn't have stickered you with quite so many tranquilizers."

"Don't say that. It's not true. Can't you see how happy I am? You should be happy with me." She looked into Maya's face. "What changed you so much, Maya? Why aren't you cheerful like you were in Munchen?"

"You're having mood swings, darling. Try not to talk so much. Let's get some rest. I'm very tired."

Therese shrank back in her seat. "Of course you're very tired. You were so brave. I'm sorry, Maya. . . . Thank you so much."

They were silent a long time. Therese wept a little more. Finally she fell asleep.

In the passing lights of rural Europe, Therese's face was a picture of peace. "You're on the other side now," Maya told her gently. "Now you're a perfect little bourgeoise. I can't believe it really works like this. I can't believe it works so well. I let a world like this happen. I did it, it was my fault, this was just the kind of world I wanted. I can't believe you're so anxious to live in a world that I couldn't stand to live in for one moment longer. I have to be an outlaw just to live and breathe, and now there's no way back for me. And the Widow is onto me now. She knows. I just know that she knows. She'd arrest me right now, except that she's patient and gentle. You know who the Widow is?"

The sleeping Therese hugged her tray a little closer. "Don't ever find out," Maya said.

Reworking the palace presented considerable difficulties. Foremost among them was the difficult fact that something was alive inside it. It had taken Benedetta and her friends quite a while to track down this troubling presence. It was Martin's dog. Plato was loose in the memory palace.

Martin had linked the dog's organic brain directly to his virtuality. This was not a medical process approved for human beings, for many good reasons. Neural activity was an emergent and highly nonlinear phenomenon. Brains grew, they metabolized from a physical organic substrate. When software tried to grow in tandem with a brain, the result was never a smooth symbiosis of thought and computation. It was usually a buzzing, blooming mess. Left alone it became artificial insanity.

Benedetta showed her the hidden wing of the palace where the dog's brain had been at work. The cyborganic mélange had grown for years in knobs and layers, immense frottages and glittering precipitates, a maze like coral and oatmeal. The neural augmentation wasn't dead yet, but they had found the links to the dog's wetware, and blocked them off. There were monster pearls in it here and there, massive spinning nodules like bad dreams that would never melt.

Since Warshaw's death, the dog's mental processes had broken through the floors in five places. The abandoned mentality jetted through the broken floors like sea urchins.

"What does this look like in code?" Maya said.

"Oh, it's such wonderful code. You couldn't parse this code in a million years."

"Do you really think it was helping him think?"

"I don't think dogs think the way we think, but this is definitely mammalian cognitive processing. Warshaw had his palace netlinked into the dog's head. Very sophisticated for the time. Of course, it's nothing compared to the stunts they work on lab animals nowadays. But for the 2060s, this was broad bandwidth and very rapid baud rate. There must be antennas woven all through the dog's spine."

"Why?"

"We speculate that he meant to hide some data inside the dog. Possibly move the whole palace into the dog's nervous system. That sort of visionary nonsense was very big in the 2060s. People believed anything in those days. They romanticized computers and mysticized virtualities. There was a lot of weird experimentation. They thought anything was possible, and they didn't have much sense. But Warshaw was no programmer. He was just old and rich. And reckless."

"Is the dog still on-line in here?"

"That's not the way to phrase it, Maya. The dog never had little doggy gloves or little doggy goggles. He never experienced the palace as a palace at all, he just infested it. Or it infested him. . . . Maybe Warshaw thought he could live in here as well, someday. Pull up all his physical traces and vanish into textures of pure media. People thought that was possible, until they tried it a bit, and learned how hard it was. Warshaw did a silly movie about that once."

"You've seen Martin Warshaw's movies? Really?"

"We have made it our business to dig them up."

"Do you like Warshaw's movies?"

"He was a primitive."

"This doesn't look primitive to me."

"But this isn't cinema at all. This is artificial life. Billions of cycles every day for thirty years."

Down in the palace basement, they had the holy-fire machineries partly stoked and lit. The dream machines. They were supposed to do certain highly arcane things to the vision sites in the brain and the auditory processing centers. You would sort of look at them and sort of hear them, and yet it never felt much like anything. Human consciousness couldn't perceive the deeply preconscious activities of the auditory and visual systems, any more than you consciously felt photons striking your retina, or felt the little bones knocking the cochlear hairs in your ears. The installations weren't blurry exactly; they simply weren't exactly there. The experience was soothing, like being underwater. Like twilight sleep in the color factory. To a semi-inaudible theme of music–not–music.

It wasn't spectacular or thrilling. It didn't burn or blast or coruscate. But it did not weary. It was the polar opposite of weariness. They were inventing very, very slow refreshments for the posthuman souls of a new world. They didn't know how to do it very well yet. They were trying different things, and testing approaches and keeping records.

Maya was not one of the test subjects, but they let her see everything, because they liked her. There were the boxes in the boxes in the boxes, the ones that bled their own geometries, the spatial kaleidoscope. Then there were the ear-flower pinwheels. You could hear the flowers moving but they never really touched the backs of your eyes. And the giant burrowing things that endlessly burrowed into the burrowing things. These were very visceral and subtle, like mental vitamins.

She could not tire of the holy fire. There was no possible way to tire of it. It did not require attention; it worked without attention. It was something that happened to one, instead of something one did. But eventually the gloves and the earphones would pinch her, or her back would start to ache. Then she would log off and look at the wall.

After the holy fire, a blank wall was intensely revelatory. She could sit and meditate on a blank wall and the sheer richness of its physicality, the utter and total thereness of its sublime and awesome thereness was sweetly overwhelming. It wasn't the inside that did things anymore, it was the outside when you came out and looked. . . .

Sometimes she would lie flat on the floor and watch the ceiling. The actress's white cats would come and sit on her chest and knead their paws and look into her face. Animal eyes from a world that knew no words and no symbols.

They were busy outside the palace, too. They had launched strikes at some of the apparently abandoned palaces, and had managed to break into three of them. They had found the physical source of Warshaw's palace; it was datastriped through a series of servers in the Pacific island of Nauru. They were collating the palace line by line out of the Nauru networks, through Morocco, through Bologna, and eventually bit by bit into the crystalline server in the actress's room in Praha. Once the altered palace was all in one machine, it would run a lot faster and more efficiently, they believed. Eventually she would be able to walk around with Warshaw's palace under her own arm. Frozen into a fist-sized chunk of optically etched computational diamond.

One day in June she spent too much time next to the vapor blizzard snowflake calliope, and when she pulled the goggles off she knew she had hurt herself a little. When she closed her eyes, the world had changed on the insides of her eyelids. They had touched the utterly intimate place where she hid when she closed her eyes. There was never true blackness when you closed your eyes while waking. Activity of a sort took place behind closed eyelids. Deprived of light, the visual cortex still worked, and tried in its gray-meat not-blind way to grip at reality. And it made a little world. The intimate world behind human eyelids was gentle formless blues and dim swimming flashbulb purples and optic flecks of dun and brown. But now they had touched it somehow. They had made it a different place. They had made it something new and not Maya.

She called Benedetta. It was trouble to call her, because Benedetta was always tight and guarded now. But she had to talk.

"Benedetta, I made a mistake."

"What kind of mistake?"

"This isn't going to work for me."

"You have to be very patient," Benedetta said very patiently. "This is a very long-term project."

"It's not going to work for me, because I'm not young. I've already been young. I was young in a different world. That world in there is your world. You're building something I can't even imagine. I can sympathize, and I can even help you build it, but I can't live there, because I'm not one of you."

"Of course you're one of us. Don't worry if it isn't having

much effect. This is nothing compared to what we'll do in a hundred years."

"I won't live a hundred more years. I'll never live to see the world beyond the singularity. It's not that I don't want to. But I just wasn't born in time."

"Maya, don't give up. Don't talk like a defeatist. You're important to our morale."

"I love you, and I'll do anything to help you, but you'll have to manage your own morale. I'm never going back in there again. I'm starting to feel and understand what it really means now. I'll never be able to stretch that far. I don't want that, and in my condition I don't even need that. It might help you with your problems, but it can't help me with mine. It will only make me worse than dead."

"Are there things worse than dead, Maya?"

"Oh, my heavens, yes." She hung up. Then she lay on her back on the bed to examine the featureless ceiling.

Some endless time later, the doorbell rang and roused her.

Maya rose like a sleepwalker, crossed the white fluffy carpet, opened the door.

A large brown dog released the bell. He dropped to all fours.

Then he lunged through the open door. She backed away, stumbling backward, and he stalked into the room.

"You hurt me," he said.

"Come in, Plato. Where are your nice clothes?"

"You hurt me."

"You don't look well. Haven't you been eating right? You should always watch what you eat. It's so important to eat properly."

"You hurt me a *lot*."

Maya backed away toward the kitchen. "Would you like a treat? I have so many treats now."

"I hurt a lot. I hurt inside my head." The dog stalked into the room, his matted head hung low. He sniffed at the floor and shook his filthy head. "You did it," he said.

One of the white cats woke up, stared in amazement, and went into bottle-brush feline terror.

"Kitty, be good!" Maya shouted quickly. "Plato, I'm going to feed you now! Everything will be fine! I'll make some calls! I'll take care of you now! We'll have a nice bath! We'll get dressed, we'll go out—"

"There are cats!" the dog howled. He attacked.

Maya screamed. White fur flew. The room exploded with animal hate. He smashed the first cat between his white-fanged jaws and it fell to the floor in convulsions. An alarm began to shriek as the cat began to die.

Maya leapt at the dog as he attacked the second cat. She tried to grab at the matted fur of his neck. He turned with enormous feral speed and ease, and bit her on the shin. It was as if she'd slammed her leg in a fanged iron door. She screamed and fell.

The cat tried hard to climb the wallpaper. The dog seized the cat's tail with his dreadful grasping paw and threw the cat down and killed him with his teeth.

Maya yanked at the door and ran away.

She had nothing. She had no shoes. She knew the dog would come for her now. Her leg was bleeding and she stank of fear, enough fear to crush the world. She ran. She ran down the hall and into an elevator. She stood there and shook and moaned until the doors closed.

There was nothing else to do now. So she caught a train.

———————

On the first day she stole clothes. This was very difficult now because she was so afraid. It was easy to steal things when you were perfectly happy and confident, because everyone loved pretty girls who were perfectly happy and confident. But nobody loved crazy girls who had funny stiff hair and who limped and who winced and who looked like a junkie and who carried no luggage.

The dog was inside the net. She couldn't imagine why she'd ever thought a net was a nice thing. A net was a thing to kill fish with. Big pieces of the dog's gray meat had grown inside the net.

He had been haunting the palace, and he had used it to track her down. He was smelling after her, and he was all over the world like a kind of vapor.

The police would find her the moment she stopped running. She was very tired and very guilty and she hurt. Whenever she sat still, blind panic gripped her, and she had to go throw up.

But in the Sinai, it was summer. This wasn't Europe. She found no release in the sensation of travel now; it felt bad and strange to be traveling. The actress was in a Red Sea resort. It was a place to go when you were very tired. The actress had naturally left strict orders not to be disturbed.

Maya convinced the staff of the spa that she had news of a death in the family. They saw that she was shattered, haunted and struck with grief, so they believed her little story and they pitied her. They were kindly people, in their little Edenic niche of desalination and pampered jungle. Their business was to care for others. They gave her a notebook and told her how to hunt for the actress's spoor.

The actress was a furry hominid with thick black nails and hairy calloused feet. She was naked and covered in wiry black fur. People could do this sort of thing conveniently if they were willing to activate some of the human junk DNA. It wasn't a medical activity that lengthened the life span, so it was the sort of thing that one did in a spa.

In certain modern circles it was considered very relaxing to retreat to a prehominid form. A few soothing months of very dim consciousness, with the hunt for food to keep one toned. The prehominid guests at the spa ate fruit and chased and killed small animals with sticks. They wore tracking devices and were feted once a week on carrion.

Maya followed the hints from the notebook. Eventually, she found Miss Jeskova. Miss Jeskova was staring out to sea and cracking raw oysters with a fist ax.

"Are you Olga Jeskova?"

Miss Jeskova loudly slurped an oyster. The notebook said something in Czestina. Maya manipulated some menus. "[Not right now,]" the machine said ambiguously.

"My name is Mia Ziemann, Miss Jeskova," she said, speaking into the notebook's inset microphone. "I'm sorry that we have to meet this way. I've come from Praha and I have some bad news for you."

"[Bad news can wait,]" said the notebook in English, crankily. "[Bad news can always wait. I'm hungry.]"

"I was living in your apartment. I was taking care of your cats. I was your cat-sitter in Praha. Do you understand me?"

Miss Jeskova chewed another oyster. Her hide twitched and she scratched herself vigorously. "[My nice little cats,]" the notebook said at last.

The staff had warned her that communication would take patience. People at the spa didn't go there to chat, but they left certain mental conduits in case there was an emergency.

"[What about my little darlings?]" said the notebook at last.

"They're dead. I'm very sorry. I was a guest in your home and your cats were killed. I feel truly terrible about it. It was all my fault. I came here as soon as I could, because I had to tell you myself."

"[My cats are dead?]" Miss Jeskova said. "[When I go home, this will make me very sad.]"

"A dog got in and killed them. It was awful, and it was all because of me. I had to come and tell you myself. I just had to." She was trembling violently.

Miss Jeskova looked at her with timeless brown eyes. "[Stop crying. You look bad. You must be hungry.]"

"I guess I am."

"[Eat these stone sweeties. So juicy and good.]" She deftly whacked another oyster with her hand ax.

Maya fished the raw oyster from its broken shell. It took a lot of courage to swallow the thing. The tactility was gruesome but it was a deeply sensual experience.

Maya studied the Red Sea. It was hard to understand why they called it Red when it was so intensely blue. Maybe they'd done something strange to it, primally changed the whole character of the ocean somehow. But there were waves rolling in, crashing against black rocks with an absolute and unhurried rhythm, under a million blue miles of hot and easy sky. "They say that drowning is really quick. It's a good death."

"[Don't be stupid. Eat.]"

Maya had another oyster. Her stomach slowly eased from an anguished knot and rumbled in ecstasy.

"I'm hungry," she said suddenly. "I can't believe how hungry I feel. Good heavens, I think I haven't eaten anything in days."

"[Eat. Dead girls are worse than dead cats.]"

Maya ate another oyster, and stared out to sea. The waves glittered rhythmically. A strange intensity began to grip her. A waking up all over, as if her skin had become one giant eyelid.

The light of the world flooded within her.

She was broken inside. She knew then and there that she would always be broken inside. She would never become a single whole woman, there were scars far past healing at the very core of her being. She was a creature of pieces and seams, and she would always be pieces and seams.

But now, for the first time, all those pieces were gazing at the same thing. All of her, gripped by the same hot light, perceiving the world outside.

Then suddenly there was no window anymore. She was standing inside the world. Inhabiting the world. Not dodging through the fractured alterity within her own skull, but living and breathing in the world that the sun shone upon. It wasn't happiness, not much like pleasure; but it was radiant experience that touched every shred inside her.

The world beneath the sun astounded her. It was a world vastly huger, and far more interesting, than any little world inside herself could ever be. That world touched her everywhere. She had only needed to really look. She was engaged within that world. Alive and aware and awake, in the clear light of day. The world was entirely, heavily, inescapably and liberatingly real.

"I feel the wind blowing through me," she murmured.

Olga only grunted.

She turned and looked at her hairy companion. "Olga, do you understand anything I'm telling you? I hardly understand it myself. I've been having such a very hard time lately. I think that—I think I've been having some kind of fit."

"[You don't understand anything,]" Olga said. "[Life is patience. You are careless, you talk too much, you hurry too much. I know how to be patient. Grief is bad, but you get over it. Guilt is bad, but you get over it. You don't know that yet. That's why I'm wiser than you even when I'm a monkey.]"

"I'm truly sorry about your cats. Really, I'd do anything to make it up to you."

"[All right, so get us more stones to eat.]"

"They're oysters, Olga. They're oysters, and sure, I'll get us some." The sun was shining on the Red Sea and it was hot and real. Wading on rocks would be fun. It would be bliss to swim. She began shedding her clothes.

"Oysters," Olga said aloud. "[Words are so funny, aren't they.]"

The scandal with Helene had locked them out of the Tête. Mere scandal couldn't stop a man of Paul's resourcefulness. He'd found them another meeting place in the Helleniki Dimokratia. He'd arranged a major immersion for them.

Greece in early summer was lovely. It was a country that could sprout a great civilization with the sweet ease of bread sprouting mold. The resort was outside the little city of Kórinthos, in the fragrant wooded hills of the Pelopónnisos. The resort was owned by a forty-year-old multimillionaire who had managed to make a terrific garbage strike in the poorly explored industrial wilds of eastern Deutschland. As one of the youngest truly rich people in Europe, the eccentric wildcatter delighted in doing things to annoy.

Now Paul and thirty of his vivid fellow-travelers were lounging around the resort's glimmering pool, greased and naked and in big toga-pinned bath towels. They were in more trouble than they had ever been in their young lives, and they were in the best of spirits about it.

"Have a grape," Benedetta said, offering a stemmed and lacquered bowl.

"Natural fruits are full of toxins," said Maya.

"These are genetic knockouts."

"Okay, give me a bunch." She ate one. It was delicious. She stuffed in a handful.

"These are fabulous," she said. "Give me more. Make me fat, ruin my stupid career."

Benedetta laughed. Benedetta nude and laughing was a creature of intense and striking loveliness. She was like a greased naiad. They were all so effortlessly lovely, these modern young people. Immortals wrapped in togas of the finest technological rhetoric. Supernaturally healthy creatures.

"I'm hungry all the time now," Maya said, munching her grapes. "It's good. Now I belong to my body again. Or my body belongs to me. . . ."

"It's more fun to share the body," said Bouboule, squeezing lotion into her palm. "I can't reach the what-you-call, the backs of my feet. Get some boy here to rub my legs. They're too lazy in all this sun, the boys need to work more."

"You look better," said Benedetta to Maya very seriously. "You mustn't run away ever again. Take things easy now, keep control, stay close to us. We will look out for you. You know that, Maya. See?" She gestured around the pool. "Isn't this lovely? Aren't we looking out for you?"

"I'm too much trouble," Maya said.

"*I'm* trouble," Bouboule insisted. "I am the trouble. Don't be greedy."

"Trouble has been very good for us," said Benedetta. "Trouble has made our name."

"You don't know enough about trouble yet," said Maya.

"But trouble made us famous. Trouble made us truly vivid. We define vivid now. Look at us! We lose the Tête, but now we relax by this beautiful pool while some rich idiot trash tycoon picks up all our bills. He thinks we're cute, because the cops say we are dangerous. He's a rich radical. Isn't it lovely that there are rich radicals? We are young European chic. This is radical chic. It's lovely, isn't it?"

"Épater les bourgeois," said Bouboule. "Succès de scandale. The old games are the good games."

"Don't you read the net, Maya? They are giving our group such nice names."

"'The Ghost Children,'" Niko spoke up sourly. "I hate that name."

"It sounds good in Français," said Bouboule.

"What's wrong with 'the Tête crowd'?" demanded Niko, restlessly. "We always just called ourselves 'the Tête crowd.'"

"It doesn't matter what we called ourselves," said Benedetta. "We should make up our own new name. We're creative people. We should take control of our own publicity. I like 'the Illuminati.'"

"It's been done," said Niko.

"The Young Immortals," said Bouboule.

"The People Who Take Paul Seriously," said Maya.

"The Cosmos-Shattering Anarchist Goddesses," said Niko. "Plus their boyfriends."

"The Subjects under Investigation," said Maya. "The Potential Defendants."

"Those names stink," said Niko, hurt.

"Not like my name does," Maya said. "I'm a crazed outlaw gerontocrat who led you all into delinquency."

Benedetta sat up, shocked. "That was stupid to say. Who says that?"

"Everyone will. Because I'm famous now, too. Once nobody knew who I was, so nobody cared. I could do anything I wanted, as long as I never made any kind of difference. Now you're actually making a difference, and I'm in the thick of it. I'm your collaborator, but I don't have any of your noble excuses. You may be visionaries, but I'm an illegal alien who embezzled a very valuable medical property." Maya tapped her sternum. "I know that I can't get away with what I've done. So I'm going to make them arrest me. I'll give myself up."

Benedetta thought this over. "I suppose you think you're being noble," she said slowly. "Well, you don't understand our strategy. They seized your network server and took your palace away from us. So what? Some pet animals died. So what? Those are only little setbacks, now that we know what is possible. We're already into other palaces. We're under the skin of the gerontocrats. The old people can't claw us out or push us aside anymore. Let them try! We'll turn them inside out."

"No, darling, it's you who can't understand. You've never been a gerontocrat, but I have. They don't care about your virtualities. They don't care about your silly problem with your infinite imagination. They pretend that they care what you think, because to admit they don't care wouldn't be polite. But they truly don't care much about dreams. They care about actualities. They care about responsibilities. They know they'll die someday. They know that you'll dance on their graves. They'll gladly forgive you anything you do, as long as they're nice and dead first. But darling, I'm not some futurist rebel, I'm a heretic here and now. I'm dancing on their feet."

"Maya, stop talking bad politics in English and do what Benedetta says," said Bouboule. "Benedetta is very smart. Oh, look! Lodewijk is kissing her!" She broke into excited Français.

Maya missed her translation wig very much. She had lost it when she fled the actress's apartment in Praha. She had lost everything she owned through running, not that she had all that much to lose. Mostly it hurt to lose her photographs. They were rather bad photographs, but they were the best she had ever made. She had carefully stored them inside the palace. Now the palace belonged to the Widow.

Niko and Bouboule were furiously excited to see Lodewijk in a sudden clinch with Yvonne. They were chattering and giggling. Even Benedetta took intense scholastic interest. If Maya paid complete attention to the gush of Français, she could decipher maybe a word in ten. Without a film of computation at her ear, these young people were impossibly distant, a generation from another culture and another continent. A generation eighty years away from her own.

She knew them, in her way: Paul, Benedetta, Marcel, Niko, Bouboule, Eugene, Lars, Julie, Eva, Max, Renée, Fernande, Pablo, Lunia, Jeanne, Victor, Berthe, Enheduanna-generally-known-as-Hedda, Berthe's weird boyfriend what's-his-face, Lodewijk, the new guy from Copenhagen, Yvonne, who'd been more or less officially Max's girl until about ten seconds ago, that intense young Russian sculptor with twelve fingers, the cute Indonesian teenager who'd been hanging out a lot lately and was supposedly having the affair with Bouboule's brother. . . . Her friends were wonderful. She had been very lucky to catch them during the brief larval phase in which they were more or less human. They loved her, and they loved one another, but they loved one another like friends and lovers should and did, and they loved her in the way that one might love a very rare and compelling set of antique portrait photographs.

Bouboule rose with oily grace from her recliner and went to tease Yvonne and Lodewijk. Niko went along to make sure that Bouboule didn't tease them too much, and also to enjoy the spectacle. Body language told her that much. Body language was a breeze without clothes.

Benedetta kicked out her slender legs on the woven lounger and turned to Maya. "He sent Yvonne so many poems, you see," she said helpfully. "I just had to cry when I read them. I can't believe that Danish poetry can make me cry."

"Really, Benedetta, you don't have to explain it to me. It's my own fault for losing my nice shiny back-combed translator."

"I like to explain things to you, Maya. I want you to understand."

"I understand too much too well already." She thought about it. "Benedetta, there is one thing I truly don't understand. Why doesn't Paul have a lover? I never see Paul with anyone."

"Maybe he's too considerate," Benedetta said.

"What do you mean, 'maybe'? Are you telling me you don't already know all about it?" She smiled. "Is this Benedetta I'm talking to?"

"It's not that we didn't try," Benedetta said. "Of course we all tried to make time with Paul. Who wouldn't want to be Mrs.

Ideologue? Who wouldn't want to be the genius's favorite girl? Right? Completely lost in his heroic shadow. I want to pick up Paul's dirty socks. I want to sew on his little buttons. That's the life for me. Isn't it? I want to gaze in silent adoration at darling Paul while he talks theory to my colleagues for fourteen hours straight. I want them to look at me and see that I have his heart in my little clutch bag. So that they can all die inside."

"Are you serious, Benedetta? Oh, you are. You're serious. Oh, darling, that's too bad."

"Did you ever have a really good talk with Paul? I have. Despite everything."

"Yes, I have," Maya said. "He once patted me on the hand."

"I think it's the cop. That's my working hypothesis. The Widow's our real rival. It's his crush. A terrible crush. Isn't that the proper word in English, 'crush'? Anyway, it's Helene. He wants Helene. He loves to feast with panthers."

"Oh, no. That can't be true."

"He respects Helene. He takes her very seriously. He talks to her, even when he doesn't have to talk to her. He wants something from Helene. He wants her validation, isn't that the word? He wants to conquer the Widow, like climbing the Matterhorn. He needs to make her believe in him."

"Oh, poor Paul, poor Benedetta. Poor everybody."

"What does this matter to me?" said Benedetta, all light-hearted bitterness. "I'll live for a thousand years. If I had Paul even for a hundred years, it would only be an episode. If I had Paul now, what would I do with Paul later, when things become inter-esting? As for the Widow, he can forget all about that. Helene is a creature of habit. She'll never love any man who will outlive her."

"Oh. Well, that explains a lot. I guess."

"See, Maya? You're not human. We're not human. But we can understand. We're artifice people. We always know it, before we can speak it aloud. We always understand much better than we think."

A gong rang. It was Marcel. He shouted something in Fran-çais, and then in Deutsch, and then in English. The time had come for the immersion.

"I'm not going in," Maya said.

"You should swim with us, Maya. It's good for you."

"I don't think so."

"This isn't serious virtuality. It's not holy fire. The immersion pool is only a rich man's toy. But it's pretty. And technically sweet."

Shimmering liquid gushed as the others whooped and dived in. No one surfaced.

Benedetta wrapped her lustrous hair in a Psyche knot and pinned it. "I'm going in. I think I'll have sex today."

"Who with, for heaven's sake?"

"Well, if I can't find someone willing to bother, maybe I'll try by myself." She smiled, ran, and dived headlong. White bubbles rose, and she was gone.

Paul patrolled the edge of the pool. Gazing in. Smiling. The picture of satisfaction.

"That's everyone but you and me," he called out.

She waved. "Don't mind me, you go ahead."

He shook his head. He drew near, walking slowly, barefooted. "I can't leave you sitting here looking so sad."

"Paul, why don't you go?"

"You've been talking politics with Benedetta," Paul concluded analytically. "We didn't take these risks, and make this effort, just to add to our own unhappiness. That would only represent a moral defeat for us. We must have a good time with our youth, or there's so little point in being young. So you see, you simply must come in with us."

"Things like this frighten me."

"Then I'll teach you about it," said Paul, perching cautiously on the foot of her lounge chair. "Think of the virtuality pool as a kind of crème de menthe. All right? On the top layer is a breathable silicone fluid. We've put a trace of anandamine in it, just for fun. On the bottom is a malleable liquid. It's something like the fusible liquids that our friend Eugene uses to cast sculpture. But it's much more advanced and much more friendly, so we can swim inside it. It's a buoyant, tactile, breathable, immersible virtuality."

Maya said nothing. She tried to look very attentive.

"The best part is the platform. The platform is a fluidic computer. It uses liquid moving through tiny locks and channels to form its logic gates. You see? We dive into the pool and we can actually *breathe* the very stuff of computation! And the computer instantiates itself as it runs. Soft liquid for software, hardened liquid for hardware. It abolishes certain crucial category distinctions. It's a deeply poetic scheme. Also, it's the sort of thing that makes gerontocrats have fits." Paul laughed cheerfully.

"All right, I understand it now. It's enormously clever, isn't it? Now please go on in."

He looked at her seriously, for the first time. He seemed to gaze completely through her head.

"Are you angry with me, Maya?"

"No."

"Have I done something to hurt or offend you? Please be honest."

"No, I'm not hurting, honestly."

"Then please don't refuse me when I ask you to share this experience with us. We'll walk into the shallow end together. Very gently. I'll stay very close. All right?"

She sighed. "All right."

He led her by the hand like a man escorting a duchess to a quadrille. The fluid swarmed with millions of prismatic flakes. Little floating sensors, maybe. Sensors small enough to breathe. The fluid was at blood heat. They waded in. Their legs seemed to dissolve.

Inhaling it was far easier than she had ever imagined. A mouthful of it dissolved on her tongue like sorbet, and when the fluid touched her lungs they reacted with startled pleasure, like sore feet suddenly massaged. Even her eyeballs loved it. The fluid closed over her head. Visibility was very short, no farther than her fingertips. Paul held her hand. Patches of him emerged from the glittering murk: hands, elbows, a flash of naked hip.

They descended slowly, swimming. Down to the white viscous surface of the crème de menthe. It was like smart clay. It reacted to her touch with unmistakable enthusiasm. Paul dug out a double handful and it boiled in his floating hands, indescribably active, like a poem becoming a jigsaw. The stuff was boiling over with machine intelligence. Somehow more alive than flesh; it grew beneath her questing fingers like a Bach sonata. Matter made virtual. Real dreams.

Someone frog-kicked past her and burrowed headlong into the mass of it, like a skier drowning joyfully in some impossible hot snowbank. Now she was beginning to get the hang of it. It was beyond eros, beyond skin. Skinlessness. Skinless memory. Bloody nostalgia, somatic déjà vu, neural *mono no aware*. Memories she was not allowed to have. From sensations she was not allowed to feel.

Memory came upon her like a hammer full of needles. It was nothing like pain. These were sensations far stronger than the personality. They were experiences that consciousness could not contain. Enormous powers riddling the flesh that the mind could make no sense of. A software crash for the soul.

When she came to, she was flat on her back. Paul was heaving at her ribs, hard flat-handed punches of resuscitation. Fluid gushed from her nose and mouth, and she coughed up a bucketful.

"I blew apart," she gasped.

"Maya, don't try to talk."

"It blew my mind. . . ."

He pressed his ear between her breasts and listened to her heartbeat.

"Where is that ambulance?" Benedetta demanded. "My God, it's been an hour." She was wrapped in a towel, and shivering.

Paul said, "That was so stupid of me. I've read about Neo-Telomeric treatment. They suspend you in a virtuality. . . . I should have thought that this might happen." He kept heaving at her lungs.

Maya rolled her head on the floor and tried to look around. There was a dried and glittering snail trail where Paul had hauled her from the pool across the chilly tiles. In the distance the others clustered, talking anxiously, looking her way. Her feet were up on blocks.

She began trembling violently.

"She'll have another convulsion if you don't stop," Benedetta said.

"It's better to convulse than to stop breathing," he said, pushing hard.

Benedetta knelt beside her, her face in anguish. "Stop it, Paul," she said. "She's breathing. I think she's conscious." She looked up. "Will she die?"

"She almost died there in my arms. When I pulled her from the pool, the pupils of her eyes were two different sizes."

"Can't she live ten more years? That's hardly anything, isn't it? Just ten years? I know she'll die and I'll have to mourn her, but why should she die now?"

"Life is too short," Paul said. "Life will always be too short."

"I like to think so," Benedetta said. "Truly, I hope so. I believe it with all my heart."

———————

The medical cops took her to Praha. It had something to do with a possible network-abuse case against her. Apparently most of the evidence was in Praha.

However no one at the Access Bureau was willing to arrest her. The Czech Access Bureau cops apparently despised and distrusted Greek medical cops; it seemed to be some kind of weird European interservice rivalry. She did what she could to explain her circumstances. Once the Access Bureau cops down on the first floor began to fully grasp the situation, they became quite annoyed with her. They told her they would get in touch with her, and tried to convince her to leave the premises and go back with her escorts to some other country.

Maya was disgusted by the prospect of yet more time in a hospital, and refused to go. She asked them to find Helene Vauxcelles-Serusier. With profound reluctance, they said they would do this for her, and they assigned her a number.

She and Brett sat down in an elbow-shaped waiting room on a pair of nasty pink plastic chairs. After an hour, the Helleniki medical escorts carefully checked Maya's tracking handcuffs and her tiara monitor. They were satisfied by this inspection, so they left. After this, pretty much nothing happened.

"Boy, this is a lot harder than I thought it was going to be," said Brett.

"It's good of you to stick with me through this, Brett. I know it's boring."

"No, no," said Brett, adjusting her spex, "it's a real privilege to be your personal media coverage. I'm so touched that you had your friends call me, and give me this great opportunity. It's a fascinating experience. I've always been so terrified of the authorities. I had no idea their indifference to us was so complete and so total. They really hold young people in complete contempt."

"That's not it. Everyone has explained to them that I'm not a young person. It's probably because I'm American. I mean, even nowadays, it's always extra trouble to deal with people from outside the jurisdiction."

Brett took off her spex and gazed at the floor's worn and ancient tiling. "I wish I hated you, Mia."

"Why?" she said.

"Because you're everything I always wanted to be. It should have been *me* involved with exciting European artifice people. It should have been me up on the catwalk. You stole my life. And now you've even made a difference. You've even hurt them. I never even dreamed that I could hurt them."

"I'm sorry," Maya said.

"I dreamed about doing so much. I never had the nerve to really do much of anything. I could have done something. Maybe. Don't you think? You're pretty, but I'm as pretty as you. You sleep with anybody, well, I'll sleep with anybody, too. I'm from the same town as you. I'm twenty, but I'm just as smart as you were when you were twenty. Aren't I?"

"Of course you are."

"I have some talent. I can make clothes. You can't make clothes. What is it you have that I don't have?"

Maya sighed. "Well, here I am sitting in a police station. Maybe you should tell me all about it."

"You're not young. That's it, isn't it? You stole my life because you're older than me, and stronger than me. So for you, it was always easy. I mean, maybe you can panic, maybe you can be wracked with guilt, maybe you can even be terrified out of your skin by some stupid wired-up dog. But even when you don't know who you are, you *still* know who you are. You're five times older than me, and five times stronger than me. And you just won't get out of the way."

"The Tête people are young. They're young like you."

"Yeah, and they love you, don't they? When you were my age, they'd have thought you were a hick and an idiot. Just like they think I'm a hick and an idiot. Because that's what I am. They're smart and gifted and really sophisticated, and the very best I can do is lurk outside their gates and watch them and envy them terribly. At my age, you wouldn't have done any better than me. You would have done a lot worse. You wouldn't even let your boyfriend take you to Europe. You dumped him and married some biotechnician. You turned into a bureaucrat, Mia."

Maya closed her eyes and leaned back in the comfortless chair. It was all so true, and all so beside the point. "I wish you wouldn't call me Mia."

"Well, I wish you wouldn't call me Brett."

"Well, okay . . . call me Mia if you have to."

"I hate it that you don't even hate me back. You're just bringing me along because I'm like a little good-luck charm to you. I'm like your hamster. And you couldn't even keep your hamster."

"That hamster creeped me out big-time. And you're starting to seriously bug me, too."

"You even *talk* just like some woman from a hundred years ago. Everybody in the whole world must be a complete idiot! I mean, once we really look at you, it's so obvious! Your hair is terrible. Do you know you have big lines in your neck? I mean, they're not wrinkles, they're not allowed to be wrinkles—but boy, they sure aren't natural."

"Brett, stop it. You're not talking any sense. First you say that I'm stealing your life, and then you say you couldn't do anything with it anyway. So what's your big problem exactly? Sure, maybe you'd have done a lot better than me, eighty years ago. But hey, you weren't around then. You can't romanticize the past to somebody like me. I was *there* in the past, all right? Eighty years ago, we basically lived like savages. We had plagues and revolutions and mass die-off and big financial crashes. People shot each other with guns when I was young. Compared to eighty years ago, this is heaven! And now you're just abusing me, and not making one bit of sense."

"But Mia, I can't make perfect sense like you can. I'm only twenty years old."

"Oh, don't cry, for heaven's sake."

"I'm twenty years old and I'm an adult. But nothing I do is important. I can't even get a chance to prove that I'm stupid. I suspect that I probably am, and I could live with that, I swear I could. I'd do something else, I wouldn't work in artifice, I'd just live like a little animal. I'd make babies and maybe I'd potter around in a garden or something. But I can't even manage that much, in this big safe lovely world you've built for me. I can't get anywhere at all."

Two Czech policemen arrived. They weren't network cops, medical cops, or artifice cops. Apparently they were just common or garden cops from Praha. They produced phonetic cards from their pink uniforms and read her an extensive list of civil rights in heavily accented English. They then placed her under arrest and booked her into the local legal system. She was charged with immigration violations and working without a permit.

They threw Brett out of the building. Brett yelled and fussed vigorously in English, but the Czech cops were patient and they put up with it and they threw her out and dusted their hands. Maya was stripped, and then dressed in dun prison coveralls. They left the monitors on her wrists and the tiara on her head.

The Praha cops took her a few blocks away to a high-rise, and installed her in a very clean holding tank. There she was able to reflect with relief that she had not yet been charged with:

(a) network abuse, (b) medical fraud, (c) complicity in illegal discharge into an urban sewer system, (d) abetting the posthumous escape of an organized criminal, or (e) any number of episodes of transportation toll fraud.

Nobody bothered with her for a couple of days. She was fed on a standard and extremely healthy medical diet. She was allowed to watch television and was given a deck of cards. Robots wheeled by every hour or so and engaged her in a very limited English conversation. The jail was almost entirely deserted, very little used, and therefore extremely quiet. There were a few gypsies somewhere in a decontamination wing; at night she could hear them singing.

On the third day she threw away the tiara. She couldn't get the bracelets loose, however.

On the fourth day Helene had her brought out for interrogation. Helene had a tiny office on the top floor of the Access Bureau. Maya was astonished at how old and small and shabby Helene's office was. It was definitely Helene's own office, because there were neatly framed little hand-drawn originals on the walls that probably were worth more than the entire building. But Maya herself had worked for decades in offices far better equipped.

Helene was out of mufti and in a very dashing belted pink uniform. Other than that, there was a window and a chair and a desk. And a little white dog. From behind the desk rose a very big brown dog.

Maya stared. "Hello, Plato."

The dog cocked his ears and said nothing.

"Plato doesn't talk now," Helene said. "He's resting."

The dog was still rather gaunt, but his coat was glossy and his nose was wet. He wore no clothing, but Helene had given him a lovely new collar. "Plato looks a lot better. I'm glad."

"Please sit down, Mrs. Ziemann."

"Why don't we get on a first-name basis so I won't have to mangle your beautiful last name with my terrible Français."

Helene considered this. "Ciao Maya."

"Ciao Helene." She sat.

"I'm sorry, but business kept me out of the city a few days."

"That's all right. What's a few days to the likes of us?"

"How good of you to be so public-spirited. I wish you'd shown that much patience under medical surveillance."

"Touché," Maya murmured.

Helene said nothing. She gazed dreamily out the office window.

Maya said nothing in return. She examined the peeling lacquer on her fingernails.

Maya was the first to break. "I can wait as long as you can," Maya blurted, boasting, and lying. "I love your decor."

"Do you know they spent a hundred thousand marks on your treatment?"

"A hundred thousand, three hundred and twelve."

"And you took it in your head to dash off for a little European vacation."

"Would it help if I said I was sorry? Of course I'm not a bit sorry, but if it would help anybody, then I'd act real polite."

"What *does* make you sorry, Maya?"

"Nothing much. Well, I'm very sorry that I lost my photographs."

"Is that all?" Helene rummaged deftly in her desk. She produced a disk. "Here."

"Oh!" Maya clutched the disk eagerly. "You copied them! Oh, I can't believe I have them back." She kissed the disk. "Thank you so much!"

"You know they're bad photographs, don't you?"

"Yes, I know that, but I'm getting better."

"Well, you could hardly help *that*. You've managed some Novak pastiches. But you have no talent."

Maya stared. "I don't think that's up to you to judge."

"Of course it's up to me to judge," Helene said patiently. "Who better? I knew Patzelt and Pauli and Becker. I married Capasso. I knew Ingrid Harmon when no one else thought she could paint. You're not an artist, Mrs. Ziemann."

"I don't think I'm doing so badly for a student only four months old."

"Art doesn't come out of a metabolic support tank. If art

came out of support tanks, it would make a complete mockery of genuine talent and inspiration. Those photographs are banal."

"Paul doesn't think so."

"Paul . . ." She sighed. "Paul is not an artist. He's a theoretician, a very young and very self-involved and very bad theoretician. When they thought they could mix art and science like whiskey and soda, they made an elementary blunder. It is crass and it's a solecism. Science is not art. Science is a set of objective techniques to reveal reproducible results. Machines could do science. Art is not a reproducible result. Creativity is a profoundly subjective act. You're a woman of damaged and fragmented subjectivity."

"I'm a woman of a *different* subjectivity. And I'd sure rather mix art and science than mix art critique and police authority."

"I'm not an artist. I only care for them."

"If you despise science so much, why aren't you dead?"

Helene said nothing.

"What are you so afraid of?" Maya said. "I hate to shatter your lovely mythos there, but if art can come out of a camera, it's got no problem crawling out of a support tank. You haven't been in the right support tanks. I have the holy fire now. That's a silly name for it, I guess, but it's as real as dirt, so why should I care what you call it?"

"Show me, then," said Helene, folding her arms. "Show me one thing truly fine. Show me something truly impressive, that you or your little friends have done. I don't count computer hacking, any idiot can break forty-year-old security systems. I don't count new forms of media, any fool gets cheap novelty from a new medium. They're clever, but they have no profundity! The Tête crowd loves to whine and complain, but artists today have every advantage. Education. Leisure. Excellent health. Free food, free shelter. Unlimited travel. All the time in the world to perfect their craft. All the information that the net can feed them, the world's whole heritage of art. And what have they given us? Profoundly bad taste."

"What do you want from them? Your world made them. Your world made me. What do you want from me?"

Helene shrugged. "What can I do with you?"

"Come on, Helene. Don't tell me you haven't already made up your mind about *that*."

Helene spread her hands. "The children don't understand. They truly think the world is fossilizing. They have no idea how close we are to chaos. The children want power. Power without responsibility, discretion, or maturity. They want to alter their brains! And you helped them to try it! Aren't your brains altered enough?"

"Maybe. I know they're pretty altered. Believe me, I can feel it. But really, I couldn't tell you."

"You can't tell me. How very reassuring that is. Imagine if there were genuine rebels in the modern world. Crazy rebels, true old-fashioned fanatics, but crawling out of brand-new support tanks. Did you know you can take any common tincture set and make enough nerve gas to poison a city? Here you are, darling, wrapping up in your sweet little furoshiki scarf and breaking the laws of nature with uninhibited force. . . . They think that you are cute. *You* think that you are cute. They think everything is under stifling control. *Nothing* is under control. Half the modern population has given up on objective reality. They are out of their minds on entheogens. They all think they see God, and if it weren't for the fact that they love and trust their government, they'd butcher each other."

"It's sure a good thing you government types are so lovable, then."

"You were government. You're a medical economist. Aren't you? You know very well how much trouble we've taken. How much labor that great effort has been. You are robbing poor, honest people so that you can have fun running off with the public's investment in your body. Is that fair? It's a miracle that we've built a just society where the rich and powerful don't trample and steal the very lives of other people."

"Yeah, I voted for all that," Maya said.

"These children take the world we built for granted. They think they're immortals. They might even be right, but they think they *deserve* immortality. They think that the increase in human life span is some mystical technological impulse. It's not mystical. There's nothing mystical about it. Real people are working very hard to achieve that progress. People are breaking their hearts, and giving everything they have, to invent new ways to postpone death. You're not an artist, but at least once you were helping society. Now you're actively doing harm."

"They've really hurt you, haven't they?"

"Yes, they have done real harm."

"I'm glad they hurt you."

"I'm glad that you said that," Helene said serenely. "I thought you were crazy, a woman of diminished moral capacity. Now I can see that you're actively malicious."

"What are you going to do to me? You can't make me be Mia."

"Of course I can't do that. I wish I could, but it's too late for that. We can't do anything about a failed experiment. Experiments fail, it happens, that's why they are experiments. But we can stop the failures; and we can try something more productive."

"Aha."

"You're a medical economist. You used to judge these processes yourself. Didn't you? How would you judge a treatment that produces cheats and mad people?"

"Helene, are you really telling me that the other NTDCD patients are behaving as oddly as I am?"

"No, I certainly am not. More than half of them have been model patients. Those are the people I truly pity. They took those treatments in good faith and fulfilled their duty to society, and now they will be stranded. Marooned in a dead extension. Because of reckless malcontents like you."

"That's wonderful news." Maya laughed. "That makes me feel so happy! It's so lovely to know I have brothers and sisters. . . . And you've even given me my pictures back! They're bad pictures, but at least they're real proof I'm not Mia."

"They're not proof of anything."

"They are. Well, they will be. I'll prove that I'm better now. I'll prove that I'm *better* than Mia. Go ahead, cut me off of treatments. I'll prove I'm valuable, I'll make everybody admit it. I'm worth much more to this world than a hundred thousand lousy marks."

"You won't prove it to me."

"We'll see about that. What do you know, anyway? You're rich and famous, and a lot of men adored you, and you're one of the major art collectors of the twenty-first century. Big deal, what does all that prove? Tell me who's your favorite photographer."

"I'd have to think." Helene thought about it. "Helmut Weisgerber."

"What, the guy who did that Arctic landscape stuff? The mountain climber? You really like Weisgerber?"

"I liked him well enough to marry him."

"You really think Weisgerber was better than Capasso? But Eric Capasso was so sensual and lively. Capasso must have been a lot of fun."

"Capasso had a great gift, but he was melodramatic. At heart he was a stage designer. But Weisgerber—nothing can touch a classic Weisgerber."

"I have to admit I really love Weisgerber's *Dead Leaf* series."

"I commissioned those."

"Really, Helene? That must have been fantastic. . . ."

There was a timid knock at the door.

"I ordered us a mineralka," Helene explained. "They're very slow here." She raised her voice. *"Entrez."*

The door opened. It was Brett.

"Come in, Brett. We were just having a little discussion on aesthetics."

Brett put her backpack on the floor.

"Brett, this is Helene. Helene, Brett. I mean Natalie. Sorry."

"This is a restricted area," Helene said, rising from her chair. "I'm afraid I'll have to ask you to leave."

"So I broke in," Brett said, adjusting her spex. "I thought you might be beating her with a rubber hose or something, so I came in to document it."

"We were talking about photography," Maya said.

"She gonna give you behavior mod?"

"No, I think the plan is to shut down my extension treatment. Apparently it's been causing a lot of civil trouble."

"Oh, yeah. That's real important. A bunch of rich geronto-crats and some twisted extension treatment. That must be really fascinating." Brett wandered to the window and looked out. "Nice view. If you like power plants."

Helene stared at her in astonishment. "Miss, this is a police interrogation. It's confidential. You have no business here."

"What are you going to do to those artifice kids?"

"That subject hasn't come up yet," Maya said.

"You mean, they're disturbing the universe, and you two old cows are sitting here talking about photography." Brett flipped the window latch with her thumb. "Typical."

"I really must ask you to leave," said Helene. "You're not merely being rude, you are breaking the law."

"If I only had a gun," Brett said, "I'd kill both of you." She opened the window.

"Brett, what are you doing?"

Brett ducked under the window frame and stepped out onto the ledge.

"Stop her," Maya said quickly. "Arrest her!"

"Stop her how? I don't have a weapon."

"Why don't you have a weapon, for heaven's sake?"

"Do I look like I carry a weapon?" Helene walked to the window. "Young woman, please come in at once."

"I'm going to jump," Brett said indistinctly.

Maya rushed to the window. Brett sidled away rapidly out of their reach.

"Brett, this is stupid. Please don't do this. You don't have to do this. You can talk to us, Brett. Come back inside now."

"You don't want to talk to me. I can't say anything that matters to you. You just don't want to be embarrassed, that's all."

"Please come in," Maya begged. "I know you're brave. You don't have to prove anything to me."

Brett raised her cupped hands to her face. There was a stiff breeze outside and her hair was flying. "Hey, everybody!" she shouted down into the street. "I'm gonna jump!"

Maya and Helene jostled for space inside the window frame. "I'm going out after her," Maya announced, putting her knee on the sill.

"No, you're not. You're in police custody. Sit down."

"I won't!"

Helene turned and said something in Français to the dogs. The white dog left at a brisk little run, slipping through the open door. Plato stood up, fixed his silent eyes on Maya, and growled deep in his throat. Maya sat down.

Helene leaned out the window.

"Get out of my sight, cop," shouted Brett. "I have a perfect right to kill myself. You can't take that away from me."

"I agree that is your civil right," Helene said. "No one is trying to deprive you of your rights. But you're not thinking clearly. You're very distraught, and it's clear you have been taking drugs. Killing yourself will not change anything."

"Of course it will," said Brett. "It will change everything, for me."

"This is very wrong," said Helene intensely. She was doing her best to be soothing. "It will hurt everyone who loves you. If you're doing this for a cause, it will only discredit you in the eyes of all sensible people." Helene glanced back hastily into the room. "Is she one of Paul's people?" she hissed. "I've never seen her."

"She's just some kid," Maya said.

"What was her name again?"

"Natalie."

Helene stuck her head out again. "Natalie, look here! Natalie, stop it! Natalie, talk to me."

"You think I want to live forever," Natalie said. And she jumped.

Maya rushed to the window. Natalie was lying crushed in the midst of a distant little crowd. People were talking into netlinks, calling for help and advice.

"I can't bear to look," Helene said, and shuddered. She pulled back into the room, and took Maya by the arm.

Maya wrenched free.

"I've seen this so many times," Helene said wearily. "They just do it. They just take possession of themselves and end their lives. It's an act of enormous will."

"You should have let me go out there after her."

Helene shut the window with a bang. "You are in my charge, you are under arrest. You are not going anywhere, and you are not killing yourself. Sit down."

Plato rose and began to bark. Helene caught at his collar. "Poor things," she said, and wiped her eyes. "We have to let them go. There is no choice. . . . Poor things, they are only human beings."

Maya slapped her face.

Helene looked at her in shocked surprise, then, slowly, turned her other cheek. "Do you feel better now, darling? Try the other one."

6

America had never quite caught on about trains. Americans were historically obsessed with individual cars. Maya couldn't afford a car. She could hitchhike sometimes if she wanted to. Mostly she could walk.

So she was walking through rural Pennsylvania. She had come to love the simple physical process of putting one foot in front of another. She liked the clarity of walking, the way that walking put you outside the rules and deep inside a tangible, immediate world. Nothing illegal about walking all by yourself. Walking cost nothing, and it wasn't traceable. A sweet and quiet way to drop off somebody else's stupid official map.

She had a sun hat, and a backpack, and a change of clothes. She had a cheap camera. She had a canteen and a little spare food; the sort of food one could chew on quite a while. She had a rather old but very decent pair of well-engineered and highly indestructible walking shoes. And she had nobody bothering her. She was alone, she was just herself now. To gently become herself, with no one watching and counting her heartbeats, free to savor the infinite thereness of the world, free to get her own grip on the quotidian—it was a series of little astonishments.

She liked Pennsylvania because there was so little fuss made about this particular corner of the world. She much preferred this sort of place now. All the fussy and glamorous places were far too brittle. Of course it was hard to find any genuine place to hide, in an era when all law, almost all media, and even most art could be phoned in; but the places that seemed entirely quotidian were the best locales for an exotic hopeful-monster like herself.

Europe was a boutique. America was a farm. Sometimes there were bicyclists in rural Pennsylvania. Occasionally hikers. There weren't many like herself, people perfectly enchanted just to walk and look. This wasn't a popular tourist niche in the North American continent, but the local Amish attracted a certain interest.

A car passed her outside Perkasie. The car pulled over, stopped, and a pair of well-dressed Indonesian tourists stepped out. They shrugged on shiny new backpacks and then headed her way. They walked hastily. Maya, who would not let anyone hurry her now, trudged along peaceably.

As the two approached her, the man tugged the woman's sleeve. They waved excitedly, then shouted something.

Maya stopped and waited for them. "Ciao," she said, a little warily.

"Hello?" the woman said.

Maya looked at her, and was thunderstruck. The stranger wore Indonesian couture, rather shiny and chic, but the stranger was American. She was familiar: much more than familiar. She looked and felt fantastically important, absolutely compelling, a personage like destiny. Maya was flooded with occult recognition, an impossible visceral surge of tenderness and heartache. She gaped as if an angel had descended.

"Are you Mia Ziemann?" the man said.

Maya closed her mouth and shook her head resolutely. "No, I'm Maya."

"Then what have you done with my mother?" the woman demanded.

Maya stared at her. "Chloe!"

Chloe's eyes widened. She relaxed a bit. She tried to smile. "Mom, it's me."

"No wonder I love you so much," Maya said with relief, and she laughed.

It was funny to have lost so much, and yet lost so very little. The details were all gone sideways, somehow out of her mental reach now, but not the disorienting intensity of her love for her child. She scarcely knew this person, and yet she loved Chloe more than she could have thought possible.

It no longer felt much like motherhood. Motherhood had been very real, very quotidian, a primal human relationship, full of devotion and effort and strain, fraught with bitter calculation and the intimate battle of wills. But now, all those complexities had been blown away like sand. The presence of this strange woman filled her with oceanic joy. The very existence of Chloe was a cosmic triumph. It felt like walking with a boddhisattva.

"I hope you remember Suhaery?" Chloe said. "Surely you must remember him, right?"

"You look so well, Mia," said Chloe's husband very gallantly. This Indonesian guy had been married to Chloe for forty years now. That was easily twice as long as Mia had ever been able to manage her. Mia had been—she could still feel this, some dim tingle of ancient resentment—politely horrified to find her daughter running off with an Indonesian. The Indonesians, in their vast island nation, had gotten off rather easily during the plague years. They had played up that advantage enormously in the decades that followed.

But that was all far in the past now. Now Chloe and Suhaery were a middle-aged couple in their sixties. Sleek and rich and completely at ease with one another. They came from the richest country on Earth and they looked as though they were very proud about that.

"How did you manage to find me?" Maya said.

"Oh, it was terribly hard, Mom. We tried the net, the police, everything. Finally we thought to ask Mercedes. Your house-keeper."

"Oh, I guess Mercedes would know."

"She had some good guesses. Mercedes says to tell you that she's sorry she scolded you so much. She still thinks what you did was totally immoral, but so many people have asked her for interviews now . . . well, you know how it is. Celebrity."

Maya shrugged. "No, I'm afraid I don't. How is my celebrity these days?"

"Mom," said Chloe, and sighed, "you've really done it this time. Haven't you? I always knew you were never as quiet as you looked. I could always tell you were faking it. I always knew some-day you'd lose your grip and blow sky-high. That was your prob-lem, Mom: you were never in touch with genuine spirituality."

Maya looked at Suhaery. Her daughter's husband was a stout and practical Asian businessman. He was in pillar-of-strength mode, playing the stellar role of psychic anchor. Suhaery was strolling along in his clean and pressed walking shorts on a weedy roadside in an alien country. Maya realized suddenly that Suhaery was finding this all very funny. He thought his wife's relations were amusingly peculiar. He was right.

"What do you think about all this, Harry?" she asked.

"Mia, you look lovely. You're like a blossoming rose. You look like Chloe on the first day I met her."

"You shouldn't tell her that," Chloe scolded. "That sounds really strange and bad in about five different ways."

Suhaery said something wicked in Malay and chuckled heartily.

"We tried to find you in San Francisco," Chloe said, "but the people in the clinic weren't helpful at all."

"Yeah, I, uh, pretty much had it with all the clinic people."

"It would have been smarter to go back under controlled care, Mom. I mean, obviously you've blown most of your value as an experimental subject. But still."

"I thought about doing that, I really did," Maya said. "I mean, if I'd run back to those meatheads and humbled myself and lived under medically defined circumstances, I probably could have repaired my medical ratings a lot, but you know something? I got no use for 'em. They're the bourgeoisie, they're philistines. I'm sick of 'em. It's not that I blame them for what happened to me, but . . . well . . . I'm busy now. I have better things to do."

"Such as?"

"I just like to walk around. Earth, sky, stars, sun. You know."

"You're kidding, right?"

"Well, I do photography. . . . The Amish, they're such good material and they're so good about it. . . . I mean, Amish children look incredibly like normal children, they *are* normal children, but then you can trace them decade by decade. Amish people around seventy . . . The natural human aging process . . . It's amazing and terrifying! And yet there's this strange organic quality to it. . . . The Amish are wonderful. They can tell I'm some kind of impossible monster by their standards, but they're so sweet and good about it. They just put up with us posthumans. Like they are doing the rest of us a favor."

Chloe thought about it. "What are you really *doing* with all this photography of Amish people?"

"Nothing much. My pictures still stink. I'm a lousy apprentice photographer and I got a lousy camera. But that's okay; I need a lot of practice. Especially in framing shots properly . . ."

Suhaery and Chloe exchanged knowing glances. Then Chloe spoke up. "Mom, Harry and I think it would be a good idea if you came back with us to Djakarta for a while."

"Why on earth would I want to do that?"

"There's plenty of room in the condo, and in Asia they're better about these things. They're more understanding."

"If only you had run to Indonesia," said Suhaery indulgently. "In Europe, they're all crazy. They never know how to rest, even when they're rich. There is something very wrong with Europeans. They just don't know how to live."

"You really want your weird mother-in-law to live under your roof, Harry?"

"You're a harmless little thing," said Suhaery kindly. "I always liked you, Mia, even when you were very afraid of me."

"Well, I can't do that. No way. Sorry."

"Mom, you need looking after. Let us look after you a little. You deserve it, you know. You sacrificed a lot for me. Years and years."

"Forget it."

Chloe sighed. "Mom, you're almost a hundred years old. And they've cut off your treatment!"

"Do I look feeble to you? I can pass for twenty. Sure, I might live even longer if I went back to the lab and kissed up to them, but I'm okay, I'm not doing anything *stupid*. I eat right, I sleep like a top, and I get plenty of exercise. You see my legs now? Look at these legs! I could kick a hole right through the side of that hex barn over there."

"Mom, stop that and listen. You're living like a bum, like some kind of tramp. All right? You're acting weird, you're not acting responsibly. These other people that went through your same treatment, they all act pretty oddly, too. I think you people have got a serious legal case. You should stand up for your rights as abused patients. You should go through proper channels. What happened to you, it's not your fault at all, and it never was. You should organize."

"Darling, if we could organize, we wouldn't be acting oddly in the first place."

"You should talk to the others. Network with them."

"I don't have net access. And I bet they don't, either."

"Mom, why not? You should be calling us. Really, Harry and I, we've both been worried sick about you. Haven't we, Harry?"

"It's true, Mia," said Suhaery loyally. "We are concerned."

Chloe drew a breath. "I can see that you're not human any longer, and I can accept that. It's fine, it happens. But you *are* my mother. You can't run off and do this to us. It's unconscionable."

"Your father did it."

"No, he didn't. Dad left *you,* but he never left me. Dad talks to me whenever I ask Dad to talk to me. And at least I always know where Dad is. I *never* know where you are anymore. *Nobody* knows. You know how long we've been searching for you on these back roads?"

"No. How long?"

"Long enough," Suhaery said, smiling. "Maybe too long. Your daughter and I are very patient people."

"Can't you just call us, at least? So we won't fret so much. Please, Mom. I don't mind if you want to walk around, but Mom, you can't ever walk away from your dharma and karma."

"Look, I don't have any money."

Suhaery slipped his brown hands neatly into his creased trouser pockets. "That's no problem. Twenty marks a week? Would that be too much?"

"Twenty marks? . . ." said Maya. "Wow."

Suhaery nodded happily. "Take a little money. What's wrong with that? It's not enough money to make any trouble for any of us. A little allowance, Mia. A family remittance. We *are* your family, you know. It would make us so happy."

"What do I have to do for this allowance?"

"Nothing! Just call us. Talk to us. Sometimes. That's all. Is that so much to ask?"

Chloe nodded eagerly. "You need some looking after, Mom. We can do that now. We can set up a little account for you. We're good at that now."

"Well . . ."

"You'd have done that for me. Wouldn't you? Heck, Mom, you *did* do it for me. Remember that allowance you gave me when I was on probation?"

"Did I?" Maya paused. "Well, okay, I guess that makes sense. Okay, have it your way."

Chloe wiped her eyes sentimentally. "Oh, I'm glad now. . . . It's funny to see you so pretty."

The allowance made a difference of sorts. Maya was no good at all at controlling money now, but a steady dribble every week bumped her up from wanderjahr status to the crumbling lower edges of society. She still had no more possessions than she could carry, but she bathed more often, and ate nicer things, and sometimes accessed networks.

Networking was not without its risks, however. Networking was how the dog found her in Des Moines. Maya found the city of Des Moines much nicer than its press would indicate. Des Moines had some very interesting buildings, the regional Indianapolis influence. Paul had been a little cynical and shortsighted on the subject of modern architecture, she could see that now. Once you learned to look for modern architecture, you could perceive waves of architectural influence percolating right through the old urban structure; a cornice here, a door there, a fungarium windowbox, even the manhole covers. . . .

She spotted the postcanine dog and his producer having breakfast as she prepared to leave the hotel. She recognized the dog at once, and she felt sorry for him. She felt quite certain that the dog would continue to follow her if she somehow escaped the hotel. But she wasn't afraid of the dog; she was no longer afraid of much of anything. The dog and his producer looked so sad to be in a cheap American hotel in Iowa, confronting flapjacks and a battery of specialized multicolored syrups.

She went to their booth. "Ciao Aquinas," she said.

"Hello," said the dog, startled. His normally perfect suit looked rumpled, perhaps because of the guide collar. His producer was blind.

The producer adjusted a translator clipped to his wattled ear. He was a Deutschlander, very elderly and very polite. "Please sit, Maya. Have you eated? Ate? Ated?"

"Okay." Maya sat.

"We came to ask for an interview," said Aquinas, in brisk and flawless English.

"Really."

"We have had both Herr Cabanne and Signorina Barsotti already."

"Who?"

"Paul and Benedetta," said the dog.

The mention of their names touched her deeply. She missed

them as she would miss a heartbeat. "How are Paul and Bene-detta?"

"Famous of course; rather troubled, unfortunately."

"But how are they really?"

"They escaped their legal difficulties. A great political success for them. But they have had a famous falling-out. A schism in their artistic movement. You hadn't heard this?"

A human waitress came over. The human attention was a typical Des Moines touch. Maya ordered waffles.

"May we ask you about this matter, on camera?"

"I hadn't heard anything about any schisms. I'm out of touch. I don't have anything to say."

"But they both speak so highly of you. They told us to come to you. They even helped us to locate you here."

"I'm amazed that you can speak English so beautifully, Aqui-nas. I've seen you speak Deutsch, and I've even heard you dubbed into Czestina, but . . ."

"It's all done with dubbing," said the dog modestly. "Dub-bing just above the level of the brain. Karl has brought a gift for you, from your friends. Go fetch it, Karl."

"Good idea," said Karl. He rose, picked up a white cane, switched it on, and trotted off unerringly.

"I really can't appear on your show," said Maya. "I don't need to play roles anymore."

"You have become an icon," the dog said.

"I don't much feel like an icon. Anyway, the best way to remain an icon is to avoid public overexposure. Isn't it?"

"How Greta Garbo of you," said the dog.

"You like old movies?" Maya said, surprised.

"Frankly, I hate old movies; I don't even much like my own quite ancient medium of television. But I'm enormously interested in the processes of celebrity."

"I've never had such a sophisticated conversation with a dog," said Maya. "I can't appear on your show, Aquinas, I hope you understand that. But I do like talking to you. In person, you're so much smaller than you look on television. And you're really interesting. I don't know if you're a dog or an artificial intelligence or whatever, but you're definitely some kind of genuine entity. You're *deep*. Aren't you? I think you should get out of pop culture. Maybe write a book."

"I can't read," the dog said.

Maya's waffles arrived. She tucked in with gusto.

"It's a shame to come to Des Moines for nothing," the dog wheedled.

"Interview the mayor," Maya said, chewing.

"I don't think that will do."

"Go back to Europe and interview Helene Vauxcelles-Serusier. Make her level with you."

"Why should I do that?" said the dog, pricking up his hairy ears. "And where would I find her?"

Karl returned to the booth. The gift had come from Paul and Benedetta. Maya shoved her waffles aside and tore open the box, and then the padding. They had sent her an antique camera. The sort of hand camera that once had processed rolls of colored film. The antique machine had been retrofitted with a digital imaging plate, and a set of network jacks. It was heavy and solid and lovely. Compared to a modern camera it felt like chiseled granite.

And there was a card with it. Handwriting.

"Don't ever believe what they say about us," scrawled Benedetta.

"First and always we will love and forgive our heretics," said Paul. His neat and perfect hand.

———

Daniel lived in Idaho now. He had gone to earth.

She could sense the border of his private little realm. Maybe twenty acres. Nothing like wire or a fence; the difference was present in the substance of the earth. Trace elements, maybe. Maybe some aspect of his peculiar practice of gardening. Could mere intelligence make trees grow faster?

The trees, the bushes, the birds, the insects even. They didn't feel quite right here. They felt as if someone were paying fantastic amounts of sustained attention to them. The branches were painterly branches, and the birds sang with operatic precision.

Her ex-husband was digging in the earth with a shovel. Daniel was about four feet high now. The bones had shrunk and the spine had compacted and the muscle had pooled out around his calves and thighs in thick Neanderthal clumps. He was old and extremely strong; he looked as though he could snap the shovel in half.

"Hello, Mia," he said in a voice rusty with disuse.

"Hello, Daniel."

"You've changed," he said, squinting. "Has it been long?"

"For me it has."

"You look like Chloe. I'd have thought you were Chloe if I didn't know better."

"I still think of you as Daniel," she confessed. "I don't know why."

Daniel said nothing. He retreated into his hut.

She followed him into his rude little shelter. It was lined with down and branches and dry shed leaves and perhaps eight trillion gigabytes of mycelial webbed information. He had put down roots here in Idaho. He had integrated himself into the depths of the Idaho landscape. He had become a genius loci, a spirit of place. Every tree, every bush, every flower, every caterpillar, genetically wired for sound. He didn't merely watch over this place—in some profound sense he had *become* this place. He had become a little piece of Idaho. In the winters, he hibernated.

"Take a little water?" Daniel croaked.

"No, thanks."

Daniel sipped collected dew from a leaf-shaped cup.

"What's new, Daniel?"

"New," Daniel mused. "Oh, there's always something new. Do something about the sky, they say. Clean it up. With spores."

"Spores," she said.

He drank more water, wiped his fantastically furrowed brow, and seemed to rally. "Yes, the sky will be the color of fungus for a while. Should make for some interesting sunsets. Atmospheric repair techniques. Very useful. Very farsighted, very wise. Good husbandry practice." Daniel was trying hard to talk to her in a language she could understand. They were both bipedal creatures who walked beneath the sky, who lived in the world of daylight. That was a kind of commonality.

"I can't believe the polity would really try a scheme like seeding the sky with fungus. I didn't think the polity had that much imagination anymore."

"Well, they don't have imagination, but it's not their idea. Other people hurt the sky in the first place. It's a response. New monster versus old monstrosity. We are as gods, Mia. We might as well get good at it."

"Are you a monster, Daniel? Whoever told you you were a god?"

"What do you think?"

He turned his lumpish back on her, left the hut, and went back to his work. He was a god, she decided. He hadn't been a god when he'd been with her. He'd been her man then, a good man. He wasn't a man any longer. Daniel was a very primitive god. A very small-scale god. A primitive steam-engine god. An amphibian god dutifully slogging the mud for some coming race of reptiles. A very minor god, maybe something like a garden gnome, a dryad, a tommy-knocker. He'd done his best with the allowable technology, but the allowable technology was just barely enough. Machines were so evanescent. Machines just flitted through the fabric of the universe like a fit through the brain of God, and in their wake people stopped being people. But people didn't stop going on.

"I need to take your picture, Daniel," she told him. "Stand under the light for me."

He didn't seem to mind. She lifted the new camera. She framed him. She knew suddenly that this was it. This was going to be her first really good picture. She could see it in the set of his shoulders, in that astonishing landscape that he called his face. The starkness of a living soul placed far beyond necessity. She understood the two of them and the world revolving, all whole and all at once, in a bright hot blaze. Her first true picture. So real and beautiful.

The camera clicked.